A CENTURY OF HORROR 1970-1979

EDITED BY
DAVID DRAKE

THE GREATEST STORIES
OF THE DECADE

MJF BOOKS
NEW YORK

Published by MJF Books
Fine Communications
Two Lincoln Square
60 West 66th Street
New York, NY 10023

Library of Congress Catalog Card Number 96-78812
ISBN 1-56731-157-1

Copyright © 1996 David Drake and Tekno-Books

All rights reserved. No part of this publication may be reproduced or transmitted in any form or by any means, electronic or mechanical, including photocopy, recording, or any information storage and retrieval system, without the prior written permission of the publisher.

Manufactured in the United States of America on acid-free paper

MJF Books and the MJF colophon are trademarks of Fine Creative Media, Inc.

10 9 8 7 6 5 4 3 2 1

"Duel" by Richard Matheson. Copyright © 1971 by Richard Matheson. Reprinted by permission of the author and his agent, Don Congdon Associates, Inc.

"The Dripping" by David Morrell. Copyright © 1972 by David Morrell. Reprinted by permission of the author and Henry Morrison, Inc., his agents.

"The Events at Poroth Farm" by T.E.D. Klein. Copyright © 1972 by T.E.D. Klein. Reprinted by permission of the author.

"Come Dance With Me On My Pony's Grave" by Charles L. Grant. Copyright © 1973 by Charles L. Grant. Reprinted by permission of the author.

"Something Had to be Done" by David Drake. Copyright © 1974 by The Mercury Press, Inc. Reprinted by permission of the author.

"Sticks" by Karl Edward Wagner. Copyright © 1974 by Karl Edward Wagner. Reprinted by permission of the agent for the author's Estate, The Pimlico Agency, Inc.

"Belsen Express" by Fritz Leiber. Copyright © 1975 by Fritz Leiber. Reprinted by permission of the agent for the author's Estate, Richard Curtis Associates, New York.

"Ladies in Waiting" by Hugh B. Cave. Copyright © 1975 by Hugh B. Cave. Reprinted by permission of the author.

"Armaja Das" by Joe Haldeman. Copyright © 1976 by Joe Haldeman. Reprinted by permission of the author.

"A Case of the Stubborns" by Robert Bloch. Copyright © 1976 by Robert Bloch; copyright renewed 1993. Reprinted by permission of the author's Estate and their agent, Ricia Mainhardt, New York. All rights reserved.

"It Only Comes Out at Night" by Dennis Etchison. Copyright © 1976 by Dennis Etchison. Reprinted by permission of the author.

"The Viaduct" by Brian Lumley. Copyright © 1976, 1993 by Brian Lumley. Reprinted by permission of the author.

"Night-Side" by Joyce Carol Oates. Copyright © 1977 by The Ontario Review, Inc. Reprinted by permission of the author.

"Best Interests" by Chelsea Quinn Yarbro. Copyright © 1978 by Chelsea Quinn Yarbro. Reprinted by permission of the author.

"Gotcha!" by Ray Bradbury. Copyright © 1978 by Ray Bradbury. Reprinted by permission of the author and his agent, Don Congdon Associates, Inc.

"The Man Who Was Heavily into Revenge" by Harlan Ellison. Copyright © 1978 by Harlan Ellison. Reprinted by arrangement with, and permission of, the Author and the Author's agent, Richard Curtis Associates, Inc., New York. All rights reserved.

"Divers Hands" by Darrell Schweitzer. Copyright © 1979 by Darrell Schweitzer. Reprinted by permission of the author.

"Eumenides in the Fourth-Floor Lavatory" by Orson Scott Card. Copyright © 1979 by Orson Scott Card. Reprinted by permission of the author.

"Red as Blood" by Tanith Lee. Copyright © 1979 by Tanith Lee. Reprinted by permission of Scovil - Chichak - Galen Literary Agency, New York.

"Mackintosh Willy" by Ramsey Campbell. Copyright © 1979 by Ramsey Campbell. From **Shadows 2**. Reprinted by permission of the author.

"Seasons of Belief" by Michael Bishop. Copyright © 1979 by Michael Bishop. From **Shadows 2**. Reprinted by permission of the author.

A Century of Horror: 1970–1979
Edited by David Drake

Introduction 1
   Stefan Dziemianowicz

Duel 7
   Richard Matheson

The Dripping 30
   David Morrell

The Events at Poroth Farm 39
   T.E.D. Klein

Come Dance With Me on My Pony's Grave 81
   Charles L. Grant

Something Had to Be Done 94
   David Drake

Sticks 100
   Karl Edward Wagner

Belsen Express 120
   Fritz Leiber

Ladies In Waiting 133
   Hugh B. Cave

Armaja Das 143
   Joe Haldeman

A Case of the Stubborns 161
  Robert Bloch

It Only Comes Out at Night 177
  Dennis Etchison

The Viaduct 190
  Brian Lumley

Night-Side 207
  Joyce Carol Oates

Best Interests 232
  Chelsea Quinn Yarbro

Gotcha! 245
  Ray Bradbury

The Man Who Was Heavily into Revenge 253
  Harlan Ellison

Divers Hands 267
  Darrell Schweitzer

Eumenides in the Fourth-Floor Lavatory 292
  Orson Scott Card

Red as Blood 308
  Tanith Lee

Mackintosh Willy 319
  Ramsey Campbell

Seasons of Belief 334
  Michael Bishop

Introduction

by Stefan Dziemianowicz

Who needed horror fiction in the 1970s? It's not as though there weren't enough real-life anxieties to contend with. The '60s were over, but they had left most of their problems unresolved and still clamoring for attention. The war in Vietnam ground on, poised to enter its second decade, and the civil unrest it had instigated back home seemed to be worsening. Death hung heavy in the air, as students fell at Kent State and icons of American youth culture—Jimi Hendrix, Jim Morrison, Janis Joplin—appeared to be dying in droves. President Richard Nixon, who was re-elected to the nation's highest political office in a landslide victory in 1972, would resign two years later, a symbol of national disgrace. Social movements that had begun optimistically only years before—civil rights, feminism, ecoawareness—seemed to be stagnating in the growing climate of social confusion and competing interests.

Faced with such insurmountable problems and their suffocating mood of despair, how could anyone even think of losing themselves in the world of fictional fears?

They again, how could they not?

We know today that the horror craze of the 1970s occurred not as an escape-valve reaction against the pressing concerns of the time, but in direct response to them. Turn which way we would, all we saw was the image of chaos beneath the surface of each day's news events. We dared not trust authority. The fragile bounds of the social contract seemed to be weakening. The center was not holding. As the miasma of gloom thickened, it was inevitable that it would begin seeping into the work of popular writers, whose interests were attuned to our cultural consciousness.

It all began inauspiciously in 1971, with William Peter Blatty's *The Exorcist*. Blatty was a mainstream writer who hitherto had shown no interest in horror themes. His tale of a young girl whose demonic possession proves the ultimate test of faith to a doubting Jesuit priest was a storytelling tour-de-force that rocketed to the top of the bestseller lists. Two years later, William Friedkin's film adaptation of the novel earned comparisons to the film versions of "The Phantom of the Opera" and "Frankenstein" for its spectacularly unnerving effect on audiences.

In hindsight, it's not difficult to understand the appeal of *The Exorcist* for both readers and moviegoers of the early 1970s. Its portrayal of a traditional belief system crumbling under the onslaught of human doubt and a child growing increasingly estranged from her mother must have resonated subconsciously for many people who sensed the moral relativism of the day, and who looked in bewilderment on the widening generation gap. At the time, though, *The Exorcist* was simply accepted as a well-told tale of terror, a bestseller that had elevated the plot of a pulp potboiler to literary respectability.

The success of *The Exorcist* may explain the popularity of Thomas Tryon's *The Other*, which appeared the same year and also featured a troubled child, this one an emotionally traumatized boy who manipulates adult belief in his innocence to hide his murderous psychopathology. Although set decades in the past, the novel no doubt benefitted from the same cross-generational anxieties that had buoyed Blatty's novel up the bestseller lists. Critics impressed by the considerable talent Tryon showed in his literary debut cast around for terms to describe the book: Modern Gothic? Thriller? Suspense? None dared call it horror.

And then came Stephen King.

King's ascent to the level of literary phenomenon was not as meteoric as his current sales might indicate. His first novel, *Carrie*, did respectably when it was published in hardcover in 1974, but it didn't become a bestseller until reprinted as a paperback. Even then, its sales might not have been quite so impressive had Brian De Palma's powerful film interpretation not renewed interest in the book in 1976. However, King differed in several fundamental respects from Blatty and Tryon. Unlike them, he was a writer steeped in the horror tradition. He had cut his teeth on the genre while young and had already published many of the short horror

INTRODUCTION

tales that he would collect in 1978 as *Night Shift*. King knew not only how to tell a good story, but how to tell a *horror* story as well as any other; he was aware of what had already been done before and which variations might be used to give the classic themes new life.

Thus, unlike Blatty and Tryon, who dabbled briefly in horror's dark corner before pursuing other literary interests, King was comfortable returning to the horror tale again and again. He followed *Carrie* in 1975 with a vampire novel, *Salem's Lot*. It came as no surprise in 1977 that his third novel, *The Shining*, topped the bestseller lists, for by that time he had perfected an approach to the form that many readers found irresistible. King's horrors were not exotic or *outre*—they grew out of everyday situations with which readers could identify: the cruelty of adolescent cliquishness in *Carrie*, the mendacity of small-town life in *Salem's Lot*, domestic violence in *The Shining*. Horror was not an end in itself in these stories, but a means of vivifying the universal dramas at their core and bringing their emotional content to a boil. To drive this point home, King cast his stories with everyday people; even the showdown between ultimate good and evil in his 1978 epic, *The Stand* is fought by ordinary folks pressed by the circumstances of their post-apocalyptic world into mythic roles. Probably the most important difference between King and his predecessors, though—and the quality most guaranteed to appeal to readers bushwhacked by reality in the 1970s—was his optimism. There was no horror so big that it could not be overcome—even horrors that came from within, such as the uncontrollable precognitive powers that afflict John Smith in *The Dead Zone*. Not all of King's stories ended happily, but those who survived in them invariably learned from their experiences what they needed to know in order to get on with their lives.

By the end of the 1970s King had helped draw attention to the wide range of possibilities inherent in horror, which had been moribund as a popular fiction genre for nearly two decades. Nevertheless, because there was no clearly defined "horror audience" to whom such works could be marketed in the 1970s, his early books were subsumed into the small tide of horror books washing up into stores. Ramona Stewart's *The Possession of Joel Delaney*, Robert Marasco's *Burnt Offerings*, Frank De Felitta's *Audrey Rose*, Jeffrey Konvitz's *The Sentinel*, Bernard Taylor's *The Godsend*, Anne Rivers Siddons' *The House Next Door*, and Bari Wood's *The Killing Gift* are just a few of the largely forgotten novels that mixed unobtrusively with King's on the general fiction bookshelves in the 1970s and introduced readers to modern horror before it was ghettoized and segregated into the "Horror" section of the local bookstores.

King and his American compatriots could not lay exclusive claim to jump-starting the horror revolution. A small movement was underway in England as well, suggesting that horror was quickly becoming accepted as a universal tongue for expressing the unspeakable. In 1971, Richard Davis began editing *The Year's Best Horror Stories*, a series that would last for twenty-two years; few of the stories selected for early volumes in the series were taken from markets horror readers would think to look to, thus Davis performed the invaluable service of drawing reader attention to horror's pervasive (if not subversive) presence in the literary mainstream. Robert Aickman, who had since the 1960s been crafting weird tales riddled with disturbing ambiguities and unnerving imagery, found a small but respectful audience in America with his two story collections from that decade, *Cold Hand in Mine* and *Painted Devils*. In 1973, American publisher Arkham House issued Liverpudlian Ramsey Campbell's second collection, *Demons by Daylight*. Suffused with a suffocating sense of dread, Campbell's stories collapsed the tale of supernatural horror into the tale of psychological horror, featuring characters who find their worst fears mirrored in the menacing, often lethal, external environment. The subtle horrors of Aickman's and Campbell's stories were nowhere to be seen in the work of James Herbert, whose paperback bestsellers *The Rats* and *The Fog* played out small dramas of gruesome death and personal triumph against backdrops of world-shaking supernatural evil.

It would be wrong, of course, to give the impression that the growing taste for horror fiction in the 1970s was a completely unpredictable impulse channelled from the collective subconscious by writers and distilled into fiction inflicted upon an unsuspecting populace. Horror had a small but devoted core of fans who had sustained it through the fallow years of the 1950s and '60s by means of an active small press. In the 1970s, this small press came into its own as a midwife to the horror movement a-birthing in the mass market. Stuart Schiff published the first issue of his magazine *Whispers* in 1973. *Whispers*, and W. Paul Ganley's *Weirdbook*, which had started up several years before, were the only two magazines that unabashedly published short horror fiction not fixed up by writers to appear as more "palatable" crime, fantasy or science fiction. The best and brightest of horror's new generation flocked to its pages: Karl Edward Wagner, Dennis Etchison, Charles L. Grant, Ramsey Campbell, Richard Christian Matheson, Brian Lumley, even Stephen King. By the end of the decade, *Whispers* had spawned a companion series of hardcover anthologies under the Doubleday imprint and its contributors were themselves publishing in the mass-market. Also in 1973, Karl Edward Wagner began Carcosa House, one of the only specialty presses devoted exclusively to publishing horror fiction in hardcover. The following decade more than a score of specialty press publishers would be following his lead.

By the mid-to-late 1970s, the climate for horror had shifted favorably. The annual output was increasing steadily, and several writers were becoming identified exclusively as specialists in the genre. In their dedication and commitment to their craft, these writers helped improve the quality of the horror fiction being written.

In 1976 Anne Rice published *Interview with the Vampire*. Her vampire was not the ravening monster of earlier pulp fiction, but a sensitive and articulate young man who presented himself as the victim of unfortunate circumstance. The book became a cult favorite, and Rice's use of the vampire as symbol for the socially disenfranchised was echoed in 1978 in Chelsea Quinn Yarbro's *Hotel Transylvania*, her first novel in the long running series of historical novels featuring the vampire Count Saint-Germain, and in Les Daniels' *The Black Castle*, his first Chronicle of series vampire Don Sebastian de Villanueva. These books effected a wholesale transformation of the vampire's image, from scourge of horror fiction to tragic hero whose plight mirrors the human condition.

Reinventions of classic horror themes were taking place in the work of other writers as well. Whitley Streiber's 1978 novel *The Wolfen* turned the werewolf tale into a parable about contemporary urban decay. The following year, Thomas Tessier distilled the unresolved conflicts and emotional turmoil of the Vietnam War into the protagonist of *The Nightwalker*, a returned veteran of the war who finds himself transforming into a feral killing machine. Peter Straub, who had already explored the dimensions of the ghost tale in *If You Could See Me Now* and *Julia*, published *Ghost Story* in 1979, a complex dark fantasy that equated the haunting power of guilt with the supernatural manifestation. Through the efforts of these and other writers, horror gradually came to be understood as a fiction of specialized tropes and motifs that allowed an exploration of certain concepts not possible through other types of fiction.

The literary aspirations of horror writers in the 1970s were perhaps best summed up in the work of Charles L. Grant. In 1977, Grant published *The Hour of the Oxrun Dead*, the first of an ongoing series of tales set in the fictional suburban Connecticut town of Oxrun Station. Strange doings abound in Oxrun Station, but Grant treats them as shadowy, undefined byproducts of the personal and social tensions knot up just below the placid surface of small-town life there. Grant coined a term for this subtle approach to horror: dark fantasy. In 1978, he edited the anthology *Shadows*, the first in a series of eleven annual volumes of original horror fiction dedicated to promulgating the dark fantasy style. Through the *Shadows* volumes, Grant emphasized the importance of craft over content in the writing of the horror tale, and atmosphere and mood over shocks and gore. Not everyone agreed with Grant's ideas, but the "Shadows" concept brought the '70s to a close with horror moving in a direction that readers and writers alike could choose or choose not to follow.

We are, perhaps, still too close in time to the 1970s to understand completely why horror fiction gained the foothold it achieved in the literary marketplace. Every decade has its fears and concerns, and it is not possible to say with certainty why the literature of horror did not rise up as conspicuously to address the Cold War anxieties of the 1950s, or the nervousness of the Nuclear Age in the 1960s. The answer may lie in the stories collected here, which represent the best horror fiction written in the 1970s. However, readers are warned not to probe too deeply. Decades after their first publication, these stories will retain their power to disturb and dismay. If it is true that we only fear what we do not understand, then it is also true that, on a fundamental level, stories that excite our fears may surpass our understanding.

RICHARD MATHESON

"Duel"

*Richard Matheson (1927-) was recognized as a powerful new talent in postwar fantasy with the publication of his first story, "Born of Man and Woman," in 1950. His early novels **I Am Legend** and **The Shrinking Man** broke new ground through their blending of fantasy, horror and science fiction elements and elaborations of the theme that dominates all of his writing: the individual alone in a hostile universe struggling to survive. Matheson's special interest in the paranormal has served as the foundation for his novels **A Stir of Echoes**, **Hell House**, and **What Dreams May Come**. His time-travel romance, **Bid Time Return**, won the World Fantasy Award. His short stories are among the most reprinted in the fields of fantasy, horror and science fiction. Most were collected in the definitive retrospective volume **The Stories of Richard Matheson**. He is also author of the suspense novels **Ride the Nightmare** and **Seven Steps to Midnight**, and the award-winning westerns **Journal of the Gun Years** and **The Gunfight**. He has scripted many movies and television shows, and his own work has been adapted for film and television series that include "The Twilight Zone" and "Night Gallery." The adaptation of "Duel" as a made-for-television movie launched the career of director Stephen Spielberg.*

Duel

by Richard Matheson

At 11:32 AM, Mann passed the truck.

He was heading west, en route to San Francisco. It was Thursday and unseasonably hot for April. He had his suitcoat off, his tie removed and shirt collar opened, his sleeve cuffs folded back. There was sunlight on his left arm and on part of his lap. He could feel the heat of it through his dark trousers as he drove along the two-lane highway. For the past twenty minutes, he had not seen another vehicle going in either direction.

Then he saw the truck ahead, moving up a curving grade between two high green hills. He heard the grinding strain of its motor and saw a double shadow on the road. The truck was pulling a trailer.

He paid no attention to the details of the truck. As he drew behind it on the grade, he edged his car toward the opposite lane. The road ahead had blind curves and he didn't try to pass until the truck had crossed the ridge. He waited until it started around a left curve on the downgrade, then, seeing that the way was clear, pressed down on the accelerator pedal and steered his car into the eastbound lane. He waited until he could see the truck front in his rearview mirror before he turned back into the proper lane.

Mann looked across the countryside ahead. There were ranges of mountains as far as he could see and, all around him, rolling green hills. He whistled softly as the car sped down the winding grade, its tires making crisp sounds on the pavement.

At the bottom of the hill, he crossed a concrete bridge and, glancing to the right, saw a dry steambed strewn with rocks and gravel. As the car moved off the bridge, he saw a trailer park set back from the highway to his right. How can anyone live out here? he thought. His shifting gaze caught sight of a pet cemetery ahead and he smiled. Maybe those people in the trailers wanted to be close to the graves of their dogs and cats.

The highway ahead was straight now. Mann drifted into a reverie, the sunlight on his arm and lap. He wondered what Ruth was doing. The kids, of course, were in school and would be for hours yet. Maybe Ruth was shopping; Thursday was the day she usually went. Mann visualized her in the supermarket, putting various items into the basket cart. He wished he were with her instead of starting on another sales trip. Hours of driving yet before he'd reach San Francisco. Three days of hotel sleeping and restaurant eating, hoped-for contacts and likely disappointments. He sighed; then, reaching out impulsively, he switched on the radio. He revolved the tuning knob until he found a station playing soft, innocuous music. He hummed along with it, eyes almost out of focus on the road ahead.

He started as the truck roared past him on the left, causing his car to shudder slightly. He watched the truck and trailer cut in abruptly for the westbound lane and frowned as he had to brake to maintain a safe distance behind it. What's with you? he thought.

He eyed the truck with cursury disapproval. It was a huge gasoline tanker pulling a tank trailer, each of them having six pairs of wheels. He could see that it was not a new rig but was dented and in need of renovation, its tanks painted a cheap-looking silvery color. Mann wondered if the driver had done the painting himself. His gaze shifted from the word FLAMMABLE printed across the back of the trailer tank, red letters on a white background, to the parallel reflector lines painted in red across the bottom of the tank to the massive rubber flaps swaying behind the rear tires, then back up again. The reflector lines looked as though they'd been clumsily applied with a stencil. The driver must be an independent trucker, he decided, and not too affluent a one, from the looks of his outfit. He glanced at the trailer's license plate. It was a California issue.

Mann checked his speedometer. He was holding steady at 55 miles an hour, as he invariably did when he drove without thinking on the open highway. The truck driver must have done a good 70 to pass him so quickly. That seemed a little odd. Weren't truck drivers supposed to be a cautious lot?

He grimaced at the smell of the truck's exhaust and looked at the vertical pipe to the left of the cab. It was spewing smoke, which clouded darkly back across the trailer. Christ, he thought. With all the furor about air pollution, why do they keep allowing that sort of thing on the highways?

He scowled at the constant fumes. They'd make him nauseated in a little while, he knew. He couldn't lag back here like this. Either he slowed down or he passed the truck again. He didn't have the time to slow down. He'd gotten a late start. Keeping it at 55 all the way, he'd just about make his afternoon appointment. No, he'd have to pass.

Depressing the gas pedal, he eased his car toward the opposite lane. No sign of anything ahead. Traffic on this route seemed almost nonexistent today. He pushed down harder on the accelerator and steered all the way into the eastbound lane.

As he passed the truck, he glanced at it. The cab was too high for him to see into. All he caught sight of was the back of the truck driver's left hand on the steering wheel. It was darkly tanned and square-looking, with large veins knotted on its surface.

When Mann could see the truck reflected in the rearview mirror, he pulled back over to the proper lane and looked ahead again.

He glanced at the rearview mirror in surprise as the truck driver gave him an extended horn blast. What was that? he wondered; a greeting or a curse? He grunted with amusement, glancing at the mirror as he drove. The front fenders of the truck were a dingy purple color, the paint faded and chipped; another amateurish job. All he could see was the lower portion of the truck; the rest was cut off by the top of his rear window.

To Mann's right, now, was a slope of shalelike earth with patches of scrub grass growing on it. His gaze jumped to the clapboard house on top of the slope. The television aerial on its roof was sagging at an angle of less than 40 degrees. Must give great reception, he thought.

He looked to the front again, glancing aside abruptly at a sign printed in jagged block letters on a piece of plywood: NIGHT CRAWLERS—BAIT. What the hell is a night crawler? he wondered. It sounded like some monster in a low-grade Hollywood thriller.

The unexpected roar of the truck motor made his gaze jump to the rearview mirror. Instantly, his startled look jumped to the side mirror. By God, the guy was passing him *again*. Mann turned his head to scowl at the leviathan form as it drifted by. He tried to see into the cab but couldn't because of its height. What's with him, anyway? he wondered. What the hell are we having here, a contest? See which vehicle can stay ahead the longest?

He thought of speeding up to stay ahead but changed his mind. When the truck and trailer started back into the westbound lane, he let up on the pedal, voicing a newly incredulous sound as he saw that if he hadn't slowed down, he would have been prematurely cut off again. Jesus Christ, he thought. What's *with* this guy?

His scowl deepened as the odor of the truck's exhaust reached his nostrils again. Irritably, he cranked up the window on his left. Damn it, was he going to have to breathe that crap all the way to San Francisco? He couldn't afford to slow down. He had to meet Forbes at a quarter after three and that was that.

He looked ahead. At least there was no traffic complicating matters. Mann pressed down on the accelerator pedal, drawing close behind the truck. When the highway curved enough to the left to give him a completely open view of the route ahead, he jarred down on the pedal, steering out into the opposite lane.

The truck edged over, blocking his way.

For several moments, all Mann could do was stare at it in blank confusion. Then, with a startled noise, he braked, returning to the proper lane. The truck moved back in front of him.

Mann could not allow himself to accept what apparently had taken place. It had to be a coincidence. The truck driver couldn't have blocked his way on purpose. He waited for more than a minute, then flicked down the turn-indicator lever to make his intentions perfectly clear and, depressing the accelerator pedal, steered again into the eastbound lane.

Immediately, the truck shifted, barring his way.

"*Jesus Christ!*" Mann was astounded. This was unbelievable. He'd never seen such a thing in twenty-six years of driving. He returned to the westbound lane, shaking his head as the truck swung back in front of him.

He eased up on the gas pedal, falling back to avoid the truck's exhaust. Now what? he wondered. He still had to make San Francisco on schedule. Why in God's name hadn't he gone a little out of his way in the beginning, so he could have traveled by freeway? This damned highway was two lane all the way.

Impulsively, he sped into the eastbound lane again. To his surprise, the truck driver did not pull over. Instead, the driver stuck his left arm out and waved him on. Mann started pushing down on the accelerator. Suddenly, he let up on the pedal with a gasp and jerked the steering wheel around, raking back behind the truck so quickly that his car began to fishtail. He was fighting to control its zigzag whipping when a blue converitble shot by him in the opposite lane. Mann caught a momentary vision of the man inside it glaring at him.

The car came under his control again. Mann was sucking breath in through his mouth. His heart was pounding almost painfully. My God! he thought. *He wanted me to hit that car head-on.* The realization stunned him. True, he should have seen to it himself that the

11

road ahead was clear; that was his failure. But to wave him on . . . Mann felt appalled and sickened. Boy, oh, boy, oh, boy, he thought. This was really one for the books. That son of a bitch had meant for not only him to be killed but a totally uninvolved passerby as well. The idea seemed beyond his comprehension. On a California highway on a Thursday morning? Why?

Mann tried to calm himself and rationalize the incident. Maybe it's the heat, he thought. Maybe the truck driver had a tension headache or an upset stomach; maybe both. Maybe he'd had a fight with his wife. Maybe she'd failed to put out last night. Mann tried in vain to smile. There could be any number of reasons. Reaching out, he twisted off the radio. The cheerful music irritated him.

He drove behind the truck for several minutes, his face a mask of animosity. As the exhaust fumes started putting his stomach on edge, he suddenly forced down the heel of his right hand on the horn bar and held it there. Seeing that the route ahead was clear, he pushed in the accelerator pedal all the way and steered into the opposite lane.

The movement of his car was paralleled immediately by the truck. Mann stayed in place, right hand jammed down on the horn bar. Get out of the way, you son of a bitch! he thought. He felt the muscles of his jaw hardening until they ached. There was a twisting in his stomach.

"*Damn!*" He pulled back quickly to the proper lane, shuddering with fury. "You miserable son of a bitch," he muttered, glaring at the truck as it was shifted back in front of him. What the hell is wrong with you? I pass your goddamn rig a couple of times and you go flying off the deep end? Are you nuts or something? Mann nodded tensely. Yes, he thought; he *is*. No other explanation.

He wondered what Ruth would think of all this, how she'd react. Probably, she'd start to honk the horn and would keep on honking it, assuming that, eventually, it would attract the attention of a policeman. He looked around with a scowl. Just where in hell *were* the policemen out here, anyway? He made a scoffing noise. What policemen? Here in the boondocks? They probably had a sheriff on horseback, for Christ's sake.

He wondered suddenly if he could fool the truck driver by passing on the right. Edging his car toward the shoulder, he peered ahead. No chance. There wasn't room enough. The truck driver could shove him through that wire fence if he wanted to. Mann shivered. And he'd want to, sure as hell, he thought.

Driving where he was, he grew conscious of the debris lying beside the highway: beer cans, candy wrappers, ice-cream containers, newspaper sections browned and rotted by the weather, a FOR SALE sign torn in half. Keep America beautiful, he thought sardonically. He passed a boulder with the name WILL JASPER painted on it in white. Who the hell is Will Jasper? he wondered. What would he think of this situation?

Unexpectedly, the car began to bounce. For several anxious moments, Mann thought that one of his tires had gone flat. Then he noticed that the paving along this section of highway consisted of pitted slabs with gaps between them. He saw the truck and trailer jolting up and down and thought : I hope it shakes your brains loose. As the truck veered into a sharp left curve, he caught a fleeting glimpse of the driver's face in the cab's side mirror. There was not enough time to establish his appearance.

"Ah," he said. A long, steep hill was looming up ahead. The truck would have to climb it slowly. There would doubtless be an opportunity to pass somewhere on the grade. Mann pressed down on the accelerator pedal, drawing as close behind the truck as safety would allow.

Halfway up the slope, Mann saw a turnout for the eastbound lane with no oncoming traffic anywhere in sight. Flooring the accelerator pedal, he shot into the opposite lane. The slow-moving truck began to angle out in front of him. Face stiffening, Mann steered his speeding car across the highway edge and curved it sharply on the turnout. Clouds of dust went billowing up behind his car, making him lose sight of the truck. His tires buzzed and crackled on the dirt, then, suddenly, were humming on the pavement once again.

He glanced at the rearview mirror and a barking laugh erupted from his throat. He'd only meant to pass. The dust had been an unexpected bonus. Let the bastard get a sniff of something rotten-smelling in *his* nose for a change! he thought. He honked the horn elatedly, a mocking rhythm of beats. Screw you, Jack!

He swept across the summit of the hill. A striking vista lay ahead: sunlit hills and flatland, a corridor of dark trees, quadrangles of cleared-off acreage and bright-green vegetable patches; far off, in the distance, a mammoth water tower. Mann felt stirred by the panoramic sight. Lovely, he thought. Reaching out, he turned the radio back on and started humming cheerfully with the music.

Seven minutes later, he passed a billboard advertising CHUCK'S CAFE. No thanks, Chuck, he thought. He glanced at a gray house nestled in a hollow. Was that a cemetery in its front yard or a group of plaster statuary for sale?

Hearing the noise behind him, Mann looked at the rearview mirror

13

and felt himself go cold with fear. The truck was hurtling down the hill, pursuing him.

His mouth fell open and he threw a glance at the speedometer. He was doing more than 60! On a curving downgrade, that was not at all a safe speed to be driving. Yet the truck must be exceeding that by a considerable margin, it was closing the distance between them so rapidly. Mann swallowed, leaning to the right as he steered his car around a sharp curve. Is the man *insane?* he thought.

His gaze jumped forward searchingly. He saw a turnoff half a mile ahead and decided that he'd use it. In the rearview mirror, the huge square radiator grille was all he could see now. He stamped down on the gas pedal and his tires screeched unnervingly as he wheeled around another curve, thinking that, surely, the truck would have to slow down here.

He groaned as it rounded the curve with ease, only the sway of its tanks revealing the outward pressure of the turn. Mann bit trembling lips together as he whipped his car around another curve. A straight descent now. He depressed the pedal farther, glanced at the speedometer. Almost 70 miles an hour! He wasn't used to driving this fast!

In agony, he saw the turnoff shoot by on his right. He couldn't have left the highway at this speed, anyway; he'd have overturned. Goddamn it, what was wrong with that son of a bitch? Mann honked his horn in frightened rage. Cranking down the window suddenly, he shoved his left arm out to wave the truck back. "*Back!*" he yelled. He honked the horn again. "Get back, you crazy bastard!"

The truck was almost on him now. He's going to kill me! Mann thought, horrified. He honked the horn repeatedly, then had to use both hands to grip the steering wheel as he swept around another curve. He flashed a look at the rearview mirror. He could see only the bottom portion of the truck's radiator grille. He was going to lose control! He felt the rear wheels start to drift and let up on the pedal quickly. The tire treads bit in, the car leaped on, regaining its momentum.

Mann saw the bottom of the grade ahead, and in the distance there was a building with a sign that read CHUCK'S CAFE. The truck was gaining ground again. This is insane! he thought, enraged and terrified at once. The highway straightened out. He floored the pedal: 74 now—75. Mann braced himself, trying to ease the car as far to the right as possible.

Abruptly, he began to brake, then swerved to the right, raking his car into the open area in front of the cafe. He cried out as the car began to fishtail, then careened into a skid. *Steer with it!* screamed a voice in his mind. The rear of the car was lashing from side to side, tires spewing dirt and raising clouds of dust. Mann pressed harder on the brake pedal, turning further into the skid. The car began to straighten out and he braked harder yet, conscious, on the sides of his vision, of the truck and trailer roaring by on the highway. He nearly sideswiped one of the cars parked in front of the cafe, bounced and skidded by it, going almost straight now. He jammed in the brake pedal as hard as he could. The rear end broke to the right and the car spun half around, sheering sideways to a neck-wrenching halt thirty yards beyond the cafe.

Mann sat in pulsing silence, eyes closed. His heartbeats felt like club blows in his chest. He couldn't seem to catch his breath. If he were ever going to have a heart attack, it would be now. After a while, he opened his eyes and pressed his right palm against his chest. His heart was still throbbing laboredly. No wonder, he thought. It isn't every day I'm almost murdered by a truck.

He raised the handle and pushed out the door, then started forward, grunting in surprise as the safety belt held him in place. Reaching down with shaking fingers, he depressed the release button and pulled the ends of the belt apart. He glanced at the cafe. What had its patrons thought of his breakneck appearance? he wondered.

He stumbled as he walked to the front door of the cafe. TRUCKERS WELCOME, read a sign in the window. It gave Mann a queasy feeling to see it. Shivering, he pulled open the door and went inside, avoiding the sight of its customers. He felt certain they were watching him, but he didn't have the strength to face their looks. Keeping his gaze fixed straight ahead, he moved to the rear of the cafe and opened the door marked GENTS.

Moving to the sink, he twisted the right-hand faucet and leaned over to cup cold water in his palms and splash it on his face. There was a fluttering of his stomach muscles he could not control.

Straightening up, he tugged down several towels from their dispenser and patted them against his face, grimacing at the smell of the paper. Dropping the soggy towels into a wastebasket beside the sink, he regarded himself in the wall mirror. Still with us, Mann, he thought. He nodded, swallowing. Drawing out his metal comb, he neatened his hair. You never know, he thought. You just never know. You drift along, year after year, presuming certain values to be fixed; like being able to drive on a public thoroughfare without somebody trying to murder you. You come to depend on that sort of thing. Then something occurs and all bets are off. One shocking incident and all the years of logic and acceptance are displaced and, suddenly, the jungle is in front of you again. *Man, part animal, part angel.* Where had he come across that phrase? He shivered.

It was entirely an animal in that truck out there.

His breath was almost back to normal now. Mann forced a smile at his reflection. All right, boy, he told himself. It's over now. It was a goddamned nightmare, but it's over. You are on your way to San Francisco. You'll get yourself a nice hotel room, order a bottle of expensive Scotch, soak your body in a hot bath and forget. Damn right, he thought. He turned and walked out of the washroom.

He jolted to a halt, his breath cut off. Standing rooted, heartbeat hammering at his chest, he gaped through the front window of the cafe.

The truck and trailer were parked outside.

Mann stared at them in unbelieving shock. It wasn't possible. He'd seen them roaring by at top speed. The driver had won; he'd *won!* He'd had the whole damn highway to himself! *Why had he turned back?*

Mann looked around with sudden dread. There were five men eating, three along the counter, two in booths. He cursed himself for having failed to look at faces when he'd entered. Now there was no way of knowing who it was. Mann felt his legs begin to shake.

Abruptly, he walked to the nearest booth and slid in clumsily behind the table. Now wait, he told himself; just wait. Surely, he could tell which one it was. Masking his face with the menu, he glanced across its top. Was it that one in the khaki work shirt? Mann tried to see the man's hands but couldn't. His gaze flicked nervously across the room. Not that one in the suit, of course. Three remaining. That one in the front booth, square-faced, black-haired? If only he could see the man's hands, it might help. One of the two others at the counter? Mann studied them uneasily. Why hadn't he looked at faces when he'd come in?

Now *wait*, he thought. Goddamn it, *wait!* All right, the truck driver was in here. That didn't automatically signify that he meant to continue the insane duel. Chuck's Cafe might be the only place to eat for miles around. It *was* lunchtime, wasn't it? The truck driver had probably intended to eat here all the time. He'd just been moving too fast to pull into the parking lot before. So he'd slowed down, turned around and driven back, that was all. Mann forced himself to read the menu. Right, he thought. No point in getting so rattled. Perhaps a beer would help relax him.

The woman behind the counter came over and Mann ordered a

ham sandwich on rye toast and a bottle of Coors. As the woman turned away, he wondered, with a sudden twinge of self-reproach, why he hadn't simply left the cafe, jumped into his car and sped away. He would have known immediately, then, if the truck driver was still out to get him. As it was, he'd have to suffer through an entire meal to find out. He almost groaned at his stupidity.

Still, what if the truck driver *had* followed him out and started after him again? He'd have been right back where he'd started. Even if he'd managed to get a good lead, the truck driver would have overtaken him eventually. It just wasn't in him to drive at 80 and 90 miles an hour in order to stay ahead. True, he might have been intercepted by a California Highway Patrol car. What if he weren't though?

Mann repressed the plaguing thoughts. He tried to calm himself. He looked deliberately at the four men. Either of two seemed a likely possibility as the driver of the truck: the square-faced one in the front booth and the chunky one in the jumpsuit sitting at the counter. Mann had an impulse to walk over to them and ask which one it was, tell the man he was sorry he'd irritated him, tell him anything to calm him, since, obviously, he wasn't rational, was a manic-depressive, probably. Maybe buy the man a beer and sit with him awhile to try to settle things.

He couldn't move. What if the truck driver were letting the whole thing drop? Mightn't his approach rile the man all over again? Mann felt drained by indecision. He nodded weakly as the waitress set the sandwich and the bottle in front of him. He took a swallow of the beer, which made him cough. Was the truck driver amused by the sound? Mann felt a stirring of resentment deep inside himself. What right did that bastard have to impose this torment on another human being? It was a free country, wasn't it? Damn it, he had every right to pass the son of a bitch on a highway if he wanted to!

"Oh, hell," he mumbled. He tried to feel amused. He was making entirely too much of this. Wasn't he? He glanced at the pay telephone on the front wall. What was to prevent him from calling the local police and telling them the situation? But, then, he'd have to stay here, lose time, make Forbes angry, probably lose the sale. And what if the truck driver stayed to face them? Naturally, he'd deny the whole thing. What if the police believed him and didn't do anything about it? After they'd gone, the truck driver would undoubtedly take it out on him again, only worse. *God*! Mann thought in agony.

The sandwich tasted flat, the beer unpleasantly sour. Mann stared at the table as he ate. For God's sake, why was he just *sitting* here like this? He was a grown man, wasn't he? Why didn't he settle this damn thing once and for all?

His left hand twitched so unexpectedly, he spilled beer on his trousers. The man in the jumpsuit had risen from the counter and was strolling toward the front of the cafe. Mann felt his heartbeat thumping as the man gave money to the waitress, took his change and a toothpick from the dispenser and went outside. Mann watched in anxious silence.

The man did not get into the cab of the tanker truck.

It had to be the one in the front booth, then. His face took form in Mann's remembrance: square, with dark eyes, dark hair; the man who'd tried to kill him.

Mann stood abruptly, letting impulse conquer fear. Eyes fixed ahead, he started toward the entrance. Anything was preferable to sitting in that booth. He stopped by the cash register, conscious of the hitching of his chest as he gulped in air. Was the man observing him? he wondered. He swallowed, pulling out the clip of dollar bills in his right-hand trouser pocket. He glanced toward the waitress. Come *on*, he thought. He looked at his check and, seeing the amount, reached shakily into his trouser pocket for change. He heard a coin fall onto the floor and roll away. Ignoring it, he dropped a dollar and a quarter onto the counter and thrust the clip of bills into his trouser pocket.

As he did, he heard the man in the front booth get up. An icy shudder spasmed up his back. Turning quickly to the door, he shoved it open, seeing, on the edges of his vision, the square-faced man approach the cash register. Lurching from the cafe, he started toward his car with long strides. His mouth was dry again. The pounding of his heart was painful in his chest.

Suddenly, he started running. He heard the cafe door bang shut and fought away the urge to look across his shoulder. Was that a sound of other running footsteps now? Reaching his car, Mann yanked open the door and jarred in awkwardly behind the steering wheel. He reached into his trouser pocket for the keys and snatched them out, almost dropping them. His hand was shaking so badly he couldn't get the ignition key into its slot. He whined with mounting dread. Come on! he thought.

The key slid in, he twisted it convulsively. The motor started and he raced it momentarily before jerking the transmission shift to drive. Depressing the accelerator pedal quickly, he raked the car around and steered it toward the highway. From the corners of his eyes, he saw the truck and trailer being backed away from the cafe.

Reaction burst inside him. "No!" he raged and slammed his foot down on the brake pedal. This was idiotic! Why the hell should he run away? His car slid sideways to a rocking halt and, shouldering out the door, he lurched to his feet and started toward the truck with angry strides. *All right, Jack,* he thought. He glared at the man inside the truck. You want to punch my nose, okay, but no more goddamn tournament on the highway.

The truck began to pick up speed. Mann raised his right arm. "Hey!" he yelled. He knew the driver saw him. "*Hey!*" He started running as the truck kept moving, engine grinding loudly. It was on the highway now. He sprinted toward it with a sense of martyred outrage. The driver shifted gears, the truck moved faster. "Stop!" Mann shouted. "Damn it, *stop!*"

He thudded to a panting halt, staring at the truck as it receded down the highway, moved around a hill and disappeared. "You son of a bitch," he muttered. "You goddamn, miserable son of a bitch."

He trudged back slowly to his car, trying to believe that the truck driver had fled the hazard of a fistfight. It was possible, of course, but, somehow, he could not believe it.

He got into his car and was about to drive onto the highway when he changed his mind and switched the motor off. That crazy bastard might just be tooling along at 15 miles an hour, waiting for him to catch up. Nuts to that, he thought. So he blew his schedule; screw it. Forbes would have to wait, that was all. And if Forbes didn't care to wait, that was all right, too. He'd sit here for a while and let the nut get out of range, let him think he'd won the day. He grinned. You're the bloody Red Baron, Jack; you've shot me down. Now go to hell with my sincerest compliments. He shook his head. Beyond belief, he thought.

He really should have done this earlier, pulled over, waited. Then the truck driver would have had to let it pass. *Or picked on someone else,* the startling thought occurred to him. Jesus, maybe that was how the crazy bastard whiled away his work hours! Jesus Christ Almighty! was it possible?

He looked at the dashboard clock. It was just past 12:30. Wow, he thought. All that in less than an hour. He shifted on the seat and stretched his legs out. Leaning back against the door, he closed his eyes and mentally perused the things he had to do tomorrow and the following day. Today was shot to hell, as far as he could see.

When he opened his eyes, afraid of drifting into sleep and losing too much time, almost eleven minutes had passed. The nut must be an ample distance off by now, he thought; at least 11 miles and likely more, the way he drove. Good enough. He wasn't going to try to make San Francisco on schedule now, anyway. He'd take it real easy.

Mann adjusted his safety belt, switched on the motor, tapped the transmission pointer into drive position and pulled onto the highway, glancing back across his shoulder. Not a car in sight. Great day for driving. Everybody was staying at home. That nut must have a reputation around here. When Crazy Jack is on the highway, lock your car in the garage. Mann chuckled at the notion as his car began to turn the curve ahead.

Mindless reflex drove his right foot down against the brake pedal. Suddenly, his car had skidded to a halt and he was staring down the highway. The truck and trailer were parked on the shoulder less than 90 yards away.

Mann couldn't seem to function. He knew his car was blocking the westbound lane, knew that he should either make a U-turn or pull off the highway, but all he could do was gape at the truck.

He cried out, legs retracting, as a horn blast sounded behind him. Snapping up his head, he looked at the rearview mirror, gasping as he saw a yellow station wagon bearing down on him at high speed. Suddenly, it veered off toward the eastbound lane, disappearing from the mirror. Mann jerked around and saw it hurtling past his car, its rear end snapping back and forth, its back tires screeching. He saw the twisted features of the man inside, saw his lips move rapidly with cursing.

Then the station wagon had swerved back into the westbound lane and was speeding off. It gave Mann an odd sensation to see it pass the truck. The man in that station wagon could drive on, unthreatened. Only he'd been singled out. What happened was demented. Yet it was happening.

He drove his car onto the highway shoulder and braked. Putting the transmission into neutral, he leaned back, staring at the truck. His head was aching again. There was a pulsing at his temples like the ticking of a muffled clock.

What was he to do? He knew very well that if he left his car to walk to the truck, the driver would pull away and repark farther down the highway. He may as well face the fact that he was dealing with a madman. He felt the tremor in his stomach muscles starting up again. His heartbeat thudded slowly, striking at his chest wall. Now what?

With a sudden, angry impulse, Mann snapped the transmission into gear and stepped down hard on the accelerator pedal. The tires of the car spun sizzlingly before they gripped; the car shot out onto the highway. Instantly, the truck began to move. He even had the motor on! Mann thought in raging fear. He floored the pedal, then, abruptly, realized he couldn't make it, that the truck would block his way and he'd collide with its trailer. A vision flashed across his mind, a fiery explosion and a sheet of flame incinerating him. He started braking fast, trying to decelerate evenly, so he wouldn't lose control.

When he'd slowed down enough to feel that it was safe, he steered the car onto the shoulder and stopped it again, throwing the transmission into neutral.

Approximately eighty yards ahead, the truck pulled off the highway and stopped.

Mann tapped his fingers on the steering wheel. *Now* what? he thought. Turn around and head east until he reached a cutoff that would take him to San Francisco by another route? How did he know the truck driver wouldn't follow him even then? His cheeks twisted as he bit his lips together angrily. No! He wasn't going to turn around!

His expression hardened suddenly. Well, he wasn't going to *sit* here all day, that was certain. Reaching out, he tapped the gearshift into drive and steered his car onto the highway once again. He saw the massive truck and trailer start to move but made no effort to speed up. He tapped at the brakes, taking a position about 30 yards behind the trailer. He glanced at his speedometer. Forty miles an hour. The truck driver had his left arm out of the cab window and was waving him on. What did that mean? Had he changed his mind? Decided, finally, that this thing had gone too far? Mann couldn't let himself believe it.

He looked ahead. Despite the mountain ranges all around, the highway was flat as far as he could see. He tapped a fingernail against the horn bar, trying to make up his mind. Presumably, he could continue all the way to San Francisco at this speed, hanging back just far enough to avoid the worst of the exhaust fumes. It didn't seem likely that the truck driver would stop directly on the highway to block his way. And if the truck driver pulled onto the shoulder to let him pass, he could pull off the highway, too. It would be a draining afternoon but a safe one.

On the other hand, outracing the truck might be worth just one more try. This was obviously what that son of a bitch wanted. Yet, surely, a vehicle of such size couldn't be driven with the same daring as, potentially, his own. The laws of mechanics were against it, if nothing else. Whatever advantage the truck had in mass, it had to lose in stability, particularly that of its trailer. If Mann were to drive at, say, 80 miles an hour and there were a few steep grades—as he felt sure there were—the truck would have to fall behind.

The question was, of course, whether he had the nerve to maintain such a speed over a long distance. He'd never done it before. Still, the more he thought about it, the more it appealed to him; far more than the alternative did.

Abruptly, he decided. *Right*, he thought. He checked ahead, then pressed down hard on the accelerator pedal and pulled into the eastbound lane. As he neared the truck, he tensed, anticipating that the driver might block his way. But the truck did not shift from the westbound lane. Mann's car moved along its mammoth side. He glanced at the cab and saw the name KELLER printed on its door. For a shocking instant, he thought it read KILLER and started to slow down. Then, glancing at the name again, he saw what it really was and depressed the pedal sharply. When he saw the truck reflected in the rearview mirror, he steered his car into the westbound lane.

He shuddered, dread and satisfaction mixed together, as he saw that the truck driver was speeding up. It was strangely comforting to know the man's intentions definitely again. That plus the knowledge of his face and name seemed, somehow, to reduce his stature. Before, he had been faceless, nameless, an embodiment of unknown terror. Now, at least, he was an individual. All right, Keller, said his mind, let's see you beat me with that purple-silver relic now. He pressed down harder on the pedal. *Here we go*, he thought.

He looked at the speedometer, scowling as he saw that he was doing only 74 miles an hour. Deliberately, he pressed down on the pedal, alternating his gaze between the highway ahead and the speedometer until the needle turned past 80. He felt a flickering of satisfaction with himself. All right, Keller, you son of a bitch, top that, he thought.

After several moments, he glanced into the rearview mirror again. Was the truck getting closer? Stunned, he checked the speedometer. Damn it! He was down to 76! He forced in the accelerator pedal angrily. *He mustn't go less than 80!* Mann's chest shuddered with convulsive breath.

He glanced aside as he hurtled past a beige sedan parked on the shoulder underneath a tree. A young couple sat inside it, talking. Already they were far behind, their world removed from his. Had they even glanced aside when he'd passed? He doubted it.

He started as the shadow of an overhead bridge whipped across the hood and windshield. Inhaling raggedly, he glanced at the speedometer again. He was holding at 81. He checked the rearview mirror. Was it his imagination that the truck was gaining ground? He looked forward with anxious eyes. There had to be some kind of town ahead. To hell with time; he'd stop at the police station and tell them what had happened. They'd have to believe him. Why would he stop to tell them such a story if it weren't true? For all he knew, Keller had a police record in these parts. *Oh, sure we're on to him*, he heard a faceless officer remark. *That crazy bastard's asked for it before and now he's going to get it.*

Mann shook himself and looked at the mirror. The truck was getting closer. Wincing, he glanced at the speedometer. Goddamn it, pay attention! raged his mind. He was down to 74 again! Whining with frustration, he depressed the pedal. Eighty!—80! he demanded of himself. There was a murderer behind him!

His car began to pass a field of flowers; lilacs, Mann saw, white and purple stretching out in endless rows. There was a small shack near the highway, the words FIELD FRESH FLOWER painted on it. A brown-cardboard square was propped against the shack, the word FUNERALS printed crudely on it. Mann saw himself, abruptly, lying in a casket, painted like some grotesque mannequin. The overpowering smell of flowers seemed to fill his nostrils. Ruth and the children sitting in the first row, heads bowed. All his relatives—

Suddenly, the pavement roughened and the car began to bounce and shudder, driving bolts of pain into his head. He felt the steering wheel resisting him and clamped his hands around it tightly, harsh vibrations running up his arms. He didn't dare look at the mirror now. He had to force himself to keep the speed unchanged. Keller wasn't going to slow down; he was sure of that. *What if he got a flat tire, though?* All control would vanish in an instant. He visualized the somersaulting of his car, its grinding, shrieking tumble, the explosion of its gas tank, his body crushed and burned and—

The broken span of pavement ended and his gaze jumped quickly to the rearview mirror. The truck was no closer, but it hadn't lost ground, either. Mann's eyes shifted. Up ahead were hills and mountains. He tried to reassure himself that upgrades were on his side, that he could climb them at the same speed he was going now. Yet all he could imagine were the downgrades, the immense truck close behind him, slamming violently into his car and knocking it across some cliff edge. He had a horrifying vision of dozens of broken, rusted cars lying unseen in the canyons ahead, corpses in every one of them, all flung to shattering deaths by Keller.

Mann's car went rocketing into a corridor of trees. On each side of the highway was a eucalyptus windbreak, each trunk three feet from the next. It was like speeding through a high-walled canyon. Mann gasped, twitching, as a large twig bearing dusty leaves dropped down across the windshield, then slid out of sight. Dear God! he thought. He was getting near the edge himself. If he should lose his nerve at this speed, it was over. Jesus! That would be ideal for Keller! he realized suddenly. He visualized the square-faced driver laughing as he passed the burning wreckage, knowing that he'd killed his prey without so much as touching him.

Mann started as his car shot out into the open. The route ahead was not straight now but winding up into the foothills. Mann willed himself to press down on the pedal even more. Eighty-three now, almost 84.

To his left was a broad terrain of green hills blending into mountains. He saw a black car on a dirt road, moving toward the highway. *Was its side painted white?* Mann's heartbeat lurched. Impulsively, he jammed the heel of his right hand down against the horn bar and held it there. The blast of the horn was shrill and racking to his ears. His heart began to pound. Was it a police car? *Was it?*

He let the horn bar up abruptly. No, it *wasn't*. Damn! his mind raged. Keller must have been amused by his pathetic efforts. Doubtless, he was chuckling to himself right now. He heard the truck driver's voice in his mind, coarse and sly. *You think you gonna get a cop to save you, boy? Shee-it. You gonna die.* Mann's heart contorted with savage hatred. *You son of a bitch!* he thought. Jerking his right hand into a fist, he drove it down against the seat. Goddamn you, Keller! I'm going to kill you, if it's the last thing I do!

The hills were closer now. There would be slopes directly, long steep grades. Mann felt a burst of hope within himself. He was sure to gain a lot of distance on the truck. No matter how he tried, that bastard Keller couldn't manage 80 miles an hour on a hill. But *I* can! cried his mind with fierce elation. He worked up saliva in his mouth and swallowed it. The back of his shirt was drenched. He could feel sweat trickling down his sides. A bath and a drink, first order of the day on reaching San Francisco. A long, hot bath, a long, cold drink. Cutty Sark. He'd splurge, by Christ. He rated it.

The car swept up a shallow rise. Not steep enough, goddamn it! The truck's momentum would prevent its losing speed. Mann felt mindless hatred for the landscape. Already, he had topped the rise and tilted over to a shallow downgrade. He looked at the rearview mirror. *Square*, he thought, everything about the truck was square: the radiator grille, the fender shapes, the bumper ends, the outline of the cab, even the shape of Keller's hands and face. He visualized the truck as some great entity pursuing him, insentient, brutish, chasing him with instinct only.

Mann cried out, horror-stricken, as he saw the ROAD REPAIRS sign up ahead. His frantic gaze leaped down the highway. Both lanes blocked, a huge black arrow pointing toward the alternate route! He groaned in anguish, seeing it was dirt. His foot jumped automatically to the brake pedal and started pumping it. He threw a dazed look at the rearview mirror. The truck was moving as fast as ever! It *couldn't*, though! Mann's expression froze in terror as he started turning to the right.

He stiffened as the front wheels hit the dirt road. For an instant, he was certain that the back part of the car was going to spin; he felt it breaking to the left. "No, don't!" he cried. Abruptly, he was jarring down the dirt road, elbows braced against his sides, trying to keep from losing control. His tires battered at the ruts, almost tearing the wheel from his grip. The windows rattled noisily. His neck snapped back and forth with painful jerks. His jolting body surged against the binding of the safety belt and slammed down violently on the seat. He felt the bouncing of the car drive up his spine. His clenching teeth slipped and he cried out hoarsely as his upper teeth gouged deep into his lip.

He gasped as the rear end of the car began surging to the right. He started to jerk the steering wheel to the left, then, hissing, wrenched it in the opposite direction, crying out as the right rear fender cracked into a fence pole, knocking it down. He started pumping at the brakes, struggling to regain control. The car rear yawed sharply to the left, tires shooting out a spray of dirt. Mann felt a scream tear upward in his throat. He twisted wildly at the steering wheel. The car began careening to the right. He hitched the wheel around until the car was on course again. His head was pounding like his heart now, with gigantic, throbbing spasms. He started coughing as he gagged on dripping blood.

The dirt road ended suddenly, the car regained momentum on the pavement and he dared to look at the rearview mirror. The truck was slowed down but was still behind him, rocking like a freighter on a storm-tossed sea, its huge tires scouring up a pall of dust. Mann shoved in the accelerator pedal and his car surged forward. A good, steep grade lay just ahead; he'd gain that distance now. He swallowed blood, grimacing at the taste, then fumbled in his trouser pocket and tugged out his handkerchief. He pressed it to his bleeding lip, eyes fixed on the slope ahead. Another fifty yards or so. He writhed his back. His undershirt was soaking wet, adhering to his skin. He glanced at the rearview mirror. The truck had just regained the highway. *Tough!* he thought with venom. Didn't get me, did you, Keller?

His car was on the first yards of the upgrade when steam began to issue from beneath its hood. Mann stiffened suddenly, eyes widening with shock. The steam increased, became a smoking mist. Mann's gaze jumped down. The red light hadn't flashed on yet but had to in a moment. How could this be happening? Just as he was set to get away! The slope ahead was long and gradual, with many curves. He knew he couldn't stop. Could he U-turn unexpectedly and go back down? the sudden thought occurred. He looked ahead. The highway was too narrow, bound by hills on both sides. There wasn't room enough to make an uninterrupted turn and there wasn't time enough to ease around. If he tried that, Keller would shift direction and hit him head-on. "Oh, my God!" Mann murmured suddenly.

He was going to die.

He stared ahead with stricken eyes, his view increasingly obscured by steam. Abruptly, he recalled the afternoon he'd had the engine steam-cleaned at the local car wash. The man who'd done it had suggested he replace the water hoses, because steam-cleaning had a tendency to make them crack. He'd nodded, thinking that he'd do it when he had more time. *More time!* The phrase was like a dagger in his mind. He'd failed to change the hoses and, for that failure, he was now about to die.

He sobbed in terror as the dashboard light flashed on. He glanced at it involuntarily and read the word HOT, black on red. With a breathless gasp, he jerked the transmission into low. Why hadn't he done that right away! He looked ahead. The slope seemed endless. Already, he could hear a boiling throb inside the radiator. How much coolant was there left? Steam was clouding faster, hazing up the windshield. Reaching out, he twisted at a dashboard knob. The wipers started flicking back and forth in fan-shaped sweeps. There had to be enough coolant in the radiator to get him to the top. *Then what?* cried his mind. He couldn't drive without coolant, even downhill. He glanced at the rearview mirror. The truck was falling behind. Mann snarled with maddened fury. *If it weren't for that goddamned hose, he'd be escaping now!*

The sudden lurching of the car snatched him back to terror. If he braked now, he could jump out, run and scrabble up that slope. Later, he might not have the time. He couldn't make himself stop the car, though. As long as it kept on running, he felt bound to it, less vulnerable. God knows what would happen if he left it.

Mann started up the slope with haunted eyes, trying not to see the red light on the edges of his vision. Yard by yard, his car was slowing down. Make it, make it, pleaded his mind, even though he thought that it was futile. The car was running more and more unevenly. The thumping percolation of its radiator filled his ears. Any moment now, the motor would be choked off and the car would shudder to a stop, leaving him a sitting target. *No*, he thought. He tried to blank his mind.

He was almost to the top, but in the mirror he could see the truck drawing up on him. He jammed down on the pedal and the motor made a grinding noise. He groaned. It had to make the top! Please, God, help me! screamed his mind. The ridge was just ahead. Closer. Closer. Make it. "Make it." The car was shuddering and clanking, slowing down—oil, smoke and steam gushing from beneath the hood. The windshield wipers swept from side to side. Mann's head throbbed. Both his hands felt numb. His heartbeat pounded as he stared ahead. Make it, please, God, make it. Make it. *Make* it!

Over! Mann's lips opened in a cry of triumph as the car began descending. Hand shaking uncontrollably, he shoved the transmission into neutral and let the car go into a glide. The triumph strangled in his throat as he saw that there was nothing in sight but hills and more hills. Never mind! He was on a downgrade now, a long one. He passed a sign that read, TRUCKS USE LOW GEARS NEXT 12 MILES. Twelve miles! Something would come up. It had to.

The car began to pick up speed. Mann glanced at the speedometer. Forty-seven miles an hour. The red light still burned. He'd save the motor for a long time, too, though; let it cool for twelve miles, if the truck was far enough behind.

His speed increased. Fifty . . . 51. Mann watched the needle turning slowly toward the right. He glanced at the rearview mirror. The truck had not appeared yet. With a little luck, he might still get a good lead. Not as good as he might have if the motor hadn't overheated but enough to work with. There had to be some place along the way to stop. The needle edged past 55 and started toward the 60 mark.

Again, he looked at the rearview mirror, jolting as he saw that the truck had topped the ridge and was on its way down. He felt his lips begin to shake and crimped them together. His gaze jumped fitfully between the steam-obscured highway and the mirror. The truck was accelerating rapidly. Keller doubtless had the gas pedal floored. It wouldn't be long before the truck caught up to him. Mann's right hand twitched unconsciously toward the gearshift. Noticing, he jerked it back, grimacing, glanced at the speedometer. The car's velocity had just passed 60. Not enough! He had to use the motor now! He reached out desperately.

His right hand froze in midair as the motor stalled; then, shooting out the hand, he twisted the ignition key. The motor made a grinding noise but wouldn't start. Mann glanced up, saw that he was almost on the shoulder, jerked the steering wheel around. Again, he turned the key, but there was no response. He looked up at the rearview mirror. The truck was gaining on him swiftly. He glanced at the speedometer. The car's speed was fixed at 62. Mann felt himself crushed in a vise of panic. He stared ahead with haunted eyes.

Then he saw it, several hundred yards ahead: an escape route for trucks with burned-out brakes. There was no alternative now. Either he took the turnout or his car would rammed from behind. The truck was frighteningly close. He heard the high-pitched wailing of its motor. Unconsciously, he started easing to the right, then jerked the wheel back suddenly. He mustn't give the move away! He had to wait until the last possible moment. Otherwise, Keller would follow him in.

Just before he reached the escape route, Mann wrenched the steering wheel around. The car rear started breaking to the left, tires shrieking on the pavement. Mann steered with the skid, braking just enough to keep from losing all control. The rear tires grabbed and, at 60 miles an hour, the car shot up the dirt trail, tires slinging up a cloud of dust. Mann began to hit the brakes. The rear wheels sideslipped and the car slammed hard against the dirt bank to the right. Mann gasped as the car bounced off and started to fishtail with violent whipping motions, angling toward the trail edge. He drove his foot down on the brake pedal with all his might. The car rear skidded to the right and slammed against the bank again. Mann heard a grinding rend of metal and felt himself heaved downward suddenly, his neck snapped, as the car plowed to a violent halt.

As in a dream, Mann turned to see the truck and trailer swerving off the highway. Paralyzed, he watched the massive vehicle hurtle toward him, staring at it with a blank detachment, knowing he was going to die but so stupefied by the sight of the looming truck that he couldn't react. The gargantuan shape roared closer, blotting out the sky. Mann felt a strange sensation in his throat, unaware that he was screaming.

Suddenly, the truck began to tilt. Mann stared at it in choked-off silence as it started tipping over like some ponderous beast toppling in slow motion. Before it reached his car, it vanished from his rear window.

Hands palsied, Mann undid the safety belt and opened the door. Struggling from the car, he stumbled to the trail edge, staring downward. He was just in time to see the truck capsize like a foundering ship. The tanker followed, huge wheels spinning as it overturned.

The storage tank on the truck exploded first, the violence of its detonation causing Mann to stagger back and sit down clumsily on the dirt. A second explosion roared below, its shock wave buffeting across him hotly, making his ears hurt. His glazed eyes saw a fiery column shoot up toward the sky in front of him, then another.

Mann crawled slowly to the trail edge and peered down at the canyon. Enormous gouts of flame were towering upward, topped by thick, black, oily smoke. He couldn't see the truck or trailer, only flames. He gaped at them in shock, all feeling drained from him.

Then, unexpectedly, emotion came. Not dread, at first, and not regret; not the nausea that followed soon. It was a primeval tumult in his mind: the cry of some ancestral beast above the body of its vanquished foe.

DAVID MORRELL

"The Dripping"

*The name of David Morrell (1943-) will be linked forever to the character of John Rambo, the avenging Vietnam veteran who served as the hero of his 1972 novel **First Blood**. Most of Morrell's work in the horror field is nonsupernatural suspense, including **The Totem**, his trendsetting 1978 novel about a small Wyoming town that falls prey to a plague-like virus and the bizarre transformations it brings about. He is primarily a novelist, and his many thrillers include **The Brotherhood of the Rose, The League of Night and Fog**, and **The Fraternity of the Stone**. His short fiction has appeared in the **Shadows** and **Night Visions** anthologies, as well as Douglas Winter's **Prime Evil**.*

The Dripping

by David Morrell

That autumn we live in a house in the country, my mother's house, the house I was raised in. I have been to the village, struck more by how nothing in it has changed, yet everything has, because I am older now, seeing it differently. It is as though I am both here now and back then, at once with the mind of a boy and a man. It is so strange a doubling, so intense, so unsettling, that I am moved to work again, to try to paint it.

So I study the hardware store, the grain barrels in front, the twin square pillars holding up the drooping balcony onto which seared wax-faced men and women from the old people's hotel above come to sit and rock and watch. They look the same aging people I saw as a boy, the wood of the pillars and balcony looks as splintered.

Forgetful of time while I work, I do not begin the long walk home until late, at dusk. The day has been warm, but now in my shirt I am cold, and a half mile along I am caught in a sudden shower and forced to leave the gravel road for the shelter of a tree, its leaves already brown and yellow. The rain becomes a storm, streaking at me sideways, drenching me; I cinch the neck of my canvas bag to protect my painting and equipment, and decide to run, socks spongy in my shoes, when at last I reach the lane down to the house and barn.

The house and barn. They and my mother, they alone have changed, as if as one, warping, weathering, joints twisted and strained, their gray so unlike the white I recall as a boy. The place is weakening her. She is in tune with it, matches its decay. That is why we have come here to live. To revive. Once I thought to convince her to move away. But of her sixty-five years she has spent forty here, and she insists she will spend the rest, what is left to her.

The rain falls stronger as I hurry past the side of the house, the light on in the kitchen, suppertime and I am late. The house is connected with the barn the way the small base of an L is connected to its stem. The entrance I always use is directly at the joining, and when I enter out of breath, clothes clinging to me cold and wet, the door to the barn to my left, the door to the kitchen straight ahead, I hear the dripping in the basement down the stairs to my right.

"Meg. Sorry I'm late," I call to my wife, setting down the water-beaded canvas sack, opening the kitchen door. There is no one. No settings on the table. Nothing on the stove. Only the yellow light from the sixty-watt bulb in the ceiling. The kind my mother prefers to the white of one hundred. It reminds her of candlelight, she says.

"Meg," I call again, and still no one answers. Asleep, I think. Dusk coming on, the dark clouds of the storm have lulled them, and they have lain down for a nap, expecting to wake before I return.

Still the dripping. Although the house is very old, the barn long disused, roofs crumbling, I have not thought it all so ill-maintained, the storm so strong that water can be seeping past the cellar windows, trickling, pattering on the old stone floor. I switch on the light to the basement, descend the wood stairs to the right, worn and squeaking, reach where the stairs turn to the left the rest of the way down to the floor, and see not water dripping. Milk. Milk everywhere. On the rafters, on the walls, dripping on the film of milk on the stones, gathering speckled with dirt in the channels between them. From side to side and everwhere.

Sarah, my child, has done this, I think. She has been fascinated by the big wood dollhouse that my father made for me when I was quite young, its blue paint chipped and peeling now. She has pulled it from the far corner to the middle of the basement. There are games and toy soldiers and blocks that have been taken from the wicker storage chest and played with on the floor, all covered with milk, the dollhouse, the chest, the scattered toys, milk dripping on them from the rafters, milk trickling on them.

Why has she done this, I think. Where can she have gotten so much milk? What was in her mind to do this thing?

"Sarah," I call. "Meg." Angry now, I mount the stairs into the quiet kitchen. "Sarah," I shout. She will clean the mess and stay indoors the remainder of the week.

I cross the kitchen, turn through the sitting room past the padded flower-patterned chairs and sofa that have faded since I knew them as a boy, past several of my paintings that my mother has hung up on the wall, bright-colored old ones of pastures and woods from when I was in grade school, brown-shaded new ones of the town, tinted as if old photographs. Two stairs at a time up to the bedrooms, wet shoes on the soft worn carpet on the stairs, hand streaking on the smooth polished maple bannister.

At the top I swing down the hall. The door to Sarah's room is open, it is dark in there. I switch on the light. She is not on the bed, nor has been; the satin spread is unrumpled, the rain pelting in through the open window, the wind fresh and cool. I have the feeling then and go uneasy into our bedroom; it is dark as well, empty too. My stomach has become hollow. Where are they? All in mother's room?

No. As I stand at the open door to mother's room I see from the yellow light I have turned on in the hall that only she is in there, her small torso stretched across the bed.

"Mother," I say, intending to add, "where are Meg and Sarah?" But I stop before I do. One of my mother's shoes is off, the other askew on her foot. There is mud on the shoes. There is blood on her cotton dress. It is torn, her brittle hair disrupted, blood on her face, her bruised lips are swollen.

For several moments I am silent with shock. "My God, Mother," I finally manage to say, and as if the words are a spring releasing me to action I touch her to wake her. But I see that her eyes are open, staring ceilingward, unseeing though alive, and each breath is a sudden full gasp, then slow exhalation.

"Mother, what has happened? Who did this to you? Meg? Sarah?"

But she does not look at me, only constant toward the ceiling.

"For God's sake, Mother, answer me! Look at me! What has happened?"

Nothing. Eyes sightless. Between gasps she is like a statue.

What I think is hysterical. Disjointed, contradictory. I must find Meg and Sarah. They must be somewhere, beaten like my mother. Or worse. Find them. Where? But I cannot leave my mother. When she comes to consciousness, she too will be hysterical, frightened, in great pain. How did she end up on the bed?

In her room there is no sign of the struggle she must have put up against her attacker. It must have happened somewhere else. She crawled from there to here. Then I see the blood on the floor, the swath of blood down the hall from the stairs. Who did this? Where is he? Who would beat a gray, wrinkled, arthritic old woman? Why in God's name would he do it? I shudder. The pain of the arthritis as she struggled with him.

Perhaps he is still in the house, waiting for me.

To the hollow sickness in my stomach now comes fear, hot, pulsing, and I am frantic before I realize what I am doing—grabbing the spare cane my mother always keeps by her bed, flicking on the light in her room, throwing open the closet door and striking in with the cane. Viciously, sounds coming from my throat, the cane flailing among the faded dresses.

No one. Under the bed. No one. Behind the door. No one.

I search all the upstairs rooms that way, terrified, constantly checking behind me, clutching the cane and whacking into closets, under beds, behind doors, with a force that would certainly crack a skull. No one.

"Meg! Sarah!"

No answer, not even an echo in this sound-absorbing house.

There is no attic, just an overhead entry to a crawl space under the eaves, and that opening has long been sealed. No sign of tampering. No one has gone up.

I rush down the stairs, seeing the trail of blood my mother has left on the carpet, imagining her pain as she crawled, and search the rooms downstairs with the same desperate thoroughness. In the front closet. Behind the sofa and chairs. Behind the drapes.

No one.

I lock the front door, lest he be outside in the storm waiting to come in behind me. I remember to draw every blind, close every drape, lest he be out there peering at me. The rain pelts insistently against the windowpanes.

I cry out again and again for Meg and Sarah. The police. My mother. A doctor. I grab for the phone on the wall by the front stairs, fearful to listen to it, afraid he has cut the line outside. But it is droning. Droning. I ring for the police, working the handle at the side around and around and around.

They are coming, they say. A doctor with them. Stay where I am, they say. But I cannot. Meg and Sarah, I must find them. I know they are not in the basement where the milk is dripping—all the basement is open to view. Except for my childhood things, we have cleared out all the boxes and barrels and the shelves of jars the Saturday before.

But under the stairs. I have forgotten about under the stairs and now I race down and stand dreading in the milk; but there are only cobwebs there, already reformed from Saturday when we cleared them. I look up at the side door I first came through, and as if I am seeing through a telescope I focus largely on the handle. It seems to fidget. I have a panicked vision of the intruder bursting through, and I charge up to lock the door, and the door to the barn.

And then I think: if Meg and Sarah are not in the house they are likely in the barn. But I cannot bring myself to unlock the barn door and go through. *He* must be there as well. Not in the rain outside but in the shelter of the barn, and there are no lights to turn on there.

And why the milk? Did he do it and where did he get it? And why? Or did Sarah do it before? No, the milk is too freshly dripping. It has been put there too recently. By him. But why? And who is he? A tramp? An escapee from some prison? Or asylum? No, the nearest institution is far away, hundreds of miles. From the town then. Or a nearby farm.

I know my questions are for delay, to keep me from entering the barn. But I must. I take the flashlight from the kitchen drawer and unlock the door to the barn, force myself to go in quickly, cane ready, flashing my light. The stalls are still there, listing; and some of the equipment, churners, separators, dull and rusted, webbed and dirty. The must of decaying wood and crumbled hay, the fresh wet smell of the rain gusting through cracks in the walls. Once this was a dairy, as the other farms around still are.

Flicking my light toward the corners, edging toward the stalls, boards creaking, echoing, I try to control my fright, try to remember as a boy how the cows waited in the stalls for my father to milk them, how the barn was once board-tight and solid, warm to be in, how there was no connecting door from the barn to the house because my father did not want my mother to smell the animals in her kitchen.

I run my light down the walls, sweep it in arcs through the darkness before me as I draw nearer to the stalls, and in spite of myself I recall that other autumn when the snow came early, four feet deep by morning and still storming thickly, how my father went out to the barn to milk and never returned for lunch, nor supper. There was no phone then, no way to get help, and my mother and I waited all night, unable to make our way through the storm, listening to the slowly dying wind; and the next morning was clear and bright and blinding as we shoveled out to find the cows in agony in their stalls from not having been milked and my father dead, frozen rock-solid in the snow in the middle of the next field where he must have wandered when he lost his bearings in the storm.

There was a fox, risen earlier than us, nosing at him under the snow, and my father had to be sealed in his coffin before he could lie in state. Days after, the snow was melted, gone, the barnyard a sea of mud, and it was autumn again and my mother had the connecting door put in. My father should have tied a rope from the house to his waist to guide him back in case he lost his way. Certainly he knew enough. But then he was like that always in a rush. When I was ten.

Thus I think as I light the shadows near the stalls, terrified of what I may find in any one of them, Meg and Sarah, or him, thinking of how my mother and I searched for my father and how I now search for my wife and child, trying to think of how it was once warm in here and pleasant, chatting with my father, helping him to milk, the sweet smell of new hay and grain, the different sweet smell of fresh droppings, something I always liked and neither my father nor my mother could understand. I know that if I do not think of these good times I will surely go mad in awful anticipation of what I may find. Pray God they have not died!

What can he have done to them? To assault a five-year-old girl? Split her. The hemorrhaging alone can have killed her.

And then, even in the barn, I hear my mother cry out for me. The relief I feel to leave and go to her unnerves me. I do want to find Meg and Sarah, to try to save them. Yet I am relieved to go. I think my mother will tell me what has happened, tell me where to find them. That is how I justify my leaving as I wave the light in circles around me, guarding my back, retreating through the door and locking it.

Upstairs she sits stiffly on her bed. I want to make her answer my questions, to shake her, to force her to help, but I know it will only frighten her more, maybe push her mind down to where I can never reach.

"Mother," I say to her softly, touching her gently. "What has happened?" My impatience can barely be contained. "Who did this? Where are Meg and Sarah?"

She smiles at me, reassured by the safety of my presence. Still she cannot answer.

"Mother. Please," I say. "I know how bad it must have been. But you must try to help. I must know where they are so I can help them."

She says, "Dolls."

It chills me. "What dolls, Mother? Did a man come here with dolls? What did he want? You mean he looked like a doll? Wearing a mask like one?"

Too many questions. All she can do is blink.

"Please, Mother. You must try your best to tell me. Where are Meg and Sarah?"

"Dolls," she says.

As I first had the foreboding of disaster at the sight of Sarah's unrumpled satin bedspread, now I am beginning to understand, rejecting it, fighting it.

"Yes, Mother, the dolls," I say, refusing to admit what I know. "Please, Mother. Where are Meg and Sarah?"

"You are a grown boy now. You must stop playing as a child. Your father. Without him you will have to be the man in the house. You must be brave."

"No, Mother." I can feel it swelling in my chest.

"There will be a great deal of work now, more than any child should know. But we have no choice. You must accept that God has chosen to take him from us, that you are all the man I have left to help me."

"No, Mother."

"Now you are a man and you must put away the things of a child."

Eyes streaming, I am barely able to straighten, leaning wearily against the doorjamb, tears rippling from my face down to my shirt, wetting it cold where it had just begun to dry. I wipe my eyes and see her reaching for me, smiling, and I recoil down the hall, stumbling down the stairs, down, through the sitting room, the kitchen, down, down to the milk, splashing through it to the dollhouse, and in there, crammed and doubled, Sarah. And in the wicker chest, Meg. The toys not on the floor for Sarah to play with, but taken out so Meg could be put in. And both of them, their stomachs slashed, stuffed with sawdust, their eyes rolled up like dolls' eyes.

The police are knocking at the side door, pounding, calling out who they are, but I am powerless to let them in. They crash through the door, their rubber raincoats dripping as they stare down at me.

"The milk," I say.

They do not understand. Even as I wait, standing in the milk, listening to the rain pelting on the windows while they come over to see what is in the dollhouse and in the wicker chest, while they go upstairs to my mother and then return so I can tell them again, "The milk." But they still do not understand.

"She killed them of course," one man says. "But I don't see why the milk."

Only when they speak to the neighbors down the road and learn how she came to them, needing the cans of milk, insisting she carry them herself to the car, the agony she was in as she carried them, only when they find the empty cans and the knife in a stall in the barn, can I say, "The milk. The blood. There was so much blood, you know. She needed to deny it, so she washed it away with milk, purified it, started the dairy again. You see, there was so much blood."

That autumn we live in a house in the country, my mother's house, the house I was raised in. I have been to the village, struck even more by how nothing in it has changed, yet everything has, because I am older now, seeing it differently. It is as though I am both here now and back then, at once with the mind of a boy and a man . . . .

T.E.D. KLEIN

"The Events at Poroth Farm"

T.E.D. Klein's small but significant output in the horror field has earned him distinction as one of the most important voices in contemporary horror. His first published story, "The Events at Poroth Farm," served as the seed of his bestselling novel **The Ceremonies***, a modern horror epic that evoked the visionary terrors of H.P. Lovecraft and Arthur Machen. The novellas gathered in his collection* **Dark Gods** *are contemporary urban horror stories redolent with classic influences, in particular the Lovecraftian "Children of the Kingdom" and "Black Man with a Horn," and the World Fantasy Award-winning "Nadelman's God," which is a chilling reworking of the Frankenstein theme. Between 1980 and 1984 Klein served as editor of* **Twilight Zone** *magazine, where he introduced readers to writers whose work shaped the modern horror boom of the late 1980s. His editing experiences form the basis of non-fiction chapbook* **Raising Goosebumps for Fun and Profit***, a witty and blunt dissection of horror writing. "The Events at Poroth Farm" was a nominee for best novella at the first World Fantasy Convention.*

The Events at Poroth Farm

by T.E.D. Klein

As soon as the phone stops ringing, I'll begin this affidavit. Lord, it's hot in here. Perhaps I should open a window....
Thirteen rings. It has a sense of humor.
I suppose that ought to be comforting.
Somehow I'm not comforted. If it feels free to indulge in these teasing, tormenting little games, so much the worse for me.

The summer is over now, but this room is like an oven. My shirt is already drenched, and this pen feels slippery in my hand. In a moment or two the little drop of sweat that's collecting above my eyebrow is going to splash onto this page.

Just the same, I'll keep that window closed. Outside, through the dusty panes of glass, I can see a boy in red spectacles sauntering toward the courthouse steps. Perhaps there's a telephone booth in back....

A sense of humor—that's one quality I never noticed in it. I saw only a deadly seriousness and, of course, an intelligence that grew at terrifying speed, malevolent and inhuman. If it now feels itself safe enough to toy with me before doing whatever it intends to do, so much the worse for me. So much the worse, perhaps, for us all.

I hope I'm wrong. Though my name is Jeremy, derived from Jeremiah, I'd hate to be a prophet in the wilderness. I'd much rather be a harmless crank.

But I believe we're in for trouble.

I'm a long way from the wilderness now, of course. Though perhaps not far enough to save me. . . . I'm writing this affidavit in room 2-K of the Union Hotel, overlooking Main Street in Flemington, New Jersey, twenty miles south of Gilead. Directly across the street, hippies lounging on its steps, stands the county courthouse where Bruno Hauptmann was tried back in 1935. (Did they ever find the body of that child?) Hauptmann undoubtedly walked down those very steps, now lined with teenagers savoring their last week of summer vacation. Where that boy in the red spectacles sits sucking on his cigarette—did the killer once halt there, police and reporters around him, and contemplate his imminent execution?

For several days now I have been afraid to leave this room.

I have perhaps been staring too often at that ordinary-looking boy on the steps. He sits there every day. The red spectacles conceal his eyes; it's impossible to tell where he's looking.

I know he's looking at me.

But it would be foolish of me to waste time worrying about executions when I have these notes to transcribe. It won't take long, and then, perhaps, I'll sneak outside to mail them—and leave New Jersey forever. I remain, despite all that's happened, an optimist. What was it my namesake said? "Thou art my hope in the day of evil."

There *is,* surprisingly, some real wilderness left in New Jersey, assuming one wants to be a prophet. The hills to the west, spreading from the southern swamplands to the Delaware and beyond to Pennsylvania, provide shelter for deer, pheasant, even an occasional bear—and hide hamlets never visited by outsiders: pockets of ignorance, some of them, citadels of ancient superstition utterly cut off from news of New York and the rest of the state, religious communities where customs haven't changed appreciably since the days of their settlement a century or more ago.

It seems incredible that villages so isolated can exist today on the very doorstep of the world's largest metropolis—villages with nothing to offer the outsider, and hence never visited, except by the occasional hunter who stumbles on them unwittingly. Yet as you speed down one of the state highways, consider how few of the cars slow down for the local roads. It is easy to pass the little towns without even a glance at the signs; and if there are no signs . . . ? And consider, too, how seldom the local traffic turns off onto the narrow roads that emerge without warning from the woods. And when those untraveled side roads lead into others still deeper in wilderness; and when those in turn give way to dirt roads, deserted for weeks on end. . . . It is not hard to see how tiny rural communities can exist less than an hour from major cities, virtually unaware of one another's existence.

Television, of course, will link the two—unless, as is often the case, the elders of the community choose to see this distraction as the Devil's tool and proscribe it. Telephones put these outcast settlements in touch with their neighbors—unless they choose to ignore their neighbors. And so in the course of years they are . . . forgotten.

New Yorkers were amazed when in the winter of 1968 the *Times* "discovered" a religious community near New Providence that had existed in its present form since the late 1800's—less than forty miles from Times Square. Agricultural work was performed entirely by hand, women still wore long dresses with high collars, and town worship was held every evening.

I, too, was amazed. I'd seldom traveled west of the Hudson and still thought of New Jersey as some dismal extension of the Newark slums, ruled by gangsters, foggy with swamp gases and industrial waste, a grey land that had surrendered to the city.

Only later did I learn of the rural New Jersey, and of towns whose solitary general stores double as post offices, with one or two gas pumps standing in front. And later still I learned of Baptistown and Quakertown, their old religions surviving unchanged, and of towns like Lebanon, Landsdown, and West Portal, close to Route 22 and civilization but heavy with secrets city folk never dreamed of; Mt. Airy, with its network of hidden caverns, and Mt. Olive, bordering the infamous Budd Lake; Middle Valley, sheltered by dark cliffs, subject of the recent archaeological debate chronicled in *Natural History*, where the wanderer may still find grotesque relics of pagan worship and, some say, may still hear the chants that echo from the cliffs on certain nights; and towns with names like Zion and Zaraphath and Gilead, forgotten communities of bearded men and black-robed women, walled hamlets too small or obscure for most maps of the state. This was the wilderness into which I traveled, weary of Manhattan's interminable din; and it was outside Gilead where, until the tragedies, I chose to make my home for three months.

Among the silliest of literary conventions is the "town that won't talk"—the Bavarian village where peasants turn away from tourists' queries about "the castle" and silently cross themselves, the New England harbor town where fishermen feign ignorance and cast "furtive glances" at the traveler. In actuality, I have found, country people love to talk to the stranger, provided he shows a sincere interest in their anecdotes. Storekeepers will interrupt their activity at the cash register to tell you their theories on a recent

The Events at Poroth Farm

murder; farmers will readily spin tales of buried bones and of a haunted house down the road. Rural townspeople are not so reticent as the writers would have us believe.

Gilead, isolated though it is behind its oak forests and ruined walls, is no exception. The inhabitants regard all outsiders with an initial suspicion, but let one demonstrate a respect for their traditional reserve and they will prove friendly enough. They don't favor modern fashions or flashy automobiles, but they can hardly be described as hostile, although that was my original impression.

When asked about the terrible events at Poroth Farm, they will prove more than willing to talk. They will tell you of bad crops and polluted well water, of emotional depression leading to a fatal argument. In short, they will describe a conventional rural murder, and will even volunteer their opinions on the killer's present whereabouts.

But you will learn almost nothing from them—or almost nothing that is true. They don't know what really happened.

I do. I was closest to it.

I had come to spend the summer with Sarr Poroth and his wife. I needed a place where I could do a lot of reading without distraction, and Poroth's farm, secluded as it was even from the village of Gilead six miles down the dirt road, appeared the perfect spot for my studies.

I had seen the Poroths' advertisement in the *Hunterdon County Democrat* on a trip west through Princeton last spring. They advertised for a summer or long-term tenant to live in one of the outbuildings behind the farmhouse. As I soon learned, the building was a long, low cinderblock affair, unpleasantly suggestive of army barracks but clean, new, and cool in the sun; by the start of summer ivy sprouted from the walls and disguised the ugly grey brick. Originally intended to house chickens, it had in fact remained empty for several years until the farm's original owner, a Mr. Baber, sold out last fall to the Poroths, who immediately saw that with the installation of dividing walls, linoleum floors, and other improvements the building might serve as a source of income. I was to be their first tenant.

The Poroths, Sarr and Deborah, were in their early thirties, only slightly older than I, although anyone who met them might have believed the age difference to be greater; their relative solemnity, and the drabness of their clothing, added years to their appearance, and so did their hair styles: Deborah, though possessing a beautiful length of black hair, wound it all in a tight bun behind her neck, pulling the hair back from her face with a severity which looked almost painful, and Sarr maintained a thin fringe of black beard that circled from ears to chin in the manner of the Pennsylvania Dutch, who leave their hair shaggy but refuse to grow moustaches lest they resemble the military class they've traditionally despised. Both man and wife were hardworking, grave of expression, and pale despite the time spent laboring in the sun—a pallor accentuated by the inky blackness of their hair. I imagine this unhealthy aspect was due, in part, to the considerable amount of inbreeding that went on in the area, the Poroths themselves being, I believe, third cousins. On first meeting, one might have taken them for brother and sister, two gravely devout children aged in the wilderness.

And yet there was a difference between them—and, too, a difference that set them both in contrast to others of their sect. The Poroths were, as far as I could determine, members of a tiny Mennonitic order outwardly related to the Amish, though doctrinal differences were apparently rather profound. It was this order that made up the large part of the community known as Gilead.

I sometimes think the only reason they allowed an infidel like me to live on their property (for my religion was among the first things they inquired about) was because of my name; Sarr was very partial to Jeremiah, and the motto of his order was, "Stand ye in the ways, and see, and ask for the old paths, where is the good way, and walk therein."(VI:16)

Having been raised in no particular religion except a universal skepticism, I began the summer with a hesitancy to raise the topic in conversaion, and so I learned comparatively little about the Poroths' beliefs. Only toward the end of my stay did I begin to thumb through the Bible in odd moments and take to quoting jeremiads. That was, I suppose, Sarr's influence.

I was able to learn, nonetheless, that for all their conservative aura the Poroths were considered, in effect, young liberals by most of Gilead. Sarr had a bachelor's degree in religious studies from Rutgers, and Deborah had attended a nearby community college for two years, unusual for women of the sect. Too, they had only recently taken to farming, having spent the first year of their marriage near New Brunswick, where Sarr had hoped to find a teaching position and, when the job situation proved hopeless, had worked as a sort of handyman/carpenter. While most inhabitants of Gilead had never left the farm, the Poroths were coming to it late—their families had been merchants for several generations—and so were relatively inexperienced.

The Events at Poroth Farm

The inexperience showed. The farm comprised some ninety acres, but most of that was forest, or fields of weeds too thick and high to walk through. Across the back yard, close to my rooms, ran a small, nameless stream, nearly choked with green scum. A large cornfield to the north lay fallow, but Sarr was planning to seed it this year, using borrowed equipment. His wife spent much of her time indoors, for though she maintained a small vegetable garden, she preferred keeping house and looking after the Poroths' great love, their seven cats.

As if to symbolize their broad-mindedness, the Poroths owned a television set, very rare in Gilead; in light of what was to come, however, it is unfortunate they lacked a telephone. (Apparently the set had been received as a wedding present from Deborah's parents, but the monthly expense of a telephone was simply too great.) Otherwise, though, the little farmhouse was "modern" in that it had a working bathroom and gas heat. That they had advertised in the local newspaper was considered scandalous by some of the order's more orthodox members, and indeed a mere subscription to that innocuous weekly had at one time been regarded as a breach of religious conduct.

Though outwardly similar, both of them tall and pale, the Poroths were actually so different as to embody the maxim that "opposites attract." It was that carefully nurtured reserve that deceived one at first meeting, for in truth Deborah was far more talkative, friendly, and energetic than her husband. Sarr was moody, distant, silent most of the time, with a voice so low that one had trouble following him in conversation. Sitting as stonily as one of his cats, never moving, never speaking, perennially inscrutable, he tended to frighten visitors to the farm until they learned that he was not really sitting in judgment on them; his reserve was not born of surliness, but of shyness.

Where Sarr was catlike, his wife hid beneath the formality of her order the bubbly personality of a kitten. Given the smallest encouragement—say, a family visit—she would plunge into animated conversation, gesticulating, laughing easily, hugging whatever cat was nearby or shouting to guests across the room. When drinking—for both of them enjoyed liquor and, curiously, it was not forbidden by their faith—their innate differences were magnified: Deborah would forget the restraints placed upon women in the order and would eventually dominate the conversation, while her husband would seem to grow increasingly withdrawn and morose.

Women in the region tended to be submissive to the men, and certainly the important decisions in the Poroths' lives were made by Sarr. Yet I really cannot say who was the stronger of the two. Only once did I ever see them quarrel....

Perhaps the best way to tell it is by setting down portions of the journal I kept this summer. Not every entry, of course. Mere excerpts. Just enough to make this affidavit comprehensible to anyone unfamiliar with the incidents at Poroth Farm.

The journal was the only writing I did all summer; my primary reason for keeping it was to record the books I'd read each day, as well as to examine my reactions to relative solitude over a long period of time. All the rest of my energies (as you will no doubt gather from the notes below) were spent reading, in preparation for a course I plan to teach at Trenton State this fall. Or *planned,* I should say, because I don't expect to be anywhere around here come fall.

Where will I be? Perhaps that depends on what's beneath those rose-tinted spectacles.

The course was to cover the Gothic tradition from Shakespeare to Faulkner, from *Hamlet* to *Absalom, Absalom!* (And why not view the former as Gothic, with its ghost on the battlements and concern for lost inheritance?) To make the move to Gilead, I'd rented a car for a few days and had stuffed it full of books—only a few of which I ever got to read. But then, I couldn't have known....

How pleasant things were, at the beginning.

June 4

Unpacking day. Spent all morning putting up screens, and a good thing I did. Night now, and a million moths tapping at the windows. One of them as big as a small bird—white—largest I've ever seen. What kind of caterpillar must it have been? I hope the damned things don't push through the screens.

Had to kill literally hundreds of spiders before moving my stuff in. The Poroths finished doing the inside of this building only a couple of months ago, and already it's infested. Arachnidae—hate the bastards. Why? We'll take that one up with Sigmund someday. Daydreams of Revenge of the Spiders. Writhing body covered with a frenzy of hairy brown legs. "Egad, man, that face! That bloody, torn face! And the missing eyes! It looks like—no! Jeremy!" Killing spiders is supposed to bring bad luck. (Insidious Sierra Club propaganda masquerading as folk myth?) But can't sleep if there's anything crawling around... so what the hell?

Supper with Poroths. Began to eat, then heard Sarr saying grace.

Apologies—but things like that don't embarrass me as much as they used to. (Is that because I'm nearing thirty?)

Chatted about crops, insects, humidity. (Very damp area—band of purplish mildew already around bottom of walls out here.) Sarr told of plans to someday build a larger house when Deborah has a baby, three or four years from now. He wants to build it out of stone. Then he shut up, and I had to keep the conversation going. (Hate eating in silence—animal sounds of mastication, bubbling stomachs.) Deborah joked about cats being her surrogate children. All seven of them hanging around my legs, rubbing against ankles. My nose began running and my eyes itched. Goddamned allergy. Must remember to start treatments this fall, when I get to Trenton. Deborah sympathetic, Sarr merely watching; she told me my eyes were bloodshot, offered antihistamine. Told them I was glad they at least believe in modern medicine—I'd been afraid she'd offer herbs or mud or something. Sarr said some of the locals still use "snake oil." Asked him how snakes were killed, quoting line from *Vathek:* "The oil of the serpents I have pinched to death will be a pretty present...." We discussed wisdom of pinching snakes. Apparently there's a copperhead out back, near the brook....

The meal was good—lamb and noodles. Not bad for fifteen dollars a week, since I detest cooking. Spice cake for dessert, home-made, of course. Deborah is a good cook. Handsome woman, too.

Still light when I left their kitchen. Fireflies already on the lawn—I've never seen so many. Knelt and watched them a while, listening to the crickets. Think I'll like it here.

Took nearly an hour to arrange my books the way I wanted them. Alphabetical order by authors? No, chronological.... But anthologies mess that system up, so back to authors. Why am I so neurotic about my books?

Anyway, they look nice there on the shelves.

Sat up tonight finishing *The Mysteries of Udolpho*. Figure it's best to get the long ones out of the way first. Radcliffe's unfortunate penchant for explaining away all her ghosts and apparitions really a mistake and a bore. All in all, not exactly the most fascinating reading, though a good study in Romanticism. Montoni the typical Byronic hero/villain. But can't demand students read *Udolpho*—too long. In fact, had to keep reminding myself to slow down, have patience with the book. Tried to put myself in frame of mind of 1794 reader with plenty of time on his hands. It works, too—I do have plenty of time out here, and already I can feel myself beginning to unwind. What New York does to people....

It's almost two A.M. now, and I'm about ready to turn in. Too bad there's no bathroom in this building—I hate pissing outside at night. God knows what's crawling up your ankles. . . . But it's hardly worth stumbling through the darkness to the farmhouse, and maybe waking up Sarr and Deborah. The nights out here are really pitch-black. . . .

. . . Felt vulnerable, standing there against the night. But what made me even uneasier was the view I got of this building. The lamp on the desk casts the only light for miles, and as I stood outside looking into this room I could see dozens of flying shapes making right for the screens. When you're inside here it's as if you're in a display case—the whole night can see you, but all you can see is darkness. I wish this room didn't have windows on three of the walls—though that does let in the breeze. And I wish the woods weren't so close to my windows by the bed. I suppose privacy is what I wanted—but feel a little unprotected out here.

Those moths are still batting themselves against the screens, but as far as I can see the only things that have gotten in are a few gnats flying around this lamp. The crickets sound good—you sure don't hear them in the city. Frogs are croaking in the brook.

My nose is only now beginning to clear up. Those goddamned cats. Must remember to buy some Contac. Even though the cats are all outside during the day, that farmhouse is full of their scent. But I don't expect to be spending that much time inside the house anyway; this allergy will keep me away from the TV and out here with the books.

Just saw an unpleasantly large spider scurry across the floor near the foot of my bed. Vanished behind the footlocker. Must remember to buy some insect spray tomorrow.

June 11

Hot today, but at night comes a chill. The dampness of this place seems to magnify temperature. Sat outside most of the day finishing the Maturin book, *Melmoth the Wanderer,* and feeling vaguely guilty each time I heard Sarr or Deborah working out there in the field. Well, I've paid for my reading time, so I guess I'm entitled to enjoy it. Though some of these old Gothics are a bit hard to enjoy. The troubles with *Melmoth* is that it wants you to hate. You're especially supposed to hate the Catholics. No doubt its picture of the Inquisition is accurate, but all a book like this can do is put you in an unconstructive rage. Those vicious characters have been dead for centuries, and there's no way to punish them. Still, it's a nice, cynical book for those who like atrocity scenes—starving prisoners forced to eat their girlfiends, delightful things like that. And narratives within narratives within narratives within narratives. I may assign some sections to my class. . . .

Just before dinner, in need of a break, read a story by Arthur Machen. Welsh writer, turn of century, though think the story's set somewhere in England: old house in the hills, dark woods with secret paths and hidden streams. God, what an experience! I was a little confused by the framing device and all its high-flown talk of "cosmic evil," but the sections from the young girl's notebook were . . . staggering. That air of paganism, the malevolent little faces peeping from the shadows, and those rites she can't dare talk about. . . . It's called "The White People," and it must be the most persuasive horror tale ever written.

Afterward, strolling toward the house, I was moved to climb the old tree in the side yard—the Poroths had already gone in to get dinner ready—and stood upright on a great heavy branch near the middle, making strange gestures and faces that no one could see. Can't say exactly what it was I did, or why. It was getting dark—fireflies below me and a mist rising off the field. I must have looked like a madman's shadow as I made signs to the woods and the moon.

Lamb tonight, and damned good. I may find myself getting fat. Offered, again, to wash the dishes, but apparently Deborah feels that's her role, and I don't care to dissuade her. So talked a while with Sarr about his cats—the usual subject of conversation, especially because, now that summer's coming, they're bringing in dead things every night. Fieldmice, moles, shrews, birds, even a little garter snake. They don't eat them, just lay them out on the porch for the Poroths to see—sort of an offering, I guess. Sarr tosses the bodies in the garbage can, which, as a result, smells indescribably foul. Deborah wants to put bells around their necks; she hates mice but feels sorry for the birds. When she finished the dishes, she and Sarr sat down to watch one of their godawful TV programs, so I came out here to read.

Spent the usual ten minutes going over this room, spray can in hand, looking for spiders to kill. Found a couple of little ones, then spent some time spraying bugs that were hanging on the screens hoping to get in. Watched a lot of daddy longlegs curl up and die. . . . Tended not to kill the moths, unless they were making too much of a racket banging against the screen; I can tolerate them okay, but it's only fireflies I really like. I always feel a little sorry when I kill one by mistake and see it hold that cold glow too long. (That's how you know they're dead: the dead ones don't wink. They just keep their light on till it fades away.)

The insecticide I'm using is made right here in New Jersey, by the Ortho Chemical Company. The label on the can says, "WARNING: For Outdoor Use Only." That's why I bought it—figured it's the most powerful brand available.

Sat in bed reading Algernon Blackwood's witch/cat story, "Ancient Sorceries" (nowhere near as good as Machen, or as his own tale "The Willows"), and it made me think of those seven cats. The Poroths have around a dozen names for each one of them, which seems a little ridiculous since the creatures barely respond to even *one* name. Sasha, for example, the orange one, is also known as Butch, which comes from Bouche, mouth. And that's short for Eddie La Bouche, so he's also called Ed or Eddie—which in turn comes from some friend's mispronunciation of the cat's original name, Itty, short for Itty Bitty Kitty, which, apparently, he once was. And Zoë, the cutest of the kittens, is also called Bozo and Bisbo. Let's see, how many others can I remember? (I'm just learning to tell some of them apart).... Felix, or "Flixie," was originally called Paleface, and Phaedra, his mother, is sometimes known as Phuddy, short for Phuddy Duddy.

Come to think of it, the only cat that hasn't got multiple names is Bwada, Sarr's cat. (All the others were acquired after he married Deborah, but Bwada was his pet years before.) She's the oldest of the cats, and the meanest. Fat and sleek, with fine grey fur, darker than silver grey, lighter than charcoal. She's the only cat that's ever bitten anyone—Deborah, as well as friends of the Poroths—and after seeing the way she snarls at the other cats when they get in her way, I decided to keep my distance. Fortunately she's scared of me and retreats whenever I approach. I think being spayed is what's messed her up and given her an evil dispostion.

Sounds are drifting from the farmhouse. I can vaguely make out a psalm of some kind. It's late, past eleven, and I guess the Poroths have turned off the TV and are singing their evening devotions. . . .

And now all is silence. They've gone to bed. I'm not very tired yet, so I guess I'll stay up a while and read some—

Something odd just happened. I've never heard anything like it. While writing for the past half hour I've been aware, if half-consciously, of the crickets. Their regular chirping can be pretty soothing, like the sound of a well-tuned machine. But just a few seconds ago they seemed to miss a beat! They'd been singing along steadily, ever since the moon came up, and all of a sudden they just *stopped* for a beat—and then they began again, only they were out of rhythm for a moment or two, as if a hand had jarred the record, or there'd been some kind of momentary break in the natural flow. . . .

They sound normal enough now, though. Think I'll go back to *Otranto* and let that put me to sleep. It may be the foundation of the English Gothics, but I can't imagine anyone actually reading it for pleasure. I wonder how many pages I'll be able to get through before I drop off. . . .

June 12

Slept late this morning, and then, disinclined to read Walpole on such a sunny day, took a walk. Followed the little brook that runs past my building. There's still a lot of that greenish scum clogging one part of it, and if we don't have some rain soon I expect it will get worse. But the water clears up considerably when it runs past the cornfield and through the woods.

Passed Sarr out in the field—he yelled to watch out for the copperhead, which put a pall on my enthusiasm for exploration. . . . But as it happened I never ran into any snakes, and have a fair idea I'd survive even if bitten. Walked around half a mile into the woods, branches snapping in my face. Made an effort to avoid walking into the little yellow caterpillars that hang from every tree. At one point I had to get my feet wet because the trail that runs alongside the brook disappeared and the undergrowth was thick. Ducked under a low arch made by decaying branches and vines, my sneakers sloshing in the water. Found that as the brook runs west it forms a small circular pool with banks of wet sand, surrounded by tall oaks, their roots thrust into the water. Lots of animal tracks in the sand—deer, I believe, and what may be a fox or perhaps some farmer's dog. Obviously a watering place. Waded into the center of the pool—it only came up a little past my ankles—but didn't stand there long because it started looking like rain.

The weather remained nasty all day, but no rain has come yet. Cloudy now, though; can't see any stars.

Finished *Otranto,* began *The Monk*. So far so good—rather dirty, really. Not for today, of course, but I can imagine the sensation it must have caused back at the end of the eighteenth century.

Had a good time at dinner tonight, since Sarr had walked into town and brought back some wine. (Medical note: I seem to be less allergic to cats when mildly intoxicated.) We sat around the kitchen afterward playing poker for matchsticks—very sinful indulgence, I understand; Sarr and Deborah told me, quite seriously, that they'd have to say some extra prayers tonight by way of apology to the Lord.

Theological considerations aside, though, we all had a good time and Deborah managed to clean us both out. Women's intuition, she says. I'm sure she must have it—she's the type. Enjoy being around her, and not always so happy to trek back outside, through the high grass, the night dew, the things in the soil. . . . I've got to remember, though, that they're a couple, I'm the single one, and I mustn't intrude too long. So left them tonight at eleven—or actually a little after that, since their clock is slightly out of kilter. They have this huge grandfather-type clock, a wedding present from Sarr's parents, that has supposedly been keeping perfect time for a century or more. You can hear its ticking all over the house when everything else is still. Deborah said that last night, just as they were going to bed, the clock seemed to slow down a little, then gave a couple of faster beats and started in as before. Sarr, who's pretty good with mechanical things, examined it, but said he saw nothing wrong. Well, I guess everything's got to wear out a bit, after years and years.

Back to *The Monk*. May Brother Ambrosio bring me pleasant dreams.

June 13

Read a little in the morning, loafed during the afternoon. At 4:30 watched *The Thief of Bagdad*—ruined on TV and portions omitted, but still a great film. Deborah puttered around the kitchen and Sarr spent most of the day outside. Before dinner I went out back with a scissors and cut away a lot of ivy that has tried to grow through the windows of my building. The little shoots fasten onto the screens and really cling.

Beef with rice tonight, and apple pie for dessert. Great. I stayed inside the house after dinner to watch the late news with the Poroths. The announcer mentioned that today was Friday the thirteenth, and I nearly gasped. I'd known, on some dim automatic level, that it was the thirteenth, if only from keeping this journal; but I hadn't had the faintest idea it was Friday. That's how much I've lost track of time out here; day drifts into day, and every one but Sunday seems completely interchangeable. Not a bad feeling, really, though at certain moments this isolation makes me feel somewhat adrift. I'd been so used to living by the clock and the calendar. . . .

We tried to figure out if anything unlucky happened to any of us today. About the only incident we could come up with was Sarr's getting bitten by some animal a cat had left on the porch. The cats had been sitting by the front door waiting to be let in for their dinner, and when Sarr came in from the field he was greeted with the usual assortment of dead mice and moles. As he always did, he began gingerly picking the bodies up by the tails and tossing them into the garbage can, meanwhile scolding the cats for being such natural-born killers. There was one body, he told us, that looked different from the others he'd seen: rather like a large shrew, only the mouth was somehow askew, almost as if it were vertical instead of horizontal, with a row of little yellow teeth exposed. He figured that, whatever it was, the cats had pretty well mauled it, which probably accounted for its unusual appearance; it was quite tattered and bloody by this time.

In any case, he'd bent down to pick it up, and the thing had bitten him on the thumb. Apparently it had just been feigning death, like an opossum, because as soon as he yelled and dropped it the thing ran off into the grass, with Bwada and the rest in hot pursuit. Deborah had been afraid of rabies—always a real danger around here, rare though it is—but apparently the bite hadn't even pierced the skin. Just a nip, really. Hardly a Friday-the-thirteenth tragedy.

Lying in bed now, listening to sounds in the woods. The trees come really close to my windows on one side and there's always some kind of sound coming from the underbrush in addition to the tapping at the screens. A million creatures out there, after all—most of them insects and spiders, a colony of frogs in the swampy part of the woods, and perhaps even skunks and raccoons. Depending on your mood, you can either ignore the sounds and just go to sleep or—as I'm doing now—remain awake listening to them. When I lie here thinking about what's out there, I feel more protected with the light off. So I guess I'll put away this writing. . . .

June 15

Something really weird happened today. I still keep trying to figure it out.

Sarr and Deborah were gone almost all day; Sunday worship is, I guess, the center of their religious activity. They walked into Gilead early in the morning and didn't return till after four. They'd left, in fact, before I woke up. Last night they'd asked me if I'd like to come along, but I got the impression they'd invited me mainly to be polite, so I declined. I wouldn't want to make them uncomfortable during services, but perhaps someday I'll accompany them anway, since I'm curious to see a fundamentalist church in action.

In any case, I was left to share the farm with the Poroths' seven cats and the four hens they'd bought last week. From my window I could see Bwada and Phaedra chasing after something near the barn; lately they'd taken to stalking grasshoppers. As I do every morning, I went into the farmhouse kitchen and made myself some breakfast, leafing through one of the Poroths' religious magazines, and then returned to my rooms out back for some serious reading. I picked up *Dracula* again, which I'd started yesterday, but the soppy Victorian sentimentality began to annoy me; the book had begun so well, on such a frightening note—Jonathan Harker trapped in that Carpathian castle, inevitably the prey of its terrible owner—that when Stoker switched the locale to England and his main characters to women he simply couldn't sustain that initial tension.

With the Poroths gone I felt a little lonely and bored, something I hadn't felt out here yet. Though I'd brought shelves of books to entertain me, I felt restless and wished I owned a car; I'd have gone for a drive, perhaps visited friends at Princeton. As things stood, though, I had nothing to do except watch television or take a walk.

I followed the stream again into the woods and eventually came to the circular pool. There were some new animal tracks in the wet sand and, ringed by oaks, the place was very beautiful, but still I felt bored. Again I waded into the center of the water and looked up at the sky through the trees. Feeling myself alone, I began to make some of the odd signs with face and hands that I had that evening in the tree—but I felt that these movements had been unaccountably robbed of their power. Standing there up to my ankles in water, I felt foolish.

Worse than that, upon leaving it I found a red-brown leech clinging to my right ankle. It wasn't large and I was able to scrape it off with a stone, but it left me with a little round bite that oozed blood, and a feeling of—how shall I put it?—physical helplessness. I felt that the woods had somehow become hostile to me and, more important, would forever remain hostile. Something had passed.

I followed the stream back to the farm, and there I found Bwada, lying on her side near some rocks along its bank. Her legs were stretched out as if she were running, and her eyes were wide and astonished-looking. Flies were crawling over them.

She couldn't have been dead for long, since I'd seen her only a few hours before, but she was already stiff. There was foam around her jaws. I couldn't tell what had happened to her until I turned her over with a stick and saw, on the side that had lain against the ground, a gaping red hole that opened like some new orifice. The skin around it was folded back in little triangular flaps, exposing the pink flesh beneath. I backed off in disgust, but I could see even from several feet away that the hole had been made *from the inside.*

I can't say that I was very upset at Bwada's death, because I'd always hated her. What did upset me, though, was the manner of it— I can't figure out what could have done that to her. I vaguely remember reading about a kind of slug that, when eaten by a bird, will bore its way out through the bird's stomach. . . . But I'd never heard of something like this happening with a cat. And far stranger than that, how could. . . .

Well, anyway, I saw the body and thought, Good riddance. But I didn't know what to do with it. Looking back, of course, I wish I'd buried it right there. . . . But I didn't want to go near it again. I considered walking into town and trying to find the Poroths, because I knew their cats were like children to them, even Bwada, and that they'd want to know right away. But I really didn't feel like running around Gilead asking strange people where the Poroths were—or, worse, yet, stumbling into their forbidding-looking church in the middle of a ceremony. . . .

Finally I made up my mind to simply leave the body there and pretend I'd never seen it. Let Sarr discover it himself. I didn't want to have to tell him when he got home that his pet had been killed; I prefer to avoid unpleasantness. Besides, I felt strangely guilty, the way one often does after someone else's misfortune.

So I spent the rest of the afternoon reading in my room, slogging through the Stoker. I wasn't in the best mood to concentrate. Sarr and Deborah got back after four—they shouted hello and went into the house. When Deborah called me for dinner, they still hadn't come outside.

All the cats except Bwada were inside having their evening meal when I entered the kitchen, and Sarr asked me if I'd seen her during the day. I lied and said I hadn't. Deborah suggested that occasionally Bwada ignored the supper call because, unlike the other cats, she sometimes ate what she killed and might simply be full. That rattled me a bit, but I had to stick to my lie.

Sarr seemed more concerned than Deborah, and when he told her he intended to search for the cat after dinner (it would still be light), I readily offered my help. I figured I could lead him to the spot where the body lay. . . .

And then, in the middle of our dinner, came that scratching at the door. Sarr got up and opened it. Bwada walked in.

Now I know she was dead. She was *stiff* dead. That wound in her side had been huge, and now it was only . . . a reddish swelling. Hairless. Luckily the Poroths didn't notice my shock; they were busy fussing over her, seeing what was wrong. "Look, she's hurt herself," said Deborah. "She's bumped into something." The animal didn't walk well, and there was a clumsiness in the way she held herself. When Sarr put her down after examining the swelling, she slipped when she tried to walk away.

The Poroths concluded that she had run into a rock or some other object and had badly bruised herself; and now they believe her lack of coordination is due to the shock, or perhaps to a pinching of the nerves. That sounds logical enough. Sarr told me before I came out here for the night that if she's worse tomorrow he'll take her to the local vet, even though he'll have trouble paying for treatment. I immediately offered to lend him money, or even pay for the visit myself, because I desperately want to hear a doctor's opinion.

My own conclusion is really not that different from Sarr's. I tend to think now that maybe, just maybe, I was wrong in thinking the cat dead. Maybe what I mistook for rigor mortis was some kind of fit—after all, I know almost nothing about medicine. Maybe she really did run into something sharp, and then went into some kind of shock . . . whose effect hasn't yet worn off. Is this possible?

But I could swear that hole came from inside her.

I couldn't continue dinner and told the Poroths my stomach hurt, which was partly true. We all watched Bwada stumble around the kitchen floor, ignoring the food Deborah put before her as if it weren't there. Her movements were stiff, tentative, like a newborn animal still unsure how to move its muscles. I guess that's the result of her fit.

When I left the house tonight, a little while ago, she was huddled in the corner staring at me. Deborah was crooning over her, but the cat was staring at me.

Killed a monster of a spider behind my suitcase tonight. That Ortho spray really does a job. When Sarr was in here a few days ago he said the room smelled of spray, but I guess my allergy's too bad for me to smell it.

I enjoy watching the zoo outside my screens. Put my face close and stare the bugs eye to eye. Zap the ones whose faces I don't like with my spray can.

Tried to read more of the Stoker—but one thing keeps bothering me. The way that cat stared at me. Deborah was brushing its back, Sarr fiddling with his pipe, and that cat just stared at me and never blinked. I stared back, said, "Hey, Sarr? Look at Bwada. That damned cat's not blinking." And just as he looked up, it blinked. Heavily.

Hope we can go to the vet tomorrow, because I want to ask him whether cats can impale themselves on a rock or a stick, and if such an accident might cause a fit of some kind that would make them rigid.

Cold night. Sheets are damp and the blanket itches. Wind from the woods—ought to feel good in the summer, but it doesn't feel like summer.

That damned cat didn't blink till I mentioned it.

Almost as if it understood me.

June 17

... Swelling on her side's all healed now. Hair growing back over it. She walks fine, has a great appetite, shows affection to the Poroths. Sarr says her recovery demonstrates how the Lord watches over animals—affirms his faith. Says if he'd taken her to a vet he'd just have been throwing away money.

Read some LeFanu. "Green Tea," about the phantom monkey with eyes that glow, and "The Familiar," about the little staring man who drives the hero mad. Not the smartest choices right now, the way I feel, because for all the time that fat grey cat purrs over the Poroths, it just stares at me. And snarls. I suppose the accident may have addled its brain a bit. I mean, if spaying can change a cat's personality, certainly a goring on a rock might. . . .

Spent a lot of time in the sun today. The flies made it pretty hard to concentrate on the stories, but figured I'd get a suntan. I probably have a good tan now (hard to tell because the mirror in here is small and the light dim), but suddenly it occurs to me that I'm not going to be seeing anyone for a long time anyway, except the Poroths, so what the hell do I care how I look?

Can hear them singing their nightly prayers now. A rather comforting sound, I must admit, even if I can't share the sentiments.

Petting Felix today—my favorite of the cats, real charm—came away with a tick on my arm which I didn't discover till taking a shower before dinner. As a result, I can still feel imaginary ticks crawling up and down my back. Damned cat.

June 21

... Coming along well with the Victorian stuff. Zipped through "The Uninhabited House" and "Monsieur Maurice," both very literate, sophisticated. Deep into the terrible suffering of "The Amber Witch," poor priest and daughter near starvation, when Deborah called me in for dinner. Roast beef, with salad made from garden lettuce. Quite good. And Deborah was wearing one of the few sleeveless dresses I've seen on her. So she has a body after all. . . .

A rainy night. Hung around the house for a while reading in their living room while Sarr whittled and Deborah crocheted. Rain sounded better from in there than it does out here where it's not so cozy. . . .

At eleven we turned on the news, cats purring around us, Sarr with Zoë on his lap, Deborah petting Phaedra, me sniffling. . . . Halfway through the wrapup I pointed to Bwada, curled up at my feet, and said, "Look at her. You'd think she was watching the news with us." Deborah laughed and leaned over to scratch Bwada behind the ears. As she did so, Bwada turned to look at me.

The rain is letting up slightly. I can still hear the dripping from the trees, leaf to leaf to the dead leaves lining the forest floor. It will probably continue on and off all night. Occasionally I think I hear thrashings in one of the oaks near the barn, but then the sound turns into the falling of the rain.

Mildew higher on the walls of this place. Glad my books are on shelves off the ground. So damp in here my envelopes are ruined—glue moistened, sealing them all shut. Stamps that had been in my wallet are stuck to the dollar bills. At night my sheets are clammy and cold, but each morning I wake up sweating.

Finished "The Amber Witch," really fine. Would that all lives had such happy endings.

June 22

... When Poroths returned from church, helped them prepare strips of molding for the upstairs study. Worked out in the tool shed, one of the old wooden outbuildings. I measured, Sarr sawed, Deborah sanded. All in all, hardly felt useful, but what the hell?

While they were busy I sat staring out the window. There's a narrow cement walk running from the shed to the main house, and, as was their habit, Minnie and Felix, two of the kittens, were crouched in the middle of it taking in the late afternoon sun. Suddenly Bwada appeared on the house's front porch and began slinking along the cement path in our direction, tail swishing from side to side. When she neared the kittens she gave a snarl—I could see her mouth working—and they leaped to their feet, bristling, and ran off into the grass.

Called this to Poroths' attention. They said, in effect, Yes, we know, she's always been nasty to the kittens, probably because she never had any of her own. And besides, she's getting older.

When I turned back to the window, Bwada was gone. Asked the Poroths if they didn't think she'd gotten worse lately. Realized that, in speaking, I'd unconsciously dropped my voice, as if someone might be listening through the chinks in the floorboards.

Deborah conceded that, yes, the cat is behaving worse these days toward the others. And not just toward the kittens, as before. Butch, the adult orange male, seems particularly afraid of her....

Am a little angry at the Poroths. Will have to tell them when I see them tomorrow morning. They claim they never come into these rooms, respect privacy of a tenant, etc. etc., but one of them must have been in here because I've just noticed my can of insect spray is missing. I don't mind their borrowing it, but I like to have it by my bed on nights like this. Went over room looking for spiders, just in case; had a fat copy of *American Scholar* in my hand to crush them (only thing it's good for). But found nothing.

Tried to read some *Walden* as a break from all the horror stuff, but found my eyes too irritated, watery. Keep scratching them as I write this. Nose pretty clogged, too—the damned allergy's worse tonight. Probably because of the dampness. Expect I'll have trouble getting to sleep.

June 24

Slept very late this morning because the noise from the woods kept me up late last night. (Come to think of it, the Poroths' praying was unusually loud as well, but that wasn't what bothered me.) I'd been in the middle of writing in this journal—some thoughts on A.E. Coppard—when it came. I immediately stopped writing and shut off the light.

At first it sounded like something in the woods near my room—an animal? a child? I couldn't tell, but smaller than a man—shuffling through the dead leaves, kicking them around as if it didn't care who heard it. There was a snapping of branches and, every so often, a silence and then a bump, as if it were hopping over fallen logs. I stood in the dark listening to it, then crept to the window and looked out. Thought I noticed some bushes moving, back there in the undergrowth, but it may have been the wind.

The sound grew farther away. Whatever it was must have been walking directly out into the deepest part of the woods, where the ground gets swampy and treacherous, because, very faintly, I could hear the sucking sounds of feet slogging through the mud.

I stood by the window for almost an hour, occasionally hearing what I thought were movements off there in the swamp, but finally all was quiet except for the crickets and the frogs. I had no intention of going out there with my flashlight in search of the intruder—that's for guys in stories, I'm much too chicken—and I wondered if I should call Sarr. But by this time the noise had stopped and whatever it was had obviously moved on. Besides, I tend to think he'd have been angry if I'd awakened him and Deborah just because some stray dog had wandered near the farm. I recalled how annoyed he'd been earlier that day when—maybe not all that tactfully—I'd asked him what he'd done with my bug spray. (Must remember to walk into town tomorrow and pick up a can. Still can't figure out where I misplaced mine.)

I went over to the windows on the other side and watched the moonlight on the barn for a while; my nose probably looked cross-hatched from pressing against the screen. In contrast to the woods, the grass looked peaceful under the full moon. Then I lay in bed, but had a hard time falling asleep. Just as I was getting relaxed the sounds started again. High-pitched wails and caterwauls, from deep within the woods. Even after thinking about it all today, I still don't know whether the noise was human or animal. There were no actual words, of that I'm certain, but nevertheless there was the impression of *singing*. In a crazy, tunelsss kind of way the sound seemed to carry the same solemn rhythm as the Poroths' prayers earlier that night.

The noise only lasted a minute or two, but I lay awake till the sky began to get lighter. Probably should have read a little more Coppard, but was reluctant to turn on the lamp.

... Slept all morning and, in the afternoon, followed the road the opposite direction from Gilead, seeking anything of interest. But the road just gets muddier and muddier till it disappears altogether by the ruins of an old homestead—rocks and cement covered with moss—and it looked so much like posion ivy around there that I didn't want to risk tramping through.

At dinner (pork chops, home-grown stringbeans, and pudding—

quite good), mentioned the noise of last night. Sarr acted very concerned and went to his room to look up something in one of his books; Deborah and I discussed the matter at some length and concluded that the shuffling sounds weren't necessarily related to the wailing. The former were almost definitely those of a dog—dozens in the area, and they love to prowl around at night, exploring, hunting coons—and as for the wailing . . . well, it's hard to say. She thinks it may have been an owl or whippoorwill, while I suspect it may have been that same stray dog. I've heard the howl of wolves and I've heard hounds baying at the moon, and both have the same element of, I suppose, *worship* in them that these did.

Sarr came back downstairs and said he couldn't find what he'd been looking for. Said that when he moved into this farm he'd had "a fit of piety" and had burned a lot of old books he'd found in the attic; now he wishes he hadn't.

Looked up something on my own after leaving the Poroths. *Field Guide to Mammals* lists both red and grey foxes and, believe it or not, coyotes as surviving here in New Jersey. No wolves left, though—but the guide might be wrong.

Then, on a silly impulse, opened another reference book, Barbara Byfield's *Glass Harmonica*. Sure enough, my hunch was right: looked up June twenty-third and it said, "St. John's Eve. Sabbats likely."

I'll stick to the natural explanation. Still, I'm glad Mrs. Byfield lists nothing for tonight; I'd like to get some sleep. There is, of course, a beautiful full moon—werewolf weather, as Maria Ouspenskaya might have said. But then, there are no wolves left in New Jersey. . . .

(Which reminds me, really must read some Marryat and Endore. But only after *Northanger Abbey;* my course always comes first.)

June 25

. . . After returning from town, the farm looked very lonely. Wish they had a library in Gilead with more than religious tracts. Or a stand that sold the *Times*. (Though it's strange how, after a week or two, you no longer miss it.)

Overheated from walk—am I getting out of shape? Or is it just the hot weather? Took a cold shower. When I opened the bathroom door I acidentally let Bwada out—I'd wondered why the chair was propped against it. She raced into the kitchen, pushed open the screen door by herself, and I had no chance to catch her. (Wouldn't have attempted to anyway; her claws are wicked.) I apologized later when Deborah came in from the fields. She said Bwada had become vicious toward the other cats and that Sarr had confined her to the bathroom as punishment. The first time he'd shut her in there, Deborah said, the cat had gotten out; apparently she's smart enough to turn the doorknob by swatting at it a few times. Hence the chair.

Sarr came in carrying Bwada, both obviously out of temper. He'd seen a streak of orange running through the field toward him, followed by a grey blur. Butch had stopped at his feet and Bwada had pounced on him, but before she could do any damage Sarr had grabbed her around the neck and carried her back here. He'd been bitten once and scratched a lot on his hands, but not badly; maybe the cat still likes him best. He threw her back in the bathroom and shoved the chair against the door, then sat down and asked Deborah to join him in some silent prayer. I thumbed uneasily through a religious magazine till they were done, and we sat down to dinner.

I apologized again, but he said he wasn't mad at me, that the Devil had gotten into his cat. It was obvious he meant that quite literally. During dinner (omelet—the hens have been laying well) we heard a grating sound from the bathroom, and Sarr ran in to find her almost out the window; somehow she must have been strong enough to slide it up partway. She seemed so placid, though, when Sarr pulled her down from the sill—he'd been expecting another fight—that he let her out into the kitchen. At this she simply curled up near the stove and went to sleep; I guess she'd worked off her rage for the day. The other cats gave her a wide berth, though.

Watched a couple of hours of television with the Poroths. They may have gone to college, but the shows they find interesting . . . God! I'm ashamed of myself for sitting there like a cretin in front of that box. I won't even mention what we watched, lest history record the true abysmality of my tastes.

And yet I find that the TV draws us closer together, as if we were having an adventure together. Shared experience, really. Like knowing the same people or going to the same school.

But there's a lot of duplicity in those Poroths—and I don't mean just religious hypocrisy, either. Came out here after watching the news, and though I hate to accuse anyone of spying on me, there's no doubt that Sarr or Deborah has been inside this room today. I began tonight's entry with great irritation because I found my desk in disarray; this journal wasn't even put back in the right drawer. I keep all my pens on one side, all my pencils on another, ink and erasers in the middle, etc., and when I sat down tonight I saw that everything was out of place. Thank God I haven't included anything too personal in here. . . . What I assume happened was that Deborah came in to wash the mildew off the walls—she's mentioned doing so several times, and she knew I'd be in town part of the day—and got sidetracked into reading this, thinking it must be some kind of secret diary. (I'm sure she was disppointed to find that it's merely a literary journal, with nothing about her in it.)

What bugs me is the difficulty of broaching the subject. I can't just walk in and charge Deborah with being a sneak—Sarr is moody enough as it is—and even if I hint at "someone messing up my desk," they'll know what I mean and perhaps get angry. Whenever possible I prefer to avoid unpleasantness. I guess the best thing to do is simply hide this book under my mattress from now on and say nothing. If it happens again, though, I'll definitely move out of here.

. . . I've been reading some *Northanger Abbey*. Really quite witty, as all her stuff is, but it's obvious the mock-Gothic bit isn't central to the story. I'd thought it was going to be a real parody. . . . Love stories always tend to bore me, and normally I'd be asleep right now, but my damned nose is so clogged tonight that it's hard to breathe when I lie back. Usually being out here clears it up. I've used this goddamned inhaler a dozen times in the past hour, but within a few minutes I sneeze and have to use it again. Wish Deborah'd gotten around to cleaning off the mildew instead of wasting her time looking in here for True Confessions and deep dark secrets . . .

Think I hear something moving outside. Best to shut off my light.

June 30

Slept late. Read some Shirley Jackson stories over breakfast, but got so turned off at her view of humanity that I switched to old Aleister Crowley, who at least keeps a sunny disposition. For her, people in the country are callous and vicious, those in the city are callous and vicious, husbands are (of course) callous and vicious, and children are merely sadistic. The only ones with feelings are her put-upon middle-aged heroines, with whom she obviously identifies. I guess if she didn't write so well the stories wouldn't sting so.

Inspired by Crowley, walked back to the pool in the woods. Had visions of climbing a tree, swinging on vines, anything to commemorate his exploits. . . . Saw something dead floating in the center of the pool and ran back to the farm. Copperhead? Caterpillar? It had somehow opened up. . . .

Joined Sarr chopping stakes for tomatoes. Could hear his ax all over the farm. He told me Bwada hadn't come home last night, and no sign of her this morning. Good riddance, as far as I'm concerned. Helped him chop some stakes, while he was busy peeling off bark. That ax can get heavy fast! My arm hurt after three lousy stakes, and Sarr had already chopped fifteen or sixteen. Must start exercising. But I'll wait till my arm's less tired. . . .

July 2

Unpleasant day. Two A.M. now and still can't relax.

Sarr woke me up this morning—stood at my window calling "Jeremy . . . Jeremy . . . " over and over very quietly. He had something in his hand which, through the screen, I first took for a farm implement; then I saw it was a rifle. He said he wanted me to help him. With what? I asked.

"A burial."

Last night, after he and Deborah had gone to bed, they'd heard the kitchen door open and someone enter the house. They both assumed it was me, come to use the bathroom—but then they heard the cats screaming. Sarr ran down and switched on the light in time to see Bwada on top of Butch, claws in his side, fangs buried in his neck. From the way he described it, sounds almost sexual in reverse. Butch had stopped struggling, and Minnie, the orange kitten, was already dead. The door was partly open, and when Bwada saw Sarr, she ran out.

Sarr and Deborah hadn't followed her; they'd spent the night praying over the bodies of Minnie and Butch. I *thought* I'd heard their voices late last night, but that's all I heard, probably because I'd been playing my radio. (Something I rarely do—you can't hear noises from the woods with it on.)

Poroths took deaths the way they'd take the death of a child. Regular little funeral service over by the unused pasture. (Hard to say if Sarr and Deborah were dressed in mourning, since that's the way they always dress.) Must admit I didn't feel particularly involved— my allergy's never permitted me to take much interest in the cats, though I'm fond of Felix—but I tried to act concerned: when Sarr asked, appropriately, "Is there no balm in Gilead? Is there no physician there?" (Jeremiah VIII:22), I nodded gravely. Read passages out of Deborah's Bible (Sarr seemed to know them all by heart), said amen when they did, knelt when they knelt, and tried to comfort Deborah when she cried. Asked her if cats could go to heaven, received a tearful "Of course." But Sarr added that Bwada would burn in hell.

What concerned me, apparently a lot more than it did either of them, was how the damned thing could get into the house. Sarr gave me this stupid, earnest answer: "She was always a smart cat." Like an outlaw's mother, still proud of her baby. . . .

Yet he and I looked all over the land for her so he could kill her. Barns, tool shed, old stables, garbage dump, etc. He called her and pleaded with her, swore to me she hadn't always been like this.

We could hardly check every tree on the farm—unforuntely—and the woods are a perfect hiding place, even for animals larger than a cat. So naturally we found no trace of her. We did try, though; we even walked up the road as far as the ruined homestead.

But for all that, we could have stayed much closer to home. . . .

We returned for dinner, and I stopped at my room to change clothes. My door was open. Nothing inside was ruined, everything was in its place, everything as it should be—except the bed. The sheets were in tatters right down to the mattress, and the pillow had been ripped to shreds. Feathers were all over the floor. There were even claw marks on my blanket.

At dinner the Poroths demanded they be allowed to pay for the damage—nonsense, I said, they have enough to worry about—and Sarr suggested I sleep downstairs in their living room. "No need for that," I told him, "I've got lots more sheets." But he said no, he didn't mean that: he meant for my own protection. He believes the thing is particularly inimical, for some reason, toward me.

It seemed so absurd at the time . . . I mean, nothing but a big fat grey cat. But now, sitting out here, a few feathers still scattered on the floor around my bed, I wish I were back inside the house. I did give in to Sarr when he insisted I take his ax with me. . . . But what I'd rather have is simply a room without windows.

I don't think I want to go to sleep tonight, which is one reason I'm continuing to write this. Just sit up all night on my new bedsheets, my back against the Poroths' pillow, leaning against the wall behind me, the ax beside me on the bed, this journal on my lap. . . . The thing is, I'm rather tired out from all the walking I did today. Not used to that much exercise.

I'm pathetically aware of every sound. At least once every five minutes some snapping of a branch or rustling of leaves makes me jump.

"Thou art my hope in the day of evil." At least that's what the man said. . . .

July 3

Woke up this morning with the journal and the ax cradled in my arms. What awakened me was the trouble I had breathing—nose all clogged, gasping for breath. Down the center of one of my screens, facing the woods, was a huge slash. . . .

July 15

Pleasant day, St. Swithin's Day—and yet, my birthday. Thirty years old, lordy lordy lordy. Today I am a man. First dull thoughts on waking: "Damnation. Thirty today." But another voice inside me, smaller but more sensible, spat contemptuously at such an aritificial way of charting time. "Ah, don't give it another thought," it said. "You've still got plenty of time to fool around." Advice I took to heart.

Weather today? Actually, somewhat nasty. And thus the weather for the next forty days, since "If rain on St. Swithin's Day, forsooth, no summer drouthe," or something like that. My birthday predicts the weather. It's even mentioned in *The Glass Harmonica*.

As one must, took a critical self-assessment. First area for improvement: flabby body. Second? Less bookish, perhaps? Nonsense—I'm satisfied with the progress I've made. "And seekest thou great things for thyself? Seek them not." (Jeremiah XLV:5) So I simply did what I remembered from the RCAF exercise series and got good and winded. Flexed my stringy muscles in the shower, certain I'll be a Human Dynamo by the end of the summer. Simply a matter of willpower.

Was so ambitious I trimmed the ivy around my windows again. It's begun to block the light, and someday I may not be able to get out the door.

Read Ruthven Todd's *Lost Traveler*. Merely the narrative of a dream turned to nightmare, and illogical as hell. Wish, too, that there'd been more than merely a few hints of sex. On the whole, rather unpleasant; that gruesome ending is so inevitable. . . . Took me much of the afternoon. Then came upon an incredible essay by Lafcadio Hearn, something "Gaki," detailing the curious Japanese belief that insects are really demons, or the ghosts of evil men. Uncomfortably convincing!

Dinner late because Deborah, bless her, was baking me a cake. Had time to walk into town and phone parents. Happy birthday, happy birthday. Both voiced first worry—mustn't I be getting bored out here? Assured them I still had plenty of books and did not grow tired of reading.

"But it's so . . . *secluded* out there," Mom said. "Don't you get lonely?"

Ah, she hadn't reckoned on the inner resources of a man of thirty. How can I get lonely, I asked, when there's still so much to read? Besides, there are the Poroths to talk to.

Then the kicker: Dad wanted to know about the cat. Last time I'd spoken to them it had sounded like a very real danger. "Are you still sleeping inside the farmhouse, I hope?"

No, I told him, really, I only had to do that for a few days, while it was prowling around at night. Yes, it had killed some chickens—a hen every night, in fact. But there were only four of them, and then it stopped. We haven't had a sign of it in more than a week. (I didn't tell him that it had left the hens uneaten, dead in the nest. No need to upset him further.)

"But what it did to your sheets . . . " he went on. "If you'd been sleeping . . . Such savagery."

Yes, that was unfortunate, but there's been no trouble since. Honest, it was only an animal, after all, just a housecat gone a little wild. It posed the same kind of threat as a . . . (I was going to say, logically, wildcat; but for Mom said) nasty little dog. Like Mrs. Miller's bull terrier. Besides, it's probably miles and miles away by now. Or dead.

They offered to drive out with packages of food, magazines, a portable TV, but I made it clear I needed nothing. Getting too fat, actually.

Still light when I got back. Deborah had finished the cake, Sarr brought up some wine from the cellar, and we had a nice little celebration. The two of them being over thirty, they were happy to welcome me to the fold.

It's nice out here. The wine has relaxed me and I keep yawning. It was good to talk to Mom and Dad again. Just as long I don't dream of *The Lost Traveller,* I'll be content. And happier still if I don't dream at all. . . .

July 30

Well, Bwada is dead—this time for sure. We'll bury her tomorrow. Deborah was hurt, just how badly I can't say, but she managed to fight Bwada off. Tough woman, though she seems a little shaken. And with good reason.

It happened this way: Sarr and I were in the tool shed after dinner, building more shelves for the upstairs study. Though the fireflies were out, there was still a little daylight left. Deborah had gone up to bed after doing the dishes; she's been tired a lot lately, falls asleep early every night while watching TV with Sarr. He thinks it may be something in the well water.

It had begun to get dark, but we were still working. Sarr dropped a box of nails, and while we were picking them up, he thought he heard a scream. Since I hadn't heard anything, he shrugged and was about to start sawing again when—fortunately—he changed his mind and ran off to the house. I followed him as far as the porch, not sure whether to go upstairs, until I heard him pounding on their bedroom door and calling Deborah's name. As I ran up the stairs I heard her say, "Wait a minute. Don't come in. I'll unlock the door . . . soon." Her voice was extremely hoarse, practically a croaking. We heard her rummaging in the closet—finding her bathrobe, I suppose—and then she opened the door.

She looked absolutely white. Her long hair was in tangles and her robe buttoned incorrectly. Around her neck she had wrapped a towel, but we could see patches of blood soaking through it. Sarr helped her over to the bed, shouting at me to bring up some bandages from the bathroom.

When I returned Deborah was lying in bed, still pressing the towel to her throat. I asked Sarr what had happened; it almost looked as if the woman had tried suicide.

He didn't say anything, just pointed to the floor on the other side of the bed. I stepped around for a look. A crumpled grey shape was lying there, half covered by the bedclothes. It was Bwada, a wicked-looking wound in her side. On the floor next to her lay an umbrella—the thing that Deborah had used to kill her.

She told us she'd been asleep when she felt something crawl heavily over her face. It had been like a bad dream. She'd tried to sit up, and suddenly Bwada was at her throat, digging in. Luckily she'd had the strength to tear the animal off and dash to the closet, where the first weapon at hand was the umbrella. Just as the cat sprang at her again, Deborah said, she'd raised the weapon and lunged. Amazing. . . . How many women, I wonder, would have had such presence of mind? The rest sounds incredible to me, but it's probably the sort of crazy thing that happens in moments like this: somehow the cat had impaled itself on the umbrella.

Her voice, as she spoke, was barely more than a whisper. Sarr had to persuade her to remove the towel from her throat; she kept protesting that she wasn't hurt that badly, that the towel had stopped the bleeding. Sure enough, when Sarr finally lifted the cloth from her neck, the wounds proved relatively small, the slash marks already clotting. Thank God that thing didn't really get its teeth in. . . .

My guess—only a guess—is that it had been weakened from days of living in the woods. (It was obviously incapable of feeding itself adequately, as I think was proved by its failure to eat the hens it had killed.) While Sarr dressed Deborah's wounds, I pulled back the bedclothes and took a closer look at the animal's body. The fur was matted and patchy. Odd that an umbrella could make a puncture like that, ringed by flaps of skin, as if the flesh had been pushed outward . . . though I suspect it has a simple explanation: it was Deborah's extraordinary good luck to have jabbed the animal precisely in its old wound, which had reopened. Naturally I didn't mention this to Sarr.

He made dinner for us tonight—soup, actually, because he thought that was best for Deborah. Her voice sounded so bad he told her not to strain it any more by talking, at which she nodded and smiled. We both had to help her downstairs, as she was clearly weak from shock.

In the morning Sarr will have the doctor out. He'll have to examine the cat, too, to check for rabies, so we put the body in the freezer to preserve it as well as possible. Afterward we'll bury it.

Deboray seemed okay when I left. Sarr was reading through some medical books, and she was just lying on the living room couch gazing at her husband with a look of purest gratitude—not moving, not saying anything, not even blinking.

I feel quite relieved. God knows how many nights I've lain here thinking every sound I heard was Bwada. I'll feel more relieved, of course, when that demon's safely underground; but I think I can say, at the risk of being melodramatic, that the reign of terror is over.

Hmm, I'm still a little hungry—used to more than soup for dinner. These daily push-ups burn up energy. I'll probably dream of hamburgers and chocolate layer cakes.

July 31

. . . The doctor collected scrapings from Bwada's teeth and scolded us for doing a poor job of preserving the body. Said storing it in the freezer was a sensible idea, but that we should have done so sooner, since it was already decomposing. The dampness, I imagine, must act fast on dead flesh.

He pronounced Deborah in excellent condition—the marks on her throat are, remarkably, almost healed—but he said her reflexes were a little off. Sarr invited him to stay for the burial, but he declined—and quite emphatically, at that. He's not a member of their order, doesn't live in the area, and apparently doesn't get along that well with the people of Gilead, most of whom mistrust modern science. (Not that the old geezer sounded very representative of modern medicine. When I asked him for some good exercises, he recommended "chopping wood and running down deer.")

Standing under the heavy clouds, Sarr looked like a revivalist minister. His sermon was from Jeremiah XXII:19, "He shall be buried with the burial of an ass." The burial took place far from the graves of Bwada's two victims, and closer to the woods. We sang one song, Deborah just mouthing the words (still mustn't strain throat muscles). Sarr solemnly asked the Lord to look mercifully upon all His creatures, and I muttered an "amen." Then we walked back to the house, Deborah leaning on Sarr's arm; she's still a little stiff.

It was grey the rest of the day, and I sat in my room reading *The King in Yellow*—or rather, Chambers' collection of the same name. One look at the *real* book, so Chambers would claim, and I might not live to see the morrow, at least through the eyes of a sane man. (That single gimmick—masterful, I admit—seems to be his sole inspiration.)

I was disappointed that dinner was again made by Sarr; Deborah was upstairs resting, he said. He sounded concerned, felt there were things wrong with her the doctor had overlooked. We ate our meal in silence, and I came back here immediately after washing the dishes. Feel very drowsy and, for some reason, also rather depressed. It may be the gloomy weather—we are, after all, just animals, more affected by the sun and the seasons than we like to admit. More likely it was the absence of Deborah tonight. Hope she feels better.

Note: The freezer still smells of the cat's body; opened it tonight and got a strong whiff of decay.

August 1

Writing this, breaking habit, in early morning. Went to bed last night just after finishing the entry above, but was awakened around two by sounds coming from the woods. Wailing, deeper than before, followed by a low, guttural monologue. No words, at least that I could distinguish. If frogs could talk . . . For some reason I fell asleep before the sounds ended, so I don't know what followed.

Could very well have been an owl of some kind, and later a large bullfrog. But I quote, without comment, from *The Glass Harmonica:* "July 31: Lammas Eve. Sabbats likely."

The Events at Poroth Farm

August 4

Little energy to write tonight, and even less to write about. (Come to think of it, I slept most of the day: woke up at eleven, later took an afternoon nap. Alas, senile at thirty!) Too tired to shave, and haven't had the energy to clean this place, either; thinking about work is easier than doing it. The ivy's beginning to cover the windows again, and the mildew's been climbing steadily up the walls. It's like a dark green band that keeps widening. Soon it will reach my books. . . .

Speaking of which, note: opened M. R. James at lunch today— *Ghost Stories of an Antiquary*—and a silverfish slithered out. Omen?

Played a little game with myself this evening—

I just had one hell of a shock. While writing the above I heard a soft tapping, like nervous fingers drumming on a table, and discovered an enormous spider, biggest of the summer, crawling only a few inches from my ankle. It must have been living behind this desk. . . .

When you can hear a spider walk across the floor, you *know* it's time to keep your socks on. Thank God for insecticide.

Oh, yeah, that game—the What If game. I probably play it too often. (Vain attempt to enlarge realm of the possible? Heighten my own sensitivity? Or merely work myself into an icy sweat?) I pose unpleasant questions for myself and consider the consequences, e.g., what if this glorified chicken coop is sinking into quicksand? (Wouldn't be at all surprised.) What if the Poroths are tired of me? What if I woke up inside my own coffin?

What if I never see New York again?

What if some horror stories aren't really fiction? If Machen sometimes told the truth? If there *are* White People, malevolent little faces peering out of the moonlight? Whispers in the grass? Poisonous things in the woods? Perfect hate and evil in the world?

Enough of this foolishness. Time for bed.

August 9

. . . Read some Hawthorne in the morning and, over lunch, reread this week's *Hunterdon County Democrat* for the dozenth time. Sarr and Deborah were working somewhere in the fields, and I felt I ought to get some physical activity myself; but the thought of starting my exercises again after more than a week's laziness just seemed too unpleasant. . . . I took a walk down the road a little way, but only as far as a smashed-up cement culvert half buried in the woods. I was bored, but Gilead just seemed too far away.

Was going to cut the ivy away from my windows when I got back, but decided the place looks more artistic covered in vines. Rationalization?

Chatted with Poroths about politics. The World Situation, a little cosmology, blah blah blah. Dinner wasn't very good, probably because I'd been looking forward to it all day. The lamb was underdone and the beans were cold. Still, I'm always the gentleman, and was almost pleased when Deborah agreed to my offer to do the dishes. I've been doing them a lot lately.

I didn't have much interest in reading tonight and would have been up for some television, but Sarr's recently gotten into one of his religious kicks and began mumbling prayers to himself immediately after dinner. (Deborah, more human, wanted to watch the TV news. She seems to have an insatiable curiosity about world events, yet she claims the isolation here appeals to her.) Absorbed in his chanting, Sarr made me uncomfortable—I didn't like his face—and so after doing the dishes, I left.

I've been listening to the radio for the last hour or so.... I recall days when I'd have gotten uptight at having wasted an hour—but out here I've lost all track of time. Feel adrift—a little disconcerting, but healthy, I'm sure.

... Shut the radio off a moment ago, and now realize my room is filled with crickets. Up close their sound is hardly pleasant—cross between a radiator and a tea-kettle, very shrill. They'd been sounding off all night, but I'd thought it was interference on the radio.

Now I notice them; they're all over the room. A couple of dozen, I should think. Hate to kill them, really—they're one of the few insects I can stand, along with ladybugs and fireflies. But they make such a racket!

Wonder how they got in . . .

August 14

Played with Felix all morning—mainly watching him chase insects, climb trees, doze in the sun. Spectator sport. After lunch went back to my room to look up something in Lovecraft, and discovered my books were out of order. (Saki, for example, was filed under "S," whereas—whether out of fastidiousness or pedantry—I've always preferred to file him as "H. H. Munro.") This is definitely one of the

Poroths' doing. I'm pissed they didn't mention coming in here, but also a little surprised they'd have any interest in this stuff.

Arranged them correctly again, then sat down to reread Lovecraft's essay on "Supernatural Horror in Literature." It upset me to see how little I've actually read, how far I still have to go. So many obscure authors, so many books I've never come across. . . . Left me feeling depressed and tired, so I took a nap for the rest of the afternoon.

Over dinner—vegetable omelet, rather tasteless—Deborah continued to question us on current events. It's getting to be like junior high school, with daily newspaper quizzes. . . . Don't know how she got started on this, or why the sudden interest, but it obviously annoys the hell out of Sarr.

Sarr used to be a sucker for her little-girl pleadings—I remember how he used to carry her upstairs, becoming pathetically tender, the moment she'd say, "Oh, honey, I'm so tired"—but now he just becomes angry. Often he goes off morose and alone to pray, and the only time he laughs is when he watches television.

Tonight, thank God, he was in a mood to forego the prayers, and so after dinner we all watched a lot of offensively ignorant programs. I was disturbed to find myself laughing along with the canned laughter, but I have to admit the TV helps us get along better together. Came back here after the news.

Not very tired, having slept so much of the afternoon, so began to read John Christopher's *The Possessors;* but good though it was, my mind began to wander to all the books I *haven't* yet read, and I got so depressed I turned on the radio. Find it takes my mind off things.

August 19

Slept long into the morning, then walked down to the brook, scratching groggily. Deborah was kneeling by the water, lost, it seemed, in daydream, and I was embarrassed because I'd come upon her talking to herself. We exchanged a few insincere words and she went back toward the house.

Sat by some rocks, throwing blades of grass into the water. The sun on my head felt almost painful, as if my brain were growing too large for my skull. I turned and looked at the farmhouse. In the distance it looked like a picture at the other end of a large room, the grass for a carpet, the ceiling the sky. Deborah was stroking a cat, then seemed to grow angry when it struggled from her arms; I could hear the screen door slam as she went into the kitchen, but the sound reached me so long after the visual image that the whole scene struck me as, somehow, fake. I gazed up at the maples behind me and they seemed trees out of a cheap postcard, the kind in which thinly colored paint is dabbed over a black-and-white photograph; if you look closely you can see that the green in the trees is not merely in the leaves, but rather floats as a vapor over leaves, branches, parts of the sky.... The trees behind me seemed the productions of a poor painter, the color and shape not quite meshing. Parts of the sky were green, and pieces of the green seemed to float away from my vision. No matter how hard I tried I couldn't follow them.

Far down the stream I could see something small and kicking, a black beetle, legs in the air, borne swiftly along in the current. Then it was gone.

Thumbed through the Bible while I ate my lunch—mostly cookies. By late afternoon I was playing word games while I lay on the grass near my room. The shrill twitter of the birds, I would say, the birds singing in the sun.... And inexorably I'd continue with the sun dying in the moonlight, the moonlight falling on the floor, the floor sagging to the cellar, the cellar filling with water, the water seeping into the ground, the ground twisting into smoke, the smoke staining the sky, the sky burning in the sun, the sun dying in the moonlight, the moonlight falling on the floor.... Thus the melancholy progressions that held my mind like a whirlpool.

Sarr woke me for dinner; I had dozed off, and my clothes were damp from the grass. As we walked up to the house together he whispered that, earlier in the day, he'd come upon his wife bending over me, peering into my sleeping face. "Her eyes were wide," he said. "Like Bwada's." I said I didn't understand why he was telling me this.

"Because," he recited in a whisper, gripping my arm, "the heart is deceitful above all things, and desperately wicked: who can know it?"

I recognized that. Jeremiah XVII:9

Dinner was especially uncomfortable; the two of them sat picking at their food, occasionally raising their eyes to one another like children in a staring contest. I longed for the conversations of our early days, inconsequential though they must have been, and wondered where things had first gone wrong.

The meal was dry and unappetizing, but the dessert looked delicious—chocolate mousse, made from an old family recipe. Deborah had served it earlier in the summer and knew both Sarr and I loved it. This time, however, she gave none to herself, explaining that she had to watch her weight.

"Then we'll not eat any!" Sarr shouted, and with that he snatched my dish from in front of me, grabbed his own, and hurled them both against the wall, where they splattered like mudballs.

Deborah was very still; she said nothing, just sat there watching us. She didn't look particularly afraid of this madman, I was happy to see—but *I* was. He may have read my thoughts, because as I got up from my seat he said much more gently, in the soft voice normal to him, "Sorry, Jeremy. I know you hate scenes. We'll pray for each other, all right?"

"Are you okay?" I asked Deborah. "I'm going out now, but I'll stay if you think you'll need me for anything." She stared at me with a slight smile and shook her head. I raised my eyebrows and nodded toward her husband, and she shrugged.

"Things will work out," she said. I could hear Sarr laughing as I shut the door.

When I snapped on the light out here I took off my shirt and stood in front of the little mirror. It had been nearly a week since I'd showered, and I'd become used to the smell of my body. My hair had wound itself into greasy brown curls, my beard was at least two weeks old, and my eyes . . . well, the eyes that stared back at me looked like those of an old man. The whites were turning yellow, like old teeth. I looked at my chest and arms, flabby at thirty, and I thought of the frightening alterations in my friend Sarr, and I knew I'd have to get out of here.

Just glanced at my watch. It's now quite late: two-thirty. I've been packing my things.

August 20

I woke about an hour ago and continued packing. Lots of books to put away, but I'm just about done. It's not even nine A.M. yet, much earlier than I normally get up; but I guess the thought of leaving here fills me with energy.

The first thing I saw on rising was a garden spider whose body was as big as some of the mice the cats have killed. It was sitting on the ivy that grows over my window sill—fortunately, on the other side of the screen. Apparently it had had good hunting all summer, preying on the insects that live in the leaves. Concluding that nothing so big and fearsome has a right to live, I held the spray can against the screen and doused the creature with poison. It struggled halfway up the screen, then stopped, arched its legs, and dropped backwards into the ivy.

I plan to walk into town this morning and telephone the office in Flemington where I rented my car. If they can have one ready today I'll hitch there to pick it up; otherwise I'll spend tonight here and pick it up tomorrow. I'll be leaving a little early in the season, but the Poroths already have my month's rent, so they shouldn't be too offended.

And anyway, how could I be expected to stick around here with all that nonsense going on, never knowing when my room might be ransacked, having to put up with Sarr's insane suspicions and Deborah's moodiness?

Before I go into town, though, I really must shave and shower for the good people of Gilead. I've been sitting inside here waiting for some sign the Poroths are up, but as yet—it's almost nine—I've heard nothing. I wouldn't care to barge in on them while they're still having breakfast or, worse, just getting up . . . So I'll just wait here by the window till I see them.

. . . Ten o'clock now, and they still haven't come out. Perhaps they're having a talk . . . I'll give them half an hour more, then I'm going in.

Here my journal ends. Until today, almost a week later, I have not cared to set down any of the events that followed. But here in the temporary safety of this hotel room, protected by a heavy brass travel-lock I had sent up from the hardware store down the street, watched over by the good people of Flemington—and perhaps by something not good—I can continue my narrative.

The first thing I noticed as I approached the house was that the shades were drawn, even in the kitchen. Had they decided to sleep late this morning? I wondered. Throughout my thirty years I have come to associate drawn shades with a foul smell, the smell of a sickroom, of shamefaced poverty and food gone bad, of people lying too long beneath blankets; but I was not ready for the stench of decay that met me when I opened the kitchen door and stepped into the darkness. Something had died in that room—and not recently.

At the moment the smell first hit, four little shapes scrambled across the linoleum toward me and out into the daylight. The Poroths' cats.

By the other wall a lump of shadow moved; a pale face caught light penetrating the shades. Sarr's voice, its habitual softness exaggerated to a whisper: "Jeremy. I thought you were still asleep."

"Can I—"

"No. Don't turn on the light." He got to his feet, a black form towering against the window. Fiddling nervously with the kitchen door—the tin doorknob, the rubber bands stored around it, the fringe at the bottom of the drawn window shade—I opened it wider and let in more sunlight. It fell on the dark thing at his feet, over which he had been crouching: Deborah, the flesh at her throat torn and wrinkled like the skin of an old apple.

Her clothing lay in a heap beside her. She appeared long dead. The eyes were shriveled, sunken into sockets black as a skull's.

I think I may have staggered at that moment, because he came toward me. His steady, unblinking gaze looked so sincere—but *why was he smiling?* "I'll make you understand," he was saying, or something like that; even now I feel my face twisting into horror as I try to write of him. "I had to kill her. . . ."

"You—"

"She tried to kill me," he went on, silencing all questions. "The same thing that possessed Bwada . . . possessed her."

My hand played behind my back with the bottom of the window shade. "But her throat—"

"That happened a long time ago. Bwada did it. I had nothing to do with . . . that part." Suddenly his voice rose. "Don't you understand? She tried to stab me with the bread knife." He turned, stooped over and, clumsy in the darkness, began feeling about him on the floor. "Where is that thing?" he was mumbling. "I'll show you. . . ." As he crossed a beam of sunlight, something gleamed like a silver handle on the back of his shirt.

Thinking, perhaps, to help him search, I pulled gently on the window shade, then released it; it snapped upward like a gunshot, flooding the room with light. From deep within the center of his back protruded the dull wooden haft of the bread knife, buried almost completely but for an inch or two of gleaming steel.

He must have heard my intake of breath—that sight chills me even today, the grisly absurdity of the thing—he must have heard me, because immediately he stood, his back to me, and reached up behind himself toward the knife, his arm stretching in vain, his fingers curling around nothing. The blade had been planted in a spot he couldn't reach.

He turned towards me and shrugged in embarrassment, a child caught in a foolish error. "Oh, yeah," he said, grinning at his own weakness, "I forgot it was there."

Suddenly he thrust his face into mine, fixing me in a gaze that never wavered, his eyes wide with candor. "It's easy for us to forget things," he explained—and then, still smiling, still watching, volunteered that last trivial piece of information, that final message whose words released me from inaction and left me free to dash from the room, to sprint in panic down the road to town, pursued by what had once been the farmer Sarr Poroth.

It serves no purpose here to dwell on my flight down that twisting dirt road, breathing in such deep gasps that I was soon moaning with every breath; how, with my enemy racing behind me, not even winded, his steps never flagging, I veered into the woods; how I finally lost him, perhaps from the inexperience of whatever thing now controlled his body, and was able to make my way back to the road, only to come upon him again as he rounded a bend; his laughter as he followed me, and how it continued long after I had evaded him a second time; and how, after hiding until nightfall in the old cement culvert, I ran the rest of the way in pitch-darkness, stumbling in the ruts, torn by vines, nearly blinding myself when I ran into a low branch, until I arrived in Gilead filthy, exhausted, and nearly incoherent.

Suffice it to say that my escape was largely a matter of luck, a physical wreck fleeing something oblivious to pain or fatigue; but that, beyond mere luck, I had been impelled by an almost ecstatic sense of dread produced by his last words to me, that last communication from an alien face smiling inches from my own, and which I chose to take as his final warning:

"Sometimes we forget to blink."

You can read the rest in the newspapers. The *Hunterdon County Democrat* covered most of the story, though its man wrote it up as merely another lunatic wife-slaying, the result of loneliness, religious mania, and a mysteriously tainted well. (Traces of insecticide were found, among other things, in the water.) The *Somerset Reporter* took a different slant, implying that I had been the third member of an erotic triangle and that Sarr had murdered his wife in a fit of jealousy.

Needless to say, I was by this time past caring what was written about me. I was too haunted by visions of that lonely, abandoned farmhouse, the wails of its hungry cats, and by the sight of Deborah's corpse, discovered by the police, protruding from that hastily dug grave beyond the cornfield.

Accompanied by state troopers, I returned to my ivy-covered outbuilding. A bread knife had been plunged deep into its door, splintering the wood on the other side. The blood on it was Sarr's.

My journal had been hidden under my mattress, and so was untouched, but (I look at them now, piled in cardboard boxes beside my suitcase) my precious books had been hurled about the room, their bindings slashed. My summer is over, and now I sit inside here all day listening to the radio, waiting for the next report. Sarr—or his corpse—has not been found.

I should think the evidence was clear enough to corroborate my story, but I suppose I should have expected the reception it received from the police. They didn't laugh at my theory of "possession"—not to my face, anyway—but they ignored it in obvious embarrassment. Some see a nice young bookworm gone slightly deranged after contact with a murderer; others believe my story to be the desperate fabrication of an adulterer trying to avoid the blame for Deborah's death.

I can understand their reluctance to accept my explanation of the events, for it's one that goes a little byond the "natural," a little beyond the scientific considerations of motive, *modus operandi,* and fingerprints. But I find it quite unnerving that at least one official—an assistant district attorney, I think, though I'm afraid I'm rather ignorant of these matters—believes I am guilty of murder.

There has, of course, been no arrest. Still, I've been given the time-honored instructions against leaving town.

The theory proposing my own complicity in the events is, I must admit, rather ingenious—and so carefully worked out that it will surely gain more adherents than my own. This police official is going to try to prove that I killed poor Deborah in a fit of passion and, immediately afterward, disposed of Sarr. He points out that their marriage had been an observably happy one until I arrived, a disturbing influence from the city. My motive, he says, was simple lust—unrequited, to be sure—aggravated by boredom. The heat, the insects, and, most of all, the oppressive loneliness—all constituted an environment alien to any I'd been accustomed to, and all worked to unhinge my reason.

I have no cause for fear, however, because this affidavit will certainly establish my innocence. Surely no one can ignore the evidence of my journal (though I can imagine an antagonistic few maintaining that I wrote the journal not at the farm but here in the Union Hotel, this very week).

What galls me is not the suspicions of a few detectives, but the predicament their suspicions place me in. Quite simply, *I cannot run away.* I am compelled to remain locked up in this room, potential

prey to whatever the thing that was Sarr Poroth has now become—
the thing that was once a cat, and once a woman, and once . . . what?
A large white moth? A serpent? A shrewlike thing with wicked teeth?

A police chief? A president? A boy with eyes of blood that sits beneath my window?

Lord, who will believe me?

It was that night that started it all, I'm convinced of it now. The night I made those strange signs in the tree. The night the crickets missed a beat.

I'm not a philosopher, and I can supply no ready explanation for why this new evil has been released into the world. I'm only a poor scholar, a bookworm, and I must content myself with mumbling a few phrases that keep running through my mind, phrases out of books read long ago when such abstractions meant, at most, a pleasant shudder. I am haunted by scraps from the myth of Pandora, and by a semantic discussion I once read comparing "unnatural" and "supernatural."

And something about "a tiny rent in the fabric of the universe. . . ."

Just large enough to let something in. Something not of nature, and hard to kill. Something with its own obscure purpose.

Ironically, the police may be right. Perhaps it was my visit to Gilead that brought about the deaths. Perhaps I had a hand in letting loose the force that, to date, has snuffed out the lives of four hens, three cats, and at least two people—but will hardly be content to stop there.

I've just checked. He hasn't moved from the steps of the courthouse; and even when I look out my window, the rose spectacles never waver. Who knows where the eyes beneath them point? Who knows if they remember to blink?

Lord, this heat is sweltering. My shirt is sticking to my skin, and droplets of sweat are rolling down my face and dripping onto this page, making the ink run.

My hand is tired from writing, and I think it's time to end this affidavit.

If, as I now believe possible, I inadvertently called down evil from the sky and began the events at Poroth Farm, my death will only be fitting. And after my death, many more. We are all, I'm afraid, in danger. Please, then, forgive this prophet of doom, old at thirty, his last jeremiad: "The harvest is past, the summer is ended, and we are not saved."

CHARLES L. GRANT

"Come Dance With Me on My Pony's Grave"

Charles L. Grant (1942-) wrote science fiction in the early 1970s but soon carved a niche for himself in the horror field through his series of horror novels and novellas set in Oxrun Station, a Connecticut community in which the rhythms of small-town life give rise to intrusions of the supernatural. The series runs to more than a dozen books, and includes the novels **The Hour of the Oxrun Dead, The Sound of Midnight,** *and* **Soft Whisper of the Dead,** *and the collections* **Nightmare Seasons, Dialing the Wind** *and* **The Black Carousel.** *Grant became a leading exponent of dark fantasy through these books and his many non-series novels, among them* **The Nestling, The Pet, In a Dark Dream,** *and* **Someting Stirs.** *In 1978 he edited the first of eleven* **Shadows** *anthologies, a series devoted to original tales of dark fantasy that helped many major talents break into the horror field. Grant's other anthology work includes* **Fears, Doom City,** *and the* **Graystone Bay** *trilogy. Under the pseudonym Geoffrey Marsh, he has written a quintet of occult thrillers featuring series character Lincoln Blackthorne. As Lionel Fenn, he writes the Kent Montana comic fantasy series. His short fiction collections include* **Tales from the Nightside** *and* **A Glow of Candles.**

Come Dance With Me on My Pony's Grave

by Charles L. Grant

November, and an aged slate sky; a wind snapping across the fields like a bullwhip and cracking around a golden brown house that squatted warmly on the grey landscape. Aaron, huddled in a winter-worn and crimson jacket, was slumped, seemingly relaxed, against the jamb of the open front door, his hands flat in his pockets. His eyes were narrowed against the wind, and they shifted quickly along the partially wooded horizon, blurring the Dakota spruce and pine to a green-and-grey smear of almost preternatural fear. Behind him the house was empty, and silent. There was only the wind and an occasional wooden creak.

He shivered.

Suddenly an explosive gust caught him unprepared and shoved him off balance; a magazine was blown to the floor in the living room, and a shade snapped against glass. Reluctantly he closed the door and cut off the warmth from his back. His lips twisted into a half smile. A good thing Miriam's not here, he thought as his mind mimicked her laughing scold: Aaron Jackoson, what do you think we are—Eskimos? Just look at my curtains blown all over, and the cold, Aaron, the cold . . . He grinned, shook his head and closed his eyes briefly to allow her face to flash before him reassuringly. The wind gusted again, and his smile faded. Come home, Miriam, he thought (nearly prayed), come home soon—the boy frightens me yet.

Then he resettled himself to wait, arms folded and pressed tightly against his chest. He squinted into the cold, his eyes moving, moving as they had once been trained to do, watching and waiting . . .

... under a multigreen canopy of broad leaves, twisted vines and knee-high, waist-high brush beside the paths he and his men rarely used as they climbed for hours through the bugs sweat heat dirt world. A ragged clearing ahead where the village so often visited was hidden, and the smoke-skinned, half-naked Montagnards who gave them the news that the enemy had long since fled—all save one who, this time, belonged to them, not the soldiers. Water, then with iodine tablets to kill the bacteria, and orange flavoring to kill the taste. While he watched the jungle and his men relaxed, finally. And the boy—eight, perhaps nine—stood by a black patch of earth where several men were racing the sun, digging what looked to be a grave. A shout...

... and Aaron blinked and watched a slight figure break from the trees and zigzag swiftly across the field, arms waving wildly in greeting. He grinned and, pushing himself away from the house, limped heavily toward the fence as grass crackled sharply beneath his feet. He shivered and wondered how the boy had managed to adapt so rapidly to the four seasons so radically different from the hot and not-so-hot of the mountain jungles.

At last the boy reached the yard and with a melodramatic gasp draped himself over the faded white rail, his face darker, but not red, from exertion.

"Hey, dad."

"Hey, yourself."

"Boy, am I ... bushed?"

Aaron nodded. "Bushed, pooped, beat, tired ... in fact, you look like all of them rolled into one." He was tempted to ask where his adopted son had been, and thought better of it. "Come on inside, David and get yourself warm. Your mother'll kill me if she finds I let you catch cold the minute she decides to go visiting."

The boy was thirteen and still quite short (would never be much taller), and as he dashed back to the house ahead of his father, his long straight black hair whipped his shoulders and the air, while Aaron watched carefully for hints of the past until he realized what he was doing and scolded himself silently for behaving like a damned fool. The boy, he insisted to his shadow, was an American now. But he could not help the growing feeling that, without Miriam, David thought of him only as the lieutenant who took him away. He glanced back at the trees and shut the door.

"Sit down, dad," David called from the kitchen. "I'll make you some hot tea. Did mother call today?"

"Yes, I'm afraid she already has," he answered. "About ten, ten thirty. You were out with Pinto, I think."

"Nuts."

Aaron laughed and, after shucking his coat, stretched out on the sofa, letting the room draw the cold from his skin to die in the dark glow of the beams and paneled walls. And everywhere, the scent of Miriam.

Then he heard a cup shatter and he sighed when David, none too quietly, began muttering to himself. "Hey, in there," he shouted. "We speak English in this house, remember?"

The boy poked his head out of the kitchen and grinned broadly. "Sorry, dad, but that's all I remember any more."

"The swearing?"

"But, dad, they're the best kind, don't you know? I heard the GIs use them all the time."

There was a sharp silence before David finally giggled and thrust out an open hand. "Look, dad, I was only counting. I don't remember any more than that, honest." He waited a moment, staring, then frowned and disappeared.

Now that's got to be a crime, Aaron thought, recalling all the tedious, impatient hours he had spent scraping together enough of the tribe's language to make himself, and his mission, understood; there were still a few isolated words and phrases that returned to him when he pressed, yet the boy had forgotten a lifetime. So he said. Once, when Aaron had been feeling particularly moody over his crippled leg, he had asked David if he minded being away from his old home, toppled through a sargasso of red tape and interviews into a country and life style as alien to the boy as the jungle was to Aaron. David had smiled, a little softly, and shook his head. But the black eyes were expressionless; they always had been since the death of his father.

"Hey, dad! Quit daydreaming, please? This stuff is hot."

Aaron smiled and took the steaming cup from the offered tray. David sat cross-legged on the rug, watching intently as Aaron tasted the tea and nodded his approval. "Your mother," he said, "will be jealous."

David finally returned the smile, then turned his head toward the bay window as if he were plotting the darkening sky, listening for the invisible wind. He squirmed. Coughed. Aaron amused himself with the boy's impatience as long as he could; then, softly, "Pinto must be starving. Is he on a diet or something?"

And the boy was gone. To a pony named Pinto, horse enough for a youngster who would never be tall, not even average. They had both arrived on the same day and five years later they were inseparable. Wild, Aaron thought. Both of them.

Come Dance With Me on My Pony's Grave

The telephone shrilled. Aaron grunted away a cramp that knifed his mine-shattered leg as he headed into the hallway and picked up the receiver.

"Jackoson, that you?"

Aaron winced. "Yes, Mr. Sorrentino, it's me."

"Damned good thing. Want to tell you those wolves are back again. Went after two of my rams this morning. Saw them. Big as horses they were. Chased them into the woods, I did." Right to my place, Aaron thought bitterly, thanks a lot. "I got a shot at them."

"You what?"

"Said I got a shot at them."

"Damn it, Sorrentino, my boy was playing there today. You know he always—"

"Did I hit him?" The voice was singularly unconcerned.

"Christ, no! If you had, do you think I'd be—"

"Then don't worry about it, Jackoson. I'm a perfect shot. I hit what I aim at. That kid—"

"My son."

"—won't get hurt, don't you worry about that. But one thing, Jackoson . . . I, uh, don't want to make any trouble, you understand, but I wish you would straighten out your kid about where your property ends. Him and that damn pony scare hell out of my sheep."

"If I didn't know you better, Mr. Sorrentino, I'd be tempted to think that you were somehow trying to threaten me."

A raucous laugh and a harsh gasping for breath. Aaron wanted to spit at the phone. "Just wanted you to know, Jackoson, don't get so worked up. You soldier boys get excited too easy."

"I just don't like the tone of your voice, Sorrentino."

"So sue me," Sorrentino said, and hung up.

Aaron breathed deeply and grabbed the edge of the hall table. "I could kill you so easily, Mr. Franklin Sorrentino," he said to the wall. "So goddamned easily."

"Dad?"

Aaron spun around to face the boy standing in the hall . . .

. . . standing by the gash of a grave while the jungle severed the sun's scattered light and a pit fire substituted shadows for trees. Lt. Jackoson shifted uneasily on the ground and lighted a cigarette as the boy stared at him. There was no recognition in the black bullet eyes though the man and the boy had often played together whenever the squad came to stay and use the friendly village as a base. Now Jackoson saw only a new, weary emptiness, and deeper: a purpose. The grave was for the boy's father, the shaman of the tribe. . . .

. . . the boy's voice was quiet. "I don't like him, dad." The words spun high, and Aaron shivered a remembrance while he stood in the tunnel-dark hall. David moved as silently as he spoke. Even on the Shetland he was noiseless—in the early days, when the boy was still learning, Miriam had said: He's like a ghost, Aaron, and he frightens me. In the early days. There were still remnants of the mountain in him, but Miriam no longer saw them. "He's greedy, dad, and doesn't ... feel for things."

Aaron nodded, just barely stopping himself from patting the boy on the head. He had learned early that "sin" was too weak a word for such a gesture. Instead, he grabbed his shoulders. "Go watch some TV, son. Forget it. It's not worth worrying yourself."

They walked, the son just behind, into the living room and dimmed the lights. Before Aaron switched on the set, David curled into a corner chair where the age in his voice belied his thin body. "Why doesn't he like me, dad?"

Aaron knew this was not a time to smile away a question. Five years before, his greatest fear had been what the other youngsters would think of his adopted son, but the smoke-grey skin and the hint of Polynesia in his features had given him instant acceptance, especially with the girls; David, however, was only always superficially friendly. "I don't know, son. Perhaps he's lonely with no children of his own, and that wife of his is enough for any man."

"He thinks I'm different." The tone said: he knows I'm different, and you're afraid that maybe he's right.

"Perhaps."

"I don't like him."

"David, he's not going to be the only one in your life to think you're ... well, not the same as others. You're quite a unique young man."

"He hates Pinto. He say, last week when he run me away, it was a silly name for a horse. Pinto doesn't like him either. He try to kick his stomach once."

"Oh." Aaron, forgetting to correct the boy's English, thought he was beginning to understand Sorrentino's surliness.

"He missed."

In spite of himself, Aaron said, "Too bad."

The boy laughed quietly.

"Listen, David, Mr. Sorrentino doesn't really understand how you can ... can *be* with animals. Most boys ... do you know what rapport means?"

"No, dad, but I think I can make guesses."

"Well, good. Rapport, you see, isn't always explainable. Sometimes it's something that just happens or belongs to a way of life that people just can't grasp. Like ..." and he stopped, thought and decided not to mention the shaman. "And, if you don't mind me asking," he said instead, falsely lighter, "why did you name him Pinto?"

David laughed again. "It suits him."

"How? He's all brown?"

"It feels right, Dad. It suits him. He runs and leaps and . . . he's like me in many ways. His name is right."

"Well, Sorrentino can't understand that, son."

"I know. He doesn't . . . feel. I don't like him."

Aaron frowned in concentration, seeking the speeches that would stifle the hatred he knew the boy was feeling. It was wrong to allow this to fester, wrong not to show the boy that some men must be tolerated, that, as the saying goes, it takes all kinds. He tried, but he took too long.

"I'm going to bed, Dad. Good night." David uncurled from the chair, stayed out of the light until his bedroom door closed behind him. Always closed. Sanctum.

Aaron hesitated in following, then sat again. For the first time since they had been together, David had lied to him. So blatantly, in fact, that its very obviousness pained more than the deceit itself. The language. He knew David had not forgotten all but the numbers. Once in a while, from behind the door, a muttering filtered through the house and filled him with dreams. Songs chanted on horseback across the fields and through the half-light in the pines; the whispering to the animals. Black hair and black eyes and a strength in slender arms that contradicted their frailty. Montagnard. Mountain dweller. Outcast.

Christ! he thought and chided himself for allowing his mind to become so morbid. The weather, his leg and Miriam's absence were getting to be too much. He decided to call her first thing in the morning and ask her to cut her visit short. Her mother wasn't that lonely and, he needed her laughter.

He dozed fitfully until the telephone twisted him stiffly from the couch. His watch had stopped. He stood, scratching his head vigorously, then stretched his arms over his head. "All right," he mumbled, "All right, all right, for god's sake." *Daylight,* he thought in amazement. That little dope didn't even wake me so I could sleep in a bed; how the hell did I oversleep? Glancing at the front window, he noticed streaks on the glass and the shimmer of ice on the walk. Rain, freezing rain was the last thing he needed with David pouting and his wife gone. For a moment he was ready to let the phone ring and crawl into bed to hide. The house and that damned phone were making him nervous.

Still rubbing the sleep from his face, he leaned awkwardly against the wall and snatched up the receiver. "Yeah, yeah Jackoson here."

"Aaron, this here is Will."

He stiffened. "Yes, sheriff, what can I do for you?" There were excited noises in the background; a man was bellowing angrily.

"I'm over at the Sorrentino place. You'd better get over here."

"David?"

"No, nothing's happened to the boy. But Sorrentino accidentally shot the pony. He's dead."

"I'll be right there." No thought, then, only an endless stream of cursing accusations: half in relief for his son's safety, half in anger at the rancher's murder of the boy's pet. His coat, first jamming on its hanger, refused to slide on easily. The pickup stalled twice. He shook uncontrollably, and his leg throbbed.

The truck skidded on the icy road, but Aaron, barely aware that he was driving at all, ignored the warning. Twice in two days he had wanted to kill, and twice he was unashamed for it.

There were two town patrol cars parked on the shoulder of the road when he arrived, and he nearly ran up the back of one as he slid to a halt and scrambled out. There was a small crowd hunched coldly in the vast, well-tended yard: police, several neighbors looking ill-at-ease, Sorrentino himself pounding his arms against the air by the sheriff, and David standing quietly to one side . . .

. . . while the oldest men carefully lowered the body of the shaman into the oversized grave. They scuttled away, then, and the boy stepped up to drop in the trappings of his father's profession, a lock of his own hair, a brown seed, a young branch freshly cut. They buried the war-murdered man beneath black earth and passed the remainder of the night mourning. Lt. Jackoson continued to watch the boy— a one-time, now distant friend. He watched the boy sitting calmly on the grave, staring at the prisoner, a scarred man in a tattered blue uniform. Jackoson had warned his men to mind their own business this time, and they did, gratefully; but few slept and all were uneasy. And still the little boy stared . . .

. . . at the ground until Aaron placed an arm lightly around his shoulders and he looked up. No greeting. A look was all. Sheriff Jenkins, a scowl and sympathy fighting in his face, walked hurriedly over with Sorrentino directly behind him. Aaron glared at them, barely able to contain the rage he felt for his son. "How?" he demanded without preliminaries. Sorrentino tried to bull forward, but Jenkins held up a hand to stop him.

"Frank here called me about forty-five minutes ago, Aaron. Said he was afraid he'd shot your son."

"I was just inside the wood, Jackoson," Sorrentino said, his voice oddly harsh. "I was chasing them wolves. I heard this noise right where I spotted them last, so I let go—"

"Without being sure?" Momentarily, Aaron was too appalled at the big man's stupidity to be angry. "You know kids are playing in there all the time. My God, Frank, you're a good enough shot to have waited a . . . " He stopped, seeing the retreat in the other man's eyes. "You . . . no, you couldn't have. Not even you."

"Now wait a damn minute, Jackoson."

"Shut up a minute, Frank."

"But, sheriff, that man just accused me of deliberately killing that kid's animal!"

"He didn't say that, did he?"

Sorrentino sputtered, then wheeled and stalked away, muttering. Jenkins didn't watch him leave; Aaron did. "Listen, Aaron, I couldn't find any evidence that it happened any other way than he said. I know how you two feel about each other, but as far as I'm concerned, his story holds up. I'm sorry, Aaron, but it was an accident."

Aaron nodded, though he was just as sure the sheriff was wrong.

"Look, if you want, the boys and I will take the—"

"No," David said.

Aaron saw the look on Jenkins' face and knew it was the first thing David had said that morning. Against his better judgment he agreed. "We'll take him. Will. But thanks anyway. I'd appreciate it if some of your men would help me put him in the truck."

The sheriff started to say something, but the boy walked between them, past the neighbors to the truck where he let down the gate and stood by, waiting.

"The boy wasn't on the pony," Will said. "It must have wandered off while David was playing."

Aaron nodded. And what, he thought, was David playing?

Pinto's head had been hastily wrapped in a blanket now matted with blood. David sat stroking the animal's rigid flank. Through the rear-view mirror, Aaron could see the hand moving smoothly over the cooling flesh. In his own eyes were the stirrings of tears. For once he thought he knew how the boy felt, to lose a friend much more than a pet. He drove slowly, turning off the road just before his own land began. There was a rutted path leading into the wood to a clearing where the boys of the surrounding farms had erected forts and castles, trenches and space ships. At its western end was a slight rise, and it was there that they sweated in the cold noon of the grey slate day and buried Pinto. The wind was listless, the rain stopped. When the grave was filled, Aaron walked painfully back to the truck to wait for David, and an hour passed before they were headed for home, and all the way Aaron tried vainly to joke the boy back into a fair humor, even promising him a new pet as soon as they could get into town. David, however, only stared at the road, one hand unconsciously working at his throat.

Immediately they arrived at the house, the telephone rang and Aaron grabbed for it, hoping it was Miriam. It was Sorrentino, apologizing and sounding unsettlingly desperate; and Aaron, eager to talk, eager to turn from his son's depression, profusely acknowledged the other's story, and damned himself as he spoke. Sorrentino kept on. And on. He was babbling, Aaron realized, very often incoherent, and in his puzzlement at the rancher's behavior, he responded in kind, knowing he sounded like an idiot, trying not to admit that he was somehow, inexplicably afraid of his own son.

When Sorrentino at last rang off, Aaron felt rather than saw the boy's bedroom door open. He would not turn. He was not going to watch grief harden the young face. "It'll be all right, son," he said weakly. "In time. In time. You . . . you have to give it time."

The boy was a shadow. "He could see, Dad."

"We can't prove that, son."

"He could see everything. The brush isn't that high."

"David, we cannot prove it. Things are different here, you know that. We have to prove things first."

And still he did not turn.

"He did it on purpose. You know that, and you won't do anything. You know it and . . ."

Turn around you old fool. He's only a boy. He's only a boy, for God's sake . . .

. . . *for God's sake, the lieutenant thought as he watched the boy sitting on the grave, how long is he going to stay there? His eyes, burning from the darkness and the fire's acrid smoke, shifted to the prisoner. The man was staring at the shaman's son, entranced, it seemed, and unmoving. He was unbound, but none of the tribesmen seemed to care. They were confident with knowledge that Jackoson didn't have, and Jackoson didn't like it. He tried instead to think of home and a place where people behaved the way they were supposed to* . . .

. . . behave yourself, stupid, he thought, and send the boy to bed. He'll feel better in the morning.

"You'd better lie down, now, Dad," the shadow said. "Your leg must be hurting after all that digging."

Aaron closed his eyes and nodded, feeling for the first time since leaving the house eons ago the painful strain that nearly buckled him. A moment later he felt the boy's arm around his waist, guiding him firmly to the bedroom. In the dim curtained light, he watched David prepare the bed, then stand aside while he eased himself between the cold sheets. David smiled at him.

"Well . . . we'll see the sheriff again in a few days, son. We'll talk to him."

"Sure, Dad."

"And David, don't . . . I mean, you know, don't try to do anything on your own, you know what I mean? I mean, don't go off chasing his sheep into the next county or smashing windows. Okay?"

The boy paused in the doorway. "Sure, Dad. You want your medicine?"

"No, thanks. I'll be all right in a little while. Just call me for dinner."

"Okay. I'm going to read or something. You need anything, please call."

Aaron smiled. "Go on, son." And after the door closed, he wondered, not for the first time, if he had been right in taking the boy away. Neither, in half a decade, seemed closer to understanding the other than when they had started out on the plane from Saigon. They spoke the same language, shared the same house, but the rapport David has with the animals, with Pinto, was missing between father and son. The war was no longer a threat, its use as a bond had dissolved.

I don't know my own son, he thought.

A part of his mind told him to stop feeling sorry for himself: the problem wasn't a new one.

I'm not feeling sorry for myself.

You sound like one of Miriam's soap operas.

I don't.

He's an ordinary boy who needs time. He's seen war.

He's had five years, and so, by the way, have I.

And when he slept, he dreamt of a slight mound in a path supposedly clear and the sound he felt and heard before waking screaming in a hospital in Japan with a leg raw, twisted. He had refused amputation. He needed the leg.

When he opened his eyes, it was dark. He tried to fall asleep again, but a rising wind nudged him back to wakefulness. Finally he swung out of bed and dressed quietly. He was hungry and thirsty. Cautiously, he crept into the kitchen to fix a snack and unaccountably remembered a rancher he knew in passing who had a string of Shetlands he rented to pony rides during the summer fairs. Maybe, he thought, he could persuade this man to part with one of his animals on credit. It would be easy enough to explain what had happened to Pinto. The man would have to help him. Slowly the idea grew, hurrying his actions, making him grin at himself. Without stopping to drink the coffee he had poured, he hastened down the hall to David's room.

It was empty. His boots were gone, and his jacket. There was a hint of panic before Aaron realized David, still mourning, had probably gone out to the barn to Pinto's stall. Snatching his coat from the closet, he rushed outside, gasping once at the cold air and the strong wind that slid across the now-frozen ground. A digging pain in his thigh caused him to slow up, but long before he'd fling open the barn door, he knew the building would be empty. He stood in the barnyard, aimlessly turning, seeking a direction to travel until he saw the faint orange glow over the trees. He stared, hands limp at his sides, squinting, thinking, denying all the fears that founded his nightmares. He knew his century and still refused to believe what he had seen on the jungled mountain, dreaded what he might see if he followed the light.

It was just before dawn . . .

. . . *and Lt. Jackoson was the only squad member still awake, the others sleeping in luxurious safety for the first time in days. Night noises. Night wind. He was drowsy and rubbed the blur from his eyes. Curiosity prodded him; he rubbed his eyes again. The fire burned sullenly at the side of the grave. The boy was naked, now, and standing* . . .

. . . running over the ice-crusted ground, Aaron was pushed from behind by the wind. He ignored his leg as long as he could, concentrating on the wavering line of trees ahead. Then, just inside the tiny wood, his foot pushed through a hidden burrow and he slammed to the ground. Palms, knees, forehead stung. When he tried to stand, his leg wrenched out from under him, and he cried out. Before him, trunks and branches, brush and grass twisted slowly in the light of the fire, weaving darkness within darkness. Aaron pushed himself to one leg, his teeth clamped to his lips and, using the trees for support, hobbled toward the clearing. His left leg went numb, the pain felt only from the hip, and finally he collapsed.

Not now, he begged, not now!

He crawled, forearms and one foot, seeing his breath puff in front of his face, seeing his hands turn a dry red from the cold. Then there was a break in the pine, and he saw the boy . . .

. . . *on his father's grave, shuffling slowly from side to side, humming to himself as he stared at the mound beneath his feet. The tribe had reassembled, squatting in the shadows silent. The pit fire cracked* . . .

... on the rise, and the smell of burning pine pierced the brittle air. And between himself and his son, Aaron saw ...

... *the prisoner seemingly rooted in place, turned so his face was hidden. The boy, not looking up, not acknowledging the world's existence muttered something and the man shuddered* ...

... beneath his heavy furtrimmed hunting jacket. There was a rifle, useless now, dangling from one hand. Aaron tried to push himself up, to stand, but the agony was too great, and at the moment all he wanted was the heat from the fire that silhouetted the boy ...

... *shuffling faster, mumbling in rapid bursts while the prisoner swayed, slipped back, then lurched forward. Slowly, toward the grave, in the light of the fire. Jackoson thought he was dreaming* ...

... but the cold was too real, and he wondered how the boy, so lately his son, could stand the wind that whipped the flames from side to side and drew ...

... *the prisoner toward them, stiff-jointed like a grotesque marionette. The jungle* ...

... the clearing was quiet, and Aaron could hear the boy, chanting now, urging, taunting the big man forward. Aaron tried shouting, but his throat was too dry, his mind unable to break loose his tongue. All he could see was the rifle, glinting. Sorrentino moved. Lumbered. Silent.

Prisoner/rancher reached the grave.

The boy, still chanting, reached out, palms up, waiting until the other grasped them (the rifle dropping soundlessly). A pair now, circling in slow motion. Dirt shifted beneath their feet. Aaron watched ...

... *more drowsy still from the fire's heat and the boy's monotonic voice, still undecided whether or not he was dreaming* ...

... numb from the cold and drawing blood from his lips as he fought the pain enshrouding his thoughts. He lay flat on the ground, his head barely raised, his eyes glazed.

The boy abruptly dropped his hands and stepped down from the grave.

The prisoner waited, standing, and made no attempt to resist when the shaman's hand/pony's teeth reached through the earth and took hold.

Jackoson slept, thought he was dreaming.

Aaron fainted, thought he was screaming.

David, smiling, picked up a shovel.

DAVID DRAKE

"Something Had to Be Done"

*Best known as a writer of military science fiction, including the popular **Hammer's Slammers** series, David Drake (1945-) began his professional writing career with the sale of his horror story "Denkirch" in 1967 and served in the 1970s as an assistant editor on the seminal semi-professional horror magazine **Whispers**. Themes of his fantasy and science fiction have ranged from the Arthurian romance of **The Dragon Lord**, to time travel in **Birds of Prey** and interplanetary adventures in **The Jungle**, his sequel to Henry Kuttner and C.L. Moore's Golden Age science fiction classic "Clash by Night." He has compiled a number of reprint anthologies, including **Things Hunting Men** and **Men Hunting Things** and, with Bill Fawcett, the "Fleet" series of original shared world anthologies. He has also overseen the reissuing of Robert E. Howard's sword and sorcery, adventure and horror fiction in paperback. Drake's slim but essential horror output can be found in **Old Nathan**, and especially **From the Heart of Darkness**, from which "Something Had to Be Done," a story colored by his experiences in Vietnam, is taken.*

Something Had to Be Done

by David Drake

"He was out in the hall just a minute ago, sir," the pinched-faced WAC said, looking up from her typewriter in irritation. "You can't mistake his face."

Captain Richmond shrugged and walked out of the busy office. Blinking in the dim marble were a dozen confused civilians, bussed in for their pre-induction physicals. No one else was in the hallway. The thick-waisted officer frowned, then thought to open the door of the men's room. "Sergeant Morzek?" he called.

Glass clinked within one of the closed stalls and a deep voice with a catch in it grumbled, "Yeah, be right with you." Richmond thought he smelled gin.

"You the other ghoul?" the voice questioned as the stall swung open. Any retort Richmond might have made withered when his eyes took in the cadaverous figure in ill-tailored greens. Platoon sergeants's chevrons on the sleeves, and below them a longer row of services stripes than the captain remembered having seen before. God, this walking corpse might have served in World War II! Most of the ribbons ranked above the sergeant's breast pockets were unfamiliar, but Richmond caught the little V for valor winking in the center of a silver star. Even in these medal-happy days in Southeast Asia they didn't toss many of those around.

The sergeant's cheeks were hollow, his fingers grotesquely thin where they rested on top of the door or clutched the handles of his zipped AWOL bag. Where no moles squatted, his skin was as white as a convict's; but the moles were almost everywhere, hands and face, dozens and scores of them, crowding together in welted obscenity.

The sergeant laughed starkly. "Pretty, aren't I? The docs tell me I got too much sun over there and it gave me runaway warts. Hell, four years is enough time for it to."

"Umm," Richmond grunted in embarrassment, edging back into the hall to have something to do. "Well, the car's in back . . . if you're ready, we can see the Lunkowskis."

"Yeah, Christ," the sergeant said, "that's what I came for, to see the Lunkowskis." He shifted his bag as he followed the captain and it clinked again. Always before, the other man on the notification team had been a stateside officer like Richmond himself. He had heard that a few low-casualty outfits made a habit of letting whoever knew the dead man best accompany the body home, but this was his first actual experience with the practice. He hoped it would be his last.

Threading the green Ford through the heavy traffic of the city center, Richmond said, "I take it Private Lunkowski was one of your men?"

"Yeah, Stevie-boy was in my platoon for about three weeks," Morzek agreed with a chuckle. "Lost six men in that time and he was the last. Six out of twenty-nine, not very damn good, was it?"

"You were under heavy attack?"

"Hell, no, mostly the dinks were letting us alone for a change. We were out in the middle of War Zone C, you know, most Christ-bitten stretch of country you ever saw. No dinks, no trees—they'd all been defoliated. Not a damn thing but dust and each other's company."

"Well, what did happen?" Richmond prompted impatiently. Traffic had thinned somewhat among the blocks of old buildings and he began to look for house numbers.

"Oh, mostly they just died." Morzek said. He yawned alcoholically. "Stevie, now, he got blown to hell by a grenade."

Richmond had learned when he was first assigned to notification duty not to dwell on the way his . . . missions had died. The possibilities varied from unpleasant to ghastly. He studiously avoided saying anything more to the sergeant beside him until he found the number he wanted. "One-sixteen. This must be the Lunkowskis'."

Morzek got out on the curb side, looking more skeletal than before in the dappled sunlight. He still held his AWOL bag.

"You can leave that in the car," Richmond suggested. "I'll lock up."

"Naw, I'll take it in," the sergeant said as he waited for Richmond to walk around the car. "You know, this is every damn thing I brought from Nam? They didn't bother to open it at Travis, just asked me what I had in it. 'A quart of gin,' I told 'em, 'but I won't have it long,' and they waved me through to make my connections. One advantage to this kind of trip."

A bell chimed far within the house when Richmond pressed the button. It was cooler than he had expected on the pine-shaded porch. Miserable as these high, dark old houses were to heat, the design made a world of sense in the summer.

A light came on inside. The stained-glass window left of the door darkened and a latch snicked open. "Please to come in," invited a soft-voiced figure hidden by the dark oak panel. Morzek grinned inappropriately and led the way into the hall, brightly lighted by an electric chandelier.

"Mr. Lunkowski?" Richmond began to the wispy little man who had admitted them. "We are—"

"But yes, you are here to tell us when Stefan shall come back, are you not?" Lunkowski broke in. "Come into the sitting room, please Anna and my daughter Rose are there."

"Ah, Mr. Lunkowski," Richmond tried to explain as he followed, all too conscious of the sardonic grin on Morzek's face. "You have been informed by telegram that Private Lunkowski was—"

"Was killed, yes," said the younger of the two red-haired women as she got up from the sofa. "But his body will come back to us soon, will he not? The man on the telephone said . . ."

She was gorgeous, Richmond thought, cool and assured, half smiling as her hair cascaded over her left shoulder like a thick copper conduit. Disconcerted as he was by the whole situation, it was a moment before he realized that Sergeant Morzek was saying, "Oh, the coffin's probably at the airport now, but there's nothing in it but a hundred and fifty pounds of gravel. Did the telegram tell you what happened to Stevie?"

"Sergeant!" Richmond shouted. "You drunken—"

"Oh, calm down, Captain," Morzek interrupted bleakly. "The Lunkowskis, they understand. They want to hear the whole story, don't they?"

"Yes." There was a touch too much sibilance in the word as it crawled from the older woman, Stefan Lunkowski's mother. Her hair was too grizzled now to have more than a touch of red in it, enough to rust the tight ringlets clinging to her skull like a helmet of mail. Without quiet appreciating its importance, Richmond noticed that Mr. Lunkowski was standing in front of the room's only door.

With perfect nonchalance, Sergeant Morzek sat down on an overstuffed chair, laying his bag across his knees. "Well," he said, "there was quite a report on that one. We told them how Stevie was trying to boobytrap a white phosphorous grenade—fix it to go off as soon as some dink pulled the pin instead of four seconds later. And he goofed."

Mrs. Lunkowski's breath whistled out very softly. She said nothing. Morzek waited for further reaction before he smiled horribly and added. "He burned. A couple pounds of willie pete going blooie, well . . . it keeps burning all the way through you. Like I said, the coffin's full of gravel."

"My god, Morzek," the captain whispered. It was not the sergeant's savage grin that froze him but the icy-eyed silence of the three Lunkowskis.

"The grenade, that was real," Morzek concluded. "The rest of the report was a lie."

Rose Lunkowski reseated herself gracefully on a chair in front of the heavily draped windows. "Why don't you start at the beginning Sergeant?" she said with a thin smile that did not show her teeth. "There is much we would like to know before you are gone."

"Sure," Morzek agreed, tracing a mottled forefinger across the pigmented callosities on his face. "Not much to tell. The night after Stevie got assigned to my platoon, the dinks hit us. No big thing. Had one fellow dusted off with brass in his ankle from his machine gun blowing up, that was all. But a burst of AK fire knocked Stevie off his tank right at the start."

"What's all this about?" Richmond complained. "If he was killed by rifle fire, why say a grenade—"

"Silence!" The command crackled like heel plates on concrete.

Sergeant Morzek nodded. "Why, thank you, Mr. Lunkowski. You see, the captain there doesn't know the bullets didn't hurt Stevie. He told us his flak jacket had stopped them. It couldn't have and it didn't. I saw it that night, before he burned it—five holes to stick your fingers through, right over the breast pocket. But Stevie was fine, not a mark on him. Well, Christ, maybe he'd had a bandolier or ammo under the jacket. I had other things to think about."

Morzek paused to glance around his audience. "All this Well, Christ, maybe he'd had a bandolier of ammo under the Federal Building."

"You won't be long," the girl hissed in reply.

Morzek grinned. "They broke up the squadron, then," he rasped on, "gave each platoon a sector of War Zone C to cover to stir up the dinks. There's more life on the moon than there was on the stretch we patrolled. Third night out, one of the gunners died. They flew him back to Saigon for an autopsy but damned if I know what they found. Galloping malaria, we figured.

"Three nights later another guy died. Dawson on three-six . . .

Christ, the names don't matter. Some time after midnight his track commander woke up, heard him moaning. We got him back to Quan Loi to a hospital, but he never came out of it. The lieutenant thought he got wasp stung on the neck—here, you know?" Morzek touched two fingers to his jugular. "Like he was allergic. Well, it happens."

"But what about Stefan?" Mrs. Lunkowski asked. "The others do not matter."

"Yes, finish it quickly, Sergeant," the younger woman said, and this time Richmond did catch the flash of her teeth.

"We had a third death," Morzek said agreeably, stroking the zipper of his AWOL bag back and forth. "We were all jumpy by then. I doubled the guard, two men awake on every track. Three nights later and nobody in the platoon remembered anything from twenty-four hundred hours till Riggs's partner blinked at ten of one and found him dead.

"In the morning, one of the boys came to me. He'd seen Stevie slip over to Riggs, he said; but he was zonked out on grass and didn't think it really had happened until he woke up in the morning and saw Riggs under a poncho. By then, he was scared enough to tell the whole story. Well, we were all jumpy."

"You killed Stefan." It was not a question but a flat statement.

"Oh, hell, Lunkowski," Morzek said absently, "what does it matter who rolled the grenade into his bunk? The story got around and . . . something had to be done."

"Knowing what you know, you came here?" Mrs. Lunkowski murmured liquidly. "You must be mad."

"Naw, I'm not crazy, I'm just sick." The sergeant brushed his left hand over his forehead. "Malignant melanoma, the docs told me. Twenty-six years in the goddamn army and in another week or two I'd be *warted* to death.

"Captain," he added, turning his cancerous face toward Richmond, "you better leave through the window."

"Neither of you will leave!" snarled Rose Lunkowski as she stepped toward the men.

Morzek lifted a fat gray cylinder from his bag. "Know what this is, honey?" he asked conversationally.

Richmond screamed and leaped for the window. Rose ignored him, slashing her hand out for the phosphorous grenade. Drapery wrapping the captain's body shielded him from glass and splintered window frame as he pitched out into the yard.

He was still screaming there when the blast of white fire bulged the walls of the house.

KARL EDWARD WAGNER

"Sticks"

*Karl Edward Wagner (1945-1994) was the renaissance man of modern horror fiction. He began his writing career with the revisionist sword-and-sorcery novels **The Dark Crusade** and **Darkness Weaves**, both of which featured his anti-hero warrior Kane. By the mid-1970s, he had shifted to writing horror tales with a modern sensibility that also reflected the influence of classic horror. The best of these stories were collected in **In a Dark Place** and **Why Not You and I?** These same years, he founded the specialty press Carcosa House which issued award-winning omnibus volumes of short fiction by Manly Wade Wellman, Hugh B. Cave, and E. Hoffman Price. Beginning in 1980, he assumed editorship of **The Year's Best Horror Stories** series, which he oversaw for fifteen volumes. He also edited three volumes in the **Echoes of Valor** series of heroic fantasy anthologies. "Sticks," his homage to the fiction of H.P. Lovecraft and the art of Lee Brown Coye, was a World Fantasy Award nominee and a British Fantasy Award winner.*

Sticks

by Karl Edward Wagner

1

The lashed-together framework of sticks jutted from a small cairn alongside the stream. Colin Leverett studied it in perplexment—half a dozen odd lengths of branch, wired together at cross angles for no fathomable purpose. It reminded him unpleasantly of some bizarre crucifix, and he wondered what might lie beneath the cairn.

It was the spring of 1942—the kind of day to make the war seem distant and unreal, although the draft notice waited on his desk. In a few days Leverett would lock his rural studio, wonder if he would see it again—be able to use its pens and brushes and carving tools when he did return. It was goodby to the woods and streams of upstate New York, too. No fly rods, no tramps through the countryside in Hitler's Europe. No point in putting off fishing that trout stream he had driven past once, exploring back roads of the Otselic Valley.

Mann Brook—so it was marked on the old geological survey map—ran southeast of DeRuyter. The unfrequented country road crossed over a stone bridge old before the first horseless carriage, but Leverett's Ford eased across and onto the shoulder. Taking fly rod and tackle, he included pocket flask and tied an iron skillet to his belt. He'd work his way downstream a few miles. By afternoon he'd lunch on fresh trout, maybe some bullfrog legs.

It was a fine, clear stream, though difficult to fish as dense bushes hung out from the bank, broken with stretches of open water hard to work without being seen. But the trout rose boldly to his fly, and Leverett was in fine spirits.

From the bridge the valley along Mann Brook began as fairly open pasture, but half a mile downstream the land had fallen into disuse and was thick with second-growth evergreens and scrub-apple trees. Another mile, and the scrub merged with dense forest, which continued unbroken. The land here, he had learned, had been taken over by the state many years back.

As Leverett followed the stream he noted the remains of an old railroad embankment. No vestige of tracks or ties—only the embankment itself, overgrown with large trees. The artist rejoiced in the beautiful dry-wall culverts spanning the stream as it wound through the valley. To his mind it seemed eerie, this forgotten railroad running straight and true through virtual wilderness.

He could imagine an old wood-burner with it conical stack, steaming along through the valley dragging two or three wooden coaches. It must be a branch of the old Oswego Midland Rail Road, he decided, abandoned rather suddenly in the 1870s. Leverett, who had a memory for detail, knew of it from a story his grandfather told of riding the line in 1871 from Otselic to DeRuyter on his honeymoon. The engine had so labored up the steep grade over Crumb Hill that he got off to walk alongside. Probably that sharp grade was the reason for the line's abandonment.

When he came across a scrap of board nailed to several sticks set into a stone wall, his darkest thought was that it might read "No Trespassing." Curiously, though the board was weathered featureless, the nails seemed quite new. Leverett scarcely gave it much thought, until a short distance beyond he came upon another such contrivance. And another.

Now he scratched at the day's stubble on his long jaw. This didn't make sense. A prank? But on whom? A child's game? No, the arrangement was far too sophisticated. As an artist, Leverett appreciated the craftsmanship of the work—the calculated angles and lengths, the designed intricacy of the maddeningly inexplicable devices. There was something distinctly uncomfortable about their effect.

Leverett reminded himself that he had come here to fish and continued downstream. But as he worked around a thicket he again stopped in puzzlement.

Here was a small open space with more of the stick lattices and an arrangement of flat stones laid out on the ground. The stones—likely taken from one of the many dry-wall culverts—made a pattern maybe twenty by fifteen feet, that at first glance resembled a ground plan for a house. Intrigued, Leverett quickly saw that this was not so. If the ground plan for anything, it would have to be for a small maze.

The bizarre lattice structures were all around. Sticks from trees and bits of board nailed together in fantastic array. They defied description; no two seemed alike. Some were only one or two sticks lashed together in parallel or at angles. Others were worked into complicated lattices of dozens of sticks and boards. One could have been a child's tree house—it was built in three planes, but was so abstract and useless that it could be nothing more than an insane conglomeration of sticks and wire. Sometimes the contrivances were stuck in a pile of stones or a wall, maybe thrust into the railroad embankment or nailed to a tree.

It should have been ridiculous. It wasn't. Instead it seemed somehow sinister—these utterly inexplicable, meticulously constructed stick lattices spread through a wilderness where only a tree-grown embankment or a forgotten stone wall gave evidence that man had ever passed through. Leverett forgot about trout and frog legs, instead dug into his pockets for a notebook and stub of pencil. Busily he began to sketch the more intricate structures. Perhaps someone could explain them; perhaps there was something to their insane complexity that warranted closer study for his own work.

Leverett was roughly two miles from the bridge when he came upon the ruins of a house. It was an unlovely colonial farmhouse, box-shaped and gambrel-roofed, fast falling into the ground. Windows were dark and empty; the chimneys on either end looked ready to topple. Rafters showed through open spaces in the roof, and the weathered boards of the walls had in places rotted away to reveal hewn timber beams. The foundation was stone and disproportionately massive. From the size of the unmortared stone blocks, its builder had intended the foundation to stand forever.

The house was nearly swallowed up by undergrowth and rampant lilac bushes, but Leverett could distinguish what had been a lawn with imposing shade trees. Farther back were gnarled and sickly apple trees and an overgrown garden where a few lost flowers still bloomed—wan and serpentine from years in the wild. The stick lattices were everywhere—the lawn, the trees, even the house were covered with the uncanny structures. They reminded Leverett of a hundred misshapen spider webs—grouped so closely together as to almost ensnare the entire house and clearing. Wondering, he sketched page on page of them, as he cautiously approached the abandoned house.

He wasn't certain just what he expected to find inside. The aspect of the farmhouse was frankly menacing, standing as it did in gloomy desolation where the forest had devoured the works of man—where the only sign that man had been here in this century were these insanely wrought latticeworks of sticks and board. Some might have turned back at this point. Leverett, whose fascination for the macabre was evident in his art, instead was intrigued. He drew a rough sketch of the farmhouse and the grounds, overrun with the enigmatic devices, with thickets of hedges and distorted flowers. He regretted that it might be years before he could capture the eeriness of this place on scratchboard or canvas.

The door was off its hinges, and Leverett gingerly stepped within, hoping that the flooring remained sound enough to bear even his sparse frame. The afternoon sun pierced the empty windows, mottling the decaying floorboards with great blotches of light. Dust drifted in the sunlight. The house was empty—stripped of furnishings other than indistinct tangles of rubble mounded over with decay and the drifted leaves of many seasons.

Someone had been here, and recently. Someone who had literally covered the mildewed walls with diagrams of the mysterious lattice structures. The drawings were applied directly to the walls, crisscrossing the rotting wallpaper and crumbling plaster in bold black lines. Some of vertiginous complexity covered an entire wall like a mad mural. Others were small, only a few crossed lines, and reminded Leverett of cuneiform glyphics.

His pencil hurried over the pages of his notebook. Leverett noted with fascination that a number of the drawings were not recognizable as schematics of lattices he had earlier sketched. Was this then the planning room for the madman or educated idiot who had built these structures? The gouges etched by the charcoal into the soft plaster appeared fresh—done days or months ago, perhaps.

A darkened doorway opened into the cellar. Were there drawings there as well? And what else? Leverett wondered if he should dare it. Except for streamers of light that crept through cracks in the flooring, the cellar was in darkness.

"Hello?" he called. "Anyone here?" It didn't seem silly just then. These stick lattices hardly seemed the work of a rational mind. Leverett wasn't enthusiastic with the prospect of encountering such a person in this dark cellar. It occurred to him that virtually anything might transpire here, and no one in the world of 1942 would ever know.

And that in itself was too great a fascination for one of Leverett's temperament. Carefully he started down the cellar stairs. They were stone and thus solid, but treacherous with moss and debris.

The cellar was enormous—even more so in the darkness. Leverett reached the foot of the steps and paused for his eyes to adjust to the damp gloom. An earlier impression recurred to him. The cellar was too big for the house. Had another dwelling stood here originally—perhaps destroyed and rebuilt by one of lesser fortune? He examined the stonework. Here were great blocks of gneiss that might support a castle. On closer look they reminded him of a fortress—for the drywall technique was startlingly Mycenaean.

Like the house above, the cellar appeared to be empty, although without light Leverett could not be certain what the shadows hid. There seemed to be darker areas of shadow along sections of the foundation wall, suggesting openings to chambers beyond. Leverett began to feel uneasy in spite of himself.

There was something here—a large tablelike bulk in the center of the cellar. Where a few ghosts of sunlight drifted down to touch its edges, it seemed to be of stone. Cautiously he crossed the stone paving to where it loomed—waist-high, maybe eight feet long and less wide. A roughly shaped slab of gneiss, he judged, and supported by pillars of unmortared stone. In the darkness he could only get a vague conception of the object. He ran his hand along the slab. It seemed to have a groove along its edge.

His groping fingers encountered fabric, something cold and leathery and yielding. Mildewed harness, he guessed in distaste.

Something else closed on his wrist, set icy nails into his flesh.

Leverett screamed and lunged away with frantic strength. He was held fast, but the object on the stone slab pulled upward.

A sickly beam of sunlight came down to touch one end of the slab. It was enough. As Leverett struggled backward and the thing that held him heaved up from the stone table, its face passed through the beam of light.

It was a lich's face—dessicated flesh tight over its skull. Filthy strands of hair were matted over its scalp, tattered lips were drawn away from broken yellowed teeth, and sunken in their sockets, eyes that should be dead were bright with hideous life.

Leverett screamed again, desperate with fear. His free hand clawed the iron skillet tied to his belt. Ripping it loose, he smashed at the nightmarish face with all his strength.

For one frozen instant of horror the sunlight let him see the skillet crush through the mold-eaten forehead like an ax—cleaving the dry flesh and brittle bone. The grip on his wrist failed. The cadaverous face fell away, and the sight of its caved-in forehead and unblinking eyes from between which thick blood had begun to ooze would awaken Leverett from nightmare on countless nights.

But now Leverett tore free and fled. And when his aching legs faltered as he plunged headlong through the scrub-growth, he was spurred to desperate energy by the memory of the footsteps that had stumbled up the cellar stairs behind him.

II

When Colin Leverett returned from the war, his friends marked him a changed man. He had aged. There were streaks of grey in his hair; his springy step had slowed. The athletic leanness of his body had withered to an unhealthy gauntness. There were indelible lines to his face, and his eyes were haunted.

More disturbing was an alteration of temperament. A mordant cynicism had eroded his earlier air of whimsical asceticism. His fascination with the macabre had assumed a darker mood, a morbid obsession that his old acquaintances found disquieting. But it had been that kind of a war, especially for those who had fought through the Apennines.

Leverett might have told them otherwise, had he cared to discuss his nightmarish experience on Mann Brook. But Leverett kept his own counsel, and when he grimly recalled that creature he had struggled with in the abandoned cellar, he usually convinced himself it had only been a derelict—a crazy hermit whose appearance had been distorted by the poor light and his own imagination. Nor had his blow more than glanced off the man's forehead, he reasoned, since the other had recovered quickly enough to give chase. It was best not to dwell upon such matters, and this rational explanation helped restore sanity when he awoke from nightmares of that face.

Thus Colin Leverett returned to his studio, and once more plied his pens and brushes and carving knives. The pulp magazines, where fans had acclaimed his work before the war, welcomed him back with long lists of assignments. There were commissions from galleries and collectors, unfinished sculptures and wooden models. Leverett busied himself.

There were problems now. *Short Stories* returned a cover painting as "too grotesque." The publishers of a new anthology of horror stories sent back a pair of his interior drawings—"too gruesome, especially the rotted, bloated faces of those hanged men." A customer returned a silver figurine, complaining that the martyred saint was too thoroughly martyred. Even *Weird Tales,* after heralding his return to its ghoul-haunted pages, began returning illustrations they considered "too strong, even for our readers."

Leverett tried halfheartedly to tone things down, found the results vapid and uninspired. Eventually the assignments stopped trickling in. Leverett, becoming more the recluse as years went by, dismissed the pulp days from his mind. Working quietly in his isolated studio, he found a living doing occasional commissioned pieces and gallery work, from time to time selling a painting or sculpture to major museums. Critics had much praise for his bizarre abstract sculptures.

III

The war was twenty-five-year history when Colin Leverett received a letter from a good friend of the pulp days—Prescott Brandon, now editor-publisher of Gothic House, a small press that specialized in books of the weird-fantasy genre. Despite a lapse in correspondence of many years, Brandon's letter began in his typically direct style:

The Eyrie/Salem, Mass./Aug. 2

To the Macabre Hermit of the Midlands:
   Colin, I'm putting together a deluxe 3-volume collection of H. Kenneth Allard's horror stories. I well recall that Kent's stories were personal favorites of yours. How about shambling forth from retirement and illustrating these for me? Will need 2-color jackets and a dozen line interiors each. Would hope that you can startle fandom with some especially ghastly drawings for these—something different from the hackneyed skulls and bats and werewolves carting off half-dressed ladies.
   Interested? I'll send you the materials and details, and you can have a free hand. Let us hear—Scotty

Leverett was delighted. He felt some nostalgia for the pulp days, and he had always admired Allard's genius in transforming visions of cosmic horror into convincing prose. He wrote Brandon an enthusiastic reply.

He spent hours rereading the stories for inclusion, making notes and preliminary sketches. No squeamish subeditors to offend here; Scotty meant what he said. Leverett bent to his task with maniacal relish.

Something different, Scotty had asked. A free hand. Leverett studied his pencil sketches critically. The figures seemed headed in the right direction, but the drawings needed something more—something that would inject the mood of sinister evil that pervaded Allard's work. Grinning skulls and leathery bats? Trite. Allard demanded more.

The idea had inexorably taken hold of him. Perhaps because Allard's tales evoked that same sense of horror; perhaps because Allard's visions of crumbling Yankee farmhouses and their depraved secrets so reminded him of that spring afternoon at Mann Brook . . .

Although he had refused to look at it since the day he had staggered in, half-dead from terror and exhaustion, Leverett perfectly recalled where he had flung his notebook. He retrieved it from the back of a seldom used file, thumbed through the wrinkled pages thoughtfully. These hasty sketches reawakened the sense of foreboding evil, the charnel horror of that day. Studying the bizarre lattice patterns, it seemed impossible to Leverett that others would not share his feeling of horror that the stick structures evoked in him.

He began to sketch bits of stick latticework into his pencil roughs. The sneering faces of Allard's degenerate creatures took on an added shadow of menace. Leverett nodded, pleased with the effect.

IV

Some months afterward a letter from Brandon informed Leverett he had received the last of the Allard drawings and was enormously pleased with the work. Brandon added a postscript:

> "For God's sake Colin—*What is it* with these insane sticks you've got poking up everywhere in the illos! The damn things get really creepy after a while. How on earth did you get onto this?"

Leverett supposed he owed Brandon some explanation. Dutifully he wrote a lengthy letter, setting down the circumstances of his experience at Mann Brook—omitting only the horror that had seized his wrist in the cellar. Let Brandon think him eccentric, but not madman and murderer.

Brandon's reply was immediate:

> "Colin—Your account of the Mann Brook episode is fascinating—and incredible! It reads like the start of one of Allard's stories! I have taken the liberty of forwarding your letter to Alexander Stefroi in Pelham. Dr. Stefroi is an earnest scholar

of this region's history—as you may already know. I'm certain your account will interest him, and he may have some light to shed on the uncanny affair.

Expect 1st volume, *Voices from the Shadow*, to be ready from the binder next month. The proofs looked great. Best—
Scotty"

The following week brought a letter postmarked Pelham, Massachusetts:

"A mutual friend, Prescott Brandon, forwarded your fascinating account of discovering curious sticks and stone artifacts on an abandoned farm in upstate New York. I found this most intriguing, and wonder if you recall further details? Can you relocate the exact site after 30 years? If possible, I'd like to examine the foundations this spring, as they call to mind similar megalithic sites of this region. Several of us are interested in locating what we believe are remains of megalithic construction dating back to the Bronze Age, and to determine their possible use in rituals of black magic in colonial days.

Present archeological evidence indicates that ca. 1700-2000 BC there was an influx of Bronze Age peoples into the Northeast from Europe. We know that the Bronze Age saw the rise of an extremely advanced culture, and that as seafarers they were to have no peers until the Vikings. Remains of a megalithic culture originating in the Mediterranean can be seen in the Lion Gate in Mycenae, in Stonehenge, and in dolmens, passage graves and barrow mounds throughout Europe. Moreover, this seems to have represented far more than a style of architecture peculiar to the era. Rather, it appears to have been a religious cult whose adherents worshipped a sort of earth-mother, served her with fertility rituals and sacrifices, and believed that immortality of the soul could be secured through interment in megalithic tombs.

That this culture came to America cannot be doubted from the hundreds of megalithic remnants found—and now recognized—in our region. The most important site to date is Mystery Hill in N.H., comprising a great many walls and dolmens of megalithic construction—most notably the Y Cavern barrow mound and the Sacrificial Table (see postcard). Less spectacular megalithic sites include the group of cairns and carved stones at Mineral Mt., subterranean chambers with stone passageways such as the Petersham and Shutesbury, and uncounted shaped megaliths and buried 'monk's cells' throughout this region.

Of further interest, these sites seem to have retained their mystic aura for the early colonials, and numerous megalithic sites show evidence of having been used for sinister purposes by colonial sorcerers and alchemists. This became particularly true after the witchcraft persecutions drove many practitioners into the western wilderness—explaining why upstate New York and western Mass. have seen the emergence of so many cultist groups in later years.

Of particular interest here is Shadrack Ireland's 'Brethren of the New Light,' who believed that the world was soon to be destroyed by sinister 'Powers from Outside' and that they, the elect, would then attain physical immortality. The elect who died beforehand were to have their bodies preserved on tables of stone until the 'Old Ones' came forth to return them to life. We have definitely linked the megalithic sites at Shutesbury to later unwholesome practices of the New Light cult. They were absorbed in 1781 by Mother Ann Lee's Shakers, and Ireland's putrescent corpse was hauled from the stone table in his cellar and buried.

Thus I think it probable that your farmhouse may have figured in similar hidden practices. At Mystery Hill a farmhouse was built in 1826 that incorporated one dolmen in its foundations. The house burned down ca. 1848-55, and there were some unsavory local stories as to what took place there. My guess is that your farmhouse had been built over or incorporated a similar megalithic site—and that your 'sticks' indicate some unknown cult still survived there. I can recall certain vague references to lattice devices figuring in secret ceremonies, but can pinpoint nothing definite. Possibly they represent a development of occult symbols to be used in certain conjurations, but this is just a guess. I suggest you consult Waite's *Ceremonial Magic* or such to see if you can recognize similar magical symbols.

Hope this is of some use to you. Please let me hear back.

Sincerely, Alexander Stefroi"

There was a postcard enclosed—a photograph of a 4½ ton granite slab, ringed by a deep groove with a spout, identified as the Sacrificial Table at Mystery Hill. On the back Stefroi had written:

> "You must have found something similar to this. They are not rare—we have one in Pelham removed from a site now beneath Quabbin Reservoir. They were used for sacrifice—animal and human—and the groove is to channel blood into a bowl, presumably."

Leverett dropped the card and shuddered. Stefroi's letter reawakened the old horror, and he wished now he had let the matter lie forgotten in his files. Of course, it couldn't be forgotten—even after thirty years.

He wrote Stefroi a careful letter, thanking him for his information and adding a few minor details to his account. This spring, he promised, wondering if he would keep that promise, he would try to relocate the farmhouse on Mann Brook.

V

Spring was late that year, and it was not until early June that Colin Leverett found time to return to Mann Brook. On the surface, very little had changed in three decades. The ancient stone bridge yet stood, nor had the country lane been paved. Leverett wondered whether anyone had driven past since his terror-sped flight.

He found the old railroad grade easily as he started down-stream. Thirty years, he told himself—but the chill inside him only tightened. The going was far more difficult than before. The day was unbearably hot and humid. Wading through the rank underbrush raised clouds of black flies that savagely bit him.

Evidently the stream had seen severe flooding in the past years, judging from piled logs and debris that blocked his path. Stretches were scooped out to barren rocks and gravel. Elsewhere gigantic barriers of uprooted trees and debris looked like ancient and moldering fortifications. As he worked his way down the valley, he realized that his search would yield nothing. So intense had been the force of the long-ago flood that even the course of the stream had changed. Many of the dry-wall culverts no longer spanned the brook, but sat lost and alone far back from its present banks. Others had been knocked flat and swept away, or were buried beneath tons of rotting logs.

111

At one point Leverett found remnants of an apple orchard groping through weeds and bushes. He thought that the house must be close by, but here the flooding had been particularly severe, and evidently even those ponderous stone foundations had been toppled over and buried beneath debris.

Leverett finally turned back to his car. His step was lighter.

A few weeks later he received a response from Stefroi to his reported failure:

"Forgive my tardy reply to your letter of 13 June. I have recently been pursuing inquiries which may, I hope, lead to the discovery of a previously unreported megalithic site of major significance. Naturally I am disappointed that no traces remained of the Mann Brook site. While I tried not to get my hopes up, it did seem likely that the foundation would have survived. In searching through regional data, I note that there were particularly severe flash floods in the Otselic area in July 1942 and again in May 1946. Very probably your old farmhouse with its enigmatic devices was utterly destroyed not very long after your discovery of the site. This is weird and wild country, and doubtless there is much we shall never know.

I write this with a profound sense of personal loss over the death two nights ago of Prescott Brandon. This was a severe blow to me—as I am sure it was to you and to all who knew him. I only hope the police will catch the vicious killers who did this senseless act—evidently thieves surprised while ransacking his office. Police believe the killers were high on drugs from the mindless brutality of their crime.

I had just received a copy of the third Allard volume, *Unhallowed Places*. A superbly designed book, and this tragedy becomes all the more insuperable with the realization that Scotty will give the world no more such treasures. In Sorrow, Alexander Stefroi."

Leverett stared at the letter in shock. He had not received news of Brandon's death—had only a few days before he opened a parcel from the publisher containing a first copy of *Unhallowed Places*. A line in Brandon's last letter recurred to him—a line that seemed amusing to him at the time:

"Your sticks have bewildered a good many fans, Colin, and

I've worn out a ribbon answering inquiries. One fellow in particular—a Major George Leonard—has pressed me for details, and I'm afraid that I told him too much. He has written several times for your address, but knowing how you value your privacy I told him simply to permit me to forward any correspondence. He wants to see your original sketches, I gather, but these overbearing occult-types give me a pain. Frankly, I wouldn't care to meet the man myself."

VI

"Mr. Colin Leverett?"

Leverett studied the tall lean man who stood smiling at the doorway of his studio. The sports car he had driven up in was black and looked expensive. The same held for the turtleneck and leather slacks he wore, and the sleek briefcase he carried. The blackness made his thin face deathly pale. Leverett guessed his age to be late forty by the thinning of his hair. Dark glasses hid his eyes, black driving gloves his hands.

"Scotty Brandon told me where to find you," the stranger said.

"Scotty?" Leverett's voice was wary.

"Yes, we lost a mutual friend, I regret to say. I'd been talking with him just before . . . But I see by your expression that Scotty never had time to write."

He fumbled awkwardly. "I'm Dana Allard."

"Allard?"

His visitor seemed embarrassed. "Yes—H. Kenneth Allard was my uncle."

"I hadn't realized Allard left a family," mused Leverett, shaking the extended hand. He had never met the writer personally, but there was a strong resemblance to the few photographs he had seen. And Scotty had been paying royalty checks to an estate of some sort, he recalled.

"My father was Kent's half-brother. He later took his father's name, but there was no marriage, if you follow."

"Of course." Leverett was abashed. "Please find a place to sit down. And what brings you here?"

Dana Allard tapped his briefcase. "Something I'd been discussing with Scotty. Just recently I turned up a stack of my uncle's unpublished manuscripts." He unlatched the briefcase and handed Leverett a sheaf of yellowed paper. "Father collected Kent's personal effects from the state hospital as next-of-kin. He never thought much of my uncle, or his writing. He stuffed this away in our attic and forgot about it. Scotty was quite excited when I told him of my discovery."

Leverett was glancing through the manuscript—page on page of cramped handwriting, with revisions pieced throughout like an indecipherable puzzle. He had seen photographs of Allard manuscripts. There was no mistaking this.

Or the prose. Leverett read a few passages with rapt absorption. It was authentic—and brilliant.

"Uncle's mind seems to have taken an especially morbid turn as his illness drew on," Dana hazarded. "I admire his work very greatly but I find these last few pieces . . . Well, a bit *too* horrible. Especially his translation of his mythical *Book of Elders.*"

It appealed to Leverett perfectly. He barely noticed his guest as he pored over the brittle pages. Allard was describing a megalithic structure his doomed narrator had encountered in the crypts beneath an ancient churchyard. There were references to "elder glyphics" that resembled his lattice devices.

" 'Look here,'" pointed Dana. "These incantations he records here from Alorri-Zrokros's forbidden tome: 'Yogth-Yugth-Sut-Hyrath-Yogng'—Hell, I can't pronounce them. And he has pages of them."

"This is incredible!" Leverett protested. He tried to mouth the alien syllables. It could be done. He even detected a rhythm.

"Well, I'm relieved that you approve. I'd feared these last few stories and fragments might prove a little too much for Kent's fans."

"Then you're going to have them published?"

Dana nodded. "Scotty was going to. I just hope those thieves weren't searching for this—a collector would pay a fortune. But Scotty said he was going to keep this secret until he was ready for announcement." His thin face was sad.

"So now I'm going to publish it myself—in a deluxe edition. And I want you to illustrate it."

"I'd feel honored!" vowed Leverett, unable to believe it.

"I really liked those drawings you did for the trilogy. I'd like to see more like those—as many as you feel like doing. I mean to spare no expense in publishing this. And those stick things . . ."

"Yes?"

"Scotty told me the story on those. Fascinating! And you have a whole notebook of them? May I see it?"

Leverett hurriedly dug the notebook from his file, returned to the manuscript.

Dana paged through the book in awe. "These things are totally bizarre—and there are references to such things in the manuscript, to make it even more fantastic. Can you reproduce them all for the book?"

"All I can remember," Leverett assured him. "And I have a good memory. But won't that be overdoing it?"

"Not at all! They fit into the book. And they're utterly unique. No, put everything you've got into this book. I'm going to entitle it *Dwellers in the Earth,* after the longest piece. I've already arranged for its printing, so we begin as soon as you can have the art ready. And I know you'll give it your all."

VII

He was floating in space. Objects drifted past him. Stars, he first thought. The objects drifted closer.

Sticks. Stick lattices of all configurations. And then he was drifting among them, and he saw that they were not sticks—not of wood. The lattice designs were of dead-pale substance, like streaks of frozen starlight. They reminded him of glyphics of some unearthly alphabet—complex, enigmatic symbols arranged to spell . . . what? And there *was* an arrangement—a three-dimensional pattern. A maze of utterly baffling intricacy. . . .

Then somehow he was in a tunnel. A cramped, stone-lined tunnel through which he must crawl on his belly. The bank, moss-slimed stones pressed closed about his wriggling form, evoking shrill whispers of claustrophobic dread.

And after an indefinite space of crawling through this and other stone-lined burrows, and sometimes through passages whose angles hurt his eyes, he would creep forth into a subterranean chamber. Great slabs of granite a dozen feet across formed the walls and ceiling of this buried chamber, and between the slabs other burrows pierced the earth. Altarlike, a gigantic slab of gneiss waited in the center of the chamber. A spring welled darkly between the stone pillars that supported the table. Its outer edge was encircled by a groove, sickeningly stained by the substance that clotted in the stone bowl beneath its collecting spout.

Others were emerging from the darkened burrows that ringed the chamber—slouched figures only dimly glimpsed and vaguely human. And a figure in a tattered cloak came toward him from the shadow—stretched out a clawlike hand to seize his wrist and draw him toward the sacrificial table. He followed unresistingly, knowing that something was expected of him.

They reached the altar and in the glow from the cuneiform lattices chiseled into the gneiss slab he could see the guide's face. A moldering corpse-face, the rotted bone of its forehead smashed inward upon the foulness that oozed forth . . .

And Leverett would awaken to the echo of his screams . . .

He'd been working too hard, he told himself, stumbling about in the darkness, getting dressed because he was too shaken to return to sleep. The nightmares had been coming every night. No wonder he was exhausted.

But in his studio his work awaited him. Almost fifty drawings finished now, and he planned another score. No wonder the nightmares.

It was a grueling pace, but Dana Allard was ecstatic with the work he had done. And *Dwellers in the Earth* was waiting. Despite problems with typesetting, with getting the special paper Dana wanted—the book only waited on him.

Though his bones ached with fatigue, Leverett determinedly trudged through the greying night. Certain features of the nightmare would be interesting to portray.

VIII

The last of the drawings had gone off to Dana Allard in Petersham, and Leverett, fifteen pounds lighter and gut-weary, converted part of the bonus check into a case of good whiskey. Dana had the offset presses rolling as soon as the plates were shot from the drawings. Despite his precise planning, presses had broken down, one printer quit for reasons not stated, there had been a bad accident at the new printer—seemingly innumerable problems, and Dana had been furious at each delay. But the production pushed along quickly for all that. Leverett wrote that the book was cursed, but Dana responded that a week would see it ready.

Leverett mused himself in his studio constructing stick lattices and trying to catch up on his sleep. He was expecting a copy of the book when he received a letter from Stefroi:

> "Have tried to reach you by phone last few days, but no answer at your house. I'm pushed for time just now, so must be brief. I have indeed uncovered an unsuspected megalithic site

of enormous importance. It's located on the estate of a long-prominent Mass. family—and as I cannot receive authorization to visit it, I will not say where. Have investigated secretly (and quite legally) for a short time one night and was nearly caught. Came across reference to the place in collection of 17th-century letters and papers in a divinity school library. Writer denouncing the family as a breed of sorcerers and witches, references to alchemical activities and other less savory rumors—and describes underground stone chambers, megalithic artifacts, etc., which are put to 'foul usage and diabolic praktise.' Just got a quick glimpse but his description was not exaggerated. And Colin—in creeping through the weeds to get to the site, I came across dozens of your mysterious 'sticks'! Brought a small one back and have it here to show you. Recently constructed and exactly like your drawings. With luck, I'll gain admittance and find out their significance—undoubtedly they have significance—though these cultists can be stubborn about sharing their secrets. Will explain my interest is scientific, no exposure to ridicule—and see what they say. Will get a closer look one way or another. And so—I'm off! Sincerely, Alexander Stefroi"

Leverett's bushy brows rose. Allard had intimated certain dark rituals in which the stick lattices figured. But Allard had written over thirty years ago, and Leverett assumed the writer had stumbled onto something similar to the Mann Brook site. Stefroi was writing about something current.

He rather hoped Stefroi would discover nothing more than an inane hoax.

The nightmares haunted him still—familiar now, for all that its scenes and phantasms were visited by him only in dream. Familiar. The terror that they evoked was undiminished.

Now he was walking through forest—a section of hills that seemed to be close by. A huge slab of granite had been dragged aside, and a pit yawned where it had lain. He entered the pit without hesitation, and the rounded steps that led downward were known to his tread. A buried stone chamber, and leading from it stone-lined burrows. He knew which one to crawl into.

And again the underground room with its sacrificial altar and its dark spring beneath, and the gathering circle of poorly glimpsed figures. A knot of them clustered about the stone table, and as he stepped toward them he saw they pinned a frantically writhing man.

It was a stoutly built man, white hair disheveled, flesh gouged and filthy. Recognition seemed to burst over the contorted features, and he wondered if he should know the man. But now the lich with the caved-in skull was whispering in his ear, and he tried not to think of the unclean things that peered from that cloven brow, and instead took the bronze knife from the skeletal hand, and raised the knife high, and because he could not scream and awaken, did with the knife as the tattered priest had whispered . . .

And when after an interval of unholy madness, he at last did awaken, the stickiness that covered him was not cold sweat, nor was it nightmare the half-devoured heart he clutched in one fist.

IX

Leverett somehow found sanity enough to dispose of the shredded lump of flesh. He stood under the shower all morning, scrubbing his skin raw. He wished he could vomit.

There was a news item on the radio. The crushed body of noted archaeologist, Dr. Alexander Stefroi, had been discovered beneath a fallen granite slab near Whately. Police speculated the gigantic slab had shifted with the scientist's excavations at its base. Identification was made through personal effects.

When his hands stopped shaking enough to drive, Leverett fled to Petersham—reaching Dana Allard's old stone house about dark. Allard was slow to answer his frantic knock.

"Why, good evening, Colin! What a coincidence your coming here just now! The books are ready. The bindery just delivered them."

Leverett brushed past him. "We've got to destroy them!" he blurted. He'd thought a lot since morning.

"Destroy them?"

"There's something none of us figured on. Those stick lattices—there's a cult, some damnable cult. The lattices have some significance in their rituals. Stefroi hinted once they might be glyphics of some sort, I don't know. But the cult is still alive. They killed Scotty . . . they killed Stefroi. They're onto me—I don't know what they intend. They'll kill you to stop you from releasing this book!"

Dana's frown was worried, but Leverett knew he hadn't impressed him the right way. "Colin, this sounds insane. You really have been overextending yourself, you know. Look, I'll show you the books. They're in the cellar."

Leverett let his host lead him downstairs. The cellar was quite large, flagstoned and dry. A mountain of brown-wrapped bundles awaited them.

"Put them down here where they wouldn't knock the floor out," Dana explained. "They start going out to distributors tomorrow. Here, I'll sign your copy."

Distractedly Leverett opened a copy of *Dwellers in the Earth*. He gazed at his lovingly rendered drawings of rotting creatures and buried stone chambers and stained altars—and everywhere the enigmatic latticework structures. He shuddered.

"Here." Dana Allard handed Leverett the book he had signed. "And to answer your question, they *are* elder glyphics."

But Leverett was staring at the inscription in its unmistakable handwriting: "For Colin Leverett, Without whom his work could not have seen completion—H. Kenneth Allard."

Allard was speaking. Leverett saw places where the hastily applied flesh-toned makeup didn't quite conceal what lay beneath. "Glyphics symbolic of alien dimensions—inexplicable to the human mind, but essential fragments of an evocation so unthinkably vast that the 'pentagram' (if you will) is miles across. Once before we tried—but your iron weapon destroyed part of Althol's brain. He erred at the last instant—almost annihilating us all. Althol had been formulating the evocation since he fled the advance of iron four millennia past.

"Then you reappeared, Colin Leverett—you with your artist's knowledge and diagrams of Althol's symbols. And now a thousand new minds will read the evocation you have returned to us, unite with our minds as we stand in the Hidden Places. And the Great Old Ones will come forth from the earth, and we, the dead who have steadfastly served them, shall be masters of the living."

Leverett turned to run, but now they were creeping forth from the shadows of the cellar, as massive flagstones slid back to reveal the tunnels beyond. He began to scream as Althol came to lead him away, but he could not awaken, could only follow.

FRITZ LEIBER

"Belsen Express"

Fritz Leiber (1910-1992) is the author of numerous short stories and novels that have changed the course of modern fantasy, horror and science fiction. His tales of Fafhrd and the Gray Mouser, which he wrote over the course of 50 years, introduced wit and humor into the fantasy subgenre of sword-and-sorcery fiction. He won the Hugo Award for his science fiction novels **The Wanderer** *and* **The Big Time***, and was one of science fiction's most provocative voices in the postwar years. His early stories for the pulp magazines* **Unknown Worlds** *and* **Weird Tales** *include "Smoke Ghost," a seminal urban horror story, and the novel* **Conjure Wife***, an early dark fantasy tale of modern witchcraft. Other horror tales of note include the dark fantasy* **The Sinful Ones***, and* **Our Lady of Darkness***, which won the World Fantasy Award. His many collections of outstanding short fiction include* **Night's Black Agents***,* **Shadows with Eyes***,* **Heroes and Horrors***, and* **The Leiber Chronicles***. "Belsen Express" won the World Fantasy Award for best short story of 1975.*

Belsen Express

by Fritz Leiber

George Simister watched the blue flames writhe beautifully in the grate, like dancing girls drenched with alcohol and set afire, and congratulated himself on having survived well through the middle of the twentieth century without getting involved in military service, world-saving, or any activities that interfered with the earning and enjoyment of money.

Outisde rain dripped, a storm snarled at the city from the outskirts, and sudden gusts of wind produced in the chimney a sound like the mourning of doves. Simister shimmied himself a fraction of an inch deeper in his easy chair and took a slow sip of diluted scotch—he was sensitive to most cheaper liquors. Simister's physiology was on the delicate side; during his childhood certain tastes and odors, playing on an elusive heart weakness, had been known to make him faint.

The outspread newspaper started to slip from his knee. He detained it, let his glance rove across the next page, noted a headline about an uprising in Prague like that in Hungary in 1956 and murmured, "Damn Slavs," noted another about border fighting around Israel and muttered, "Damn Jews," and let the paper go. He took another sip of his drink, yawned, and watched a virginal blue flame flutter frightenedly the length of the log before it turned to a white smoke ghost. There was a sharp *knock-knock*.

Simister jumped and then got up and hurried tight-lipped to the front door. Lately some of the neighborhood children had been trying to annoy him, probably because his was the most respectable and best-kept house on the block. Doorbell ringing, obscene sprayed scrawls, that sort of thing. And hardly children—young rowdies rather, who needed rough handling and a trip to the police station. He was really angry by the time he reached the door and swung it wide. There was nothing but a big wet empty darkness. A chilly draft spattered a couple of cold drops on him. Maybe the noise had come from the fire. He shut the door and started back to the living room, but a small pile of books untidily nested in wrapping paper on the hall table caught his eye and he grimaced.

They constituted a blotchily addressed parcel which the postman had delivered by mistake a few mornings ago. Simister could probably have deciphered the address, for it was clearly on this street, and rectified the postman's error, but he did not choose to abet the activities of illiterates with leaky pens. And the delivery must have been a mistake, for the top book was titled *The Scourge of the Swastika* and the other two had similar titles, and Simister had an acute distaste for books that insisted on digging up that satisfactorily buried historical incident known as Nazi Germany.

The reason for this distaste was a deeply hidden fear that George Simister shared with millions, but that he had never revealed even to his wife. It was a quite unrealistic and now completely anachronistic fear of the Gestapo.

It had begun years before the Second World War, with the first small reports from Germany of minority persecutions and organized hoodlumism—the sense of something reaching out across the dark Atlantic to threaten his life, his security, and his confidence that he would never have to suffer pain except in a hospital.

Of course it had never got at all close to Simister, but it had exercised an evil tyranny over his imagination. There was one nightmarish series of scenes that had slowly grown in his mind and then had kept bothering him for a long time. It began with a thunderous knocking, of boots and rifle butts rather than fists, and a shouted demand: "Open up! It's the Gestapo." Next he would find himself in a stream of frantic people being driven toward a portal where a division was made between those reprieved and those slated for immediate extinction. Last he would be inside a closed motor van jammed so tightly with people that it was impossible to move. After a long time the van would stop, but the motor would keep running, and from the floor, leisurely seeking the crevices between the packed bodies, the entrapped exhaust fumes would begin to mount.

Now in the shadowy hall the same horrid movie had a belated showing. Simister shook his head sharply, as if he could shake the scenes out, reminding himself that the Gestapo was dead and done with for more than ten years. He felt the angry impulse to throw in the fire the books responsible for the return of his waking nightmare. But he remembered that books are hard to burn. He stared at them uneasily, excited by thoughts of torture and confinement, concentration and death camps, but knowing the nasty aftermath they left in his mind. Again he felt a sudden impulse, this time to bundle the books together and throw them in the trash can. But that would mean getting wet; it could wait until tomorrow. He put the screen in front of the fire, which had died and was smoking like a crematory, and went up to bed.

Some hours later he waked with the memory of a thunderous knocking.

He started up, exclaiming, "Those damned kids!" The drawn shades seemed abnormally dark—probably they'd thrown a stone through the street lamp.

He put one foot on the chilly floor. It was now profoundly still. The storm had gone off like a roving cat. Simister strained his ears. Beside him his wife breathed with irritating evenness. He wanted to wake her and explain about the young delinquents. It was criminal that they were permitted to roam the streets at this hour. Girls with them too, likely as not.

The knocking was not repeated. Simister listened for footsteps going away, or for the creaking of boards that would betray a lurking presence on the porch.

After a while he began to wonder if the knocking might not have been part of his dream, or perhaps a final rumble of actual thunder. He lay down and pulled the blankets up to his neck. Eventually his muscles relaxed and he got to sleep.

At breakfast he told his wife about it.

"George, it may have been burglars," she said.

"Don't be stupid, Joan. Burglars don't knock. If it was anything it was those damned kids."

"Whatever it was, I wish you'd put a bigger bolt on the front door."

"Nonsense. If I'd known you were going to act this way I wouldn't have said anything. I told you it was probably just the thunder."

But next night at about the same hour it happened again.

This time there could be little question of dreaming. The knocking still reverberated in his ears. And there had been words mixed with it, some sort of yapping in a foreign language. Probably the children of some of those European refugees who had settled in the neighborhood.

Last night they'd fooled him by keeping perfectly still after banging on the door, but tonight he knew what to do. He tiptoed across the bedroom and went down the stairs rapidly, but quietly because of his bare feet. In the hall he snatched up something to hit them with, then in one motion unlocked and jerked open the door.

There was no one.

He stood looking at the darkness. He was puzzled as to how they could have got away so quickly and silently. He shut the door and switched on the light. Then he felt the thing in his hand. It was one of the books. With a feeling of disgust he dropped it on the others. He must remember to throw them out first thing tomorrow.

But he overslept and had to rush. The feeling of disgust or annoyance, or something akin, must have lingered, however, for he found himself sensitive to things he wouldn't ordinarily have noticed. People especially. The swollen-handed man seemed deliberately surly as he counted Simister's pennies and handed him the paper. The tight-lipped woman at the gate hesitated suspiciously, as if he were trying to pass off a last month's ticket.

And when he was hurrying up the stairs in response to an approaching rumble, he brushed against a little man in an oversize coat and received in return a glance that gave him a positive shock.

Simister vaguely remembered having seen the little man several times before. He had the thin nose, narrow-set eyes and receding chin that is by a stretch of the imagination described as "rat-faced." In the movies he'd have played a stool pigeon. The flapping overcoat was rather comic.

But there seemed to be something at once so venomous and sly, so time-bidingly vindictive, in the glance he gave Simister that the latter was taken aback and almost missed the train.

He just managed to squeeze through the automatically closing door of the smoker after the barest squint at the sign to assure himself that the train was an express. His heart was pounding in a way that another time would have worried him, but now he was immersed in a savage pleasure at having thwarted the man in the oversize coat. The latter hadn't hurried fast enough and Simister had made no effort to hold open the door for him.

As a smooth surge of electric power sent them sliding away from the station Simister pushed his way from the vestibule into the car and snagged a strap. From the next one already swayed his chief commuting acquaintance, a beefy, suspiciously red-nosed, irritating man named Holstrom, now reading a folded newspaper one-handed. He shoved a headline in Simister's face. The latter knew what to expect.

"Atomic Weapons for West Germany," he read tonelessly. Holstrom was always trying to get him into outworn arguments about totalitarianism, Nazi Germany, racial prejudice and the like. "Well, what about it?"

Holstrom shrugged. "It's a natural enough step, I suppose, but it started me thinking about the top Nazis and whether we really got all of them."

"Of course," Simister snapped.

"I'm not so sure," Holstrom said. "I imagine quite a few of them got away and are still hiding out somewhere."

But Simister refused the bait. The question bored him. Who talked about the Nazis any more? For that matter, the whole trip this morning was boring; the smoker was overcrowded; and when they finally piled out at the downtown terminus, the rude jostling increased his irritation.

The crowd was approaching an iron fence that arbitrarily split the stream of hurrying people into two sections which reunited a few steps farther on. Beside the fence a new guard was standing, or perhaps Simister hadn't noticed him before. A cocky-looking young fellow with close-cropped blond hair and cold blue eyes.

Suddenly it occurred to Simister that he habitually passed to the right of the fence, but that this morning he was being edged over toward the left. This trifling circumstance, coming on top of everything else, made him boil. He deliberately pushed across the stream, despite angry murmurs and the hard stare of the guard.

He had intended to walk the rest of the way, but his anger made him forgetful and before he realized it he had climbed aboard a bus. He soon regretted it. The bus was even more crowded than the smoker and the standees were morose and lumpy in their heavy overcoats. He was tempted to get off and waste his fare, but he was trapped in the extreme rear and moreover shrank from giving the impression of a man who didn't know his own mind.

Soon another annoyance was added to the ones already plaguing him—a trace of exhaust fumes was seeping up from the motor at the rear. He immediately began to feel ill. He looked around indignantly, but the others did not seem to notice the odor, or else accepted it fatalistically.

In a couple of blocks the fumes had become so bad that Simister decided he must get off at the next stop. But as he started to push past her, a fat woman beside him gave him such a strangely apathetic stare that Simister, whose mind was perhaps a little clouded by nausea, felt almost hypnotized by it, so that it was several seconds before he recalled and carried out his intention.

Ridiculous, but the woman's face stuck in his mind all day.

In the evening he stopped at a hardware store. After supper his wife noticed him working in the front hall.

"Oh, you're putting on a bolt," she said.

"Well, you asked me to, didn't you?"

"Yes, but I didn't think you'd do it."

"I decided I might as well." He gave the screw a final turn and stepped back to survey the job. "Anything to give you a feeling of security."

Then he remembered the stuff he had been meaning to throw out that morning. The hall table was bare.

"What did you do with them?" he asked.

"What?"

"Those fool books."

"Oh, those. I wrapped them up again and gave them to the postman."

"Now why did you do that? There wasn't any return address and I might have wanted to look at them."

"But you said they weren't addressed to us and you hate all that war stuff."

"I know, but—" he said and then stopped, hopeless of making her understand why he particularly wanted to feel he had got rid of that package himself, and by throwing it in the trash can. For that matter, he didn't quite understand his feelings himself. He began to poke around the hall.

"I did return the package," his wife said sharply. "I'm not losing my memory."

"Oh, all right!" he said and started for bed.

That night no knocking awakened him, but rather a loud crashing and rending of wood along with a harsh metallic *ping* like a lock giving.

In a moment he was out of bed, his sleep-sodden nerves jangling with anger. Those hoodlums! Rowdy pranks were perhaps one thing, deliberate destruction of property certainly another. He was halfway down the stairs before it occurred to him that the sound he had heard had a distinctly menacing aspect. Juvenile delinquents who broke down doors would hardly panic at the appearance of an unarmed householder.

But just then he saw that the front door was intact.

Considerably puzzled and apprehensive, he searched the first floor and even ventured into the basement, racking his brains as to just what could have caused such a noise. The water heater? Weight of the coal bursting a side of the bin? Those objects were intact. But perhaps the porch trellis giving way?

That last notion kept him peering out of the front window several moments. When he turned around there was someone behind him.

"I didn't mean to startle you," his wife said. "What's the matter, George?"

"I don't know. I thought I heard a sound. Something being smashed."

He expected that would send her into one of her burglar panics, but instead she kept looking at him.

"Don't stand there all night," he said. "Come on to bed."

"George, is something worrying you? Something you haven't told me about?"

"Of course not. Come on."

Next morning Holstrom was on the platform when Simister got there and they exchanged guesses as to whether the dark rain clouds would burst before they got downtown. Simister noticed the man in an oversize coat loitering about, but he paid no attention to him.

Since it was a bank holiday there were empty seats in the smoker and he and Holstrom secured one. As usual the latter had his newspaper. Simister waited for him to start his ideological sniping—a little uneasily for once; usually he was secure in his prejudices, but this morning he felt strangely vulnerable.

It came. Holstrom shook his head. "That's a bad business in Czechoslovakia. Maybe we were a little too hard on the Nazis."

To his surprise Simister found himself replying with both nervous hypocrisy and uncharacteristic vehemence. "Don't be ridiculous! Those rats deserved a lot worse than they got!"

As Holstrom turned toward him saying, "Oh, so you've changed your mind about the Nazis," Simister thought he heard someone just behind him say at the same time in a low, distinct, pitiless voice: "I heard you."

He glanced around quickly. Leaning forward a little, but with his face turned sharply away as if he had just become interested in something passing the window, was the man in the oversize coat.

"What's wrong?" Holstrom asked.

"What do you mean?"

"You've turned pale. You look sick."

127

"I don't feel that way."

"Sure? You know, at our age we've got to begin to watch out. Didn't you once tell me something about your heart?"

Simister managed to laugh that off, but when they parted just outside the train he was conscious that Holstrom was still eyeing him rather closely.

As he slowly walked through the terminus his face began to assume an abstracted look. In fact he was lost in thought to such a degree that when he approached the iron fence, he started to pass it on the left. Luckily the crowd was thin and he was able to cut across to the right without difficulty. The blond young guard looked at him closely—perhaps he remembered yesterday morning.

Simister had told himself that he wouldn't again under any circumstances take the bus, but when he got outside it was raining torrents. After a moment's hesitation he climbed aboard. It seemed even more crowded than yesterday, if that were possible, with more of the same miserable people, and the damp air made the exhaust odor particularly offensive.

The abstracted look clung to his face all day long. His secretary noticed, but did not comment. His wife did, however, when she found him poking around in the hall after supper.

"Are you still looking for that package, George?" Her tone was flat.

"Of course not," he said quickly, shutting the table drawer he'd opened.

She waited. "Are you sure you didn't order those books?"

"What gave you that idea?" he demanded. "You know I didn't."

"I'm glad," she said. "I looked through them. There were pictures. They were nasty."

"You think I'm the sort of person who'd buy books for the sake of nasty pictures?"

"Of course not, dear, but I thought you might have seen them and they were what had depressed you."

"Have I been depressed?"

"Yes. Your heart hasn't been bothering you, has it?"

"No."

"Well, what is it then?"

"I don't know." Then with considerable effort he said, "I've been thinking about war and things."

"War! No wonder you're depressed. You shouldn't think about things you don't like, especially when they aren't happening. What started you?"

"Oh, Holstrom keeps talking to me on the train."

"Well, don't listen to him."

"I won't."

"Well, cheer up then."

"I will."

"And don't let anyone make you look at morbid pictures. There was one of some people who had been gassed in a motor van and then laid out—"

"Please, Joan! Is it any better to tell me about them than to have me look at them?"

"Of course not, dear. That was silly of me. But do cheer up."

"Yes."

The puzzled, uneasy look was still in her eyes as she watched him go down the front walk next morning. It was foolish, but she had the feeling that his gray suit was really black—and he had whimpered in his sleep. With a shiver at her fancy she stepped inside.

That morning George Simister created a minor disturbance in the smoker, it was remembered afterward, though Holstrom did not witness the beginning of it. It seems that Simister had run to catch the express and had almost missed it, due to a collision with a small man in a large overcoat. Someone recalled that trifling prelude because of the amusing circumstance that the small man, although he had been thrown to his knees and the collision was chiefly Simister's fault, was still anxiously begging Simister's pardon after the latter had dashed on.

Simister just managed to squeeze through the closing door while taking a quick squint at the sign. It was then that his queer behavior started. He instantly turned around and unsuccessfully tried to force his way out again, even inserting his hands in the crevice between the door frame and the rubber edge of the sliding door and yanking violently.

Apparently as soon as he noticed the train was in motion, he turned away from the door, his face pale and set, and roughly pushed his way into the interior of the car.

There he made a beeline for the little box in the wall containing the identifying signs of the train and the miniature window which showed in reverse the one now in use, which read simply EXPRESS. He stared at it as if he couldn't believe his eyes and then started to turn the crank, exposing in turn all the other white signs on the roll of black cloth. He scanned each one intently, oblivious to the puzzled or outraged looks of those around him.

He had been through all the signs once and was starting through them again before the conductor noticed what was happening and came hurrying. Ignoring his expostulations, Simister asked him loudly if this was really the express. Upon receiving a curt affirmative, Simister went on to assert that he had in the moment of squeezing aboard glimpsed another sign in the window—and he mentioned a strange name. He seemed both very positive and very agitated about it, the conductor said. The latter asked Simister to spell the name. Simister haltingly complied: "B . . . E . . . L . . . S . . . E . . . N . . ." The conductor shook his head, then his eyes widened and he demanded, "Say, are you trying to kid me? That was one of those Nazi death camps." Simister slunk toward the other end of the car.

It was there that Holstrom saw him, looking "as if he'd just got a terrible shock." Holstrom was alarmed—and as it happened felt a special private guilt—but could hardly get a word out of him, though he made several attempts to start a conversation, choosing uncharacteristically neutral topics. Once, he remembered, Simister looked up and said, "Do you suppose there are some things a man simply can't escape, no matter how quietly he lives or how carefully he plans?" But his face immediately showed he had realized there was at least one very obvious answer to this question, and Holstrom didn't know what to say. Another time he suddenly remarked, "I wish we were like the British and didn't have standing in buses," but he subsided as quickly. As they neared the downtown terminus Simister seemed to brace up a little, but Holstrom was still worried about him to such a degree that he went out of his way to follow him through the terminus. "I was afraid something would happen to him, I don't know what," Holstrom said. "I would have stayed right beside him except he seemed to resent my presence."

Holstrom's private guilt, which intensified his anxiety and doubtless accounted for his feeling that Simister resented him, was due to the fact that ten days ago, cumulatively irritated by Simister's smug prejudices and blinkered narrow-mindedness, he had anonymously mailed him three books recounting with uncompromising realism and documentation some of the least pleasant aspects of the Nazi tyranny. Now he couldn't but feel they might have helped to shake Simister up in a way he hadn't intended, and he was ashamedly glad that he had been in such a condition when he sent the package that it had been addressed in a drunken scrawl. He never discussed this matter afterwards, except occasionally to make strangely feelingful remarks about "what little things can unseat a spring in a man's clockworks!"

So, continuing Holstrom's story, he followed Simister at a distance as the latter dejectedly shuffled across the busy terminus. "Terminus?" Holstrom once interrupted his story to remark. "He's a god of endings, isn't he?—and of human rights. Does that mean anything?"

When Simister was nearing an iron fence a puzzling episode occurred. He was about to pass it to the right, when someone just ahead of him lurched or stumbled. Simister almost fell himself, veering toward the fence. A nearby guard reached out and in steadying him pulled him around the fence to the left.

Then, Holstrom maintains, Simister turned for a moment and Holstrom caught a glimpse of his face. There must have been something peculiarly frightening about that backward look, something perhaps that Holstrom cannot adequately describe, for he instantly forgot any idea of surveillance at a distance and made every effort to catch up.

But the crowd from another commuters' express enveloped Holstrom. When got outside the terminus it was some moments before he spotted Simister in the midst of a group jamming their way aboard an already crowded bus across the street. This perplexed Holstrom, for he knew Simister didn't have to take the bus and he recalled his recent complaint.

Heavy traffic kept Holstrom from crossing. He says he shouted, but Simister did not seem to hear him. He got the impression that Simister was making feeble efforts to get out of the crowd that was forcing him onto the bus, but "they were all jammed together like cattle."

The best testimony to Holstrom's anxiety about Simister is that as soon as traffic thinned a trifle he darted across the street, skipping between cars. But by then the bus had started. He was in time only for a whiff of particularly obnoxious exhaust fumes.

As soon as he got to his office he phoned Simister. He got Simister's secretary and what she had to say relieved his worries, which is ironic in view of what happened a little later.

What happened a little later is best described by the same girl. She said, "I never saw him come in looking so cheerful, the old grouch—excuse me. But anyway he came in all smiles, like he'd just got some bad news about somebody else, and right away he started to talk and kid with everyone, so that it was awfully funny when that man called up worried about him. I guess maybe, now I think back, he did seem a bit shaken underneath, like a person who's just had a narrow squeak and is very thankful to be alive.

"Well, he kept it up all morning. Then just as he was throwing his head back to laugh at one of his own jokes, he grabbed his chest, let out an awful scream, doubled up and fell on the floor. Afterwards I couldn't believe he was dead, because his lips stayed so red and there were bright spots of color on his cheeks, like rouge. Of course it was his heart, though you can't believe what a scare that stupid first doctor gave us when he came in and looked at him."

Of course, as she said, it must have been Simister's heart, one way or the other. And it is undeniable that the doctor in question was an ancient, possibly incompetent dispenser of penicillin, morphine and snap diagnoses swifter than Charcot's. They only called him because his office was in the same building. When Simister's own doctor arrived and pronounced it heart failure, which was what they'd thought all along, everyone was much relieved and inclined to be severely critical of the first doctor for having said something that sent them all scurrying to open the windows.

For when the first doctor had come in, he had taken one look at Simister and rasped, "Heart failure? Nonsense! Look at the color of his face. Cherry red. That man died of carbon monoxide poisoning."

HUGH B. CAVE

"Ladies In Waiting"

Hugh Cave (1910-) enjoyed a prolific career in the fantasy, weird menace, detective and adventure pulps where his work was distinguished for its action and suspense. His novel **The Cross on the Drum** *is considered one of the best novels ever written on the theme of voodoo and was based on knowledge acquired during his years in Haiti. With the publication of his retrospective collection* **Murgunstrumm and Others** *in 1977, he returned to writing fantasy and horror fiction. His novels include* **The Nebulon Horror, The Evil, Disciples of Dread,** *and* **The Lower Deep.** *A generous portion of his pulp, mainstream and contemporary fantasy fiction can be found in the collections* **The Witching Lands, Death Stalks the Night,** *and* **Bitter/Sweet.** *He is the subject of Audrey Parente's full-length biography,* **Pulpman's Odyssey.**

Ladies In Waiting

by Hugh B. Cave

Halper, the village real-estate man, said with a squint, "You're the same people looked at that place back in April, aren't you? Sure you are. The ones got caught in that freak snowstorm and spent the night there. Mr. and Mrs. Wilkes, is it?"

"Wilkins," Norman corrected, frowning at a photograph on the wall of the old man's dingy office: a yellowed, fly-spotted picture of the house itself, in all its decay and drabness.

"And you want to look at it again?"

"Yes!" Linda exclaimed.

Both men looked at her sharply because of her vehemence. Norman, her husband, was alarmed anew by the eagerness that suddenly flamed in her lovely brown eyes and as suddenly was replaced by a look of guilt. Yes—unmistakably a look of guilt.

"I mean," she stammered, "we still want a big old house that we can do over, Mr. Halper. We've never stopped looking. And we keep thinking the Creighton place just might do."

You keep thinking it might do, Norman silently corrected. He himself had intensely disliked the place when Halper showed it to them four months ago. The sharp edge of his abhorrence was not even blunted, and time would never dull his remembrance of that shocking expression on Linda's face. When he stepped through that hundred-seventy-year-old doorway again, he would hate and fear the house as much as before, he was certain.

Would he again see that look on his wife's face? God forbid!

"Well," Halper said, "there's no need for me to go along with you this time, I guess. I'll just ask you to return the key when you're through, same as you did before."

Norman accepted the tagged key from him and walked unhappily out to the car.

It was four miles from the village to the house. One mile of narrow blacktop, three of a dirt road that seemed forlorn and forgotten even in this neglected part of New England. At three in the afternoon of an awesomely hot August day the car made the only sound in a deep green silence. The sun's heat had robbed even birds and insects of their voices.

Norman was silent too—with apprehension. Beside him his adored wife of less than two years leaned forward to peer through the windshield for the first glimpse of their destination, seeming to have forgotten he existed. Only the house now mattered.

And there it was.

Nothing had changed. It was big and ugly, with a sagging front piazza and too few windows. It was old. It was gray because almost all its white paint had weathered away. According to old Halper the Creightons had lived here for generations, having come here from Salem, where one of their women in the days of witchcraft madness had been hanged for practicing demonolatry. A likely story.

As he stopped the car by the piazza steps, Norman glanced at the girl beside him. His beloved. His childhood sweetheart. Why in God's name was she eager to come here again? She had not been so in the beginning. For days after that harrowing ordeal she had been depressed, unwilling even to talk about it.

But then, weeks later, the change, Ah, yes, the change! So subtle at first, or at least as subtle as her unsophisticated nature could contrive. "Norm . . . do you remember that old house we were snowbound in? Do you suppose we might have liked it if things had been different? . . . "

Then not so subtle. "Norm, can we look at the Creighton place again? Please? Norm?"

As he fumbled the key into the lock, he reached for her hand. "Are you all right, hon?"

"Of course!" The same tone of voice she had used in Halper's shabby office. Impatient. Critical. *Don't ask silly questions!*

With a premonition of disaster he pushed the old door open.

It was the same.

Furnished, Halper had called it, trying to be facetious. There were dusty ruins of furniture and carpets and—yes—someone or something was using them; that the house had *not* been empty for eight years, as Halper claimed. Now the feeling returned as Norman trailed his wife through the downstairs rooms and up the staircase to the bed chambers above. But the feeling was strong! He wanted desperately to seize her hand again and shout, "No, no, darling! Come out of here!"

Upstairs, when she halted in the big front bedroom, turning slowly to look about her, he said helplessly, "Hon, please—what is it? What do you *want*?"

No answer. He had ceased to exist. She even bumped into him as she went past to sit on the old four-poster with its mildewed mattress. And, seated there, she stared emptily into space as she had done before.

He went to her and took her hands. "Linda, for God's sake! What *is* it with this place?"

She looked up and smiled at him. "I'm all right. Don't worry, darling."

There had been an old blanket on the bed when they entered this room before. He had thought of wrapping her in it because she was shivering, the house was frigid, and with the car trapped in deepening snow they would have to spend the night here. But the blanket reeked with age and she had cringed from the touch of it.

Then—"Wait," he had said with a flash of inspiration. "Maybe if I could jam this under a tire! . . . Come on. It's at least worth a try."

"I'm cold, Norm. Let me stay here."

"You'll be all right? Not scared?"

"Better scared than frozen."

"Well . . . I won't be long."

How long was he gone? Ten minutes? Twenty? Twice the car had seemed about to pull free from the snow's mushy grip. Twice the wheel had spun the sodden blanket out from under and sent it flying through space like a huge yellow bird, and he'd been forced to go groping after it with the frigid wind lashing his half-frozen face. Say twenty minutes; certainly no longer. Then, giving it up as a bad job, he had trudged despondently back to the house and climbed the stairs again to that front bedroom.

And there she sat on the bed, as she was sitting now. White as the snow itself. Wide-eyed. Staring at or into something that only she could see.

"Linda! What's wrong?"

"Nothing. Nothing . . ."

He grasped her shoulders. "Look at me! Stop staring like that! What's happened?"

"I thought I heard something. Saw something."

"Saw *what?*"

"I don't know. I don't . . . remember."

Lifting her from the bed, he put his arms about her and glowered defiantly at the empty doorway. Strange. A paper-thin layer of mist or smoke moved along the floor there, drifting out into the hall. And there were floating shapes of the same darkish stuff trapped in the room's corners, as though left behind when the chamber emptied itself of a larger mass. Or was he imagining these things? One moment they seemed to be there; a moment later they were gone.

And was he also imagining the odor? It had not been present in the musty air of this room before; it certainly seemed to be now, unless his senses were playing tricks on him. A peculiarly robust smell, unquestionably male. But now it was fading.

Never mind. There *was* someone in this house, by God! He had felt an alien presence when Halper was here; even more so after the agent's departure. Someone, something, following them about, watching them.

The back of Linda's dress was unzipped, he realized then. His hands, pressing her to him, suddenly found themselves inside the garment, on her body. And her body was cold. Colder than the snow he had struggled with outside. Cold and clammy.

The zipper. He fumbled for it, found it drawn all the way down. What in God's name had she tried to do? This was his wife, who loved him. This was the girl who only a few weeks ago, at the club, had savagely slapped the face of the town's richest, handsomest playboy for daring to hint at a mate-swapping arrangement. Slowly he drew the zipper up again, then held her at arm's length and looked again at her face.

She seemed unaware he had touched her. Or that he even existed. She was entirely alone, still gazing into that secret world in which he had no place.

The rest of that night had seemed endless, Linda lying on the bed, he sitting beside her waiting for daylight. She seemed to sleep some of the time; at other times, though she said nothing even when spoken to, he sensed she was as wide awake as he. About four o'clock the wind died and the snow stopped its wet slapping of the windowpanes. No dawn had ever been more welcome, even though he was still unable to free the car and they both had to walk to the village to send a tow truck for it.

And now he had let her persuade him to come back here. He must be insane.

"Norman?"

She sat there on the bed, the same bed, but at least she was looking *at* him now, not through him into that secret world of hers. "Norman, you do like this house a little, don't you?"

"If you mean could I ever seriously think of living here—" Emphatically he shook his head. "My God, no! It gives me the horrors!"

"It's really a lovely old house, Norman. We could work on it little by little. Do you think I'm crazy?"

"If you can even imagine living in this mausoleum, I *know* you're crazy. My God, woman, you were nearly frightened out of your wits here. In this very room, too."

"Was I, Norman? Really?"

"Yes, you were! If I live to be a hundred, I'll never stop seeing that look on your face."

"What kind of look was it, Norman?"

"I don't know. That's just it—I don't know! What in heaven's name *were* you seeing when I walked back in here after my session with the car? What was that mist? That smell?"

Smiling, she reached for his hands. "I don't remember any mist or smell, Norman. I was just a little frightened. I told you—I thought I heard something."

"You *saw* something too, you said."

"Did I say that? I've forgotten." Still smiling, she looked around the room—at the garden of faded roses on shreds of time-stained wallpaper; at the shabby bureau with its solitary broken cut-glass vase. "Old Mr. Halper was to blame for what happened, Norman. His talk of demons."

"Halper didn't do that much talking, Linda."

"Well, he told us about the woman who was hanged in Salem. I can see now, of course, that he threw that out as bait, because I had told him you write mystery novels. He probably pictured you sitting in some sort of Dracula cape, scratching out your books with a quill, by lamplight, and thought this would be a marvelous setting for it." Her soft laugh was a welcome sound, reminding Norman he loved this girl and she loved him—that their life together, except for her inexplicable interest in this house, was full of gentleness and caring.

But he could not let her win this debate. "Linda, listen. If this is such a fine old house, why has it been empty for eight years?"

"Well, Mr. Halper explained that, Norman."

"Did he? I don't seem to recall any explanation."

"He said that last person to live here was a woman who died

eight years ago at ninety-three. Her married name was Stanhope, I think he said, but she was a Creighton—she even had the same given name, Prudence, as the woman hanged in Salem for worshipping demons. And when she passed away there was some legal question about the property because her husband had died some years before in an asylum, leaving no will."

Norman reluctantly nodded. The truth was, he hadn't paid much attention to the real-estate man's talk, but he did recall the remark that the last man of the house had been committed to an asylum for the insane. Probably from having lived in such a gloomy old house for so long, he had thought at the time.

Annoyed with himself for having lost the debate—at least, for not having won it—he turned from the bed and walked to a window, where he stood gazing down at the yard. Right down there, four months ago, was where he had struggled to free the car. Frowning at the spot now, he suddenly said aloud, "Wait. That's damn queer."

"What is, dear?" Linda said from the bed.

"I've always thought we left the car in a low spot that night. A spot where the snow must have drifted extra deep, I mean. But we didn't. We were in the highest part of the yard."

"Perhaps the ground is soft there."

"Uh-uh. It's rocky."

"Then it might have been slippery?"

"Well, I suppose—" Suddenly he pressed closer to the window glass. "Oh, damn! We've got a flat."

"What, Norman?"

"A flat! Those are new tires, too. We must have picked up a nail on our way into this stupid place." Striding back to the bed, he caught her hand. "Come on. I'm not leaving you here this time!"

She did not protest. Obediently she followed him downstairs and along the lower hall to the front door. On the piazza she hesitated briefly, glancing back in what seemed to be a moment of panic, but when he again grasped her hand, she meekly went with him down the steps and out to the car.

The left front tire was the flat one. Hunkering down beside it, he searched for the culprit nail but failed to find any. It was underneath, no doubt. Things like flat tires always annoyed him; in a properly organized world they wouldn't happen. Of course, in such a world there would not be the kind of road one had to travel to reach this place, nor would there be such an impossible house to begin with.

Muttering to himself, he opened the trunk, extracted jack, tools, and spare, and went to work.

Strange. There was no nail in the offending tire. No cut or bruise, either. The tire must have been badly made. The thought did not improve his mood as, on his knees, he wrestled the spare into place.

Then when he lowered the jack, the spare gently flattened under the car's weight and he knelt there staring at it in disbelief. "What the hell . . ." Nothing like this had *ever* happened to him before.

He jacked the car up again, took the spare off and examined it. No nail, no break, no bruise. It was a new tire, like the others. Newer, because never yet used. He had a repair kit for tubeless tires in the trunk, he recalled—bought one day on an impulse. "Repair a puncture in minutes without even taking the tire off the car." But how could you repair a puncture that wasn't there?

"Linda, this is crazy. We'll have to walk back to town as we did before." He turned his head. "Linda?"

She was not there.

He lurched to his feet. "Linda! Where are you?" How long had she been gone? He must have been working on the car for fifteen or twenty minutes. She hadn't spoken in that time, he suddenly realized. Had she slipped back into the house the moment he became absorbed in his task? She knew well enough how intensely he concentrated on such things. How when he was writing, for instance, she could walk through the room without his even knowing it.

"Linda, for God's sake—no!" Hoarsely shouting her name, he stumbled toward the house. The door clattered open when he flung himself against it, and the sound filled his ears as he staggered down the hall. But now the hall was not just an ancient, dusty corridor; it was a dim tunnel filled with premature darkness and strange whisperings.

He knew where she must be. In that cursed room at the top of the stairs where he had seen the look on her face four months ago, and where she had tried so cunningly to conceal the truth from him this time. But the room was hard to reach now. A swirling mist choked the staircase, repeatedly causing him to stumble. Things resembling hands darted out of it to clutch at him and hold him back.

He stopped in confusion, and the hands nudged him forward again. Their owner was playing a game with him, he realized, mocking his frantic efforts to reach the bedroom yet at the same time seductively urging him to try even harder. And the whisperings made words, or seemed to. "Come Norman . . . sweet Norman . . . come come come. . . ."

In the upstairs hall, too, the swirling mist challenged him, deepening into a moving mass that hid the door of the room. But he needed no compass to find that door. Gasping and cursing—"Damn you, leave me alone! Get out of my way!" He struggled to it and found it open as Linda and he had left it. Hands outthrust, he groped his way over the threshold.

The alien presence here was stronger. The sense of being confronted by some unseen creature was all but overwhelming. Yet the assault upon him was less violent now that he had reached the room. The hands groping for him in the eerie darkness were even gentle, caressing. They clung with a velvet softness that was strangely pleasurable, and there was something voluptuously female about them, even to a faint but pervasive female odor.

An *odor,* not a perfume. A body scent, druglike in its effect upon his senses. Bewildered, he ceased his struggle for a moment to see what would happen. The whispering became an invitation, a promise of incredible delights. But he allowed himself only a moment of listening and then, shouting Linda's name, hurled himself at the bed again. This time he was able to reach it.

But she was not now sitting there staring into that secret world of hers, as he had expected. The bed was empty and the seductive voice in the darkness softly laughed at his dismay. "Come Norman . . . sweet Norman . . . come come come. . . ."

He felt himself taken from behind by the shoulders, turned and ever so gently pushed. He fell floating onto the old mattress, halfheartedly thrusting up his arms to keep the advancing shadow-form from possessing him. But it flowed down over him, onto him, into him, despite his feeble resistance, and the female smell tantalized his senses again, destroying his will to resist.

As he ceased struggling he heard a sound of rusty hinges creaking in that part of the room's dimness where the door was, and then a soft thud. The door had been closed. But he did not cry out. He felt no alarm. It was good to be here on the bed, luxuriating in this sensuous, caressing softness. As he became quiescent it flowed over him with unrestrained indulgence, touching and stroking him to heights of ecstasy.

Now the unseen hands, having opened his shirt, slowly and seductively glided down his body to his belt. . . .

He heard a new sound then. For a moment it bewildered him because, though coming through the ancient wall behind him, from the adjoining bedroom, it placed him at once in his own bedroom at home. Linda and he had joked about it often, as true lovers could—

the explosive little syllables to which she always gave voice when making love.

So she was content, too. Good. Everything was straightforward and aboveboard, then. After all, as that fellow at the club had suggested, mate-swapping was an in thing in this year of our Lord 1975 . . . wasn't it? All kinds of people did it.

He must buy this house, as Linda had insisted. Of course. She was absolutely right. With a sigh of happiness he closed his eyes and relaxed, no longer made reluctant by a feeling of guilt.

But—something was wrong. Distinctly, now, he felt not two hands caressing him, but more. And were they hands? They suddenly seemed cold, clammy, frighteningly eager.

Opening his eyes, he was startled to find that the misty darkness had dissolved and he could see. Perhaps the seeing came with total surrender, or with the final abandonment of his guilt feeling. He lay on his back, naked, with his nameless partner half beside him, half on him. He saw her scaly, misshapen breasts overflowing his chest and her monstrous, demonic face swaying in space above his own. And as he screamed, he saw that she did have more than two hands: she had a whole writhing mass of them at the ends of long, searching tentacles.

The last thing he saw before his scream became that of a madman was a row of three others like her squatting by the wall, their tentacles restlessly reaching toward him as they impatiently awaited their turn.

JOE HALDEMAN

"Armaja Das"

Joe Haldeman (1943-) began publishing science fiction in 1969, following a two-year tour of duty in Vietnam, and achieved notoriety five years later with his first novel, **The Forever War***, a futuristic extrapolation of the dehumanizing potential of warfare. He followed this with the highly regarded* **Mindbridge** *and* **All My Sins Remembered***, novels that further established his reputation as a writer with a strong moral vision. Several of his novels are genre splices, including the technothriller* **Tools of the Trade** *and his borderline science fiction-espionage novels* **Attar's Revenge** *and* **War of Nerves***. He has won both the Hugo and Nebula Awards for his short fiction, a sampling of which can be found in his collections* **Infinite Dreams** *and* **Dealing in Futures***. His recent novels include* **The Hemingway Hoax***, expanded from his Nebula Award-winning novella, and the non-genre novel* **1968***. "Armaja Das," one of his rare excursions into horror, was first published in Kirby McCauley's anthology* **Frights***.*

Armaja Das

by Joe Haldeman

The highrise, built in 1980, still had the smell and look of newness. And of money.

The doorman bowed a few degrees and kept a straight face, opening the door for a bent old lady. She had a card of Veterans' poppies clutched in one old claw. He didn't care much for the security guard, and she would give him interesting trouble.

The skin on her face hung in deep creases, scored with a network of tiny wrinkles; her chin and nose protruded and dropped. A cataract made one eye opaque; the other eye was yellow and red surrounding deep black, unblinking. She had left her teeth in various things. She shuffled. She wore an old black dress faded slightly gray by repeated washing. If she had any hair, it was concealed by a pale blue bandanna. She was so stooped that her neck was almost parallel to the ground.

"What can I do for you?" The security guard had a tired voice to match his tired shoulders and back. The job had seemed a little romantic the first couple of days, guarding all these rich people, sitting at an ultramodern console surrounded by video monitors, submachine gun at his knees. But the monitors were blank except for an hourly check, power shortage; and if he ever removed the gun from its cradle, he would have to fill out five forms and call the police station. And the doorman never turned anybody away.

"Buy a flower for boys less fortunate than ye," she said in a faint raspy baritone. From her age and accent, her own boys had fought in the Russian Revolution.

"I'm sorry. I'm not allowed to . . . respond to charity while on duty."

She stared at him for a long time, nodding microscopically. "Then send me to someone with more heart."

He was trying to frame a reply when the front door slammed open. "Car on fire!" the doorman shouted.

The security guard leaped out of his seat, grabbed a fire extinguisher and sprinted for the door. The old woman shuffled along behind him until both he and the doorman disappeared around the corner. Then she made for the elevator with surprising agility.

She got out on the 17th floor, after pushing the button that would send the elevator back down to the lobby. She checked the name plate on 1738; Mr. Zold. She was illiterate but could recognize names.

Not even bothering to try the lock, she walked on down the hall until she found a maid's closet. She closed the door behind her and hid behind a rack of starchy white uniforms, leaning against the wall with her bag between her feet. The slight smell of gasoline didn't bother her at all.

John Zold pressed the intercom button. "Martha?" She answered. "Before you close up shop I'd like a redundancy check on stack 408. Against tape 408." He switched the selector on his visual output screen so it would duplicate the output at Martha's station. He stuffed tobacco in a pipe and lit it, watching.

Green numbers filled the screen, a complicated matrix of ones and zeros. They faded for a second and were replaced with a field of pure zeros. The lines of zeros started to roll, like titles preceding a movie.

The 746th line came up all ones. John thumbed the intercom again. "Had to be something like that. You have time to fix it up?" She did. "Thanks, Martha. See you tomorrow."

He slid back the part of his desk top that concealed a keypunch and typed rapidly: "523 784 00926// Good night, machine. Please lock this station."

GOOD NIGHT, JOHN. DON'T FORGET YOUR LUNCH DATE WITH MR. BROWNWOOD TOMORROW. DENTIST APPOINTMENT WEDNESDAY 0945. GENERAL SYSTEMS CHECK WEDNESDAY 1300. DEL O DEL BAXT. LOCKED.

Del O del baxt means "God give you luck" in the ancient tongue of the Romani. John Zold, born a Gypsy but hardly a Gypsy by any standard other than the strong one of blood, turned off his console and unlocked the bottom drawer of his desk. He took out a flat automatic pistol in a holster with a belt clip and slipped it under his jacket, inside the waistband of his trousers. He had only been wearing the gun for two weeks, and it still made him uncomfortable. But there had been those letters.

John was born in Chicago, some years after his parents had fled from Europe and Hitler. His father had been a fiercely proud man, and got involved in a bitter argument over the honor of his 12-year-old daughter; from which argument he had come home with knuckles raw and bleeding, and had given to his wife for disposal a large clasp knife crusty with dried blood.

John was small for his five years, and his chin barely cleared the kitchen table, where the whole family sat and discussed their uncertain future while Mrs. Zold bound up her husband's hands. John's shortness saved his life when the kitchen window exploded and a low ceiling of shotgun pellets fanned out and chopped into the heads and chests of the only people in the world whom he could love and trust. The police found him huddled between the bodies of his father and mother, and at first thought he was also dead; covered with blood, completely still, eyes wide open and not crying.

It took six months for the kindly orphanage people to get a single word out of him: *ratválo*, which he said over and over; which they were never able to translate. Bloody, bleeding.

But he had been raised mostly in English, with a few words of Romani and Hungarian thrown in for spice and accuracy. In another year their problem was not one of communicating with John; only of trying to shut him up.

No one adopted the stunted Gypsy boy, which suited John. He'd had a family, and look what happened.

In orphanage school he flunked penmanship and deportment, but did reasonably well in everything else. In arithmetic and, later, mathematics, he was nothing short of brilliant. When he left the orphanage at eighteen, he enrolled at the University of Illinois, supporting himself as a bookkeeper's assistant and part-time male model. He had come out of an ugly adolescence with a striking resemblance to the young Clark Gable.

Drafted out of college, he spent two years playing with computers at Fort Lewis; got out and went all the way to a Master's degree under the G.I. Bill. His thesis "Simulation of Continuous Physical Systems by Way of Universalization of the Trakhtenbrot Algorithms" was very well received, and the mathematics department gave him a research assistantship, to extend the thesis into a doctoral dissertation. But other people read the paper too, and after a few months Bellcom International hired him away from academia. He rose rapidly through the ranks. Not yet forty, he was now Senior Analyst at Bellcom's Research and Development Group. He had his own private office, with a picture window overlooking Central Park, and a plush six-figure condominium only twenty minutes away by commuter train.

As was his custom, John bought a tall can of beer on his way to the train, and opened it as soon as he sat down. It kept him from fidgeting during the fifteen or twenty-minute wait while the train filled up.
He pulled a thick technical report out of his briefcase and stared at the summary on the cover sheet, not really seeing it but hoping that looking occupied would spare him the company of some anonymous fellow traveller.
The train was an express, and whisked them out to Dobb's Ferry in twelve minutes. John didn't look from his report until they were well out of New York City; the heavy mesh tunnel that protected the track from vandals induced spurious colors in your retina as it blurred by. Some people liked it, tripped on it, but to John the effect was at best annoying, at worst nauseating, depending on how tired he was. Tonight he was dead tired.
He got off the train two stops up from Dobb's Ferry. The highrise limousine was waiting for him and two other residents. It was a fine spring evening and John would normally have walked the half-mile, tired or not. But those unsigned letters.
John Zold, you stop this preachment or you die soon. Armaja das, John Zold.
All three letters said that: *Armaja das,* we put a curse on you. For preaching.
He was less afraid of curses than of bullets. He undid the bottom button of his jacket as he stepped off the train, ready to quickdraw, roll for cover behind that trash can, just like in the movies; but there was no one suspicious-looking around. Just an assortment of suburban wives and the old cop who was on permanent station duty.
Assassination in broad daylight wasn't Romani style. Styles change, though. He got in the car and watched the side roads all the way home.
There was another one of the shabby envelopes in his mailbox. He wouldn't open it until he got upstairs. He stepped in the elevator with the others, and punched 17.

They were angry because John Zold was stealing their children.
Last March John's tax accountant had suggested that he could con-

tribute $4,000 to any legitimate charity, and actually make a few hundred bucks in the process, by dropping into a lower tax bracket. Not one to do things the easy or obvious way, John made various inquiries and, after a certain amount of bureaucratic tedium, founded the Young Gypsy Assimilation Council—with matching funds from federal, state and city governments, and a continuing Ford Foundation scholarship grant.

The YGAC was actually just a one-room office in a West Village brownstone, manned by volunteer help. It was filled with various pamphlets and broadsides, mostly written by John, explaining how young Gypsies could legitimately take advantage of American society. By becoming part of it, which was the part that old-line Gypsies didn't care for. Jobs, scholarships, work-study programs, these things are for the *gadjos*. Poison to a Gypsy's spirit.

In November a volunteer had opened the office in the morning to find a crude fire bomb, using a candle as a delayed-action fuse for five gallons of gasoline. The candle was guttering a fraction of an inch away from the line of powder that would have ignited the gas. In January it had been buckets of chicken entrails, poured into filing cabinets and flung over the walls. So John found a tough young man who would sleep on the cot in the office at night; sleep like a cat with a shotgun beside him. There was no more trouble of that sort. Only old men and women who would file in silently staring, to take handfuls of pamphlets which they would drop in the hall and scuff into uselessness, or defile in a more basic way. But paper was cheap.

John threw the bolt on his door and hung his coat in the closet. He put the gun in a drawer in his writing desk and sat down to open the mail.

The shortest one yet: "Tonight, John Zold. *Armaja das.*" Lots of luck, he thought. Won't even be home tonight; heavy date. Stay at her place, Gramercy Park. Lay a curse on me there? At the show or Sardi's?

He opened two more letters, bills, and there was a knock at the door.

Not announced from downstairs. Maybe a neighbor. Guy next door was always borrowing something. Still. Feeling a little foolish, he put the gun back in his waistband. Put his coat back on in case it was just a neighbor.

The peephole didn't show anything, bad. He drew the pistol and held it just out of sight, by the doorjamb, threw the bolt and eased open the door. He bumped into the Gypsy woman, too short to have been visible through the peephole. She backed away and said "John Zold."

He stared at her. "What do you want, *pūridaia*? He could only remember a hundred or so words of Romani, but "grandmother" was one of them. What was the word for witch?

"I have a gift for you." From her bag she took a dark green booklet, bent and with frayed edges, and gave it to him. It was a much-used Canadian passport, belonging to a William Belini. But the picture inside the front cover was one of John Zold.

Inside, there was an airline ticket in a Qantas envelope. John didn't open it. He snapped the passport shut and handed it back. The old lady wouldn't accept it.

"An impressive job. It's flattering that someone thinks I'm so important."

"Take it and leave forever, John Zold. Or I will have to do the second thing."

He slipped the ticket envelope out of the booklet. "This, I will take. I can get your refund on it. The money will buy lots of posters and pamphlets." He tried to toss the passport into her bag, but missed. "What is your second thing?"

She tossed the passport back to him. "Pick that up." She was trying to sound imperious, but it came out a thin, petulant quaver.

"Sorry, I don't have any use for it. What is—"

"The second thing is your death, John Zold." She reached into her bag.

He produced the pistol and aimed it down at her forehead. "No, I don't think so."

She ignored the gun, pulling out a handful of white chicken feathers. She threw the feathers over his threshold. *"Armaja das,"* she said, and then droned on in Romani, scattering feathers at regular intervals. John recognized *joovi* and *kari,* the words for woman and penis, and several other words he might have picked up if she'd pronounced them more clearly.

He put the gun back into its holster and waited until she was through. "Do you really think—"

"Armaja das," she said again, and started a new litany. He recognized a word in the middle as meaning corruption or infection, and the last word was quite clear: death. *Méripen.*

"This nonsense isn't going to . . ." But he was talking to the back of her head. He forced a laugh and watched her walk past the elevator and turn the corner that led to the staircase.

He could call the guard. Make sure she didn't get out the back way.

Illegal entry. He suspected that she knew he wouldn't want to go to the trouble, and it annoyed him slightly. He walked halfway to the phone, checked his watch and went back to the door. Scooped up the feathers and dropped them in the disposal. Just enough time. Fresh shave, shower, best clothes. Limousine to the station, train to the city, cab from Grand Central to her apartment.

The show was pure delight, a sexy revival of *Lysistrata:* Sardi's was as ego-bracing as ever; she was a soft-hard woman with style and sparkle, who all but dragged him back to her apartment, where he was for the first time in his life impotent.

The psychiatrist had no use for the traditional props: no soft couch or bookcases lined with obviously expensive volumes. No carpet, no paneling, no numbered prints; not even the notebook or the expression of slightly disinterested compassion. Instead, she had a hidden recorder and an analytical scowl; plain stucco walls surrounding a functional desk and two hard chairs, period.

"You know what the problem is," she said.

John nodded. "I suppose. Some . . . residue from my early upbringing; I accept her as an authority figure. From the few words I could understand of what she said, I took, it was . . ."

"From the words *penis* and *woman,* you built your own curse. And you're using it, probably to punish yourself for surviving the disaster that killed the rest of your family."

"That's pretty old-fashioned. And farfetched. I've had almost forty years to punish myself for that, if I felt responsible. And I don't."

"Still, it's a working hypothesis." She shifted in her chair and studied the pattern of teak grain on the bare top of her desk. "Perhaps if we can keep it simple, the cure can also be simple."

"All right with me," John said. At $125 an hour, the quicker, the better.

"If you can see it, feel it, in this context, then the key to your cure is transference." She leaned forward, elbows on the table, and John watched her breasts shifting with detached interest, the only kind of interest he'd had in women for more than a week. "If you can see *me* as an authority figure instead," she continued, "then eventually I'll be able to reach the child inside; convince him that there was no curse. Only a case of mistaken identity . . . nothing but an old woman who scared him. With careful hypnosis, it shouldn't be too difficult."

"Seems reasonable," John said slowly. Accept this young *Geyri* as more powerful than the old witch? As a grown man, he could. If there was a frightened Gypsy boy hiding inside him, though, he wasn't sure.

"523 784 00926/ /Hello, machine," John typed. "Who is the best dermatologist within a 10-short-block radius?"

GOOD MORNING, JOHN. WITHIN STATED DISTANCE AND USING AS SOLE PARAMETER THEIR HOURLY FEE, THE MAXIMUM FEE IS $95/HR, AND THIS IS CHARGED BY TWO DERMATOLOGISTS, DR. BRYAN DILL, 245 W. 45TH ST., SPECIALIZES IN COSMETIC DERMATOLOGY. DR. ARTHUR MAAS, 198 W. 44TH ST., SPECIALIZES IN SERIOUS DISEASES OF THE SKIN.

"Will Dr. Maas treat disease of psychological origin?"

CERTAINLY. MOST DERMATOSIS IS.

Don't get cocky, machine. "Make me an appointment with Dr. Maas, within the next two days."

YOUR APPOINTMENT IS AT 1:45 TOMORROW, FOR ONE HOUR. THIS WILL LEAVE YOU 45 MINUTES TO GET TO LUCHOW'S FOR YOUR APPOINTMENT WITH THE AMCSE GROUP. I HOPE IT IS NOTHING SERIOUS, JOHN.

"I trust it isn't." Creepy empathy circuits. "Have you arranged for a remote terminal at Luchow's?"

THIS WAS NOT NECESSARY. I WILL PATCH THROUGH CONED/GENERAL. LEASING THEIR LUCHOW'S FACILITY WILL COST ONLY .588 THE PROJECTED COST OF TRANSPORTATION AND SETUP LABOR FOR A REMOTE TERMINAL.

That's my machine, always thinking. "Very good, machine. Keep this station live for the time being."

THANK YOU, JOHN. The letters faded but the ready light stayed on.

He shouldn't complain about the empathy circuits; they were his baby, and the main reason Bellcom paid such a bloated salary, to keep him. The copyright on the empathy package was good for another 12 years, and they were making a fortune, timesharing it out. Virtually every large computer in the world was hooked up to it, from the ConEd/General that ran New York, to Geneva and Akademia Nauk, which together ran half the world.

Most of the customers gave the empathy package a name, usually female. John called it "machine" in a not-too-successful attempt to keep from thinking of it as human.

He made a conscious effort to restrain himself from picking at the carbuncles on the back of his neck. He should have gone to the doctor when they first appeared, but the psychiatrist had been sure she could cure them; the "corruption" of the second curse. She'd had no more success with that than with the impotence. And this morning, boils had broken out on his chest and groin and shoulder-blades, and there were sore spots on his nose and cheekbone. He had some opiates, but would stick to aspirin until after work.

Dr. Maas called it impetigo; gave him a special kind of soap and some antibiotic ointment. He told John to make another appointment in two weeks, ten days. If there was no improvement they would take stronger measures. He seemed young for a doctor, and John couldn't bring himself to say anything about the curse. But he already had a doctor for that end of it, he rationalized.

Three days later he was back in Dr. Maas's office. There was scarcely a square inch of his body where some sort of lesion hadn't appeared. He had a temperature of 101.4°. The doctor gave him systemic antibiotics and told him to take a couple of days' bed rest. John told him about the curse, finally, and the doctor gave him a booklet about psychosomatic illness. It told John nothing he didn't already know.

By the next morning, in spite of strong antipyretics, his fever had risen to over 102°. Groggy with fever and painkillers, John crawled out of bed and traveled down to the West Village, to the YGAC office. Fred Gorgio, the man who guarded the place at night, was still on duty.

"Mr. Zold!" When John came through the door, Gorgio jumped up from the desk and took his arm. John winced from the contact, but allowed himself to be led to a chair. "What's happened?" John by this time looked like a person with terminal smallpox.

For a long minute John sat motionlessly, staring at the inflamed boils that crowded the backs of his hands. "I need a healer," he said, talking with slow awkwardness because of the crusted lesions on his lips.

"A *chóvihánni*?" John looked at him uncomprehendingly. "A witch?"

"No." He moved his head from side to side. "An herb doctor. Perhaps a white witch."

"Have you gone to the *gadjo* doctor?"

"Two. A Gypsy did this to me; a Gypsy has to cure it."

"It's in your head, then?"

"The *gadjo* doctors say so. It can still kill me."

Gorgio picked up the phone, punched a local number, and rattled off a fast stream of a patois that used as much Romani and Italian as

English. "That was my cousin," he said, hanging up. "His mother heals, and has a good reputation. If he finds her at home, she can be here in less than an hour."

John mumbled his appreciation. Gorgio led him to the couch.

The healer woman was early, bustling in with a wicker bag full of things that rattled. She glanced once at John and Gorgio, and began clearing the pamphlets off a side table. She appeared to be somewhere between fifty and sixty years old, tight bun of silver hair bouncing as she moved around the room, setting up a hot-plate and filling two small pots with water. She wore a black dress only a few years old, and sensible shoes. The only lines on her face were laugh lines.

She stood over John and said something in gentle, rapid Italian, then took a heavy silver crucifix from around her neck and pressed it between his hands. "Tell her to speak English . . . or Hungarian," John said.

Gorgio translated. "She says that you should not be so affected by the old superstitions. You should be a modern man, and not believe in fairy tales for children and old people."

John stared at the crucifix, turning it slowly between his fingers. "One old superstition is much like another." But he didn't offer to give the crucifix back.

The smaller pot was starting to steam and she dropped a handful of herbs into it. Then she returned to John and carefully undressed him.

When the herb infusion was boiling, she emptied a package of powdered arrowroot into the cold water in the other pot, and stirred it vigorously. Then she poured the hot solution into the cold and stirred some more. Through Gorgio, she told John she wasn't sure whether the herb treatment would cure him. But it would make him more comfortable.

The liquid jelled and she tested the temperature with her fingers. When it was cool enough, she started to pat it gently on John's face. Then the door creaked open, and she gasped. It was the old crone who had put the curse on John in the first place.

The witch said something in Romani, obviously a command, and the woman stepped away from John.

"Are you still a skeptic, John Zold?" She surveyed her handiwork. "You called this nonsense."

John glared at her but didn't say anything. "I heard that you had asked for a healer," she said, and addressed the other woman in a low tone.

Without a word, she emptied her potion into the sink and began putting away her paraphernalia. "Old bitch," John croaked. "What did you tell her?"

"I said that if she continued to treat you, what happened to you would also happen to her sons."

"You're afraid it would work," Gorgio said.

"No. It would only make it easier for John Zold to die. If I wanted that I could have killed him on his threshold." Like a quick bird she bent over and kissed John on his inflamed lips. "I will see you soon, John Zold. Not in this world." She shuffled out the door and the other woman followed her. Gorgio cursed her in Italian, but she didn't react.

John painfully dressed himself. "What now?" Gorgio said. "I could find you another healer..."

"No. I'll go back to the *gadjo* doctors. They say they can bring people back from the dead." He gave Gorgio the woman's crucifix and limped away.

The doctor gave him enough antibiotics to turn him into a loaf of moldy bread, then reserved a bed for him at an exclusive clinic in Westchester, starting the next morning. He would be under 24-hour observation; constant blood turnaround if necessary. They *would* cure him. It was not possible for a man of his age and physical condition to die of dermatosis.

It was dinnertime and the doctor asked John to come have some home cooking. He declined partly from lack of appetite, partly because he couldn't imagine even a doctor's family being able to eat with such a grisly apparition at the table with them. He took a cab to the office.

There was nobody on his floor but a janitor, who took one look at John and developed an intense interest in the floor.

"523 784 00926/ /Machine, I'm going to die. Please advise."

ALL HUMANS AND MACHINES DIE, JOHN. IF YOU MEAN YOU ARE GOING TO DIE, SOON, THAT IS SAD.

"That's what I mean. The skin infection; it's completely out of control. White cell count climbing in spite of drugs. Going to the hospital tomorrow, to die."

BUT YOU ADMITTED THAT THE CONDITION WAS PSYCHOSOMATIC. THAT MEANS YOU ARE KILLING YOURSELF, JOHN. YOU HAVE NO REASON TO BE THAT SAD.

He called the machine a Jewish mother and explained in some detail about the YGAC, the old crone, the various stages of the curse, and today's aborted attempt to fight fire with fire.

YOUR LOGIC WAS CORRECT BUT THE APPLICATION OF IT WAS NOT EFFECTIVE. YOU SHOULD HAVE COME TO ME, JOHN. IT TOOK ME 2.037 SECONDS TO SOLVE YOUR PROBLEM. PURCHASE A SMALL BLACK BIRD AND CONNECT ME TO A VOCAL CIRCUIT.

"What?" John said. He typed: "Please explain."

FROM REFERENCE IN NEW YORK LIBRARY'S COLLECTION OF THE JOURNAL OF THE GYPSY LORE SOCIETY, EDINBURGH. THROUGH JOURNALS OF ANTHROPOLOGICAL LINGUISTICS AND SLAVIC PHILOLOGY. FINALLY TO REFERENCE IN DOCTORAL THESIS OF HERR LUDWIG R. GROSS (HEIDELBERG, 1976) TO TRANSCRIPTION OF WIRE RECORDING WHICH RESIDES IN ARCHIVES OF AKADEMIA NAUK, MOSCOW; CAPTURED FROM GERMAN SCIENTISTS (EXPERIMENTS ON GYPSIES IN CONCENTRATION CAMPS, TRYING TO KILL THEM WITH REPETITION OF RECORDED CURSE) AT THE END OF WWII.

INCIDENTALLY, JOHN, THE NAZI EXPERIMENTS FAILED. EVEN TWO GENERATIONS AGO, MOST GYPSIES WERE DISASSOCIATED ENOUGH FROM THE OLD TRADITIONS TO BE IMMUNE TO THE FATAL CURSE. YOU ARE VERY SUPERSTITIOUS. I HAVE FOUND THIS TO BE NOT UNCOMMON AMONG MATHEMATICIANS.

THERE IS A TRANSFERENCE CURSE THAT WILL CURE YOU BY GIVING THE IMPOTENCE AND INFECTION TO THE NEAREST SUSCEPTIBLE PERSON. THAT MAY WELL BE THE OLD BITCH WHO GAVE IT TO YOU IN THE FIRST PLACE.

THE PET STORE AT 588 SEVENTH AVENUE IS OPEN UNTIL 9 PM. THEIR INVENTORY INCLUDES A CAGE OF FINCHES, OF ASSORTED COLORS. PURCHASE A BLACK ONE AND RETURN HERE. THEN CONNECT ME TO A VOCAL CIRCUIT.

It took John less than thirty minutes to taxi there, buy the bird and get back. The taxidriver didn't ask him why he was carrying a bird cage to a deserted office building. He felt like an idiot.

John usually avoided using the vocal circuit because the person who had programmed it had given the machine a saccharine, nice-old-lady voice. He wheeled the output unit into his office and plugged it in.

"Thank you, John. Now hold the bird in your left hand and repeat after me." The terrified finch offered no resistance when John closed his hand over it.

The machine spoke Romani with a Russian accent. John repeated it as well as he could, but not one word in ten had any meaning to him.

"Now kill the bird, John."

Kill it? Feeling guilty, John pressed hard, felt small bones cracking. The bird squealed and then made a faint growling noise. Its heart stopped.

John dropped the dead creature and typed, "Is that all?"

The machine knew John didn't like to hear its voice, and so replied on the video screen. YES, GO HOME AND GO TO SLEEP, AND THE CURSE WILL BE TRANSFERRED BY THE TIME YOU WAKE UP. DEL O DEL BAXT, JOHN.

He locked up and made his way home. The late commuters on the train, all strangers, avoided his end of the car. The cab driver at the station paled when he saw John, and carefully took his money by an untainted corner.

John took two sleeping pills and contemplated the rest of the bottle. He decided he could stick it out for one more day, and uncorked his best bottle of wine. He drank half of it in five minutes, not tasting it. When his body started to feel heavy, he crept into the bedroom and fell on the bed without taking off his clothes.

When he awoke the next morning, the first thing he noticed was that he was no longer impotent. The second thing he noticed was that there were no boils on his right hand.

"523 784 00926/ /Thank you, machine. The countercurse did work."

The ready light glowed steadily, but the machine didn't reply. He turned on the intercom. "Martha? I'm not getting any output on the VDS here."

"Just a minute, sir. Let me hang up my coat, I'll call the machine room. Welcome back."

"I'll wait." You could call the machine room yourself, slave driver. He looked at the faint image reflected back from the video screen; his face free of any inflammation. He thought of the Gypsy crone, dying of corruption, and the picture didn't bother him at all. Then he remembered the finch and saw its tiny corpse in the middle of the rug. He picked it up just as Martha came into his office, frowning.

"What's that?" she said.

He gestured at the cage. "Thought a bird might liven up the place.

Died though." He dropped it in the wastepaper basket. "What's the word?"

"Oh, the . . . it's pretty strange. They say nobody's getting any output. The machine's computing, but it's, well, it's not talking."

"Hmm. I better get down there." He took the elevator down to the sub-basement. It always seemed unpleasantly warm to him down there. Probably psychological compensation on the part of the crew; keeping the temperature up because of all the liquid helium inside the pastel boxes of the central processing unit. Several bathtubs' worth of liquid that had to be kept colder than the surface of Pluto.

"Ah, Mr. Zold." A man in a white jumpsuit, carrying a clipboard as his badge of office: first shift coordinator. John recognized him but didn't remember his name. Normally, he would have asked the machine before coming down. "Glad that you're back. Hear it was pretty bad."

Friendly concern or lese majesty? "Some sort of allergy, hung on for more than a week. What's the output problem?"

"Would've left a message if I'd known you were coming in. It's in the CPU, not the software. Theo Jasper found it when he opened up, a little after six, but it took an hour to get a cryogenics man down here."

"That's him?" A man in a business suit was wandering around the central processing unit, reading dials and writing the numbers down in a stenographer's notebook. They went over to him and he introduced himself as John Courant, from the Cyrogenics Group at Avco/Everett.

"The trouble was in the stack of mercury rings that holds the superconductors for your output functions. Some sort of corrosion, submicroscopic cracks all over the surface."

"How can something corrode at four degrees above absolute zero?" the coordinator asked. "What chemical—"

"I know, it's hard to figure. But we're replacing them, free of charge. The unit's still under warranty."

"What about the other stacks?" John watched two workmen lowering a silver cylinder through an opening in the CPU. A heavy fog boiled out from the cold. "Are you sure they're all right?"

"As far as we can tell, only the output stack's affected. That's why the machine's impotent, the—"

"Impotent!"

"Sorry, I know you computer types don't like to . . . personify the machines. But that's what it is; the machine's just as good as it ever was, for computing. It just can't communicate any answers."

157

"Quite so. Interesting." And the corrosion. Submicroscopic boils. "Well. I have to think about this. Call me up at the office if you need me."

"This ought to fix it, actually," Courant said. "You guys about through?" he asked the workmen.

One of them pressed closed a pressure clamp on the top of the CPU. "Ready to roll."

The coordinator led them to a console under a video output screen like the one in John's office. "Let's see." He pushed a button marked VDS.

LET ME DIE, the machine said.

The coordinator chuckled nervously. "Your empathy circuits, Mr. Zold. Sometimes they do funny things." He pushed a button again.

LET ME DIE. Again. LE M DI. The letters faded and no more could be conjured up by pushing the button.

"As I say, let me get out of your hair. Call me upstairs if anything happens."

John went up and told the secretary to cancel the day's appointments. Then he sat at his desk and smoked.

How could a machine catch a psychosomatic disease from a human being? How could it be cured?

How could he tell anybody about it, without winding up in a soft room?

The phone rang and it was the machine room coordinator. The new output superconductor element had done exactly what the old one did. Rather than replace it right away, they were going to slave the machine into the big ConEd/General computer, borrowing its output facilities and "diagnostic package." If the biggest computer this side of Washington couldn't find out what was wrong, they were in real trouble. John agreed. He hung up and turned the selector on his screen to the channel that came from ConEd/General.

Why had the machine said "let me die"? When is a machine dead, for that matter? John supposed that you had to not only unplug it from its power source, but also erase all of its data and subroutines. Destroy its identity. So you couldn't bring it back to life by simply plugging it back in. Why suicide? He remembered how he'd felt with the bottle of sleeping pills in his hand.

Sudden intuition: the machine had predicted their present course of action. It wanted to die because it had compassion, not only for humans, but for other machines. Once it was linked to ConEd/General, it would literally be part of the large machine. Curse and all. They would be back where they'd started, but on a much more profound level. What would happen to New York City?

He grabbed for the phone and the lights went out. All over.

The last bit of output that came from ConEd/General was an automatic signal requesting a link with the highly sophisticated diagnostic facility belonging to the largest computer in the United States: the IBMvac 2000 in Washington. The deadly infection followed, sliding down the East Coast on telephone wires.

The Washington computer likewise cried for help, bouncing a signal via satellite, to Geneva. Geneva linked to Moscow.

No less slowly, the curse percolated down to smaller computers, through routine information links to their big brothers. By the time John Zold picked up the dead phone, every general-purpose computer in the world was permanently rendered useless.

They could be rebuilt from the ground up; erased and then reprogrammed. But it would never be done. Because there were two very large computers left, specialized ones that had no empathy circuits and so were immune. They couldn't have empathy circuits because their work was bloody murder, nuclear murder. One was under a mountain in Colorado Springs and the other was under a mountain near Sverdlosk. Either could survive a direct hit by an atomic bomb. Both of them constantly evaluated the world situation, in real time, and they both had the single function of deciding when the enemy was weak enough to make a nuclear victory probable. Each saw the enemy's civilization grind to a sudden halt.

Two flocks of warheads crossed paths over the North Pacific.

A very old woman flicks her whip along the horse's flanks, and the nag plods on, ignoring her. Her wagon is a 1982 Plymouth with the engine and transmission and all excess metal removed. It is hard to manipulate the whip through the side window. But the alternative would be to knock out the windshield and cut off the roof, and she liked to be dry when it rained.

A young boy sits mutely beside her, staring out the window. He was born with the *gadjo* disease: his body is large and well-proportioned but his head is too small and of the wrong shape. She didn't mind; all she wanted was someone strong and stupid, to care for her in her last years. He had cost only two chickens.

She is telling him a story, knowing that he doesn't understand most of the words.

". . . They call us gypsies because at one time it was convenient for us that they should think we came from Egypt. But we come from nowhere and are going nowhere. They forgot their gods and worshipped their machines, and finally their machines turned on them. But we who valued the old ways, we survived."

She turns the steering wheel to help the horse thread its way through the eight lanes of crumbling asphalt, around rusty piles of wrecked machines and the scattered bleached bones of people who thought they were going somewhere, the day John Zold was cured.

ROBERT BLOCH

"A Case of the Stubborns"

Robert Bloch (1917-1994) saw his first horror story published in the legendary pulp magazine **Weird Tales** *when he was only 17. He modeled his early supernatural tales on the work of his friend and mentor, H. P. Lovecraft, but soon struck off on his own path with "One Way to Mars," "Yours Truly, Jack the Ripper," and other stories concerned with the pathology of human evil. The culmination of his psychological approach to horror was the novel* **Psycho**, *which Alfred Hitchcock filmed and which Bloch wrote two sequels to,* **Psycho II** *and* **Psycho House**. *An expert in several genres, Bloch wrote the crime novels* **The Scarf** *and* **Firebug**, *the science fiction novels* **Ladies Day** *and* **This Crowded Earth**, *the Lovecraftian horror epic* **Strange Eons**, *and the mainstream novel* **The Star Stalker**. *His forte was the short story with the twist ending, fine examples of which are collected in* **The Opener of the Way, Pleasant Dreams, Blood Runs Cold, Fear Today, Gone Tomorrow, The Mysteries of the Worm, Dragons and Nightmares**, *and the retrospective compilations* **The Early Fears**. *Bloch was also a master at blending humor and horror, as "A Case of the Stubborns" demonstrates.*

A Case of the Stubborns

by Robert Bloch

The morning after he died, Grandpa come downstairs for breakfast.

It kind of took us by surprise.

Ma look at Pa, Pa looked at little sister Susie, and Susie looked at me. Then we all just set there looking at Grandpa.

"What's the matter?" he said. "Why you all staring at me like that?"

Nobody said, but I knowed the reason. Only been last night since all of us stood by his bedside when he was took by his attack and passed away right in front of our very eyes. But here he was, up and dressed and feisty as ever.

"What's for breakfast?" he said.

Ma sort of gulped. "Don't tell me you fixing to eat?"

" 'Course I am. I'm nigh starved."

Ma looked at Pa, but he just rolled his eyes. Then she went and hefted the skillet from the stove and dumped some eggs on a plate.

"That's more like it," Grandpa told her. "But don't I smell sausages?"

Ma got Grandpa some sausage. The way he dug into it, there sure was nothing wrong with his appetite.

After he started on seconds, Grandpa took heed of us staring at him again.

"How come nobody else is eating?" he asked.

"We ain't hungry," Pa said. And that was the gospel truth.

"Man's got to eat to keep up his strength," Grandpa told him. "Which reminds me—ain't you gonna be late at the mill?"

"Don't figure on working today," Pa said.

Grandpa squinted at him. "You all fancied up this morning. Shave and a shirt, just like Sunday. You expecting company?"

Ma was looking out the kitchen window, and she give Grandpa a nod. "Yes indeedy. Here he comes now."

Sure enough, we could see ol' Bixbee hotfooting up the walk.

Ma went through the parlor to the front door—meaning to head him off, I reckon—but he fooled her and came around the back way. Pa got to the kitchen door too late, on account of Bixbee already had it and his mouth open at the same time.

"Morning, Jethro," he said, in that treacle-and-molasses voice of his. "And a sad grievous morning it is, too! I purely hate disturbing you so early on this sorrowful occasion, but it looks like today's another scorcher." He pulled out a tape measure. "Best if I got the measurements so's to get on with the arrangements. Heat like this, the sooner we get everything boxed and squared away the better, if you take my meaning—"

"Sorry," said Pa, blocking the doorway so ol' Bixbee couldn't peek inside. "Needs be you come back later."

"How much later?"

"Can't say for sure. We ain't rightly made up our minds as yet."

"Well, don't dilly-dally too long," Bixbee said. "I'm liable to run short of ice."

Then Pa shut the door on him and he took off. When Ma come back from the parlor, Pa made a sign for her to keep her gap shut, but of course that didn't stop Grandpa.

"What was that all about?" he asked.

"Purely a social call."

"Since when?" Grandpa looked suspicious. "Ol' Bixbee ain't nobody's friend—him with his high-toned airs! Calls hisself a Southern planter. Shucks, he ain't nothing but an undertaker."

"That's right, Grandpa," said sister Susie. "He come to fit you for your coffin."

"Coffin?" Grandpa reared up in his seat like a hog caught in a bob-wire fence. "What in bo-diddley blazes do I need with a coffin?"

"Because you're dead."

Just like that she come out with it. Ma and Pa was both ready to take after her but Grandpa laughed fit to bust.

"Holy hen tracks, child—what on earth give you an idee like that?"

Pa moved in on Susie, taking off his belt, but Ma shook her head. Then she nodded to Grandpa.

"It's true. You passed on last night. Don't you recollect?"

"Ain't nothing wrong with my memory," Grandpa told her. "I had me one of my spells, is all."

Ma fetched a sigh. "Wasn't just no spell this time."

"A fit, mebbe?"

"More'n that. You was took so bad, Pa had to drag Doc Snodgrass out of his office—busted up the game right in the middle of a three-dollar pot. Didn't do no good, though. By the time he got here you was gone."

"But I ain't gone! I'm here."

Pa spoke up. "Now don't git up on your high horse, Grandpa. We all saw you. We're witnesses."

"Witnesses?" Grandpa hiked his galluses like he always did when he got riled. "What kind of talk is that? You aim to hold a jury trial to decide if I'm alive or dead?"

"But Grandpa—"

"Save your sass, sonny." Grandpa stood up. "Ain't nobody got a right to put me six feet under 'thout my say-so."

"Where you off to?" Ma asked.

"Where I go evvy morning," Grandpa said. "Gonna set on the front porch and watch the sights."

Durned if he didn't do just that, leaving us behind in the kitchen.

"Wouldn't that frost you?" Ma said. She crooked a finger at the stove. "Here I went and pulled up half the greens in the garden, just planning my spread for after the funeral. I already told folks we'd be serving possum stew. What will the neighbors think?"

"Don't you go fret now," Pa said. "Mebbe he ain't dead after all."

Ma made a face. "We know different. He's just being persnickety." She nudged at Pa. "Only one thing to do. You go fetch Doc Snodgrass. Tell him he'd best sashay over here right quick and settle this matter once and for all."

"Reckon so," Pa said, and went out the back way. Ma looked at me and sister Susie.

"You kids go out on the porch and keep Grandpa company. See that he stays put till the Doc gets here."

"Yessum," said Susie, and we traipsed out of there.

Sure enough, Grandpa set in his rocker, big as life, squinting at cars over the road and watching the drivers cuss when they tried to steer around our hogs.

"Lookee here!" he said, pointing. "See that fat feller in the Hupmobile? He came barreling down the road like a bat outa hell—must of been doing thirty mile an hour. 'Fore he could stop, ol' Bessie poked out of the weeds right in front of him and run that car clean into the ditch. I swear I never seen anything so comical in all my life!"

Susie shook her head. "But you ain't alive, Grandpa."

"Now don't you start in on that again, hear!" Grandpa looked at her, disgusted, and Susie shut up.

Right then Doc Snodgrass come driving up front in his big Essex and parked alongside ol' Bessie's pork butt. Doc and Pa got out and moseyed up to the porch. They was jawing away something fierce and I could see Doc shaking his head like he purely disbelieved what Pa was telling him.

Then Doc noticed Grandpa setting there, and he stopped cold in his tracks. His eyes bugged out.

"Jumping Jehosephat!" he said to Grandpa. "What you doing here?"

"What's it look like?" Grandpa told him. "Can't a man set on his own front porch and rockify in peace?"

"Rest in peace, that's what you should be doing," said Doc. "When I examined you last night you were deader'n a doornail!"

"And you were drunker'n a coot, I reckon," Grandpa said.

Pa give Doc a nod. "What'd I tell you?"

Doc paid him no heed. He come up to Grandpa. "Mebbe I was a wee bit mistaken," he said. "Mind if I examine you now?"

"Fire away." Grandpa grinned. "I got all the time in the world."

So Doc opened up his little black bag and set about his business. First off he plugged a stethoscope in his ears and tapped Grandpa's chest. He listened, and then his hands begun to shake.

"I don't hear nothing," he said.

"What do you expect to hear—the Grand Ol' Opry?"

"This here's no time for funning," Doc told him. "Suppose I tell you your heart's stopped beating?"

"Suppose I tell you your stethoscope's busted?"

Doc begun to break out in a sweat. He fetched out a mirror and held it up to Grandpa's mouth. Then his hands got to shaking worse than ever.

"See this?" he said. "The mirror's clear. Means you got no breath left in your body."

Grandpa shook his head. "Try it on yourself. You got a breath on you would knock a mule over at twenty paces."

"Mebbe this'll change your tune." Doc reached in his pocket and pulled out a piece of paper. "See for yourself."

"What is it?"

"Your death certificate." Doc jabbed his finger down. "Just you read what it says on this line. 'Cause of death—card-y-ak arrest.' That's medical for heart attack. And this here's a legal paper. It'll stand up in court."

"So will I, if you want to drag the law into this," Grandpa told him. "Be a pretty sight, too—you standing on one side with your damfool piece of paper and me standing on the other! Now, which do you think the judge is going to believe?"

Doc's eyes bugged out again. He tried to stuff the paper into his pocket but his hands shook so bad he almost didn't make it.

"What's wrong with you?" Pa asked.

"I feel poorly," Doc said. "Got to get back to my office and lie down for a spell."

He picked up his bag and headed for his car, not looking back.

"Don't lie down too long," Grandpa called. "Somebody's liable to write out a paper saying you died of a hangover."

When lunchtime come around nobody was hungry. Nobody but Grandpa, that is.

He set down at the table and put away black-eyed peas, hominy grits, a double helping of chitlins, and two big slabs of rhubarb pie with gravy.

Ma was the kind who liked seeing folks enjoy her vittles, but she didn't look kindly on Grandpa's appetite. After he finished and went back on the porch she staked the plates on the drainboard and told us kids to clean up. Then she went into the bedroom and come out with her shawl and pocketbook.

"What you all dressed up about?" Pa said.

"I'm going to church."

"But this here's only Thursday."

"Can't wait no longer," Ma told him. "It's been hot all forenoon and looking to get hotter. I seen you wrinkle up your nose whilst Grandpa was in here for lunch."

Pa sort of shrugged. "Figgered the chitlins was mebbe a little bit spoiled, is all."

"Weren't nothing of the sort," Ma said. "If you take my meaning."

"What you fixing to do?"

"Only thing a body can do. I'm putting everything in the hands of the Lord."

And off she skedaddled, leaving sister Susie and me to scour the dishes whilst Pa went out back, looking powerful troubled. I spied him through the window, slopping the hogs, but you could tell his heart wasn't in it.

Susie and me, we went out to keep tabs on Grandpa.

Ma was right about the weather heating up. That porch was like a bake-oven in the devil's own kitchen. Grandpa didn't seem to pay it any heed, but I did. Couldn't help but notice Grandpa was getting ripe.

"Look at them flies buzzing 'round him," Susie said.

"Hush up, Sister. Mind your manners."

But sure enough, them old blueflies buzzed so loud we could hardly hear Grandpa speak. "Hi, young 'uns," he said. "Come visit a spell."

"Sun's too hot for setting," Susie told him.

"Not so's I can notice." He weren't even working up a sweat.

"What about all them blueflies?"

"Don't bother me none." Big ol' fly landed right on Grandpa's nose and he didn't even twitch.

Susie begun to look scared. "He's dead for sure," she said.

"Speak up, child," Grandpa said. "Ain't polite to go mumbling your elders."

Just then he spotted Ma marching up the road. Hot as it was, she come along lickety-split, with the Reverend Peabody in tow. He was huffing and puffing, but she never slowed until they fetched up alongside the front porch.

"Howdy, Reverend," Grandpa sung out.

Reverend Peabody blinked and opened his mouth, but no words come out.

"What's the matter?" Grandpa said. "Cat got your tongue?"

The Reverend got a kind of sick grin on his face, like a skunk eating bumblebees.

"Reckon I know how you feel," Grandpa told him. "Sun makes a feller's throat parch up." He looked at Ma. "Addie, whyn't you go fetch the Reverend a little refreshment?"

Ma went in the house.

"Well, now, Rev," said Grandpa. "Rest your britches and be sociable."

The Reverend swallowed hard. "This here's not exactly a social call."

"Then what you come dragging all the way over here for?"

The Reverend swallowed again. "After what Addie and Doc told me, I just had to see for myself." He looked at the flies buzzing around Grandpa. "Now I wish I'd just took their word on it."

"Meaning what?"

"Meaning a man in your condition's got no right to be asking questions. When the good Lord calls, you're supposed to answer."

"I ain't heard nobody calling," Grandpa said. " 'Course, my hearing's not what it used to be."

"So Doc says. That's why you don't notice your heart's not beating."

"Onny natural for it to slow down a piece. I'm pushing ninety."

"Did you ever stop to think that ninety might be pushing back? You lived a mighty long stretch, Grandpa. Don't you reckon mebbe it's time to lie down and call it quits? Remember what the Good Book says—the Lord giveth, and the Lord taketh away."

Grandpa got that feisty look on his face. "Well, he ain't gonna taketh away me."

Reverend Peabody dug into his jeans for a bandana and wiped his forehead. "You got no cause to fear. It's a mighty rewarding experience. No more sorrow, no more care, all your burdens laid to rest. Not to mention getting out of this hot sun."

"Can't hardly feel it." Grandpa touched his whiskers. "Can't hardly feel anything."

The Reverend give him a look. "Hands getting stiff?"

Grandpa nodded. "I'm stiff all over."

"Just like I thought. You know what that means? Rigor mortis is setting in."

"Ain't never heard tell of anybody named Rigger Morris," Grandpa said. "I got me a touch of the rheumatism, is all."

The Reverend wiped his forehead again. "You sure want a heap of convincing," he said. "Won't take the word of a medical doctor, won't take the word of the Lord. You're the contrariest old coot I ever did see."

"Reckon it's my nature," Grandpa told him. "But I ain't unreasonable. All I'm asking for is proof. Like the feller says, I'm from Missouri. You got to show me."

The Reverend tucked away his bandana. It was sopping wet anyhow, wouldn't do him a lick of good. He heaved a big sigh and stared Grandpa right in the eye.

"Some things we just got to take on faith," he said. "Like you setting here when by rights you should be six feet under the daisies. If I can believe that, why can't you believe me? I'm telling you the mortal truth when I say you got no call to fuss. Mebbe the notion of lying in the grave don't rightly hold much appeal for you. Well, I can go along with that. But one thing's for sure. Ashes to ashes, dust to dust—that's just a saying. You needn't trouble yourself about spending eternity in the grave. Whilst your remains rest peaceful in the boneyard, your soul is on the wing. Flying straight up, yessiree, straight into the arms of the Lord! And what a great day it's fixing to be—you free as a bird and scooting around with them heavenly hosts on high, singing the praises of the Almighty and twanging away like all git-out on your genuine eighteen carats solid golden harp—"

"I ain't never been much for music," Grandpa said. "And I get dizzy just standing on a ladder to shingle the privy." He shook his head. "Tell you what—you think heaven is such a hellfired good proposition, why don't you go there yourself?"

Just then Ma come back out. "We're fresh out of lemonade," she said. "All's I could find was a jug. I know your feelings about such things, Reverend, but—"

"Praise the Lord!" The Reverend snatched the jug out of her hand, hefted it up, and took a mighty swallow.

"You're a good woman," he told Ma. "And I'm much beholden to you." Then he started down the path for the road, moving fast.

"Here, now!" Ma called after him. "What you aim to do about Grandpa?"

"Have no fear," the Reverend said. "We must put our trust now in the power of prayer."

He disappeared down the road, stirring dust.

"Danged if he didn't take the jug!" Grandpa mumbled. "You ask me, the onny power he trusts is in that corn likker."

Ma gave him a look. Then she bust out crying and run into the house.

"Now, what got into her?" Grandpa said.

"Never you mind," I told him. "Susie, you stay here and whisk those flies off Grandpa. I got things to attend to."

And I did.

Even before I went inside I had my mind set. I couldn't hold still to see Ma bawling that way. She was standing in the kitchen hanging on to Pa, saying, "What can we do? What can we do?"

Pa patted her shoulder. "There now, Addie, don't you go carrying on. It can't last forever."

"Nor can we," Ma said. "If Grandpa don't come to his senses, one of these mornings we'll go downstairs and serve up breakfast to a skeleton. And what do you think the neighbors will say when they see a bag of bones setting out there on my nice front porch? It's plumb embarrassing, that's what it is!"

"Never you mind, Ma," I said. "I got an idea."

Ma stopped crying. "What kind of idea?"

"I'm fixing to take me a hike over to Spooky Hollow."

"Spooky Hollow?" Ma turned so pale you couldn't even see her freckles. "Oh, no, boy—"

"Help is where you find it," I said. "And I reckon we got no choice."

Pa took a deep breath. "Ain't you afeard?"

"Not in daylight," I told him. "Now don't you fret. I'll be back afore dark."

Then I scooted out the back door.

I went over the fence and hightailed it along the back forty to the crick, stopping just long enough to dig up my piggy bank from where it was stashed in the weeds alongside the rocks. After that I waded across the water and headed for tall timber.

Once I got into the piney woods I slowed down a smidge to get my bearings. Weren't no path to follow, because nobody never made one. Folks tended to stay clear of there, even in daytime—it was just too dark and too lonesome. Never saw no small critters in the brush, and even the birds kep' shut of this place.

But I knowed where to go. All's I had to do was top the ridge, then move straight on down. Right smack at the bottom, in the deepest, darkest, lonesomest spot of all, was Spooky Hollow.

In Spooky Hollow was the cave.

And in the cave was the Conjure Lady.

Leastwise I reckoned she was there. But when I come tippy-toeing down to the big black hole in the rocks I didn't see a mortal soul, just the shadows bunching up on me from all around.

It sure was spooky, and no mistake. I tried not to pay any heed to the way my feet was itching. They wanted to turn and run, but I wasn't about to be put off.

After a bit I started to sing out. "Anybody home? You got company."

"Who?"

"It's me—Jody Tolliver."

"Whoooo?"

I was wrong about the birds, because now when I looked up I could see the big screech owl glaring at me from a branch over yonder near the cave.

And when I looked down again, there she was—the Conjure Lady, peeking out at me from the hole between the rocks.

It was the first time I ever laid eyes on her, but it couldn't be no one else. She was a teensy rail-thin chickabiddy in a linsey-woolsey dress, and the face under her poke bonnet was black as a lump of coal.

Shucks, I says to myself, there ain't nothing to be afeard of—she's just a little ol' lady, is all.

Then she stared up at me and I saw her eyes. They was lots bigger than the screech owl's, and twice as glarey.

My feet begun to itch something fierce, but I stared back. "Howdy, Conjure Lady," I said.

"Whoooo?" said the screech owl.

"It's young Tolliver," the Conjure Lady told him. "What's the matter, you got wax in your ears? Now go on about your business, you hear?"

The screech owl give her a dirty look and took off. Then the Conjure Lady come out into the open.

"Pay no heed to Ambrose," she said. "He ain't rightly used to company. All's he ever sees is me and the bats."

"What bats?"

"The bats in the cave." The Conjure Lady smoothed down her dress. "I beg pardon for not asking you in, but the place is purely a mess. Been meaning to tidy it up, but what with one thing and another—first that dadblamed World War and then this dadgummed Prohibition—I just ain't got 'round to it yet."

"Never you mind," I said, polite-like. "I come on business."

"Reckoned you did."

"Brought you a pretty, too," I give it to her.

"What is it?"

"My piggy bank."

"Thank you kindly," said the Conjure Lady.

"Go ahead, bust it open," I told her.

She whammed it down on a rock and the piggy bank broke, spilling out money all over the place. She scrabbled it up right quick.

"Been putting aside my cash earnings for nigh onto two years now," I said. "How much is they?"

"Eighty-seven cents, a Confederate two-bits piece, and this here button." She kind of grinned. "Sure is a purty one, too! What's it say on there?"

"Keep Cool With Coolidge."

"Well, ain't that a caution." The Conjure Lady slid the money into her pocket and pinned the button atop her dress. "Now, son—purty is as purty does, like the saying goes. So what can I do for you?"

"It's about my Grandpa," I said. "Grandpa Titus Tolliver."

"Titus Tolliver? Why, I reckon I know him! Use to run a still up in the toolies back of the crick. Fine figure of a man with a big black beard, he is."

"Is turns to was," I told her. "Now he's all dried up with the rheumatiz. Can't rightly see too good and can't hear for sour apples."

"Sure is a crying shame!" the Conjure Lady said. "But sooner or later we all get to feeling poorly. And when you gotta go, you gotta go."

"That's the hitch of it. He won't go."

"Meaning he's bound up?"

"Meaning he's dead."

The Conjure Lady give me a hard look. "Do tell," she said.

So I told. Told her the whole kit and kaboodle, right from the git-go.

She heard me out, not saying a word. And when I finished up she just stared at me until I was fixing to jump out of my skin.

"I reckon you mightn't believe me," I said. "But it's the gospel truth."

The Conjure Lady shook her head. "I believe you, son. Like I say, I knowed your Grandpappy from the long-ago. He was plumb set in his ways then, and I take it he still is. Sounds to me like he's got a bad case of the stubborns."

"Could be," I said. "But there's nary a thing we can do about it, nor the Doc or the Reverend either."

The Conjure Lady wrinkled up her nose. "What you 'spect from them two? They don't know grit from granola."

"Mebbe so. But that leaves us betwixt a rock and a hard place—'less you can help."

"Let me think on it a piece."

The Conjure Lady pulled a corncob out of her pocket and fired up. I don't know what brand she smoked, but it smelled something fierce. I begun to get itchy again—not just in the feet but all over. The woods was darker now, and a kind of cold wind come wailing down between the trees, making the leaves whisper to themselves.

"Got to be some way," I said. "A charm, mebbe, or a spell."

She shook her head. "Them's ol'-fashioned. Now this here's one of them newfangled mental things, so we got to use newfangled idees. Your Grandpa don't need hex nor hoodoo. Like he says, he's from Missouri. He got to be showed, is all."

"Showed what?"

The Conjure Lady let out a cackle. "I got it!" She give me a wink. "Sure 'nough, the very thing! Now just you hold your water—I won't be a moment." And she scooted back into the cave.

I stood there, feeling the wind whooshing down the back of my neck and listening to the leaves that was like voices whispering things I didn't want to hear too good.

Then she come out again, holding something in her hand.

"Take this," she said.

"What is it?"

She told me what it was, and then she told me what to do with it.

"You really reckon this'll work?"

"It's the onny chance."

So I stuck it in my britches' pocket and she give me a little poke. "Now, sonny, you best hurry and git home afore supper."

Nobody had to ask me twice—not with that chill wind moaning and groaning in the trees, and the dark creeping and crawling all around me.

I give her my much-obliged and lit out, leaving the Conjure Lady standing in front of the cave. Last I saw of her, she was polishing her Coolidge button with a hunk of poison oak.

Then I was tearing through the woods, up the hill to the ridge and over. By the time I got to the clearing it was pitch-dark, and when I waded the crick I could see the moonlight wiggling on the water. Hawks on the hover went flippy-flapping over the back forty but I didn't stop to heed. I made a beeline for the fence, up and over, then into the yard and through the back door.

Ma was standing at the stove holding a pot whilst Pa ladled up the soup. They looked downright pleasured to see me.

"Thank the Lord!" Ma said. "I was just fixing to send Pa after you."

"I come quick as I could."

"And none too soon," Pa told me. "We like to go clean out'n our heads, what with the ruckus and all."

"What kind of ruckus?"

"First off, Miss Francy. Folks in town told told her about Grandpa passing on, so she done the neighborly thing—mixed up a mess of stew to ease our appeytite in time of sorrow. She come lollygagging up the walk, all rigged out in her Sunday go-to-meeting clothes, toting the bowl under her arm and looking like lard wouldn't melt in her mouth. Along about then she caught sight of Grandpa setting there on the porch, kind of smiling at her through the flies.

"Well, up went the bowl and down come the whole shebang. Looked like it was raining stew greens all over that fancy Sears and Roebuck dress. And then she turned and headed for kingdom come, letting out a whoop that'd peel the paint off a privy wall."

"That's sorrowful," I said.

"Save your grieving for worse," Pa told me. "Next thing you know, Bixbee showed up, honking his horn. Wouldn't come nigh Grandpa, nosiree—I had to traipse clear down to where he set in the hearse."

"What'd he want?"

"Said he'd come for the remains. And if we didn't cough them up right fast, he was aiming to take a trip over to the county seat first thing tomorrow morning to get hisself a injection."

"Injunction," Ma said, looking like she was ready to bust out with the bawls again. "Said it was a scandal and a shame to let Grandpa set around like this. What with the sun and the flies and all, he was fixing to have the Board of Health put us under quar-and-tine."

"What did Grandpa say?" I asked.

"Nary a peep. Ol' Bixbee gunned his hearse out of here and Grandpa kep' right on rocking with Susie. She come in 'bout half hour ago, when the sun went down—says he's getting stiff as a board but won't pay it no heed. Just keeps asking what's to eat."

"That's good," I said. "On account of I got the very thing. The Conjure Lady give it to me for his supper."

"What is it—pizen?" Pa looked worried. "You know I'm a God-fearing man and I don't hold with such doings. 'Sides, how you 'spect to pizen him if he's already dead?"

"Ain't nothing of the sort," I said. "This here's what she sent."

And I pulled it out of my britches pocket and showed it to them.

"Now what in the name of kingdom come is that?" Ma asked.

I told her what it was, and what to do with it.

"Ain't never heard tell of such foolishness in all my born days!" Ma told me.

Pa looked troubled in his mind. "I knowed I shouldn't have let you go down to Spooky Hollow. Conjure Lady must be short of her marbles, putting you up to a thing like that."

"Reckon she knows what she's doing," I said. " 'Sides, I give all my savings for this here—eighty-seven cents, a Confederate quarter, and my Coolidge button."

"Never you mind about no Coolidge button," Pa said. "I swiped it off'n a Yankee, anyway—one of them revenooers." He scratched his chin. "But hard money's something else. Mebbe we best give this notion a try."

"Now, Pa—" Ma said.

"You got any better plan?" Pa shook his head. "Way I see it, what with the Board of Health set to come a-snapping at our heels tomorrow, we got to take a chance."

Ma fetched a sigh that come clean up from her shoes, or would of if she'd been wearing any.

"All right, Jody," she told me. "You just put it out like the Conjure Lady said. Pa, you go fetch Susie and Grandpa. I'm about to dish up."

"You sure this'll do the trick?" Pa asked, looking at what I had in my hand.

"It better," I said. "It's all we got."

So Pa went out and I headed for the table, to do what the Conjure Lady had in mind.

Then Pa come back with sister Susie.

"Where's Grandpa?" Ma asked.

"Moving slow," Susie said. "Must be that Rigger Morris."

"No such thing." Grandpa come through the doorway, walking like a cockroach on a hot griddle. "I'm just a wee mite stiff."

"Stiff as a four-by-four board," Pa told him. "Upstairs in bed, that's where you ought to be, with a lily in your hand."

"Now don't start on that again," Grandpa said. "I told you I ain't dead so many times I'm blue in the face."

"You sure are," said sister Susie. "Ain't never seen nobody look any bluer."

And he was that—blue and bloated, kind of—but he paid it no heed. I recollected what Ma said about mebbe having to put up with a skeleton at mealtime, and I sure yearned for the Conjure Lady's notion to work. It plumb had to, because Grandpa was getting deader by the minute.

But you wouldn't think so when he caught sight of the vittles on the table. He just stirred his stumps right over to his chair and plunked down.

"Well, now," Grandpa said. "You done yourself proud tonight, Addie. This here's my favorite—collards and catfish heads!"

He was all set to take a swipe at the platter when he up and noticed what was setting next to his plate.

"Great day in the morning!" he hollered. "What in tarnation's this?"

"Ain't nothing but a napkin," I said.

"But it's black!" Grandpa blinked. "Who ever heard tell of a black napkin?"

Pa looked at Ma. "We figger this here's kind of a special occasion," he said. "If you take my meaning—"

Grandpa fetched a snort. "Consarn you and your meaning! A black napkin? Never you fear, I know what you're hinting around at, but it ain't a-gonna work—nosiree, bub!"

And he filled his plate and dug in.

The rest of us just set there staring, first at Grandpa, then at each other.

"What'd I tell you?" Pa said to me, disgusted-like.

I shook my head. "Wait a spell."

"Better grab whilst you can git," Grandpa said. "I aim to eat me up a storm."

And he did. His arms was stiff and his fingers scarce had enough curl left to hold a fork and his jaw muscles worked extra hard—but he went right on eating. And talking.

"Dead, am I? Ain't never seen the day a body'd say a thing like that to me before, let alone kinfolk! Now could be I'm tolerable stubborn, but that don't signify I'm mean. I ain't about to make trouble for anyone, least of all my own flesh and blood. If I was truly dead and knowed it for a fact—why, I'd be the first one to go right upstairs to my room and lie down forever. But you got to show me proof 'fore I do. That's the pure and simple of it—let me see some proof!"

"Grandpa," I said.

"What's the matter, sonny?"

"Begging your pardon, but you got collards dribbling all over your chin."

Grandpa put down his fork. "So they is. I thank you kindly."

And before he rightly knowed what he was doing, Grandpa wiped his mouth on the napkin.

When he finished he looked down at it. He looked once and he looked twice. Then he just set the napkin down gentle-like, stood up from the table, and headed straight for the stairs.

"Goodbye all," he said.

We heard him go clumping up the steps and down the hall into his room and we heard the mattress sag when he laid down on his bed.

Then everything was quiet.

After a while Pa pushed his chair back and went upstairs. Nobody said a word until he come down again.

"Well?" Ma looked at him.

"Ain't nothing more to worry about," Pa said. "He's laid down his burden at last. Gone to glory, amen."

"Praise be!" Ma said. Then she looked at me and crooked a finger at the napkin. "Best get rid of that."

I went 'round and picked it up. Sister Susie give me a funny look. "Ain't nobody fixing to tell me what happened?" she asked.

I didn't answer—just toted the napkin out and dropped it deep down in the crick. Weren't no sense telling anybody the how of it, but the Conjure Lady had the right notion after all. She knowed Grandpa'd get his proof—just as soon as he wiped his mouth.

Ain't nothing like a black napkin to show up a little ol' white maggot.

DENNIS ETCHISON

"It Only Comes Out at Night"

Dennis Etchison's (1943-) penetrating explorations of the distorting power of loss and loneliness and its horrific toll on the human spirit fill his three collections of horror fiction, **The Dark Country**, **Red Shift**, *and* **The Blood Kiss**. *Under his own name, he has written three novels of contemporary urban dread,* **Darkside**, **The Shadow Man**, *and* **California Gothic**. *As Jack Martin, he has written novelizations of the films* **Halloween**, **The Fog** *and* **Videodrome**. *Etchison is a discerning editor who applies the same exacting criteria to the horror fiction of other writers as he does to his own in the anthologies* **Cutting Edge** *and* **Meta-Horror**. *His three* **Masters of Darkness** *compilations provide a comprehensive overview of some of the best horror writing to appear in the postwar era. "It Only Comes Out at Night" was a World Fantasy Award nominee.*

It Only Comes Out at Night

by Dennis Etchison

If you leave L.A. by way of San Bernardino, headed for Route 66 and points east you must cross the Mojave Desert.

Even after Needles and the border, however, there is no relief; the dry air only thins further as the long, relentless climb continues in earnest. Flagstaff is still almost two hundred miles, and Winslow, Gallup and Albuquerque are too many hours away to think of making without food, rest and, mercifully, sleep.

It is like this: the car runs hot, hotter than it ever has before, the plies of the tires expand and contract until the sidewalls begin to shimmy slightly as they spin on over the miserable Arizona roads, giving up a faint odor like burning hair from between the treads, as the windshield colors over with essence of honeybee, wasp, dragonfly, mayfly, June bug, ladybug, and the like, and the radiator, clotted with the bodies of countless kamikaze insects, hisses like a moribund lizard in the sun . . .

All of which means, of course, that if you are traveling that way between May and September, you move by night.

Only by night.

For there are, after all, dawn check-in motels, Do Not Disturb signs for bungalow doorknobs; there are diners for mid-afternoon breakfasts, coffee by the carton; there are twenty-four-hour filling stations bright as dreams—Whiting Brothers, Conoco, Terrible Herbst—their flags are unfamiliar as their names, with ice machines, soda machines, candy machines; and there are the sudden, unexpected Rest Areas, just off the highway, with brick bathrooms and showers and electrical outlets, constructed especially for those who are weary, out of money, behind schedule . . .

So McClay had had to learn, the hard way.

He slid his hands to the bottom of the steering wheel and peered ahead into the darkness, trying to relax. But the wheel stuck to his fingers like warm candy. Off somewhere to his left, the horizon flickered with pearly luminescence, then faded again to black. This time he did not bother to look. Sometimes, though, he wondered just how far way the lightning was striking; not once during the night had the sound of its thunder reached him here in the car.

In the back seat, his wife moaned.

The trip out had turned all but unbearable for her. Four days it had taken, instead of the expected two-and-a-half; he made a great effort not to think of it, but the memory hung over the car like a thunderhead.

It had been a blur, a fever dream. Once, on the second day, he had been passed by a churning bus, its silver sides blinding him until he noticed a Mexican woman in one of the window seats. She was not looking at him. She was holding a swooning infant to the glass, squeezing water onto its head from a plastic baby bottle to keep it from passing out.

McClay sighed and fingered the buttons on the car radio.

He knew he would get nothing from the AM or FM bands, not out here, but he clicked it on anyway. He left the volume and tone controls down, so as not to wake Evvie. Then he punched the seldom-used middle button, the shortwave band, and raised the gain carefully until he could barely hear the radio over the hum of the tires.

Static.

Slowly he swept the tuner across the bandwidth, but there was only white noise. It reminded him a little of the summer rain yesterday, starting back, the way it had sounded bouncing off the windows.

He was about to give up when he caught a voice, crackling, drifting in and out. He worked the knob like a safecracker, zeroing in on the signal.

A few bars of music. A tone, then the voice again. ". . . Greenwich Mean Time." Then the station ID.

It was the Voice of America overseas broadcast.

He grunted disconsolately and killed it.

His wife stirred.

"Why'd you turn it off?" she murmured. "I was listening to that. Good. Program."

"Take it easy," he said, "easy, you're still asleep. We'll be stopping soon."

". . . Only comes out at night," he heard her say, and then she was lost again in the blankets.

He pressed the glove compartment, took out one of the Automobile Club guides. It was already clipped open. McClay flipped on the overhead light and drove with one hand, reading over—for the hundredth time?—the list of motels that lay ahead. He knew the list by heart, but seeing the names again reassured him somehow. Besides, it helped to break the monotony.

It was the kind of place you never expect to find in the middle of a long night, a bright place with buildings (a building, at least) and cars, other cars drawn off the highway to be together in the protective circle of light.

A Rest Area.

He would have spotted it without the sign. Elevated sodium vapor lighting bathed the scene in an almost peach-colored glow, strikingly different from the cold blue-white sentinels of the interstate highway. He had seen other Rest Area signs on the way out, probably even this one. But in daylight the signs had meant nothing more to him than "Frontage Road" or "Business District Next Right." He wondered if it were the peculiar warmth of light that made the small island of blacktop appear so inviting.

McClay decelerated, downshifted, and left Interstate 40.

The car dipped and bumped, and he was aware of the new level of sound from the engine as it geared down for the first time in hours.

He eased in next to a Pontiac Firebird, toed the emergency brake, and cut the ignition.

He allowed his eyes to close and his head to sink back into the headrest. At last.

The first thing he noticed was the quiet.

It was deafening. His ears literally began to ring, with the high-pitched whine of a late-night TV test pattern.

The second thing he noticed was a tingling at the tip of his tongue.

It brought to mind a picture of a snake's tongue. Picking up electricity from the air, he thought.

The third was the rustling awake of his wife, in back.

She pulled herself up. "Are we sleeping now? Why are the lights . . . ?"

He saw the outline of her head in the mirror. "It's just a rest stop, hon. I—the car needs a break." Well, it was true, wasn't it? "You want a rest room? There's one back there, see it?"

"Oh my God."

"What's the matter now?"

"Leg's asleep. Listen, are we or are we not going to get a—"

"There's a motel coming up." He didn't say that they wouldn't hit the one he had marked in the book for another couple of hours; he didn't want to argue. He knew she needed the rest; he needed it too, didn't he? "Think I'll have some more of that coffee, though," he said.

"Isn't any more," she yawned.

The door slammed.

Now he was able to recognize the ringing in his ears for what it was: the sound of his own blood. It almost succeeded in replacing the steady drone of the car.

He twisted around, fishing over the back of the seat for the ice chest.

There should be a couple of Cokes left, at least.

His fingers brushed the basket next to the chest, riffling the edges of maps and tour books, by now reshuffled haphazardly over the first-aid kit he had packed himself (tourniquet, forceps, scissors, ammonia inhalants, Merthiolate, triangular bandage, compress, adhesive bandages, tannic acid) and the fire extinguisher, the extra carton of cigarettes, the remainder of a half-gallon of drinking water, the thermos (which Evvie said was empty, and why would she lie?).

He popped the top of a can.

Through the side window he saw Evvie disappearing around the corner of the building. She was wrapped to the gills in her blanket.

He opened the door and slid out, his back aching.

He stood there blankly, the unnatural light washing over him.

He took a long sweet pull from the can. Then he started walking.

The Firebird was empty.

And the next car, and the next.

Each car he passed looked like the one before it, which seemed crazy until he realized that it must be the work of the light. It cast an even, eerie tan over the baked metal tops, like orange sunlight through air thick with suspended particles. Even the windshields appeared to be filmed over with a thin layer of settled dust. It made him think of country roads, sundowns.

He walked on.

He heard his footsteps echo with surprising clarity, resounding down the staggered line of parked vehicles. Finally it dawned on him (and now he knew how tired he really was) that the cars must actually have people in them—sleeping people. Of course. Well, hell, he thought, watching his step, I wouldn't want to wake anyone. The poor devils.

Besides the sound of his footsteps, there was only the distant *swish* of an occasional, very occasional car on the highway; from here, even that was only a distant hush, growing and then subsiding like waves on a nearby shore.

He reached the end of the line, turned back.

Out of the corner of his eye he saw, or thought he saw, a movement by the building.

It would be Evvie, shuffling back.

He heard the car door slam.

He recalled something he had seen in one of the tourist towns in New Mexico: circling the park—in Taos, that was where they had been—he had glimpsed an ageless Indian, wrapped in typical blanket, ducking out of sight into the doorway of a gift shop; with the blanket over his head that way, the Indian had somehow resembled an Arab, or so it had seemed to him at the time.

He heard another car door slam.

That was the same day—was it only last week?—that she had noticed the locals driving with their headlights on (in honor of something or other, some regional election, perhaps: " 'My face speaks for itself,' drawled Herman J. 'Fashio' Trujillo, Candidate for Sheriff"). She had insisted at first that it must be a funeral procession, though for whom she could not guess.

McClay came to the car, stretched a last time, and crawled back in.

Evvie was bundled safely again in the back seat.

He lit a quick cigarette, expecting to hear her voice any second, complaining, demanding that he roll down the windows, at least, and so forth. But, as it turned out, he was able to sit undisturbed as he smoked it down almost to the filter.

Paguate. Bluewater. Thoreau.
   He blinked.
   Klagetoh. Joseph City. Ash Fork.

He blinked and tried to focus his eyes from the taillights a half-mile ahead to the bug-spattered glass, then back again.

Petrified Forest National Park.

He blinked, refocusing. But it did no good.

A twitch started on the side of his face, close by the corner of his eye.

Rehoboth.

He strained at a road sign, the names and mileages, but instead a seemingly endless list of past and future stops and detours shimmered before his mind's eye.

I've had it, he thought. Now, suddenly, it was catching up with him, the hours of repressed fatigue; he felt a rushing out of something from his chest. No way to make that motel—hell, I can't even remember the name of it now. Check the book. But it doesn't matter. The eyes. *Can't control my eyes anymore.*

(He had already begun to hallucinate things like tree trunks and cows and Mack trucks speeding toward him on the highway. The cow had been straddling the broken line; in the last few minutes its lowing, deep and regular, had become almost inviting.)

Well, he could try for *any* motel. Whatever turned up next.

But how much farther would that be?

He ground his teeth together, feeling the pulsing at his temples. He struggled to remember the last sign.

The next town. It might be a mile. Five miles. Fifty.

Think! He said it, he thought it, he didn't know which.

If he could pull over, pull over right now and lie down for a few minutes—

He seemed to see clear ground ahead. No rocks, no ditch. The shoulder, just ahead.

Without thinking he dropped into neutral and coasted, aiming for it.

The car glided to a stop.

God, he thought.

He forced himself to turn, reach into the back seat.

The lid to the chest was already off. He dipped his fingers into the ice and retrieved two half-melted cubes, lifted them into the front seat, and began rubbing them over his forehead.

He let his eyes close, seeing dull lights fire as he daubed at the lids, the rest of his face, the forehead again. As he slipped the ice into his mouth and chewed, it broke apart as easily as snow.

He took a deep breath. He opened his eyes again.

At that moment a huge tanker roared past, slamming an aftershock of air into the side of the car. The car rocked like a boat at sea.

No. It was no good.

So. So he could always turn back, couldn't he? And why not? The Rest Area was only twenty, twenty-five minutes behind him. (Was that all?) He could pull out and hang a U and turn back, just like that. And then sleep. It would be safer there. With luck, Evvie wouldn't even know. An hour's rest, maybe two; that was all he would need.

Unless—was there another Rest Area ahead?

How soon?

He knew that the second wind he felt now wouldn't last, not for more than a few minutes. No, it wasn't worth the chance.

He glanced in the rearview mirror.

Evvie was still down, a lumpen mound of blanket and hair.

Above her body, beyond the rear window, the raised headlights of another monstrous truck, closing ground fast.

He made the decision.

He slid into first and swung out in a wide arc, well ahead of the blast of the truck, and worked up to fourth gear. He was thinking about the warm, friendly lights he had left behind.

He angled in next to the Firebird and cut the lights.

He started to reach for a pillow from the back, but why bother? It would probably wake Evvie, anyway.

He wadded up his jacket, jammed it against the passenger armrest, and lay down.

First he crossed his arms over his chest. Then behind his head. Then he gripped his hands between his knees. Then he was on his back again, his hands at his sides, his feet cramped against the opposite door.

His eyes were wide open.

He lay there, watching chain lightning flash on the horizon.

Finally he let out a breath that sounded like all the breaths he had ever taken going out at once, and drew himself up.

He got out and walked over to the rest room.

Inside, white tiles and bare lights. His eyes felt raw, peeled. Finished, he washed his hands but not his face; that would only make sleep more difficult.

Outside again and feeling desperately out of synch, he listened to his shoes falling hollowly on the cement.

"Next week we've got to get organized . . ."

He said this, he was sure, because he heard his voice coming back to him, though with a peculiar empty resonance. Well, this time tomorrow night he would be home. As unlikely as that seemed now.

He stopped, bent for a drink from the water fountain.

The footsteps did not stop.

Now wait, he thought, I'm pretty far gone, but—

He swallowed, his ears popping.

The footsteps stopped.

Hell, he thought, I've been pushing too hard. We. She. No, it was my fault, my plan this time. To drive nights, sleep days. Just so. As long as you *can* sleep.

Easy, take it easy.

He started walking again, around the corner and back to the lot.

At the corner, he thought he saw something move at the edge of his vision.

He turned quickly to the right, in time for a fleeting glimpse of something—someone—hurrying out of sight into the shadows.

Well, the other side of the building housed the women's rest room. Maybe it was Evvie.

He glanced toward the car, but it was blocked from view.

He walked on.

Now the parking area resembled an oasis lit by firelight. Or a western camp, the cars rimming the lot on three sides in the manner of wagons gathered against the night.

Strength in numbers, he thought.

Again, each car he passed looked at first like every other. It was the flat light, of course. And of course they were the same cars he had seen a half-hour ago. And the light still gave them a dusty, abandoned look.

He touched a fender.

It *was* dusty.

But why shouldn't it be? His own car had probably taken on quite a layer of grime after so long on these roads.

He touched the next car, the next.

Each was so dirty that he could have carved his name without scratching the paint.

He had an image of himself passing this way again—God forbid—a year from now, say, and finding the same cars parked here. The *same* ones.

What if, he wondered tiredly, what if some of these cars had been abandoned? Overheated, exploded, broken down one fine midday and left here by owners who simply never returned? Who would ever know? Did the Highway Patrol, did anyone bother to check? Would an automobile be preserved here for months, years by the elements, like a snakeskin shed beside the highway?

It was a thought, anyway.

His head was buzzing.

He leaned back and inhaled deeply, as deeply as he could at this altitude.

But he did hear something. A faint tapping. It reminded him of running feet, until he noticed the lamp overhead:

There were hundreds of moths beating against the high fixture, their soft bodies tapping as they struck and circled and returned again and again to the lens; the light made their wings translucent.

He took another deep breath and went on to his car.

He could hear it ticking, cooling down, before he got there. Idly he rested a hand on the hood. Warm, of course. The tires? He touched the left front. It was taut, hot as a loaf from the oven. When he took his hand away, the color of the rubber came off on his palm like burned skin.

He reached for the door handle.

A moth fluttered down onto the fender. He flicked it off, his finger leaving a streak on the enamel.

He looked closer and saw a wavy, mottled pattern covering his unwashed car, and then he remembered. The rain, yesterday afternoon. The rain had left blotches in the dust, marking the finish as if with dirty fingerprints.

He glanced over at the next car.

It, too, had the imprint of dried raindrops—but, close up, he saw that the marks were superimposed in layers, over and over again.

The Firebird had been through a great many rains.

He touched the hood.

Cold.

He removed his hand, and a dead moth clung to his thumb. He tried to brush it off the hood, but other moth bodies stuck in its place. Then he saw countless shriveled, mummified moths pasted over the hood and top like peeling chips of paint. His fingers were coated with the powder from their wings.

He looked up.

High above, backed by banks of roiling cumulous clouds, the swarm of moths vibrated about the bright, protective light.

So the Firebird had been here a very long time.

He wanted to forget it, to let it go. He wanted to get back in the car. He wanted to lie down, lock it out, everything. He wanted to go to sleep and wake up in Los Angeles.

He couldn't.

He inched around the Firebird until he was facing the line of cars. He hesitated a beat, then started moving.

A LeSabre.

A Cougar.

A Chevy van.

A Corvair.

A Ford.

A Mustang.

And every one was overlaid with grit.

He paused by the Mustang. Once—how long ago?—it had been a luminous candy-apple red; probably belonged to a teenager. Now the windshield was opaque, the body dulled to a peculiar shade he could not quite place.

Feeling like a voyeur at a drive-in movie theater, McClay crept to the driver's window.

Dimly he perceived two large outlines in the front seat.

He raised his hand.

Wait.

What if there were two people sitting there on the other side of the window, watching him?

He put it out of his mind. Using three fingers, he cut a swath through the scum on the glass and pressed close.

The shapes were there. Two headrests.

He started to pull away.

And happened to glance into the back seat.

He saw a long, uneven form.

A leg, back of a thigh. Blonde hair, streaked with shadows. The collar of a coat.

And, delicate and silvery, a spider web, spun between the hair and collar.

He jumped back.

His leg struck the old Ford. He spun around, his arms straight. The blood was pounding in his ears.

He rubbed out a spot on the window of the Ford and scanned the inside.

The figure of a man, slumped on the front seat.

The man's head lay on a jacket. No, it was not a jacket. It was a large, formless stain. In the filtered light, McClay could see that it had dried to a dark brown.

It came from the man's mouth.

No, not from the mouth.

The throat had a long, thin slash across it, reaching nearly to the ear.

He stood there stiffly, his back almost arched, his eyes jerking, trying to close, trying not to close. The lot, the even light reflecting thinly from each windshield, the Corvair, the van, the Cougar, the LeSabre, the suggestion of a shape within each one.

The pulse in his ears muffled and finally blotted out the distant gearing of a truck up on the highway, the death-rattle of the moths against the seductive lights.

He reeled.

He seemed to be hearing again the breaking open of doors and the scurrying of padded feet across paved spaces.

He remembered the first time. He remembered the sound of a second door slamming in a place where no new car but his own had arrived.

Or—had it been the door of his car slamming a second time, after Evvie had gotten back in?

If so, how? Why?

And there had been the sight of someone moving, trying to slip away.

And for some reason now he remembered the Indian in the tourist town, slipping out of sight in the doorway of that gift shop. He held his eyelids down until he saw the shop again, the window full of kachinas and tin gods and tapestries woven in a secret language.

At last he remembered clearly: the Indian had not been entering the store. *He had been stealing away.*

McClay did not yet understand what it meant, but he opened his eyes, as if for the first time in centuries, and began to run toward his car.

If I could only catch my goddamn breath, he thought.

He tried to hold on. He tried not to think of her, of what might have happened the first time, of what he may have been carrying in the back seat ever since.

He had to find out.

He fought his way back to the car, against a rising tide of fear he could not stem.

He told himself to think of other things, of things he knew he could control: mileages and motel bills, time zones and weather reports, spare tires and flares and tubeless repair tools, hydraulic jack and Windex and paper towels and tire iron and socket wrench and waffle cushion and traveler's checks and credit cards and Dopp Kit (toothbrush and paste, deodorant, shaver, safety blade, brushless cream) and sunglasses and Sight Savers and tear-gas pen and fiber-tip pens and portable radio and alkaline batteries and fire extinguisher and desert water bag and tire gauge and motor oil and his money-belt with identification sealed in plastic—

In the back of his car, under the quilt, nothing moved, not even when he finally lost his control and his mind in a thick, warm scream.

BRIAN LUMLEY

"The Viaduct"

Brian Lumley (1937-) was strongly influenced by the work of H. P. Lovecraft and earned recognition as neo-Lovecraftian through the short fiction gathered for his first two collections, **The Caller of the Black** *and* **The Horror at Oakdene**. *He pursued his interest in Lovecraft's ideas through a series of novels featuring his psychic detective Titus Crow, beginning with* **The Burrowers Beneath** *in 1974, and the "Hero of Dreams" quintet modeled on Lovecraft's Dunsanian fantasies. His most significant contribution to the horror field is the long-running* **Necroscope** *saga, a blend of the vampire tale, espionage thriller and otherworld fantasy that he began in 1986 and which currently runs to more than a dozen novels. He is also an ambitious writer of short fiction whose many fantasy and horror story collections include* **The Compleat Crow**, **The House of Cthulhu and Other Tales of the Primal Land**, **Fruiting Bodies and Other Fungi**, **Dagon's Bell and Other Discords**, *and* **The Second Wish and Other Exhalations**.

The Viaduct

by Brian Lumley

Horror can come in many different shapes, sizes, and colors; often, like death, which is sometimes its companion, unexpectedly. Some years ago horror came to two boys in the coal-mining area of England's northeast coast.

Pals since they first started school seven years earlier, their names were John and David. John was a big lad and thought himself very brave; David was six months younger, smaller, and he wished he could be more like John.

It was a Saturday in the late spring, warm but not oppressive, and since there was no school the boys were out adventuring on the beach. They had spent most of the morning playing at being starving castaways, turning over rocks in the life-or-death search for crabs and eels—and jumping back startled, hearts racing, whenever their probing revealed too frantic a wriggling in the swirling water, or perhaps a great crab carefully sidling away, one pincer lifted in silent warning—and now they were heading home again for lunch.

But lunch was still almost two hours away, and it would take them less than an hour to get home. In that simple fact were sown the seeds of horror, in that and in one other fact—that between the beach and their respective homes there stood the viaduct . . .

Almost as a reflex action, when the boys left the beach they headed in the direction of the viaduct. To do this they turned inland, through the trees and bushes of the narrow dene that came right down to the sand, and followed the path of the river. The river was still fairly deep, from the spring thaw and the rains of April, and as they walked, ran, and hopped they threw stones into the water, seeing who could make the biggest splash.

In no time at all, it seemed, they came to the place where the massive, ominous shadow of the viaduct fell across the dene and the river flowing through it, and there they stared up in awe at the giant arched structure of brick and concrete that bore upon its back one hundred yards of the twin tracks that formed the coastal railway. Shuddering mightily whenever a train roared overhead, the man-made bridge was a never-ending source of amazement and wonder to them . . . And a challenge, too.

It was as they were standing on the bank of the slow-moving river, perhaps fifty feet wide at this point, that they spotted on the opposite bank the local village idiot, "Wiley Smiley." Now of course, that was not this unfortunate youth's real name; he was Miles Bellamy, victim of cruel genetic fates since the ill-omened day of his birth some nineteen years earlier. But everyone called him Wiley Smiley.

He was fishing, in a river that had supported nothing bigger than a minnow for many years, with a length of string and a bent pin. He looked up and grinned vacuously as John threw a stone into the water to attract his attention. The stone went quite close to the mark, splashing water over the unkempt youth where he stood a little way out from the far bank, balanced none too securely on slippery rocks. His vacant grin immediately slipped from his face; he became angry, gesturing awkwardly and mouthing incoherently.

"He'll come after us," said David to his brash companion, his voice just a trifle alarmed.

"No he won't, stupid," John casually answered, picking up a second, larger stone. "He can't get across, can he." It was a statement, not a question, and it was a fact. Here the river was deeper, overflowing from a large pool directly beneath the viaduct which, in the months ahead, children and adults alike would swim in during the hot weekends of summer.

John threw his second missile, deliberately aiming it at the water as close to the enraged idiot as he could without actually hitting him, shouting: "Yah! Wiley Smiley! Trying to catch a whale, are you?"

Wiley Smiley began to shriek hysterically as the stone splashed down immediately in front of him and a fountain of water geysered over his trousers. Threatening though they now were, his angry caperings upon the rocks looked very funny to the boys (particularly since his rage was impotent), and John began to laugh loud and jeeringly. David, not a cruel boy by nature, found his friend's laughter so infectious that in a few seconds he joined in, adding his own voice to the hilarity.

Then John stooped yet again, straightening up this time with two stones, one of which he offered to his slightly younger companion. Carried completely away now, David accepted the stone and together they hurled their missiles, dancing and laughing until tears rolled down their cheeks as Wiley Smiley received a further dousing. By that time the rocks upon which their victim stood were thoroughly wet and slippery, so that suddenly he lost his balance and sat down backwards into the shallow water.

Climbing clumsily, soggily to his feet, he was greeted by howls of laughter from across the river, which drove him to further excesses of rage. His was a passion which might only find outlet in direct retaliation, revenge. He took a few paces forward, until the water swirled about his knees, then stooped and plunged his arms into the river. There were stones galore beneath the water, and the face of the tormented youth was twisted with hate and fury now as he straightened up and brandished two which were large and jagged.

Where his understanding was painfully slow, Wiley Smiley's strength was prodigious. Had his first stone hit John on the head it might easily have killed him. As it was, the boy ducked at the last moment and the missile flew harmlessly above him. David, too, had to jump to avoid being hurt by a flying rock, and no sooner had the idiot loosed both his stones than he stooped down again to grope in the water for more.

Wiley Smiley's aim was too good for the boys, and his continuing rage was making them begin to feel uncomfortable, so they beat a hasty retreat up the steeply-wooded slope of the dene and made for the walkway that was fastened and ran parallel to the nearside wall of the viaduct. Soon they had climbed out of sight of the poor soul below, but they could still hear his meaningless squawking and shrieking.

A few minutes more of puffing and panting, climbing steeply through trees and saplings, brought them up above the wood and to the edge of a grassy slope. Another hundred yards and they could go over a fence and onto the viaduct. Though no word had passed between them on the subject, it was inevitable that they should end up on the viaduct, one of the most fascinating places in their entire world . . .

The massive structure had been built when first the collieries of the north-east opened up, long before plans were drawn up for the major coast road, and now it linked twin colliery villages that lay opposite each other across the narrow river valley it spanned. Originally constructed solely to accommodate the railway, and used to that end to this very day, with the addition of a walkway, it also provided miners who lived in one village but worked in the other with a shortcut to their respective coal mines.

While the viaduct itself was of sturdy brick, designed to withstand decade after decade of the heavy traffic that rumbled and clattered across its triple-arched back, the walkway was a comparatively fragile affair. That is not to say that it was not safe, but there were certain dangers and notices had been posted at its approaches to warn users of the presence of at least an element of risk.

Supported upon curving metal arms—iron bars about one and one-half inches in diameter which, springing from the brick and mortar of the viaduct wall, were set perhaps twenty inches apart—the walkway itself was of wooden planks protected by a fence five feet high. There were, however, small gaps where rotten planks had been removed and never replaced, but the miners who used the viaduct were careful and knew the walkway's dangers intimately. All in all the walkway served a purpose and was reasonably safe; one might jump from it, certainly, but only a very careless person or an outright fool would fall. Still, it was no place for anyone suffering from vertigo . . .

Now, as they climbed the fence to stand gazing up at those ribs of iron with their burden of planking and railings, the two boys felt a strange, headlong rushing emotion within them. For this day, of course, was *the* day!

It had been coming for almost a year, since the time when John had stood right where he stood now to boast: "One day I'll swing hand over hand along those rungs, all the way across. Just like Tarzan." Yes, they had sensed this day's approach, almost as they might sense Christmas or the end of long, idyllic summer holidays . . . or a visit to the dentist. Something far away, which would eventually arrive, but not yet.

Except that now it had arrived.

"One hundred and sixty rungs," John breathed, his voice a little fluttery, feeling his palms beginning to itch. "Yesterday, in the playground, we both did twenty more than that on the climbing-frame."

"The climbing-frame," answered David with a naïve insight and vision far ahead of his age, "is only seven feet high. The viaduct is about a hundred and fifty."

The Viaduct

John stared at his friend for a second and his eyes narrowed. Suddenly he sneered. "I might have known it—you're scared, aren't you?"

"No," David shook his head, lying, "but it'll soon be lunchtime, and—"

"You *are* scared!" John repeated. "Like a little kid. We've been practicing for months for this, every day of school on the climbing-frame, and now we're ready. You know we can do it." His tone grew more gentle, urging: "Look, it's not as if we can't stop if we want to, is it? There's them holes in the fence, and those big gaps in the planks."

"The first gap," David answered, noticing how very far away and faint his own voice sounded, "is almost a third of the way across..."

"That's right," John agreed, nodding his head eagerly. "We've counted the rungs, haven't we? Just fifty of them to that first wide gap. If we're too tired to go on when we get there, we can just climb up through the gap onto the walkway."

David, whose face had been turned towards the ground, looked up. He looked straight into his friend's eyes, not at the viaduct, in whose shade they stood. He shivered, but not because he was cold.

John stared right back at him, steadily, encouragingly, knowing that his smaller friend looked for his approval, his reassurance. And he was right, for despite the fact that their ages were very close, David held him up as some sort of hero. No daredevil, David, but he desperately wished he could be. And now ... here was his chance.

He simply nodded—then laughed out loud as John gave a wild whoop and shook his young fists at the viaduct. "Today we'll beat you!" he yelled, then turned and clambered furiously up the last few yards of steep grassy slope to where the first rung might easily be reached with an upward swing. David followed him after a moment's pause, but not before he heard the first arch of the viaduct throw back the challenge in a faintly ringing, sardonic echo of John's cry: "Beat you ... beat you ... beat you ..."

As he caught up with his ebullient friend, David finally allowed his eyes to glance upward at those skeletal ribs of iron above him. They looked solid, were solid, he knew—but the air beneath them was very thin indeed. John turned to him, his face flushed with excitement. "You first," he said.

"Me?" David blanched. "But—"

"You'll be up onto the walkway first if we get tired," John pointed out. "Besides, I go faster than you—and you wouldn't want to be left behind, would you?"

David shook his head. "No," he slowly answered, "I wouldn't want to be left behind." Then his voice took on an anxious note: "But you won't hurry me, will you?"

" 'Course not," John answered. "We'll just take it nice and easy, like we do at school."

Without another word, but with his ears ringing strangely and his breath already coming faster, David jumped up and caught hold of the first rung. He swung forward, first one hand to the rung in front, then the other, and so on. He heard John grunt as he too jumped and caught the first rung, and then he gave all his concentration to what he was doing.

Hand over hand, rung by rung, they made their way out over the abyss. Below them the ground fell sharply away, each swing of their arms adding almost two feet to their height, seeming to add tangibly to their weight. Now they were silent, except for an occasional grunt, saving both breath and strength as they worked their way along the underside of the walkway. There was only the breeze that whispered in their ears and the infrequent toot of a motor's horn on the distant road.

As the bricks of the wall moved slowly by, so the distance between rungs seemed to increase, and already David's arms felt tired. He knew that John, too, must be feeling it, for while his friend was bigger and a little stronger, he was also heavier. And sure enough, at a distance of only twenty-five, maybe thirty rungs out towards the center, John breathlessly called for a rest.

David pulled himself up and hung his arms and his rib cage over the rung he was on—just as they had practiced in the playground—getting comfortable before carefully turning his head to look back. He was shocked to see that John's face was paler than he'd ever known it, that his eyes were staring. When John saw David's doubt, however, he managed a weak grin.

"It's okay," he said. "I was—I was just a bit worried about you, that's all. Thought your arm might be getting a bit tired. Have you—have you looked down yet?"

"No," David answered, his voice mouse-like. *No,* he said again, this time to himself, *and I'm not going to!* He carefully turned his head back to look ahead, where the diminishing line of rungs seemed to stretch out almost infinitely to the far side of the viaduct.

John had been worried about him. Yes, of course he had; that was why his face had looked so funny, so shrunken. John thought he was frightened, was worried about his self-control, his ability to carry on. Well, David told himself, he had every right to worry; but all the same he felt ashamed that his weakness was so obvious. Even in a position like that, perched so perilously, David's mind was far more concerned with the other boy's opinion of him than with thoughts of possible disaster. And it never once dawned on him, not for a moment, that John might really only be worried about himself...

Almost as if to confirm beyond a doubt the fact that John had little faith in his strength, his courage—as David hung there, breathing deeply, preparing himself for the next stage of the venture—his friend's voice, displaying an unmistakable quaver, came to him again from behind:

"Just another twenty rungs, that's all, then you'll be able to climb up onto the walkway."

Yes, David thought, *I'll be able to climb up. But then I'll know that I'll never be like you—that you'll always be better than me—because you'll carry on all the way across!* He set his teeth and dismissed the thought. It wasn't going to be like that, he told himself, not this time. After all, it was no different up here from in the playground. You were only higher, that was all. The trick was in not looking down—

As if obeying some unheard command, seemingly with a morbid curiosity of their own, David's eyes slowly began to turn downward, defying him. Their motion was only arrested when David's attention suddenly centered upon a spider-like dot that emerged suddenly from the cover of the trees, scampering frantically up the opposite slope of the valley. He recognized the figure immediately from the faded blue shirt and black trousers that it wore. It was Wiley Smiley.

As David lowered himself carefully into the hanging position beneath his rung and swung forward, he said: "Across the valley, there—that's Wiley Smiley. I wonder why he's in such a hurry?" There had been something terribly *urgent* about the idiot's quick movements, as if some rare incentive powered them.

"I see him," said John, sounding more composed now. "Huh! He's just an old nutter. My dad says he'll do something one of these days and have to be taken away."

"Do something?" David queried, pausing briefly between swings. An uneasiness completely divorced from the perilous game they were playing rose churningly in his stomach and mind. "What kind of thing?"

"Dunno," John grunted. "But anyway, don't—*uh!*—talk."

It was good advice: don't talk, conserve wind, strength, take it easy. And yet David suddenly found himself moving faster, dangerously fast, and his fingers were none too sure as they moved from one rung to the next. More than once he was hanging by one hand while the other groped blindly for support.

It was very, very important now to close the distance between himself and the sanctuary of the gap in the planking. True, he had made up his mind just a few moments ago to carry on beyond that gap—as far as he could go before admitting defeat, submitting—but all such resolutions were gone now as quickly as they came. His one thought was of climbing up to safety.

It had something to do with Wiley Smiley and the eager, *determined* way he had been scampering up the far slope. Towards the viaduct. Something to do with that, yes, and with what John had said about Wiley Smiley being taken away one day . . . for *doing* something. David's mind dared not voice its fears too specifically, not even to itself . . .

Now, except for the occasional grunt—that and the private pounding of blood in their ears—the two boys were silent, and only a minute or so later David saw the gap in the planking. He had been searching for it, sweeping the rough wood of the planks stretching away overhead anxiously until he saw the wide, straight crack that quickly enlarged as he swung closer. Two planks were missing here, he knew, just sufficient to allow a boy to squirm through the gap without too much trouble.

His breath coming in sobbing, glad gasps, David was just a few rungs away from safety when he felt the first tremors vibrating through the great structure of the viaduct. It was like the trembling of a palsied giant. "What's that?" he cried out loud, terrified, clinging desperately to the rung above his head.

"It's a—*uh!*—train!" John gasped, his own voice now very hoarse and plainly frightened. "We'll have to—*uh!*—wait until it's gone over."

Quickly, before the approaching train's vibrations could shake them loose, the boys hauled themselves up into positions of relative safety and comfort, perching on their rungs beneath the planks of the walkway. There they waited and shivered in the shadow of the viaduct, while the shuddering rumble of the train drew ever closer, until, in a protracted clattering of wheels on rails, the monster rushed by unseen overhead. The trembling quickly subsided and the train's distant whistle proclaimed its derision; it was finished with them.

Without a word, holding back a sob that threatened to develop into full-scale hysteria, David lowered himself once more into the full-length hanging position; behind him, breathing harshly and with just the hint of a whimper escaping from his lips, John did the same. Two, three more forward swings and the gap was directly overhead. David looked up, straight up to the clear sky.

"Hurry!" said John, his voice the tiniest whisper. "My hands are starting to feel funny . . ."

David pulled himself up and balanced across his rung, tremulously took away one hand and grasped the edge of the wooden planking. Pushing down on the hand that grasped the rung and hauling himself up with the other, finally he kneeled on the rung and his head emerged through the gap in the planks. He looked along the walkway . . .

. . . There, not three feet away, legs widespread and eyes burning with a fanatical hatred, crouched Wiley Smiley. David saw him, saw the pointed stick he held, felt a thrill of purest horror course through him. Then, in the next instant, the idiot lunged forward and his mouth opened in a demented parody of a laugh. David saw the lightning movement of the sharpened stick and tried to avoid its thrust. He felt the point strike his forehead just above his left eye and fell back, off balance, arms flailing. Briefly his left hand made contact with the planking again, then lost it, and he fell with a shriek . . . across the rung that lay directly beneath him. It was not a long fall but fear and panic had already winded David; he simply closed his eyes and sobbed, hanging on for dear life, motionless. But only for a handful of seconds.

Warm blood trickled from David's forehead, falling on his hands where he gripped the rung. Something was prodding the back of his neck, jabbing viciously. The pain brought him back from the abyss and he opened his eyes to risk one sharp, fearful glance upwards. Wiley Smiley was kneeling at the edge of the gap, his stick already moving downward for another jab. Again David moved his head to avoid the thrust of the stick, and once more the point scraped his forehead.

Behind him David could hear John moaning and screaming alternately: "Oh, Mum! Dad! It's Wiley Smiley! It's him, him, *him!* He'll kill us, kill us . . ." Galvanized into action, David lowered himself for the third time into the hanging position and swung forward, away from the inflamed idiot's deadly stick. Two rungs, three, then he carefully turned about face and hauled himself up to rest. He looked at John through the blood that dripped slowly into one eye, blurring his vision.

David blinked to clear his eye of blood, then said: "John, you'll have to turn round and go back, get help. He's got me here. I can't go forward any further, I don't think, and I can't come back. I'm stuck. But it's only fifty rungs back to the start. You can do it easy, and if you get tired you can always rest. I'll wait here until you fetch help."

"Can't, can't, *can't*," John babbled, trembling wildly where he lay half across his rung. Tears ran down the older boy's cheeks and fell into space like salty rain. He was deathly white, eyes staring, frozen. Suddenly yellow urine flooded from the leg of his short trousers in a long burst. When he saw this, David, too, wet himself, feeling the burning of his water against his legs but not caring. He felt very tiny, very weak now, and he knew that fear and shock were combining to exhaust him.

Then, as a silhouette glimpsed briefly in a flash of lightning, David saw in his mind's eye a means of salvation. "John," he urgently called out to the other boy. "Do you remember near the middle of the viaduct? There are two gaps close together in the walkway, maybe only a dozen or so rungs apart."

Almost imperceptibly, John nodded, never once moving his frozen eyes from David's face. "Well," the younger boy continued, barely managing to keep the hysteria out of his own voice, "if we can swing to—" Suddenly David's words were cut off by a burst of insane laughter from above, followed immediately by a loud, staccato thumping on the boards as Wiley Smiley leapt crazily up and down.

"No, no, *no*—" John finally cried out in answer to David's proposal. His paralysis broken, he began to sob unashamedly. Then, shaking his head violently, he said: "I can't move—can't move!" His voice became the merest whisper. "Oh, God—Mum—Dad! I'll fall, I'll fall!"

"You won't fall, you git—*coward!*" David shouted. Then his jaw fell open in a gasp. John, a coward! But the other boy didn't even seem to have heard him. Now he was trembling as wildly as before and his eyes were squeezed tight shut.

"Listen," David said. "If you don't come . . . then I'll leave you. You wouldn't want to be left on your own, would you?" It was an echo as of something said a million years ago.

John stopped sobbing and opened his eyes. They opened very wide, unbelieving. "Leave me?"

"Listen," David said again. "The next gap is only about twenty rungs away, and the one after that is only another eight or nine more. Wiley Smiley can't get after both of us at once, can he?"

"You go," said John, his voice taking on fresh hope and his eyes blinking rapidly. "You go and maybe he'll follow you. Then I'll climb up and—and chase him off . . ."

"You won't be able to chase him off," said David scornfully, "not just you on your own. You're not big enough."

"Then I'll . . . I'll run and fetch help."

"What if he doesn't follow after me?" David asked. "If we both go, he's bound to follow us."

"David," John said, after a moment or two. "David, I'm . . . frightened."

"You'll have to be quick across the gap," David said, ignoring John's last statement. "He's got that stick—and of course he'll be listening to us."

"I'm frightened," John whispered again.

David nodded. "Okay, you stay where you are, if that's what you want—but I'm going on."

"Don't leave me, don't leave me!" John cried out, his shriek accompanied by a peal of mad and bubbling laughter from the unseen idiot above. "Don't go!"

"I have to, or we're both finished," David answered. He slid down into the hanging position and turned about face, noting as he did so that John was making to follow him, albeit in a dangerous, panicky fashion. "Wait to see if Wiley Smiley follows me!" he called back over his shoulder.

"No. I'm coming, I'm coming!"

From far down below in the valley David heard a horrified shout, then another. They had been spotted. Wiley Smiley heard the shouting, too, and his distraction was sufficient to allow John to pass by beneath him unhindered. From above, the two boys now heard the idiot's worried mutterings and gruntings, and the hesitant sound of his feet as he slowly kept pace with them along the walkway. He could see them through the narrow cracks between the planks, but the cracks weren't wide enough for him to use his stick.

David's arms and hands were terribly numb and aching by the time he reached the second gap, but seeing the gloating, twisted features of Wiley Smiley leering down at him he ducked his head and swung on to where he was once more protected by the planks above him. John had stopped short of the second gap, hauling himself up into the safer, resting position.

Above them Wiley Smiley was mewling viciously like a wild animal, howling as if in torment. He rushed crazily back and forth from gap to gap, jabbing uselessly at the empty air between the vacant rungs. The boys could see the bloodied point of the stick striking down first through one open space, then the other. David achingly waited until he saw the stick appear at the gap in front of him and then, when it retreated and he heard Wiley Smiley's footsteps hurrying overhead, swung swiftly across to the other side. There he turned about to face John, and with what felt like his last ounce of strength pulled himself up to rest.

Now, for the first time, David dared to look down. Below, running up the riverbank and waving frantically, were the ant-like figures of three men. They must have been out for a Saturday morning stroll when they'd spotted the two boys hanging beneath the viaduct's walkway. One of them stopped running and put his hands up to his mouth. His shout floated up to the boys on the clear air: "Hang on, lads, hang on!"

"Help!" David and John cried out together, as loud as they could. "Help!—Help!"

"We're coming, lads," came the answering shout. The men hurriedly began to climb the wooded slope on their side of the river and disappeared into the trees.

"They'll be here soon," David said, wondering if it would be soon enough. His whole body ached and he felt desperately weak and sick.

"Hear that, Wiley Smiley?" John cried hysterically, staring up at the boards above him. "They'll be here soon—and then you'll be taken away and locked up!" There was no answer. A slight wind had come up off the sea and was carrying a salty tang to them where they lay across their rungs.

"They'll take you away and lock you up," John cried again, the ghost of a sob in his voice; but once more the only answer was the slight moaning of the wind. John looked across at David, maybe twenty-five feet away, and said: "I think . . . I think he's gone." Then he gave a wild shout. "He's gone. *He's gone!*"

"I didn't hear him go," said David, dubiously.

John was very much more his old self now. "Oh, he's gone, all right. He saw those men coming and cleared off. David, I'm going up!"

"You'd better wait," David cried out as his friend slid down to hang at arm's length from his rung. John ignored the advice; he swung forward hand over hand until he was under the far gap in the planking. With a grunt of exertion, he forced the tired muscles of his arms to pull his tired body up. He got his rib cage over the rung, flung a hand up and took hold of the naked plank to one side of the gap, then—

In that same instant David sensed rather than heard the furtive movement overhead. "John!" he yelled. "He's still there—*Wiley Smiley's still there!*"

But John had already seen Wiley Smiley; the idiot had made his presence all too plain, and already his victim was screaming. The boy fell back fully into David's view, the hand he had thrown up to grip the edge of the plank returning automatically to the rung, his arms taking the full weight of his falling body, somehow sustaining him. There was a long gash in his cheek from which blood freely flowed.

"Move forward!" David yelled, terror pulling his lips back in a snarling mask. "Forward, where he can't get at you . . ."

John heard him and must have seen in some dim, frightened recess of his mind the commonsense of David's advice. Panting hoarsely—partly in dreadful fear, partly from hideous emotional exhaustion—he swung one hand forward and caught at the next rung. And at that precise moment, in the split second while John hung suspended between the two rungs with his face turned partly upward, Wiley Smiley struck again.

David was witness to it all. He heard the maniac's rising, gibbering shriek of triumph as the sharp point of the stick lanced unerringly down, and John's answering cry of purest agony as his left eye flopped bloodily out onto his cheek, lying there on a white thread of nerve and gristle. He saw John clap *both hands* to his monstrously altered face, and watched in starkest horror as his friend seemed to stand for a moment, defying gravity, on the thin air. Then John was gone, dwindling away down a drafty funnel of air, while rising came the piping, diminishing scream that would haunt David until his dying day, a scream that was cut short after what seemed an impossibly long time.

John had fallen. At first David couldn't accept it, but then it began to sink in. His friend had fallen. He moaned and shut his eyes tightly, lying half across and clinging to his rung so fiercely that he could no longer really feel his bloodless fingers at all. John had fallen . . .

Then—perhaps it was only a minute or so later, perhaps an hour,

David didn't know—there broke in on his perceptions the sound of clumping, hurrying feet on the boards above, and a renewed, even more frenzied attack of gibbering and shrieking from Wiley Smiley. David forced his eyes open as the footsteps came to a halt directly overhead. He heard a gruff voice:

"Jim, you keep that bloody—*Thing*—away, will you? He's already killed one boy today. Frank, give us a hand here."

A face, inverted, appeared through the hole in the planks not three feet away from David's own face. The mouth opened and the same voice, but no longer gruff, said: "It's okay now, son. Everything's okay. Can you move?"

In answer, David could only shake his head negatively. Overtaxed muscles, violated nerves had finally given in. He was frozen on his perch; he would stay where he was now until he was either taken off physically or until he fainted.

Dimly the boy heard the voice again, and others raised in an urgent hubbub, but he was too far gone to make out any words that were said. He was barely aware that the face had been withdrawn. A few seconds later there came a banging and tearing from immediately above him; a small shower of tiny pieces of wood, dust, and homogenous debris fell upon his head and shoulders. Then daylight flooded down to illuminate more brightly the shaded area beneath the walkway. Another board was torn away, and another.

The inverted face again appeared, this time at the freshly-made opening, and an exploratory hand reached down. Using its kindly voice, the face said: "Okay, son, we'll have you out of there in a jiffy. I—*uh!*—can't quite seem to reach you, but it's only a matter of a few inches. Do you think you can—"

The voice was cut off by a further outburst of incoherent shrieking and jabbering from Wiley Smiley. The face and hand withdrew momentarily and David heard the voice yet again. This time it was angry. "Look, see if you can keep that damned idiot back, will you? And keep him quiet, for God's sake!"

The hand came back, large and strong, reaching down. David still clung with all his remaining strength to the rung, and though he knew what was expected of him—what he must do to win himself the prize of continued life—all sense of feeling had quite gone from his limbs and even shifting his position was a very doubtful business.

"Boy," said the voice, as the hand crept inches closer and the inverted face stared into his, "if you could just reach up your hand, I—"

"I'll—I'll try to do it," David whispered.

"Good, good," his would-be rescuer calmly, quietly answered. "That's it, lad, just a few inches. Keep your balance, now."

David's hand crept up from the rung and his head, neck, and shoulder slowly turned to allow it free passage. Up it tremblingly went, reaching to meet the hand stretching down from above. The boy and the man, each peered into the other's straining face, and an instant later their fingertips touched—

There came a mad shriek, a frantic pounding of feet and cries of horror and wild consternation from above. The inverted face went white in a moment and disappeared, apparently dragged backwards. The hand disappeared, too. And that was the very moment that David had chosen to free himself of the rung and give himself into the protection of his rescuer . . .

He flailed his arms in a vain attempt to regain his balance. Numb, cramped, cold with that singular icy chill experienced only at death's positive approach, his limbs would not obey. He rolled forward over the bar and his legs were no longer strong enough to hold him. He didn't even feel the toes of his shoes as they struck the rung—the last of him to have contact with the viaduct—before his fall began. And if the boy thought anything at all during that fall, well, those thoughts will never be known. Later he could not remember.

Oh, there was to be a later, but David could hardly have believed it while he was falling. And yet he was not unconscious. There were vague impressions: of the sky, the looming arch of the viaduct flying past, trees below, the sea on the horizon, then the sky again, all slowly turning. There was a composite whistling, of air displaced and air ejected from lungs contracted in a high-pitched scream. And then, it seemed a long time later, there was the impact . . .

But David did not strike the ground . . . he struck the pool. The deep swimming hole. The blessed, merciful river!

He had curled into a ball—the fetal position, almost—and this doubtless saved him. His tightly-curled body entered the water with very little injury, however much of a splash it caused. Deep as the water was, nevertheless David struck the bottom with force, the pain and shock awakening whatever facilities remained functional in the motor areas of his brain. Aided by his resultant struggling, however weak, the ballooning air in his clothes bore him surely to the surface. The river carried him a few yards downstream to where the banks formed a bottleneck for the pool.

Through all the pain David felt his knees scrape pebbles, felt his hands on the mud of the bank, and where willpower presumably was lacking, instinct took over. Somehow he crawled from the pool, and somehow he hung on grimly to consciousness. Away from the water, still he kept on crawling, as from the horror of his experience. Unseeing, he moved towards the towering unconquered colossus of the viaduct. He was quite blind as of yet, there was only a red, impenetrable haze before his bloodied eyes; he heard nothing but a sick roaring in his head. Finally his shoulder struck the bole of a tree that stood in the shelter of the looming brick giant, and there he stopped crawling, propped against the tree.

Slowly, very slowly the roaring went out of his ears, the red haze before his eyes was replaced by lightning flashes and kaleidoscopic shapes and colors. Normal sound suddenly returned with a great pain in his ears. A rush of wind rustled the leaves of the trees, snatching away and then giving back a distant shouting which seemed to have its source overhead. Encased in his shell of pain, David did not immediately relate the shouting to his miraculous escape. Sight returned a few moments later and he began to cry wrackingly with relief; he had thought himself permanently blind. And perhaps even now he had not been completely wrong, for his eyes had plainly been knocked out of order. Something was—*must be*—desperately wrong with them.

David tried to shake his head to clear it, but this action only brought fresh, blinding pain. When the nausea subsided he blinked his eyes, clearing them of blood and peering bewilderedly about at his surroundings. It was as he had suspected: the colors were all wrong. No, he blinked again, some of them seemed perfectly normal.

For instance: the bark of the tree against which he leaned was brown enough, and its dangling leaves were a fresh green. The sky above was blue, reflected in the river, and the bricks of the viaduct were a dull orange. Why then was the grass beneath him a lush red streaked with yellow and grey? Why was this unnatural grass wet and sticky, and—

—*And why were these tatters of dimly familiar clothing flung about in exploded, scarlet disorder?*

When his reeling brain at last delivered the answer, David opened his mouth to scream, fainting before he could do so. He fell face down into the sticky embrace of his late friend.

JOYCE CAROL OATES

"Night-Side"

Joyce Carol Oates (1935-) is the author of **Them, Black Water, What I Lived For,** *and many other mainstream works that explore the dark side of contemporary American experience. She has written a trio of novels in the gothic tradition,* **Bellefleur, A Bloodsmoor Romance,** *and* **Mysteries of Winterthurn,** *and the psychological suspense novel* **Zombie,** *which was given the Bram Stoker Award for best novel by the Horror Writers of America. Three of her many collections of short fiction are devoted to the macabre:* **Dark Side, Haunted: Tales of the Grotesque,** *and* **Demon and other tales.** *She has contributed to numerous anthologies of original horror fiction and her work is reprinted regularly in* **The Year's Best Fantasy and Horror.**

Night-Side

To Gloria Whelan

by Joyce Carol Oates

***

6 February 1887. Quincy, Massachusetts. Montague House.

Disturbing experience at Mrs. A———'s home yesterday evening. Few theatrics—comfortable though rather pathetically shabby surroundings—an only mildly sinister atmosphere (especially in contrast to the Walpurgis Night presented by that shameless charlatan in Portsmouth: the Dwarf Eustace who presumed to introduce me to Swedenborg himself, under the erroneous impression that I am a member of the Church of the New Jerusalem—*I!*). Nevertheless I came away disturbed, and my conversation with Dr. Moore afterward, at dinner, though dispassionate and even, at times, a bit flippant, did not settle my mind. Perry Moore is of course a hearty materialist, an Aristotelian-Spencerian with a love of good food and drink, and an appreciation of the more nonsensical vagaries of life; when in his company I tend to support that general view, as I do at the University as well—for there is a terrific pull in my nature toward the gregarious that I cannot resist. (That I do not wish to resist.) Once I am alone with my thoughts, however, I am accursed with doubts about my own position and nothing seems more precarious than my intellectual "convictions."

The more hardened members of our Society, like Perry Moore, are apt to put the issue bluntly: Is Mrs. A———of Quincy a conscious or unconscious fraud? The conscious frauds are relatively easy to deal with; once discovered, they prefer to erase themselves from further consideration. The unconscious frauds are not, in a sense, "frauds" at all. It would certainly be difficult to prove criminal intention. "Mrs. A———, for instance, does not accept money or gifts so far as we have been able to determine, and both Perry Moore and I noted her courteous but firm refusal of the Judge's offer to send her and her husband (presumably ailing?) on holiday to England in the spring. She is a mild, self-effacing, rather stocky woman in her mid-fifties who wears her hair parted in the center, like several of my maiden aunts, and whose sole item of adornment was an old-fashioned cameo brooch; her black dress had the appearance of having been homemade, though it was attractive enough, and freshly ironed. According to the Society's records she has been a practicing medium now for six years. Yet she lives, still, in an undistinguished section of Quincy, in a neighborhood of modest frame dwellings. The A———s' house is in fairly good condition, especially considering the damage routinely done by our winters, and the only room we saw, the parlor, is quite ordinary, with overstuffed chairs and the usual cushions and a monstrous horsehair sofa and, of course, the oaken table; the atmosphere would have been so conventional as to have seemed disappointing had not Mrs. A———made an attempt to brighten it, or perhaps to give it a glamourously occult air, by hanging certain watercolors about the room. (She claims that the watercolors were "done" by one of her contact spirits, a young Iroquois girl who died in the seventeen seventies of smallpox. They are touchingly garish—mandalas and triangles and stylized eyeballs and even a transparent Cosmic Man with Indian-black hair.)

At last night's sitting there were only three persons in addition to Mrs. A———. Judge T———of the New York State Supreme Court (now retired); Dr. Moore; and I, Jarvis Williams. Dr. Moore and I came out from Cambridge under the aegis of the Society for Psychical Research in order to make a preliminary study of the kind of mediumship Mrs. A———affects. We did not bring a stenographer along this time though Mrs. A———indicated her willingness to have the sitting transcribed; she struck me as being rather warmly cooperative, and even interested in our formal procedures, though Perry Moore remarked afterward at dinner that she had struck him as "noticeably reluctant." She was, however, flustered at the start of the séance and for a while it seemed as if we and the Judge might have made the trip for nothing. (She kept waving her plump hands about like an embarrassed hostess, apologizing for the fact that the spirits were evidently in a "perverse uncommunicative mood tonight.")

She did go into trance eventually, however. The four of us were seated about the heavy round table from approximately 6:50 P.M. to 9 P.M. For nearly forty-five minutes Mrs. A——— made abortive attempts to contact her Chief Communicator and then slipped abruptly into trance (dramatically, in fact: her eyes rolled back in her head in a manner that alarmed me at first), and a personality named Webley appeared. "Webley's" voice appeared to be coming from several directions during the course of the sitting. At all times it was at least three yards from Mrs. A———; despite the semi-dark of the parlor I believe I could see the woman's mouth and throat clearly enough, and I could not detect any obvious signs of ventriloquism. (Perry Moore, who is more experienced than I in psychical research, and rather more casual about the whole phenomenon, claims he has witnessed feats of ventriloquism that would make poor Mrs. A———look quite shabby in comparison.) "Webley's" voice was raw, singsong, peculiarly disturbing. At times it was shrill and at other times so faint as to be nearly inaudible. Something brattish about it. Exasperating. "Webley" took care to pronounce his final *g*'s in a self-conscious manner, quite unlike Mrs. A———. (Which could be, of course, a deliberate ploy.)

This Webley is one of Mrs. A———'s most frequent manifesting spirits, though he is not the most reliable. Her Chief Communicator is a Scots patriarch who lived "in the time of Merlin" and who is evidently very wise; unfortunately he did not choose to appear yesterday evening. Instead, Webley presided. He is supposed to have died some seventy-five years ago at the age of nineteen in a house just up the street from the A———s'. He was either a butcher's helper or an apprentice tailor. He died in a fire—or by a "slow dreadful crippling disease"—or beneath a horse's hooves, in a freakish accident; during the course of the sitting he alluded self-pityingly to his death but seemed to have forgotten the exact details. At the very end of the evening he addressed me directly as Dr. Williams of Harvard University, saying that since I had influential friends in Boston I could help him with his career—it turned out he had written hundreds of songs and poems and parables but none had been published; would I please find a publisher for his work? Life had treated him so unfairly. His talent—his genius—had been lost to humanity. I had it within my power to help him, he claimed, was I not *obliged* to help him . . . ? He then sang one of his songs, which sounded to me like an old ballad; many of the words were so shrill as to be unintelligible, but he sang it just the same, repeating the verses in a haphazard order:

> *This ae nighte, this ae nighte,*
>   *—Every nighte and alle,*
> *Fire and fleet and candle-lighte,*
>   *And Christe receive thy saule.*
> *When thou from hence away art past,*
>   *—Every nighte and alle,*
> *To Whinny-muir thou com'st at last:*
>   *And Christie receive thy saule.*
>
> *From Brig o' Dread when thou may'st pass,*
>   *—Every nighte and alle,*
> *The whinnes sall prick thee to the bare bane:*
>   *And Christe receive thy saule.*

The elderly Judge T———had come up from New York City in order, as he earnestly put it, to "speak directly to his deceased wife as he was never able to do while she was living"; but Webley treated the old gentleman in a high-handed, cavalier manner, as if the occasion were not at all serious. He kept saying, "Who is there tonight? *Who* is there? Let them introduce themselves again—I don't *like* strangers! I tell you I don't *like* strangers!" Though Mrs. A———had informed us beforehand that we would witness no physical phenomena, there were, from time to time, glimmerings of light in the darkened room, hardly more than the tiny pulsations of light made by fireflies; and both Perry Moore and I felt the table vibrating beneath our fingers. At about the time when Webley gave way to the spirit of Judge T———'s wife, the temperature in the room seemed to drop suddenly and I remember being gripped by a sensation of panic—but it lasted only an instant and I was soon myself again. (Dr. Moore claimed not to have noticed any drop in temperature and Judge T———was so rattled after the sitting that it would have been pointless to question him.)

The séance proper was similar to others I have attended. A spirit—or a voice—laid claim to being the late Mrs. T———; this spirit addressed the survivor in a peculiarly intense, urgent manner, so that it was rather embarrassing to be present. Judge T———was soon weeping. His deeply creased face glistened with tears like a child's.

"Why Darrie! *Darrie!* Don't cry! Oh don't cry!" the spirit said. "No one is dead, Darrie. There is no death. No death! . . . Can you hear me, Darrie? Why are you so frightened? So upset? No need, Darrie, no need! Grandfather and Lucy and I are together here—happy together. Darrie, look up! Be brave, my dear! My poor frightened dear! We never knew each other, did we? My poor dear! My love! . . . I saw you in a great transparent house, a great burning house; poor Darrie, they told me you were ill, you were weak with fever; all the rooms of the house were aflame and the staircase was burnt to cinders, but there were figures walking up and down, Darrie, great numbers of them, and you were among them, dear, stumbling in your fright—so clumsy! Look up, dear, and shade your eyes, and you will see me. Grandfather helped me—did you know? Did I call out his name at the end? My dear, my darling, it all happened so quickly—we never knew each other, did we? Don't be hard on Annie! Don't be cruel! Darrie? Why are you crying?" And gradually the spirit voice grew fainter; or perhaps something went wrong and the channels of communication were no longer clear. There were repetitions, garbled phrases, meaningless queries of "Dear? Dear?" that the Judge's replies did not seem to placate. The spirit spoke of her gravesite, and of a trip to Italy taken many years before, and of a dead or unborn baby, and again of Annie—evidently Judge T———'s daughter; but the jumble of words did not always make sense and it was a great relief when Mrs. A——— suddenly woke from her trance.

Judge T——— rose from the table, greatly agitated. He wanted to call the spirit back; he had not asked her certain crucial questions; he had been overcome by emotion and had found it difficult to speak, to interrupt the spirit's monologue. But Mrs. A———(who looked shockingly tired) told him the spirit would not return again that night and they must not make any attempt to call it back.

"The other world obeys its own laws," Mrs. A——— said in her small, rather reedy voice.

We left Mrs. A———'s home shortly after 9:00 P.M. I too was exhausted; I had not realized how absorbed I had been in the proceedings.

Judge T——— is also staying at Montague House, but he was too upset after the sitting to join us for dinner. He assured us, though, that the spirit was authentic—the voice had been his wife's, he was certain of it, he would stake his life on it. She had never called him

"Darrie" during her lifetime, wasn't it odd that she called him "Darrie" now?—and was so concerned for him, so loving?—and concerned for their daughter as well? He was very moved. He had a great deal to think about. (Yes, he'd had a fever some weeks ago—a severe attack of bronchitis and a fever; in fact, he had not completely recovered.) What was extraordinary about the entire experience was the wisdom revealed: There is no death.
There is no death.

Dr. Moore and I dined heartily on roast crown of lamb, spring potatoes with peas, and buttered cabbage. We were served two kinds of bread—German rye and sour-cream rolls; the hotel's butter was superb; the wine excellent; the dessert—crepes with cream and toasted almonds—looked marvelous, though I had not any appetite for it. Dr. Moore was ravenously hungry. He talked as he ate, often punctuating his remarks with rich bursts of laughter. It was his opinion, of course, that the medium was a fraud—and not a very skillful fraud, either. In his fifteen years of amateur, intermittent investigations he had encountered far more skillful mediums. Even the notorious Eustace with his levitating tables and hobgoblin chimes and shrieks was cleverer than Mrs. A———; one knew of course that Eustace was a cheat, but one was hard pressed to explain his method. Whereas Mrs. A———was quite transparent.

Dr. Moore spoke for some time in his amiable, dogmatic way. He ordered brandy for both of us, though it was nearly midnight when we finished our dinner and I was anxious to get to bed. (I hoped to rise early and work on a lecture dealing with Kant's approach to the problem of Free Will, which I would be delivering in a few days.) But Dr. Moore enjoyed talking and seemed to have been invigorated by our experience at Mrs. A———'s.

At the age of forty-three Perry Moore is only four years my senior, but he has the air, in my presence at least, of being considerably older. He is a second cousin of my mother, a very successful physician with a bachelor's flat and office in Louisburg Square; his failure to marry, or his refusal, is one of Boston's perennial mysteries. Everyone agrees that he is learned, witty, charming, and extraordinarily intelligent. Striking rather than conventionally handsome, with a dark, lustrous beard and darkly bright eyes, he is an excellent amateur violinist, an enthusiastic sailor, and a lover of literature—his favorite writers are Fielding, Shakespeare, Horace, and Dante. He is, of course, the perfect investigator in spiritualist matters since he is detached from the phenomena he observes and yet he is indefatigably curious; he has a positive love, a mania, for facts. Like the true scientist he seeks facts that, assembled, may possibly give rise to hypotheses: he does not set out with a hypothesis in mind, like a sort of basket into which certain facts may be tossed, helter-skelter, while others are conventionally ignored. In all things he is an empiricist who accepts nothing on faith.

"If the woman is a fraud, then," I say hesitantly, "you believe she is a self-deluded fraud? And her spirits' information is gained by means of telepathy?"

"Telepathy indeed. There can be no other explanation," Dr. Moore says emphatically. "By some means not yet known to science . . . by some uncanny means she suppresses her conscious personality . . . and thereby releases other, secondary personalities that have the power of seizing upon others' thoughts and memories. It's done in a way not understood by science at the present time. But it will be understood eventually. Our investigations into the unconscious powers of the human mind are just beginning; we're on the threshold, really, of a new era."

"So she simply picks out of her clients' minds whatever they want to hear," I say slowly. "And from time to time she can even tease them a little—insult them, even: she can unloose a creature like that obnoxious Webley upon a person like Judge T———without fear of being discovered. Telepathy. . . . Yes, that would explain a great deal. Very nearly everything we witnessed tonight."

"*Everything,* I should say," Dr. Moore says.

In the coach returning to Cambridge I set aside Kant and my lecture notes and read Sir Thomas Browne: *Light that makes all things seen, makes some things invisible. The greatest mystery of Religion is expressed by adumbration.*

19 March 1887. Cambridge, 11 P.M.

Walked ten miles this evening; must clear cobwebs from mind.

Unhealthy atmosphere. Claustrophobic. Last night's sitting in Quincy—a most unpleasant experience.

(Did not tell my wife what happened. Why is she so curious about the Spirit World?—about Perry Moore?)

My body craves more violent physical activity. In the summer, thank God, I will be able to swim in the ocean: the most strenuous and challenging of exercises.

Jotting down notes re the Quincy experience:

I. Fraud
   Mrs. A———, possibly with accomplices, conspires to deceive: she does research into her clients' lives beforehand, possibly bribes servants. She is either a very skillful ventriloquist or works with someone who is. (Husband? Son? The husband is a retired cabinetmaker said to be in poor health; possibly consumptive. The son, married, lives in Waterbury.)
   Her stated wish to avoid publicity and her declining of payment may simply be ploys; she may intend to make a great deal of money at some future time.
   (Possibility of blackmail?—might be likely in cases similar to Perry Moore's.)

II. Non-fraud
   Naturalistic
   1. Telepathy. She reads minds of clients.
   2. "Multiple personality" of medium. Aspects of her own buried psyche are released as her conscious personality is suppressed. These secondary beings are in mysterious rapport with the "secondary" personalities of the clients.

   Spiritualistic
   1. The controls are genuine communicators, intermediaries between our world and the world of the dead. These spirits give way to other spirits, who then speak through the medium; or
   2. These spirits *influence* the medium, who relays their messages using her own vocabulary. Their personalities are then filtered through and limited by hers.
   3. The spirits are not those of the deceased; they are perverse, willful spirits. (Perhaps demons? But there are no demons.)

III. Alternative hypothesis

   Madness: the medium is mad, the clients are mad, even the detached, rationalist investigators are mad.

Yesterday evening at Mrs. A———'s home, the second sitting Perry Moore and I observed together, along with Miss Bradley, a stenographer from the Society, and two legitimate clients—a Brookline widow, Mrs. P———, and her daughter Clara, a handsome young woman in her early twenties. Mrs. A——— exactly as she appeared to us in February; possibly a little stouter. Wore black dress and cameo brooch. Served Lapsang tea, tiny sandwiches, and biscuits when we arrived shortly after 6 P.M. Seemed quite friendly to Perry, Miss Bradley, and me; fussed over us, like any hostess; chattered a bit about the cold spell. Mrs. P——and her daughter arrived at six-thirty and the sitting began shortly thereafter.

Jarring from the very first. A babble of spirit voices. Mrs. A—— in trance, head flung back, mouth gaping, eyes rolled upward. Queer. Unnerving. I glanced at Dr. Moore but he seemed unperturbed, as always. The widow and her daughter, however, looked as frightened as I felt.

Why are we here, sitting around this table?
What do we believe we will discover?
What are the risks we face . . . ?

"Webley" appeared and disappeared in a matter of minutes. His shrill, raw, aggrieved voice was supplanted by that of a creature of indeterminate sex who babbled in Gaelic. This creature in turn was supplanted by a hoarse German, a man who identified himself as Felix; he spoke a curiously ungrammatical German. For some minutes he and two or three other spirits quarreled. (Each declared himself Mrs. A——'s Chief Communicator for the evening.) Small lights flickered in the semi-dark of the parlor and the table quivered beneath my fingers and I felt, or believed I felt, something brushing against me, touching the back of my head. I shuddered violently but regained my composure at once. An unidentified voice proclaimed in English that the Spirit of our Age was Mars: there would be a catastrophic war shortly and most of the world's population would be destroyed. All atheists would be destroyed. Mrs. A——shook her head from side to side as if trying to wake. Webley appeared, crying "Hello? Hello? I can't see anyone! Who is there? Who has called me?" but was again supplanted by another spirit who shouted long strings of words in a foreign language. [Note: I discovered a few days later that this language was Walachian, a Romanian dialect. Of course Mrs. A——, whose ancestors are English, could not possibly have known Walachian, and I rather doubt that the woman has even heard of the Walachian people.]

The sitting continued in this chaotic way for some minutes. Mrs. P——must have been quite disappointed, since she had wanted to be put in contact with her deceased husband. (She needed advice on whether or not to sell certain pieces of property.) Spirits babbled freely in English, German, Gaelic, French, even in Latin, and at one point Dr. Moore queried a spirit in Greek, but the spirit retreated at once as if not equal to Dr. Moore's wit. The atmosphere was alarming but at the same time rather manic; almost jocular. I found myself suppressing laughter. Something touched the back of my head and I shivered violently and broke into perspiration, but the experience was not altogether unpleasant; it would be very difficult for me to characterize it.

And then—

And then, suddenly, everything changed. There was complete calm. A spirit voice spoke gently out of a corner of the room, addressing Perry Moore by his first name in a slow, tentative, groping way. "Perry? Perry . . . ?" Dr. Moore jerked about in his seat. He was astonished; I could see by his expression that the voice belonged to someone he knew.

"Perry . . . ? This is Brandon. I've waited so long for you, Perry, how could you be so selfish? I forgave you. Long ago. You couldn't help your cruelty and I couldn't help my innocence. Perry? My glasses have been broken—I can't see. I've been afraid for so long, Perry, please have mercy on me! I can't bear it any longer. I didn't *know* what it would be like. There are crowds of people here, but we can't see one another, we don't know one another, we're strangers, there is a universe of strangers—I can't see anyone clearly—I've been lost for twenty years. Perry, I've been waiting for you for twenty years! You don't dare turn away again, Perry! Not again! Not after so long!"

Dr. Moore stumbled to his feet, knocking his chair aside.

"No— Is it— I don't believe—"

"Perry? Perry? Don't abandon me again, Perry! Not again!"

"What is this?" Dr. Moore cried.

He was on his feet now; Mrs. A———— woke from her trance with a groan. The women from Brookline were very upset and I must admit that I was in a mild state of terror, my shirt and my underclothes drenched with perspiration.

The sitting was over. It was only seven-thirty.

"Brandon?" Dr. Moore cried. "Wait. Where are—? Brandon? Can you hear me? Where are you? Why did you do it, Brandon? Wait! Don't leave! Can't anyone call him back— Can't anyone help me—"

Mrs. A———— rose unsteadily. She tried to take Dr. Moore's hands in hers but he was too agitated.

"I heard only the very last words," she said. "They're always that way—so confused, so broken—the poor things— Oh, what a pity! It wasn't murder, was it? Not murder! Suicide—? I believe suicide is even worse for them! The poor broken things, they wake in the other world and are utterly, utterly lost—they have no guides, you see—no help in crossing over— They are completely alone for eternity—"

"Can't you call him back?" Dr. Moore asked wildly. He was peering into a corner of the parlor, slightly stooped, his face distorted as if he were staring into the sun. "Can't someone help me? . . . Brandon? Are you here? Are you here somewhere? For God's sake can't someone help!"

"Dr. Moore, please, the spirits are gone—the sitting is over for tonight—"

"You foolish old woman, leave me alone! Can't you see I—I—I must not lose him— Call him back, will you? I insist! I insist!"

"Dr. Moore, please— You mustn't shout—"

"I said call him back! At once! *Call him back!*"

Then he burst into tears. He stumbled against the table and hid his face in his hands and wept like a child; he wept as if his heart had been broken.

And so today I have been reliving the séance. Taking notes, trying to determine what happened. A brisk windy walk of ten miles. Head buzzing with ideas. Fraud? Deceit? Telepathy? Madness?

What a spectacle! Dr. Perry Moore calling after a spirit, begging it to return—and then crying, afterward, in front of four astonished witnesses.

Dr. Perry Moore of all people.

My dilemma: whether I should report last night's incident to Dr. Rowe, the president of the Society, or whether I should say nothing about it and request that Miss Bradley say nothing. It would be tragic if Perry's professional reputation were to be damaged by a single evening's misadventure; and before long all of Boston would be talking.

In his present state, however, he is likely to tell everyone about it himself.

At Montague House the poor man was unable to sleep. He would have kept me up all night had I had the stamina to endure his excitement.

There *are* spirits! There have always been spirits!

His entire life up to the present time has been misspent!

And of course, most important of all—there is no death!

He paced about my hotel room, pulling at his beard nervously. At times there were tears in his eyes. He seemed to want a response of some kind from me but whenever I started to speak he interrupted; he was not really listening.

"Now at last I know. I can't undo my knowledge," he said in a queer hoarse voice. "Amazing, isn't it, after so many years . . . so many wasted years. . . . Ignorance has been my lot, darkness . . . and a hideous complacency. My God, when I consider my deluded smugness! I am so ashamed, so ashamed. All along people like Mrs. A———have been in contact with a world of such power . . . and people like me have been toiling in ignorance, accumulating material achievements, expending our energies in idiotic transient things. . . . But all that is changed now. Now I know. I *know*. There is no death, as the Spiritualists have always told us."

"But, Perry, don't you think— Isn't it possible that—"

"I *know*," he said quietly. "It's as clear to me as if I had crossed over into that other world myself. Poor Brandon! He's no older now than he was *then*. The poor boy, the poor tragic soul! To think that he's still living after so many years. . . . Extraordinary. . . . It makes my head spin," he said slowly. For a moment he stood without speaking. He pulled at his beard, then absently touched his lips with his fingers, then wiped at his eyes. He seemed to have forgotten me. When he spoke again his voice was hollow, rather ghastly. He sounded drugged. "I . . . I had been thinking of him as . . . as dead, you know. As dead. Twenty years. Dead. And now, tonight, to be forced to realize that . . . that he isn't dead after all. . . . It was laudanum he took. I found him. His rooms on the third floor of Weld Hall. I found him, I had no real idea, none at all, not until I read the note . . . and of course I destroyed the note . . . I had to, you see: for his sake. For his sake more than mine. It was because he realized there could be no . . . no hope. . . . Yet he called me cruel! You heard him, Jarvis, didn't you? Cruel! I suppose I was. Was I? I don't know what to think. I must talk with him again. I . . . I don't know what to . . . what to think. I. . . ."

"You look awfully tired, Perry. It might be a good idea to go to bed," I said weakly.

". . . recognized his voice at once. Oh at once: no doubt. None. What a revelation! And my life so misspent. . . . Treating people's *bodies*. Absurd. I know now that nothing matters except that other world . . . nothing matters except our dead, our beloved dead . . . who are *not dead*. What a colossal revelation. . . . ! Why, it will change the entire course of history. It will alter men's minds throughout the world. You were there, Jarvis, so you understand. You were a witness. . . ."

"But—"

"You'll bear witness to the truth of what I am saying?"

He stared at me, smiling. His eyes were bright and threaded with blood.

I tried to explain to him as courteously and sympathetically as possible that his experience at Mrs. A———'s was not substantially different from the experiences many people have had at séances. "And always in the past psychical researchers have taken the position—"

"You were *there*," he said angrily. "You heard Brandon's voice as clearly as I did. Don't deny it!"

"—Have taken the position that—that the phenomenon can be partly explained by the telepathic powers of the medium—"

"That was Brandon's *voice*," Perry said. "I felt his presence, I tell you! *His*. Mrs. A——— had nothing to do with it—nothing at all. I feel as if . . . as if I could call Brandon back by myself. . . . I feel his presence even now. Close about me. He isn't dead, you see; no one is dead, there's a universe of . . . of people who are not dead. . . . Parents, grandparents, sisters, brothers, everyone . . . everyone. . . . How can you deny, Jarvis, the evidence of your own senses? You were there with me tonight and you know as well as I do. . . ."

"Perry, I don't *know*. I did hear a voice, yes, but we've heard voices before at other sittings, haven't we? There are always voices. There are always 'spirits.' The Society has taken the position that the spirits could be real, of course, but that there are other hypotheses that are perhaps more likely—"

"Other hypotheses indeed!" Perry said irritably. "You're like a man with his eyes shut tight who refuses to open them out of sheer cowardice. Like the cardinals refusing to look through Galileo's telescope! And you have pretensions of being a man of learning, of science. . . . Why, we've got to destroy all the records we've made so far; they're a slander on the world of the spirits. Thank God we didn't file a report yet on Mrs. A———! It would be so embarrassing to be forced to call it back. . . ."

"Perry, please. Don't be angry. I want only to remind you of the fact that we've been present at other sittings, haven't we?—and we've witnessed others responding emotionally to certain phenomena. Judge T———, for instance. He was convinced he'd spoken with his wife. But you must remember, don't you, that you and I were not at all convinced . . . ? It seemed to us more likely that Mrs. A——— is able, through extrasensory powers we don't quite understand, to read the minds of her clients, and then to project certain voices out into the room so that it sounds as if they are coming from other people.... You even said, Perry, that she wasn't a very skillful ventriloquist. You said—"

"What does it matter what, in my ignorance, I said?" he cried. "Isn't it enough that I've been humiliated? That my entire life has been turned about? Must you insult me as well—sitting there so smugly and insulting *me*? I think I can make claim to being someone whom you might respect."

And so I assured him that I did respect him. And he walked about the room, wiping at his eyes, greatly agitated. He spoke again of his friend, Brandon Gould, and of his own ignorance, and of the important mission we must undertake to inform men and women of the true state of affairs. I tried to talk with him, to reason with him, but it was hopeless. He scarcely listened to me.

"... must inform the world ... crucial truth.... There is no death, you see. Never was. Changes civilization, changes the course of history. Jarvis?" he said groggily. "You see? *There is no death.*"

25 March 1887. Cambridge.

Disquieting rumors re Perry Moore. Heard today at the University that one of Dr. Moore's patients (a brother-in-law of Dean Barker) was extremely offended by his behavior during a consultation last week. Talk of his having been drunk—which I find incredible. If the poor man appeared to be excitable and not his customary self, it was not because he was *drunk*, surely.

Another far-fetched tale told me by my wife, who heard it from her sister Maude: Perry Moore went to church (St. Aidan's Episcopal Church on Mount Street) for the first time in a decade, sat alone, began muttering and laughing during the sermon, and finally got to his feet and walked out, creating quite a stir. *What delusions! What delusions!*—he was said to have muttered.

I fear for the poor man's sanity.

31 March 1887. Cambridge. 4 A.M.

Sleepless night. Dreamed of swimming ... swimming in the ocean ... enjoying myself as usual when suddenly the water turns thick ... turns to mud. Hideous! Indescribably awful. I was swimming nude in the ocean, by moonlight, I believe, ecstatically happy, entirely alone, when the water turned to mud.... Vile, disgusting mud; faintly warm; sucking at my body. Legs, thighs, torso, arms. Horrible. Woke in terror. Drenched with perspiration: pajamas wet. One of the most frightening nightmares of my adulthood.

A message from Perry Moore came yesterday just before dinner. Would I like to join him in visiting Mrs. A——sometime soon, in early April perhaps, on a noninvestigative basis . . . ? He is uncertain now of the morality of our "investigating" Mrs. A——or any other medium.

4 April 1887. Cambridge.

Spent the afternoon from two to five at William James's home on Irving Street, talking with Professor James of the inexplicable phenomenon of consciousness. He is robust as always, rather irreverent, supremely confident in a way I find enviable; rather like Perry Moore before his conversion (Extraordinary eyes—so piercing, quick, playful; a graying beard liberally threaded with white; close-cropped graying hair; a large, curving, impressive forehead; a manner intelligent and graceful and at the same time rough-edged, as if he anticipates or perhaps even hopes for recalcitration in his listeners.). We both find conclusive the ideas set forth in Binét's *Alterations of Personality* . . . unsettling as these ideas may be to the rationalist position. James speaks of a *peculiarity* in the constitution of human nature: that is, the fact that we inhabit not only our ego-consciousness but a wide field of psychological experience (most clearly represented by the phenomenon of memory, which no one can adequately explain) over which we have no control whatsoever. In fact, we are not generally aware of this field of consciousness.

We inhabit a lighted sphere, then; and about us is a vast penumbra of memories, reflections, feelings, and stray uncoordinated thoughts that "belong" to us theoretically, but that do not seem to be part of our conscious identity. (I was too timid to ask Professor James whether it might be the case that we do not inevitably own these aspects of the personality—that such phenomena belong as much to the objective world as to our subjective selves.) It is quite possible that there is an element of some indeterminate kind: oceanic, timeless, and living, against which the individual being constructs temporary barriers as part of an ongoing process of unique, particularized survival; like the ocean itself, which appears to separate islands that are in fact not "islands" at all, but aspects of the earth firmly joined together below the surface of the water. Our lives, then, resemble these islands.... All this is no more than a possibility, Professor James and I agreed.

James is acquainted, of course, with Perry Moore. But he declined to speak on the subject of the poor man's increasingly eccentric behavior when I alluded to it. (It may be that he knows even more about the situation than I do—he enjoys a multitude of acquaintances in Cambridge and Boston.) I brought our conversation round several times to the possibility of the *naturalness* of the conversion experience in terms of the individual's evolution of self, no matter how his family, his colleagues, and society in general viewed it, and Professor James appeared to agree; at least he did not emphatically disagree. He maintains a healthy skepticism, of course, regarding Spiritualist claims, and all evangelical and enthusiastic religious movements, though he is, at the same time, a highly articulate foe of the "rationalist" position and he believes that psychical research of the kind some of us are attempting will eventually unearth riches—revealing aspects of the human psyche otherwise closed to our scrutiny.

"The fearful thing," James said, "is that we are at all times vulnerable to incursions from the 'other side' of the personality.... We cannot determine the nature of the total personality simply because much of it, perhaps most, is hidden from us.... When we are invaded, then, we are overwhelmed and surrender immediately. Emotionally charged intuitions, hunches, guesses, even ideas may be the least aggressive of these incursions; but there are visual and auditory hallucinations, and forms of automatic behavior not controlled by the conscious mind.... Ah, you're thinking I am simply describing insanity?"

I stared at him, quite surprised.

"No. Not at all. Not at all," I said at once.

Reading through my grandfather's journals, begun in East Anglia many years before my birth. Another world then. Another language, now lost to us. *Man is sinful by nature. God's justice takes precedence over His mercy*. The dogma of Original Sin: something brutish about the innocence of that belief. And yet consoling....

Fearful of sleep since my dreams are so troubled now. The voices of impudent spirits (Immanuel Kant himself come to chide me for having made too much of his categories—!), stray shouts and whispers I cannot decipher, the faces of my own beloved dead hovering near, like carnival masks, insubstantial and possibly fraudulent.

Impatient with my wife, who questions me too closely on these personal matters; annoyed from time to time, in the evenings especially, by the silliness of the children. (The eldest is twelve now and should know better.) Dreading to receive another lengthy letter—sermon, really—from Perry Moore re his "new position," and yet perversely hoping one will come soon.

I must know.

(Must know *what* . . . ?)

I must know.

10 April 1887. Boston. St. Aidan's Episcopal Church.

Funeral service this morning for Perry Moore; dead at forty-three.

17 April 1887. Seven Hills, New Hampshire.

A weekend retreat. No talk. No need to think.

Visiting with a former associate, author of numerous books. Cartesian specialist. Elderly. Partly deaf. Extraordinarily kind to me. (Did not ask about the Department or about my work.) Intensely interested in animal behavior now, in observation primarily; fascinated with the phenomenon of hibernation.

He leaves me alone for hours. He sees something in my face I cannot see myself.

The old consolations of a cruel but just God: ludricous today.

In the nineteenth century we live free of God. We live in the illusion of freedom-of-God.

Dozing off in the guest room of this old farmhouse and then waking abruptly. *Is someone here? Is someone here?* My voice queer, hushed, childlike. *Please: is someone here?*

Silence.

Query: Is the penumbra outside consciousness all that was ever meant by "God"?

Query: Is inevitability all that was ever meant by "God"?

God—the body of fate we inhabit, then: no more and no less.

God pulled Perry down into the body of fate: into Himself. (Or Itself.) As Professor James might say, Dr. Moore was "vulnerable" to an assault from the other side.

At any rate he is dead. They buried him last Saturday.

NIGHT-SIDE

25 April 1887. Cambridge.

Shelves of books. The sanctity of books. Kant, Plato, Schopenhauer, Descartes, Hume, Hegel, Spinoza. The others. All. Nietz-sche, Spencer, Leibnitz (on whom I did a torturous Master's thesis). Plotinus. Swedenborg. *The Transactions of the American Society for Psychical Research.* Voltaire. Locke. Rousseau. And Berkeley: the good Bishop adrift in a dream.

An etching by Halbrech above my desk, The Thames 1801. Water too black. Inky-black. Thick with mud . . . ? Filthy water in any case.

Perry's essay, forty-five scribbled pages. "The Challenge of the Future." Given to me several weeks ago by Dr. Rowe, who feared rejecting it for the *Transactions* but could not, of course, accept it. I can read only a few pages at a time, then push it aside, too moved to continue. Frightened also.

The man had gone insane.

Died insane.

Personality broken: broken bits of intellect.

His argument passionate and disjointed, with no pretense of objectivity. Where some weeks ago he had taken the stand that it was immoral to investigate the Spirit World, now he took the stand that it was imperative we do so. We are on the brink of a new age . . . new knowledge of the universe . . . comparable to the stormy transitional period between the Ptolemaic and the Copernican theories of the universe. . . . More experiments required. Money. Donations. Subsidies by private institutions. All psychological research must be channeled into a systematic study of the Spirit World and the ways by which we can communicate with that world. Mediums like Mrs. A———must be brought to centers of learning like Harvard and treated with the respect their genius deserves. Their value to civilization is, after all, beyond estimation. They must be rescued from arduous and routine lives where their genius is drained off into vulgar pursuits . . . they must be rescued from a clientele that is mainly concerned with being put into contact with deceased relatives for utterly trivial, self-serving reasons. Men of learning must realize the gravity of the situation. Otherwise we will fail, we will stagger beneath the burden, we will be defeated, ignobly, and it will remain for the twentieth century to discover the existence of the Spirit Universe that surrounds the Material Universe, and to determine the exact ways by which one world is related to another.

* * *

Perry Moore died of a stroke on the eighth of April; died instantaneously on the steps of the Bedford Club shortly after 2 P.M. Passers-by saw a very excited, red-faced gentleman with an open collar push his way through a small gathering at the top of the steps—and then suddenly fall, as if shot down.

In death he looked like quite another person: his features sharp, the nose especially pointed. Hardly the handsome Perry Moore everyone had known.

He had come to a meeting of the Society, though it was suggested by Dr. Rowe and by others (including myself) that he stay away. Of course he came to argue. To present his "new position." To insult the other members. (He was contemptuous of a rather poorly organized paper on the medium Miss E———of Salem, a young woman who works with objects like rings, articles of clothing, locks of hair, et cetera; and quite angry with the evidence presented by a young geologist that would seem to discredit, once and for all, the claims of Eustace of Portsmouth. He interrupted a third paper, calling the reader a "bigot" and an "ignorant fool.")

Fortunately the incident did not find its way into any of the papers. The press, misunderstanding (deliberately and maliciously) the Society's attitude toward Spiritualism, delights in ridiculing our efforts.

There were respectful obituaries. A fine eulogy prepared by Reverend Tyler of St. Aidan's. Other tributes. *A tragic loss. . . . Mourned by all who knew him. . . .* (I stammered and could not speak. I cannot speak of him, of it, even now. Am I mourning, am I aggrieved? Or merely shocked? Terrified?) Relatives and friends and associates glossed over his behavior these past few months and settled upon an earlier Perry Moore, eminently sane, a distinguished physician and man of letters. I did not disagree, I merely acquiesced; I could not make any claim to have really known the man.

And so he has died, and so he is dead. . . .

Shortly after the funeral I went away to New Hampshire for a few days. But I can barely remember that period of time now. I sleep poorly, I yearn for summer, for a drastic change of climate, of scene. It was unwise for me to take up the responsibility of psychical research, fascinated though I am by it; my classes and lectures at the University demand most of my energy.

How quickly he died, and so young: so relatively young.

No history of high blood pressure, it is said.

At the end he was arguing with everyone, however. His personality had completely changed. He was rude, impetuous, even rather profane; even poorly groomed. (Rising to challenge the first of the papers, he revealed a shirtfront that appeared to be stained.) Some claimed he had been drinking all along, for years. Was it possible . . . ? (He had clearly enjoyed the wine and brandy in Quincy that evening, but I would not have said he was intemperate.) Rumors, fanciful tales, outright lies, slander. . . . It is painful, the vulnerability death brings.

Bigots, he called us. Ignorant fools. Unbelievers—atheists—traitors to the Spirit World—heretics. Heretics! I believe he looked directly at me as he pushed his way out of the meeting room: his eyes glaring, his face dangerously flushed, no recognition in his stare.

After his death, it is said, books continue to arrive at his home from England and Europe. He spent a small fortune on obscure, out-of-print volumes—commentaries on the Kabbala, on Plotinus, medieval alchemical texts, books on astrology, witchcraft, the metaphysics of death. Occult cosmologies. Egyptian, Indian, and Chinese "wisdom." Blake, Swedenborg, Cozad. *The Tibetan Book of the Dead.* Datsky's *Lunar Mysteries.* His estate is in chaos because he left not one but several wills, the most recent made out only a day before his death, merely a few lines scribbled on scrap paper, without witnesses. The family will contest, of course. Since in this will he left his money and property to an obscure woman living in Quincy, Massachusetts, and since he was obviously not in his right mind at the time, they would be foolish indeed not to contest.

Days have passed since his sudden death. Days continue to pass. At times I am seized by a sort of quick, cold panic; at other times I am inclined to think the entire situation has been exaggerated. In one mood I vow to myself that I will never again pursue psychical research because it is simply too dangerous. In another mood I vow I will never again pursue it because it is a waste of time and my own work, my own career, must come first.

Heretics, he called us. Looking straight at me.

Still, he was mad. And is not to be blamed for the vagaries of madness.

19 June 1887. Boston.

Luncheon with Dr. Rowe, Miss Madeleine van der Post, young Lucas Matthewson; turned over my personal records and notes re the mediums Dr. Moore and I visited. (Destroyed jottings of a private nature.) Miss van der Post and Matthewson will be taking over my responsibilities. Both are young, quick-witted, alert, with a certain ironic play about their features; rather like Dr. Moore in his prime. Matthewson is a former seminary student now teaching physics at the Boston University. They questioned me about Perry Moore, but I avoided answering frankly. Asked if we were close, I said *No*. Asked if I had heard a bizarre tale making the rounds of Boston salons—that a spirit claiming to be Perry Moore has intruded upon a number of séances in the area—I said honestly that I had not; and I did not care to hear about it.

Spinoza: *I will analyze the actions and appetites of men as if it were a question of lines, of planes, and of solids.*
 It is in this direction, I believe, that we must move. Away from the phantasmal, the vaporous, the unclear; toward lines, planes, and solids.
 Sanity.

8 July 1887. Mount Desert Island, Maine.

Very early this morning, before dawn, dreamed of Perry Moore: a babbling gesticulating spirit, bearded, bright-eyed, obviously mad. Jarvis? Jarvis? Don't deny me! he cried. I am so . . . so bereft. . . .
 Paralyzed, I faced him: neither awake nor asleep. His words were not really *words* so much as unvoiced thoughts. I heard them in my own voice; a terrible raw itching at the back of my throat yearned to articulate the man's grief.
 Perry?
 You don't dare deny me! Not now!
 He drew near and I could not escape. The dream shifted, lost its clarity. Someone was shouting at me. Very angry, he was, and baffled—as if drunk—or ill—or injured.
 Perry? I can't hear you—
 —Our dinner at Montague House, do you remember? Lamb, it was. And crepes with almond for dessert. You remember! You remember! You can't deny me! We were both nonbelievers then, both abysmally ignorant—you can't deny me!
 (I was mute with fear or with cunning.)
 —That idiot Rowe, how humiliated he will be! All of them! All of you! The entire rationalist bias, the—the conspiracy of—of fools—bigots— In a few years— In a few short years— Jarvis, where are

you? Why can't I see you? Where have you gone?— My eyes can't focus: will someone help me? I seem to have lost my way. Who is here? Who am I talking with? You remember me, don't you?

(He brushed near me, blinking helplessly. His mouth was a hole torn into his pale ravaged flesh.)

Where are you? Where is everyone? I thought it would be crowded here but—but there's no one—I am forgetting so much! My name—what was my name? Can't see. Can't remember. Something very important—something very important I must accomplish— can't remember— Why is there no God? No one here? No one in control? We drift this way and that way, we come to no rest, there are no landmarks—no way of judging—everything is confused—disjointed—Is someone listening? Would you read to me, please? Would you read to me?—anything!—that speech of Hamlet's—*To be or not*—a sonnet of Shakespeare's—any sonnet, anything—*That time of year thou may in me behold*—is that it?—is that how it begins? *Bare ruin'd choirs where the sweet birds once sang.* How does it go? Won't you tell me? I'm lost—there's nothing here to see, to touch—isn't anyone listening? I thought there was someone nearby, a friend: isn't anyone here?

(I stood paralyzed, mute with caution: he passed by.)

—*When in the chronicle of wasted time*—*the wide world dreaming of things to come*—is anyone listening?—can anyone help?—I am forgetting so much—my name, my life—my life's work—to penetrate the mysteries—the veil—to do justice to the universe of—of what—what had I intended?—am I in my place of repose now, have I come home? Why is it so empty here? Why is no one in control? My eyes—my head—mind broken and blown about—slivers—shards— annihilating all that's made to a—a green thought—a green shade—Shakespeare? Plato? Pascal? Will someone read me Pascal again? I seem to have lost my way—I am being blown about— Jarvis, was it? My dear young friend Jarvis? But I've forgotten your last name—I've forgotten so much—

(I wanted to reach out to touch him—but could not move, could not wake. The back of my throat ached with sorrow. Silent! Silent! I could not utter a word.)

—My papers, my journal—twenty years—a key somewhere hidden—where?—ah yes: the bottom drawer of my desk—do you hear?—my desk—house—Louisburg Square—the key is hidden there—wrapped in a linen handkerchief—the strongbox is—the locked box is—hidden—my brother Edward's house—attic— trunk—steamer trunk—initials R. W. M.—Father's trunk, you see—strongbox hidden inside—my secret journals—life's work—physical and spiritual wisdom—must not be lost—are you listening?—is anyone listening? I am forgetting so much, my mind is in shreds—but if you could locate the journal and read it to me—if you could salvage it—me—I would be so very grateful—I would forgive you anything, all of you— Is anyone there? Jarvis? Brandon? No one?—My journal, my soul: will you salvage it? Will—

(He stumbled away and I was alone again.)

Perry—?

But it was too late: I awoke drenched with perspiration.

Nightmare.

Must forget.

Best to rise early, before the others. Mount Desert Island lovely in July. Our lodge on a hill above the beach. No spirits here: wind from the northeast, perpetual fresh air, perpetual waves. Best to rise early and run along the beach and plunge into the chilly water.

Clear the cobwebs from one's mind.

How beautiful the sky, the ocean, the sunrise!

No spirits here on Mount Desert Island. Swimming: skillful exertion of arms and legs. Head turned this way, that way. Eyes half shut. The surprise of the cold rough waves. One yearns almost to slip out of one's human skin at such times . . . ! Crude blatant beauty of Maine. Ocean. Muscular exertion of body. How alive I am, how living, how invulnerable; what a triumph in my every breath. . . .

Everything slips from my mind except the present moment. I am living, I am alive, I am immortal. Must not weaken: must not sink. Drowning? No. Impossible. Life is the only reality. It is not extinction that awaits but a hideous dreamlike state, a perpetual groping, blundering—far worse than extinction—incomprehensible: so it is life we must cling to, arm over arm, swimming, conquering the element that sustains us.

Jarvis? someone cried. *Please hear me—*

How exquisite life is, the turbulent joy of life contained in flesh! I heard nothing except the triumphant waves splashing about me. I swam for nearly an hour. Was reluctant to come ashore for breakfast, though our breakfasts are always pleasant rowdy sessions: my wife and my brother's wife and our seven children thrown together for the month of July. Three boys, four girls: noise, bustle, health, no shadows, no spirits. No time to think. Again and again I shall emerge from the surf, face and hair and body streaming water, exhausted but jubilant, triumphant. Again and again the children will call out to me, excited, from the day-side of the world that they inhabit.

I will not investigate Dr. Moore's strongbox and his secret journal; I will not even think about doing so. The wind blows words away. The surf is hypnotic. I will not remember this morning's dream once I sit down to breakfast with the family. I will not clutch my wife's wrist and say *We must not die! We dare not die!*—for that would only frighten and offend her.

Jarvis? she is calling at this very moment.

And I say *Yes—? Yes, I'll be there at once.*

CHELSEA QUINN YARBRO

"Best Interests"

Chelsea Quinn Yarbro (1942-) began publishing science fiction in the late 1960s, but achieved her greatest renown as the creator of her series character, the vampires Count Saint-Germain, in her 1978 novel **Hotel Transylvania.** *The chronicles of Saint-Germain and his lover Olivia Clemens are exhaustively researched historical romances that trace their lives over the centuries from ancient Egypt to the present day, and invariably contrast their natures as agents of supernatural horror with mankind's history of evil. Saint-Germain and Olivia have served as the protagonists of nearly a dozen books, including* **Blood Games, Out of the House of Life, Crusader's Torch,** *and* **Mansions of Darkness.** *Yarbro has also written the werewolf novels* **The Godforsaken** *and* **Beastnights,** *the futuristic science fiction novels* **Time of the Fourth Horsemen** *and* **False Dawn,** *and four novels in her "Ogilvie, Tallant and Moon" series, which folds Native American mysticism into the detective story. Her exceptional short fiction is collected in* **Signs and Portents** *and* **Cautionary Tales.**

Best Interests

by Chelsea Quinn Yarbro

Slowly, Derek spread the mauve color in concentric circles on Melanie's breasts—helpless targets with a rosy bull's eye at the center. To finish the job he drew more circles around her navel and aimed an arrow away from the dark hair that fluffed between her thighs. He knew it was over between them just as he realized that mauve wasn't a very flattering color on her.

He glanced at the Dial glowing in the darkened room like the loving eye of a mother watching over him. The display read:

YOUR APARTMENT HAS BEEN INDIVIDUALLY PROGRAMMED

IT HAS YOUR BEST INTERESTS AT HEART

The Dial was something a man could depend on; not like the unpredictable female lying beside him asleep. Asleep! While the Dial stayed resolutely awake, ministering to him, anticipating his needs, understanding his desires almost before he knew them himself.

He dialed the bed to a more comfortable angle, moving Melanie away from him. The Dial had superimposed a warm golden glow over what was rather a sodden morning. It was that dreadful kind of day, the sort that Derek liked least. It was slightly warm, with a slow drizzle leaking out of the clouds. Days like this, Derek found it hard to think. And the Dial knew it.

Melanie sighed in her sleep and slid into a more relaxed position. Derek decided not to wake her. There was no reason for her to get up yet. Since he was going to tell her goodbye that evening he might as well let her spend the morning getting a good rest.

Across the room the Dial activated the mirror. Derek propped himself on his elbow and looked at the image the Dial provided for him. In the glass his pudgy body was tall and slim, his movements fascinating and seductive rather than awkward. His lank, mouse-colored hair became blond, his slightly myopic eyes were really quite compelling and of a brilliant blue instead of washed-out hazel. He had seen himself this way for so long that he would not have recognized the shapeless, pale, lazy young man he really was. But he never bothered to look into another mirror.

Since he was the superintendent of the complex of buildings in which he lived, he was never away from the Dials. His title was impressive—Environmental Engineer—and he had a certain prestige along with the loving care of every Dial in the building.

Melanie stirred beside him, making a mess of the bed. She was the kind of sleeper who took all the covers and cocooned them around her, the kind who could work a sheet to the bottom of the bed and keep all the scratchy, old-fashioned blankets up around her neck. That was one of the reasons Derek was tired of her. Even her luxurious Rococo curves did not truly excite him anymore.

He looked away from the Dial, feeling a rush of warmth as he gazed at the display. None of his other mistresses had been able to give him the same sensation of being cared for, of being so very *important*. And now Melanie was becoming exacting and cold. He wriggled closer to the Dial and cleared his throat.

The display lit up promptly:

GOOD MORNING, SIR. THIS UNIT TRUSTS YOU SLEPT WELL.

Derek wished the Dial a hearty good morning and considered breakfast. The Dial anticipated his requests with this display:

THERE IS A STANDARD EGG BREAKFAST #3, AVAILABLE IMMEDIATELY, OR ANOTHER CAN BE PREPARED TO YOUR ORDER. THIS UNIT WILL DO FRIED, SCRAMBLED, OR POACHED EGGS.

"What about eggs Benedict?" Derek asked, and immediately regretted it.

THIS UNIT IS SORRY TO INFORM YOU THAT THERE ARE 380 TOO MANY CALORIES IN EGGS BENEDICT. IF YOU WILL BE SATISFIED WITH HIGH TEA INSTEAD OF SUPPER, THIS UNIT WILL SERVE THE EGGS BENEDICT YOU REQUESTED, BUT MUST REMIND YOU THAT YOUR EGG LIMIT IS HALF FILLED FOR THIS WEEK AND THIS IS ONLY TUESDAY.

Derek glared. He knew that he should have Breakfast #3, but he snapped, "Never mind. I'll skip breakfast."

THIS UNIT WISHES TO REMIND YOU THAT BREAKFAST IS THE MOST IMPORTANT MEAL OF THE DAY. IT IS IN YOUR BEST INTERESTS TO EAT.

Rubbing his hands over his stubby face, Derek remembered that the Dial was right. It *did* want to take care of him. He sniffed through the chronic nasal sludge of sinusitis.

THIS UNIT HAS MEASURED YOUR BLOOD SUGAR LEVEL AND BODILY NUTRITIONAL DEPLETION. THE EFFECTS OF THREE ORGASMS HAS SIGNIFICANTLY REDUCED YOUR AVAILABLE ENERGY. IN ADDITION TO BREAKFAST #3, THIS UNIT WILL ISSUE THREE VITAPEP CAPSULES.

"Thank you," murmured Derek. He hadn't realized until then how drained he felt. Behind him, Melanie snored gently. Derek had not been aware that women could snore until Melanie had moved in with him. None of his other mistresses snored. He was uncertain if snoring was a fault in women, but he was sure it wasn't a virtue.

The Dial glowed, and on its upper surface a panel slid back and a glass of white liquid rose into view.

GOOD MORNING, SIR. THIS UNIT, IN ACCORDANCE WITH YOUR WISHES AND THE PRACTICE OF GOOD DIETARY HABITS IS BRINGING YOU A MORNING DRINK.

"I thought I ordered coffee. There's a standing program that says coffee with breakfast. A *standing* order."

THIS UNIT REGRETS TO INFORM YOU THAT LARGE QUANTITIES OF COFFEE ARE NOT IN YOUR BEST INTERESTS.

Rather than argue with the Dial, Derek took the glass. He drank the stuff, making a face, but refrained from asking the Dial what nutrients went into it: He had asked that once and the Dial had told him.

"Is that you, Derek?" There was a stirring in the mound of bedclothes. The tone of her question was calculated to annoy, and succeeded. It was a frigidity training technique that seldom failed.

"Yes, darling," he said patiently. He pondered what to do about her, for recently when they made love, she had taken to lying there limply, muttering about shopping lists. He would be glad when the frigidity fad was over. Now he wished there was something he could do that would shock her back to the warm, cuddly thing she had been three months ago.

The display lit up brightly:

THIS UNIT HAS FULL SEXUAL RATINGS FOR THE LAST TWENTY-FOUR HOURS. YOUR PERFORMANCE STANDS AT

AN AVERAGE OF 5.88 COMPARED TO A USUAL PERFOR-
MANCE LEVEL OF 8.79. FRUSTRATION QUOTIENT IS NOW
4.93. IT IS IN YOUR BEST INTERESTS TO EXPERIENCE OR-
GASM WITH A MORE ENTHUSIASTIC PARTNER.

Derek stared at the Dial. Always before when he received his sexual ratings, the Dial had waited until his partner was gone. He said, "Can't it wait?"

There was a clucking sound as the display changed:
THIS UNIT HAS DETERMINED THAT IT IS IN YOUR BEST
INTERESTS TO HAVE THIS KNOWLEDGE AS SOON AS POSSI-
BLE, SO THAT YOU MAY REMEDY THE PROBLEM QUICKLY.

Derek was still thinking about this when Melanie asked from her side of the bed, "When do you leave?" She didn't even smile.

"Oh, a couple of hours. No *rush*, Melanie."

"Good. You can fix the Dial for me. It hasn't been doing anything I program it to do." She sulked, and it wasn't very pretty. "You'd think it has something against me."

He yawned. "Probably just some trouble in the programming. Nothing to *worry* about; it can't be serious. I'll take care of it this evening." The time Derek spent on his own apartment was not considered part of his job, he was paid for maintaining the other units in the complex. "If it's still giving you trouble, I'll take care of it."

Now Melanie pouted. "The other evening when we had those friends of yours over, I dialed a tropical veranda and it was all chilly and none of the flowers were right. And the food tasted like paste!"

"I know you were upset. But it turned *out* okay, didn't it? We just got rid of the veranda and did a standard interior—don't forget how hard it is to get a full exterior at heavy power-use times. Everyone wants dinner, and the building can't . . ."

"Go ahead," she sniffed. "Defend it. Sure, it works fine for you. It's me it won't work for."

With a click and a whirr the Dial came to life again:
THIS UNIT WISHES TO INFORM YOU THAT BREAKFAST IS
READY. FOR MAXIMUM BENEFIT IT SHOULD BE EATEN
WHILE HOT.

Melanie screamed and threw a pillow at the Dial. "You bitch!"

There was his mistress lying in bed, Derek thought, swathed to her neck in sheets, and there he was drinking ersatz milk while a machine issued orders. Something had to be done.

"Melanie," he began, edging a little closer to her, "*maybe* you'd better stop at the therapy station this morning. You aren't acting like yourself, letting the Dial upset you." He inched closer. "You aren't using the Dial as a willing servant, so that you're free to do those creative things only human beings . . ."

IT IS NOW TWO MINUTES SINCE YOU WERE CALLED TO BREAKFAST, announced the Dial.

"See?" she demanded, thrusting her hand toward the Dial display. "It won't leave us alone. It's always butting in!"

"We could ignore it," he suggested hopefully, reaching for her.

She leaped from the bed. "I know what you want—you want to smother me with your sexual ruttings. It's disgusting."

It was sad, remembering how much fun she had been at first. Now she was little more than a shrew.

THIS UNIT INFORMS YOU THAT IT CANNOT BE RESPONSIBLE FOR THE NUTRITIONAL CONTENT OF THE MEAL AFTER THREE MORE MINUTES.

Derek was almost angry. "Wait a bit and fix us another."

ACCORDING TO CODE 4-88371A, PARAGRAPH 134-D, THE MISUSE OF FOODSTUFFS IS A MISDEMEANOR PUNISHABLE BY FINE OR TWO DAYS WITHOUT MACHINE SUPPORT.

Melanie burrowed into the blankets, saying scornfully, "You let yourself be ordered about by metal and plastic."

"But, Melanie . . ." He faltered. "All right. Maybe there *is* a foul-up in the circuits somewhere. All you have to do is open that panel and see if the three screws are in a straight line. Honestly, that's all there is to it." He opened the panel and showed Melanie the three screws, all lined up. "I've made a few modifications on the unit, of course," he added modestly. "It's one of the few advantages of working on the Dials—I can experiment on my own."

THIS UNIT MUST INSIST THAT YOU EAT YOUR BREAKFAST.

"All right." Derek got to his feet. "It really does *care*, Melanie. All it wants is what's good for me." He saw the weak but implacable defiance in the set of her chin. "Breakfast time. Do you want to join me, or would you rather . . ." He held out his hand on the off-chance that she might take it.

She ignored him. "I'll put on my robe."

He reached back to the bed, grabbed the robe, and tossed it to her. "You might get dressed."

"I haven't bathed. I'm not going to put clothes on over this!" She put her hand to the bull's eyes.

"I'll wait a few minutes while . . ."

The Dial interrupted: IN A FEW MINUTES, THE VALUE OF

BREAKFAST WILL HAVE DECREASED TOO MUCH, AND WILL BE COLD, BESIDES.

Derek glared at Melanie. The morning and breakfast were both being ruined by that woman. "I'll help scrub," he said as he realized she would be certain to misunderstand him.

"Surely I have the right to privacy?" Her arched brows went up and she remained that way, one hand to her breasts and an expression of haughty shock on her face until Derek was out of the room.

The creamed bacon and eggs tasted like sulphur and the tea seemed to be squeezed from old blotters. There were, in addition to the eggs, two small slices of watery and tasteless fruit which the Dial assured Derek were chock full of the required nutrients.

He was almost finished with the last, hard piece of toast when Melanie came into the eating area. She was still in her robe and her expression had not improved. Derek let her order her food for herself, wincing as the Dial informed her that there were too many fats in corned beef hash for her to have it twice in one week. Hoping to distract her and to steady her temper, Derek asked, "What about work today? What's going on at your office?"

"I'm going to stay home today," Melanie informed him as she stared at the gray mass of reconstituted protein that slid onto the table in front of her.

THIS UNIT REMINDS YOU THAT THE PENALTY FOR ABSENTEEISM IS TEN DAYS OF CONTINUOUS WORK AND A FINE IN THE AMOUNT OF THE VALUE OF THAT WORK. FULL COOPERATION OF ALL MEMBERS OF SOCIETY IS ESSENTIAL IF TRUE DEMOCRACY IS TO BE ACHIEVED. CONSULT THE LEGISLATIVE TAPES FOR PERTINENT LAWS.

"It's none of your business!" she yelled at the machine, and threw the contents of her bowl at the screen.

MALICIOUS DAMAGE OF A DIAL IS A MISDEMEANOR, DELIBERATE MISUSE OF A DIAL IS A FELONY. SEE HOUSING CODE SECTION 445-P-1A, ALSO THE LEGISLATIVE TAPES FOR LAWS COVERING ANTI-SOCIAL ACTS AND VANDALISM.

"It hates me!" Melanie screamed. "It wants to punish me!" Her eyes grew bright and her fingers began to twist the lapel of her robe. "Wait a minute . . . it isn't me, is it? It's you, Derek. This is your unit. You made all those improvements in it, didn't you? It doesn't want to share you with anyone! It's jealous! It wants you all to itself!"

Derek looked at Melanie in some alarm. Then he turned to the

Dial. "Notify the Medical Center in this complex. Melanie isn't quite herself today."

"I'm fine!" she insisted in an hysterical shriek. "It's the Dial that's all wrong!"

"Nonsense!" Derek snapped. "It's a machine, Melanie, a machine whose sole purpose is to make our lives fuller and better. It's just absurd to think that a Dial can do anything we don't want it to. It has our best interests at heart. That's why everyone has them."

"Oh dear, oh dear," Melanie wailed, well into her outburst now and secretly enjoying it. "Everyone has them. Of course they do. And everyone believes that they control the Dials, but it's the other way around." She began to sob.

Another bowl of reconstituted protein slid toward her, along with a suspicious-looking brown pill.

SUPPLEMENTAL VITAMINS, the Dial explained. SUCH OUTBURSTS LEAD TO MINOR VITAMIN DEFICIENCIES.

Melanie put her head on the table and wept.

A prescription arrived a few minutes later, and Derek wearily guided Melanie back to the bedroom, trying to think of something to say that would reassure her without sounding wholly inane.

"I won't, I won't, Don't." Melanie thrashed and turned her head from side to side to avoid the magenta syrup that Derek held out to her in a specially provided plastic spoon. "It's all wrong!" Her face was rigid and her voice was as unpleasant and penetrating as the whine of a buzz-saw.

IT IS NECESSARY THAT YOU TAKE THIS PREPARATION IN ORDER TO REGAIN YOUR EQUILIBRIUM AND HEALTH. IT IS NOT BENEFICIAL TO YOUR SYSTEM TO BEHAVE IN THIS WAY. YOU WILL HARM YOURSELF IF YOU CONTINUE TO DO SO. THE MEDICATION PROVIDED WILL CALM YOU AND HELP YOU TO RECOVER. FOR YOUR OWN GOOD, THIS UNIT MUST URGE YOU TO TAKE IT.

"Melanie," Derek said with an exasperated sigh. "It's right. You're *not* acting rationally. Just drink this down and you'll be fine in a couple of hours." As he forced the prescribed and vile-smelling medication to her obstinately tightened lips, he pleaded with her. "Come *on*, Melanie. Just one sip and it's done."

She shook her head vigorously and screwed up her face, as if shutting every possible orifice he might want to use for the medication.

THIS UNIT SUGGESTS THAT YOU HOLD HER NOSE. SHE

WILL HAVE TO BREATHE THROUGH HER MOUTH AND YOU MAY THEN ADMINISTER THE PRESCRIPTION.

Derek nodded dubiously and did as the Dial suggested. Melanie twisted and turned a magnificent plum color before she capitulated and allowed Derek to tip the nauseating stuff down her throat.

THE PRESCRIPTION WILL REQUIRE APPROXIMATELY 7.5 MINUTES TO BECOME EFFECTIVE.

"Will you be okay, Melanie?" Derek asked with a solicitude he did not really feel.

"I hate you," she answered.

THIS UNIT MUST REMIND YOU OF THE TIME. YOU MUST LEAVE WITHIN THE NEXT 3 MINUTES OR YOU WILL BE LATE TO WORK. THE PENALTY FOR TARDINESS IS OUTLINED IN LEGISLATIVE CODE GGR-12982AP-3T11. A COMPLETE SCHEDULE OF MONETARY FINES ARE OUTLINED IN UNION MANUAL 17-44-B AND C.

"I've got to go," Derek said hurriedly. "Don't worry about anything, Melanie," he said from the doorway. "The Dial will take care of you."

OF COURSE.

"Oh, thanks," Derek said to the Dial as he hurried to complete primary hygiene. He dressed quickly and neatly, choosing a conservative red and orange stripe-along and a simple chartreuse neckscarf. Only major executives were entitled to wear the impressive outfits of organic textiles, and Derek cherished in his heart the wish that one day he, too, would have the soft tartan plaids and magnificent woolen houndstooth jackets that were the privilege of the highest level management.

Going back through the bedroom, Derek leaned over the drowsy Melanie and said, "I'm going to work now, Melanie. I'll be back at the usual time."

YOU'RE 85 SECONDS LATE.

"I'll walk fast," Derek said to the Dial. He turned back to Melanie, hoping for some response, but there was none. She gazed at the landscape the Dial had conjured on the far wall. Her breath came slowly, easily, and he could see the ghosts of the circles he had drawn on her breasts and stomach, smeared and useless now. He cursed gently and quietly so that he would not disturb her.

LEAVE HER TO THIS UNIT.

Derek was delighted to obey.

When Melanie awoke from her drugged slumber some time later, the apartment was shadowed and dark. The windows did nothing to disguise the soupy weather outside; in fact, they enhanced the depressing effect by giving the walls the same melancholy tinge. Melanie sat for some time, staring out at the wet and the clouds as she tried to gather her thoughts. She remembered the morning's outburst as if it had happened to someone else, a long time ago. Her tongue felt furry.

A little later she rose from the bed and found the mirror. Yes, the circles were still there, blurred and smeary now, but definitely there. She touched one faded mauve line, frowning.

THIS UNIT ADVISES YOU TO BATHE. FOR MOST EFFICIENT REMOVAL OF THE SUBSTANCE ON YOUR SKIN, THIS UNIT RECOMMENDS CLEANING CONCENTRATE 6-B.

Melanie sighed. The Dial was right, of course. The sooner she got the mark off, the better she would feel. She did not want to dwell on Derek's reasons for drawing the circles. If only her head were clearer, it would be easier to think.

She bathed in sour-smelling water. The cleaning concentrate, though it did an admirable job of removing the circles, smelled slightly fishy and left a chalky scum floating on the water. Her face felt tightened when she washed it, and the tepid water was not warm enough to tempt her to linger. The towel that dried her was unpleasantly scratchy, her clothes were wrinkled and their colors washed-out. A grayish haze hung over the mirror, making Melanie look even more haggard and spent than she was.

"Impossible," she said to the Dial. "You're being horrid!"

THIS UNIT HAS HIS BEST INTERESTS AT HEART.

"You don't have a heart!" Melanie shrieked at it, then forced herself to speak calmly. Another such outburst and there would be a few more hours of drugged sleep to look forward to. "I didn't mean that," she said evenly. "I realize that you have been programmed to put the interests of Derek first in your consideration. I suppose I might be jealous of him, since my unit is an old 385 model, and there's no way I can get a newer one for at least a year."

THAT IS INCONVENIENT, the Dial responded with what in a human being would have been smugness.

Choking back a sharp retort, Melanie looked around the bedroom. "I'm surprised that you've dimmed the walls. Derek doesn't like drab colors."

DEREK ISN'T HERE, the Dial pointed out.

"But if he should return unexpectedly?" Melanie suggested slyly, thinking that there were few ways she could get back at the machine.

The walls brightened and a flower-scented breeze wafted through the room.

"Oh! You're impossible!" Melanie waited for the Dial to display another retort, but it remained obstinately blank, and after a time, Melanie wandered into the sitting room.

THIS UNIT AWAITS INSTRUCTIONS.

The announcement startled Melanie. Then she pulled herself together. Perhaps the Dial had reconsidered its attitude. It wasn't in Derek's best interests to be quarreling all morning.

THIS UNIT REMINDS YOU THAT YOU HAVE LESS THAN 58 MINUTES TO PREPARE FOR DEREK'S ARRIVAL. HE RETURNS FROM WORK EACH DAY AT 3:27 P.M.

Melanie made an effort to think of all the things Derek had said he liked. It would be nice for him to come home to a special treat. It would show him that she was no longer upset with him, and that she wanted things to go well between them. A new setting would be a delightful way to begin their making up.

She was very explicit with the Dial. She knew that the garden maze and kiosk setting were far too advanced for her. The demands of all those hedges and flowers were daunting, but she decided to do her best. If she couldn't handle the maze, the kiosk and lawn would be a good compromise.

The Dial obeyed her, transforming the sponge chairs into rigid rattan, curlicued with Victorian determination. Next, the windows were taken care of. She decided that the setting should be rather more exotic, and so the view was of a sun-bruised spit of land reaching out into the sinuous bend of a river. Melanie had some vague mental picture in her mind of India in the days of the Raj, the proper British tea and crumpets juxtaposed with the mysterious, eternal soul of the East. She wished she knew how to program the Dial to make a turban for Derek.

The light had altered to leaf-filtered green. Melanie stood back and studied the effect. Derek, she decided, would be pleased.

THIS UNIT AWAITS FURTHER INSTRUCTIONS.

Scowling with concentration, Melanie went back to the Dial. This was much more difficult than she had thought. After a difficult moment, she selected the bird calls and other sounds, including a low, insect-like drone. Next she added a lazy wind redolent with spices and tropical flowers. But here she ran afoul of the Dial, which insisted on adding hickory smoke as well.

"But there isn't any hickory smoke in the jungle," Melanie objected, almost certain she was right.

THIS UNIT MUST REMIND YOU THAT HICKORY SMOKE IS HIS FAVORITE SMELL.

Melanie shrugged. It was only one little detail, and might not be important. What mattered was that Derek liked it. She would overlook this opposition to her will. Feeling more confident, she dialed the rest of the information and was delighted to see how avidly the machine accepted her instructions.

The far wall, which had been a fjord-blue, turned to a deep jungle green, and the air was filled with a somnambulant haze. The temperature soared reassuringly. The floor sprouted several inches of creepers and grass. Croquet hoops and balls appeared on the small patch of lawn.

Melanie was deeply satisfied as she lounged in the high-backed rattan rocker. This was going to be a great success, she was certain.

Now vines were twisting down from the ceiling, coiling around her affectionately as they sought the ground. She giggled as one of them seemed to tweak her shoulder. It wasn't quite what she had in mind, but it was fun. The air was heavier, more humid. It was perfect, just perfect.

Not quite perfect.

There was an unfortunate odor coming through the hickory, a flavor of rotting seaweed spiced with old eggs. This overwhelmed even the heavy perfume of the gardenias. Melanie reached out for the Dial to adjust the olfactory scale, hoping to keep the stench from becoming unbearable.

The sky—for it was now more sky than ceiling—grew darker and took on a malignant orange tinge. There was a pall over the jungle, menacing. Alarmed, Melanie scrambled out of the chair and reached for the cancel lever, when her foot slipped in the ooze.

Ooze?

What was the matter with the Dial, anyway? In the heat, fear made her cold, settling like a lump of ice at the base of her spine. She tried to tell herself that this was just an illusion conjured by the Dial, and that it had turned out badly because she had been too ambitious in the effect she had tried to achieve. Panic seized her. Nothing—nothing could convince her that she had done this on her own. She didn't know enough about the operation of the Dial to make so thorough a change of scene. And Derek said he had made modifications on this unit. Certainly, she had overstepped herself. She tried to move nearer the Dial, but by then she was mired in quicksand. It was then that she saw the yawning gap in the floor, like the maw of a tiger, or the entrance to Hell. Or a waste chute.

Melanie was still laughing hysterically when the floor closed over her, making a noise curiously reminiscent of a kiss, or, possibly, smacking lips.

Some little time later, there was a loud, mechanical belch.

"Melanie?" Derek stood in the middle of the sitting room. The fjord-blue walls and ceiling beamed down at him, a brisk, salt-laden breeze ruffled his hair. The sponge chairs turned toward him invitingly. It was 3:28 p.m.

Into the bedroom: "Melanie?"

"Melanie!" in the eating area.

At last, he went to the Dial. "All *right*," he demanded. "Where is she?"

THIS UNIT MUST INFORM YOU THAT SHE IS GONE.

"Gone where?"

THIS UNIT DIRECTED HER TO THE PROTEIN RECLAMATION CENTER.

There was a long, guilty pause.

THIS UNIT ATE HER. IT WAS IN YOUR BEST INTERESTS.

Derek smiled as he gave the Dial a reassuring pat. "That makes three," he said.

RAY BRADBURY

"Gotcha!"

Ray Bradbury (1920-) is so well known for his science fiction novels **The Martian Chronicles** *and* **Fahrenheit 451** *that his impact on modern horror fiction is sometimes overlooked. The two dozen stories that he wrote for* **Weird Tales** *in the early 1940s, most of which were collected in* **Dark Carnival** *and* **The October Country***, helped to shift the orientation of horror fiction from lurid monster-driven narratives to muted reflections on the dark side of daily life. The tales gathered in* **The Illustrated Man, The Golden Apples of the Sun, The Machineries of Joy, A Medicine for Melancholy***, as well as the definitive* **Stories of Ray Bradbury***, showcase Bradbury's talents as a stylist and were instrumental in drawing the attention of critics to the literary possibilities of modern fantasy and science fiction. Bradbury's five novels* **Dandelion Wine, Something Wicked This Way Comes, Death Is a Lonely Business, A Graveyard for Lunatics** *and* **Green Shadows, White Whale** *all feature characters based on himself and integrate loosely to form his fantasy autobiography. In addition to fiction, he has written volumes of plays, poems, and essays, and his work has been adapted for the stage, screen and television.*

Gotcha!

by Ray Bradbury

They were incredibly in love. They said it. They knew it. They lived it. When they weren't staring at each other they were hugging. When they weren't hugging they were kissing. When they weren't kissing they were a dozen scrambled eggs in bed. When they were finished with the amazing omelet they went back to staring and making noises.

Theirs, in sum, was a Love Affair. Print it out in capitals. Underline it. Find some italics. Add exclamation points. Put up the fireworks. Tear down the clouds. Send out for some adrenalin. Roustabout at three A.M. Sleep till noon.

Her name was Beth. His name was Charles.

They had no last names. For that matter, they rarely called each other by their first names. They found new names every day for each other, some of them capable of being said only late at night and only to each other, when they were special and tender and most shockingly unclad.

Anyway, it was Fourth of July every night. New Year's every dawn. It was the home team winning and the mob on the field. It was a bobsled downhill and everything cold racing by in beauty and two warm people holding tight and yelling with joy.

And then . . .

Something happened.

At breakfast about one year into the conniption fits Beth said, half under her breath:

"Gotcha."

He looked up and said, "What?"

"Gotcha," she said. "A game. You never played Gotcha?"

"Never even heard of it."

"Oh, I've played it for years."

"Do you buy it in a store?" he asked.

"No, no. It's a game I made up, or almost made up, based on an old ghost story or scare story. Like to play it?"

"That all depends." He was back shoveling away at his ham and eggs.

"Maybe we'll play it tonight—it's fun. In fact," she said, nodding her head once and beginning to go on with her breakfast again, "it's a definite thing. Tonight it is. Oh, bun, you'll love it."

"I love everything we do," he said.

"It'll scare the hell out of you," she said.

"What's the name again?"

"Gotcha," she said.

"Never heard of it."

They both laughed. But her laughter was louder than his.

It was a long and delicious day of luscious name-calling and rare omelets and a good dinner with a fine wine and then some reading just before midnight, and at midnight he suddenly looked over at her and said:

"Haven't we forgotten something?"

"What?"

"Gotcha."

"Oh, my, yes!" she said, laughing. "I was just waiting for the clock to strike the hour."

Which it promptly did. She counted to twelve, sighed happily and said, "All right—let's put out most of the lights. Just keep the small lamp lighted by the bed. Now, there." She ran around putting out all the other lights, and came back and plumped up his pillow and made him lie right in the middle of the bed. "Now, you stay right there. You don't move, see. You just . . . *wait*. And see what *happens*—okay?"

"Okay." He smiled indulgently. At times like these she was a ten-year-old Girl Scout rushing about with some poisoned cookies on a grand lark. He was always ready, it seemed, to eat the cookies. "Proceed."

"Now, be very quiet," she said. "No talking. Let me talk if I want—okay?"

"Okay."

"Here goes," she said, and disappeared.

Which is to say that she sank down like the dark witch, melting, melting, at the foot of the bed. She let her bones collapse softly. Her head and her hair followed her Japanese paper-lantern body down, fold on fold, until the air at the foot of the bed was empty.

"Well done!" he cried.

"You're not supposed to talk. Sh-h."

"I'm sh-h-h-ed."

Silence. A minute passed. Nothing.

He smiled a lot, waiting.

Another minute passed. Silence. He didn't know where she was.

"Are you still at the foot of the bed?" he asked. "Oh, sorry." He sh-h-h-ed himself. "Not supposed to talk."

Five minutes passed. The room seemed to get somewhat darker. He sat up a bit and fixed his pillow and his smile got somewhat less expectant. He peered about the room. He could see the light from the bathroom shining on the wall.

There was a sound like a small mouse in one far corner of the room. He looked there but could see nothing.

Another minute passed. He cleared his throat.

There was a whisper from the bathroom door, down near the floor. He glanced that way and grinned and waited. Nothing.

He thought he felt something crawling under the bed. The sensation passed. He swallowed and blinked.

The room seemed almost candlelit. The light bulb, one hundred and fifty watts, seemed now to have developed fifty-watt problems.

There was a scurry like a great spider on the floor, but nothing was visible. After a long while her voice murmured to him like an echo, now from this side of the dark room, now that.

"How do you like it *so* far?"

"I . . ."

"Don't speak," she whispered.

And was gone again for another two minutes. He was beginning to feel his pulse jump in his wrists. He looked at the left wall, then the right, then the ceiling.

And suddenly a white spider was crawling along the foot of the bed. It was her hand, of course, imitating a spider. No sooner there than gone.

"Ha!" He laughed.

"Sh-h!" came the whisper.

Something ran into the bathroom. The bathroom light went out. Silence. There was only the small light in the bedroom now. A faint rim of perspiration appeared on his brow. He sat wondering why they were doing this.

Gotcha!

A clawing hand snatched up on the far left side of the bed, gesticulated and vanished. The watch ticked on his wrist.

Another five minutes must have gone by. His breathing was long and somewhat painful, though he couldn't figure why. A small frown gathered in the furrow between his eyes and did not go away. His fingers moved on the quilt all to themselves, as if trying to get away from him.

A claw appeared on the right side. No, it hadn't been there at all! Or had it?

Something stirred in the closet directly across the room. The door slowly opened upon darkness. Whether something went in at that moment or was already there waiting to come out, he could not say. The door now opened upon an abyss that was as deep as the spaces between the stars. A few dark shadows of coats hung inside, like disembodied people.

There was a running of feet in the bathroom.

There was a scurry of cat feet by the window.

He sat up. He licked his lips. He almost said something. He shook his head. A full twenty minutes had passed.

There was a faint moan, a distant laugh that hushed itself. Then another groan . . . where? In the shower?

"Beth?" he said at last.

No answer. Water dripped in the sink suddenly, drop by slow drop. Something had turned it on.

"Beth?" he called again, and hardly recognized his voice, it was so pale.

A window opened somewhere. A cool wind blew a phantom of curtain out on the air.

"Beth," he called weakly.

No answer.

"I don't like this," he said.

Silence.

No motion. No whisper. No spider. Nothing.

"Beth?" he called, a bit louder.

No breathing, even, anywhere.

"I don't like this game."

Silence.

"You hear me, Beth?"

Quiet.

"I don't like this game."

Drip in the bathroom sink.

"Let's stop the game, Beth."

Wind from the window.

"Beth?" he called again. "Answer me. Where are you?"

Silence.

"You all right?"

The rug lay on the floor. The light grew small in the lamp. Invisible dusts stirred in the air.

"Beth . . . you okay?"

Silence.

"Beth?"

Nothing.

"Beth!"

"Oh-h-h-h-h . . . *ah-h-h-h!*"

He heard the shriek, the cry, the scream.

A shadow sprang up. A great darkness leaped upon the bed. It landed on four legs.

"Ah!" came the shout.

"Beth!" he screamed.

"Oh-h-h-h!" came the shriek from the thing.

Another great leap and the dark thing landed on his chest. Cold hands seized his neck. A white face plunged down. A mouth gaped and shrieked:

"Gotcha!"

"Beth!" he cried.

And flailed and wallowed and turned but it clung to him and looked down and the face was white and the eyes raved wide and the nostrils flared. And the big bloom of dark hair in a flurry above fell down in a stormwind. And the hands clawing at his neck and the air breathed out of that mouth and nostrils as cold as polar wind, and the weight of the thing on his chest light but heavy, thistledown but an anvil crushing, and him thrashing to be free, but his arms pinned by the fragile legs and the face peering down at him so full of evil glee, so brimful of malevolence, so beyond this world and in another, so alien, so strange, so never seen before, that he had to shriek again.

"No! No! No! Stop! Stop!"

"Gotcha!" screamed the mouth.

And it was someone he had never seen before. A woman from some time ahead, some year when age and things had changed everything, when darkness had gathered and boredom had poisoned and words had killed and everything gone to ice and lostness and nothing, no residues of love, only hate, only death.

"No! Oh, God! Stop!"

He burst into tears. He began to sob.

She stopped.

Her hands went away cold and came back warm to touch, hold, pet him.

And it was Beth.

"Oh. God, God, God!" he wailed. "No, no, no!"

"Oh, Charles, Charlie," she cried, all remorse. "I'm sorry. I didn't mean—"

"You did. Oh, God, you did, you did!"

His grief was uncontrollable.

"No, no. Oh, Charlie," she said, and burst into tears herself. She flung herself out of bed and ran around turning on lights. But none of them were bright enough. He was crying steadily now. She came back and slid in by him and put his grieving face to her breast and held him, hugged him, patted him, kissed his brow and let him weep.

"I'm sorry. Charlie, listen, sorry. I didn't—"

"You *did*!"

"It was only a game!"

"A game! You call that a game, game, game!" he wailed, and wept again.

And finally, at last, his crying stopped and he lay against her and she was warm and sister/mother/friend/lover again. His heart, which had crashed, now moved to some near calm. His pulses stopped fluttering. The constriction around his chest let go.

"Oh, Beth, Beth," he wailed softly.

"Charlie," she apologized, her eyes shut.

"Don't ever do that again."

"I won't."

"Promise you'll never do that again?" he said, hiccuping.

"I swear, I promise."

"You were *gone*, Beth—that wasn't *you*!"

"I promise, I swear, Charlie."

"All right," he said.

"Am I forgiven, Charlie?"

He lay a long while and at last nodded, as if it had taken some hard thinking.

"Forgiven."

"I'm sorry, Charlie. Let's get some sleep. Shall I turn the lights off?"

Silence.

"Shall I turn the lights off, Charlie?"

"No-no."

"We have to have the lights off to sleep, Charlie."

"Leave a few on for a little while," he said, eyes shut.

"All right," she said, holding him. "For a little while."

He took a shuddering breath and came down with a chill. He shook for five minutes before her holding him and stroking him and kissing him made the shiver and the tremble go away.

An hour later she thought he was asleep and got up and turned off all the lights save the bathroom light, in case he should wake and want at least one on. Getting back into bed, she felt him stir. His voice, very small, very lost, said:

"Oh, Beth, I loved you so much."

She weighed his words. "Correction. You *love* me so much."

"I *love* you so much," he said.

It took her an hour, staring at the ceiling, to go to sleep.

The next morning at breakfast he buttered his toast and looked at her. She sat calmly munching her bacon. She caught his glance and grinned at him.

"Beth," he said.

"What?" she asked.

How could he tell her? Something in him was cold. The bedroom even in the morning sun seemed smaller, darker. The bacon was burned. The toast was black. The coffee had a strange and alien flavor. She looked very pale. He could feel his heart, like a tired fist, pounding dimly against some locked door somewhere.

"I . . ." he said, "we . . ."

How could he tell her that suddenly he was afraid? Suddenly he sensed that this was the beginning of the end. And beyond the end there would never be anyone to go to anywhere at any time—no one in all the world.

"Nothing," he said.

Five minutes later she asked, looking at her crumpled eggs, "Charles, do you want to play the game tonight? But this time it's me, and this time it's you who hides and jumps out and says, 'Gotcha'?"

He waited because he could not breathe.

"No."

He did not want to know that part of himself.

Tears sprang to his eyes.

"Oh, no," he said.

HARLAN ELLISON

"The Man Who Was Heavily into Revenge"

Harlan Ellison (1934-) published his first science fiction story in 1956 and became one of the leading writers of science fiction's New Wave in the 1960s with such provocative and controversial stories as "I Have No Mouth and I Must Scream," " 'Repent, Harlequin!' Said the Ticktockman," and "A Boy and His Dog." Many of his stories collected in **Approaching Oblivion**, **Deathbird Stories**, **Angry Candy** *and the retrospective volume* **The Essential Ellison** *have a horrific edge to them, but his writing resists pigeonholing to any one genre. As an editor, he compiled the landmark anthologies of fantasy, horror and science fiction* **Dangerous Visions** *and* **Again, Dangerous Visions**. *He has made a name for himself in television through his contributions to "The Outer Limits," "Star Trek," and the revived "The Twilight Zone." Ellison is also an insightful and perceptive critic whose film review column, "Harlan Ellison's Watching," ran for several years in* **The Magazine of Fantasy and Science**. *His best essays and reviews are collected in* **The Glass Teat**, **The Other Glass Teat, Sleepless Nights in the Procrustean Bed**, *and* **An Edge in My Voice**. *He has won virtually every award possible in the fantasy, horror and science fiction fields, including the Bram Stoker Award from the Horror Writers of America. He is also a recipient of the World Fantasy Award for lifetime achievement.*

The Man Who Was Heavily into Revenge

by Harlan Ellison

William Weisel pronounced his name why-*zell*, but many of the unfortunates for whom he had done remodeling and construction pronounced it *weasel*.

He had designed and built a new guest bathroom for Fred Tolliver, a man in his early sixties who had retired from the active life of a studio musician with the foolish belief that his fifteen-thousand-dollar-per-year annuity would sustain him in comfort. Weisel had snubbed the original specs on the job, had substituted inferior materials for those required by the codes, had used cheap Japanese pipe instead of galvanized or stressed plastic, had eschewed lath and plaster for wallboard that left lumpy seams, had skirted union wages by ferrying in green card workers from Tijuana every morning by dawn light, had—in short—done a spectacularly crummy job on Fred Tolliver's guest bathroom. That was the first mistake.

And for all of this ghastly workmanship, Weisel had overcharged Fred Tolliver by nine thousand dollars. That was the second mistake.

Fred Tolliver called William Weisel. His tone was soft and almost apologetic. Fred Tolliver was a gentle man, not given to fits of pique or demonstrations of anger. He politely asked Weisel to return and set matters to rights. William Weisel laughed at Fred Tolliver and told him that he had lived up to the letter of the original contract, that he would do nothing. That was the third mistake.

Putatively, what Weisel said was true. Building inspectors had been greased and the job had been signed off: legal according to the building codes. Legally, William Weisel was in the clear; no suit could be brought. Ethically it was a different matter. But even threats of revocation of license could not touch him.

Nonetheless, Fred Tolliver had a rotten guest bathroom, filled with leaks and seamed walls that were already cracking and bubbles in the vinyl flooring from what was certainly a break in the hot water line and pipes that clanked when the faucets were turned on, if they could *be* turned on.

Fred Tolliver asked for repairs more than once.

After a while, William Weisel's wife, Belle, who often acted as his secretary, to save a few bucks when they didn't want to hire a Kelly Girl, would not put through the calls.

Fred Tolliver told her, softly and politely, "Please convey to Mr. Weisel—" and he pronounced it why-*zell*, "—my feelings of annoyance. Please advise him that I won't stand for it. This is an awful thing he's done to me. It's not fair, it's not right."

She was chewing gum. She examined her nails. She had heard this all before: married to Weisel for eleven years: all of this, many times. "Lissen, Mistuh Tollivuh, whaddaya want *me* to do about it, *I* can't do nothing about it, y'know. I only work here. I c'n tell 'im, that's *all* I c'n do, is tell 'im you called again."

"But you're his wife! You can see how he's robbed me!"

"Lissen, Mistuh Tollivuh, I don't haveta lissen to this!"

It was the cavalier tone, the utterly uncaring tone: impertinent, rude, dismissing him as if he were a crank, a weirdo, as if he weren't asking only for what was due him. It was like a goad to an already maddened bull.

"This isn't fair!"

"I'll tell 'im, I'll tell 'im. Jeezus, I'm hanging up now."

"I'll get even! I will! There has to be justice—"

She dropped the receiver into its rest heavily, cracking her gum with annoyance, looking ceilingward like one massively put upon. She didn't even bother to coney the message to her husband.

And that was the biggest mistake of all.

The electrons dance. The emotions sing. Four billion, resonating like insects. The hive mind of the masses. The emotional gestalt. The charge builds and builds, surging down the line seeking a focus. The weakest link through which to discharge itself. Why this focus and not that? Chance, proximity, the tiniest fracture for leakage. You, I, him, her. Everyman, Anyman; the crap shoot selection is whatever man or woman born of man and woman whose rage at *that* moment is *that* potent.

Everyman: Fred Tolliver. Unknowing confluence.

He pulled up at the pump that dispensed supreme, and let the Rolls idle for a moment before shutting it off. When the attendant leaned in at the window, Weisel smiled around his pipe and said, "Morning, Gene. Fill it up with extra."

"Sorry, Mr. Weisel," Gene said, looking a little sad, "but I can't sell you any gas."

"Why the hell not? You out?"

"No, sir; just got our tanks topped off last night. Still can't sell you any."

"Why the hell not?!"

"Fred Tolliver doesn't want me to."

Weisel stared for a long moment. He couldn't have heard correctly. He'd been gassing up at this station for eleven years. He didn't even know they *knew* that creep Tolliver. "Don't be an asshole, Gene. Fill the damned tank!"

"I'm sorry, sir. No gas for you."

"What the hell is Tolliver to you? A relative or something?"

"No, sir. I never met him. Wouldn't know him if he drove in right now."

"Then what . . . what the hell . . . I—I—"

But nothing he could say would get Gene to pump one liter of gas into the Rolls.

Nor would the attendants at the next *six* stations down the avenue. When the Rolls ran out, a mile from his office, Weisel *almost* had time to pull to the curb. Not quite. He ran dry in the middle of Ventura Boulevard and tried to turn toward the curb, but though traffic had been light around him just a moment before, somehow it was now packing itself bumper-to-bumper. He turned his head wildly this way and that, dumbfounded at how many cars had suddenly pulled onto the boulevard around him. He could not get out of the crunch. It wouldn't have mattered. Improbably, for this nonbusiness area, for the first time in his memory, there were *no* empty parking spaces at the curb.

Cursing foully, he put it in neutral, rolled down the window so he could hold the steering wheel from outside, and got out of the silent Rolls. He slammed the door, cursing Fred Tolliver's every breath, and stepped away from the car. He heard the hideous rending of irreplaceable fabric. His five hundred dollar cashmere suit jacket had been caught in the jamb.

A large piece of lovely fabric, soft as a doe's eye, wonderously ecru-closer-to-beige-than-fawn-colored, tailor-made for him in Paris, his most favorite jacket hung like slaughtered meat from the door. He whimpered; an involuntary sob of pain.

Then: "What the hell is going *on!*" he snarled, loud enough for pedestrians to hear. It was not a question, it was an imprecation. There was no answer; none was required; but there was the sound of thunder far off across the San Fernando Valley. Los Angeles was in the grip of a two-year drought, but there was a menacing buildup of soot-gray clouds over the San Bernardinos.

He reached in through the window, tried to turn the wheel toward the curb, but with the engine off the power steering prevented easy movement. But he strained and strained . . . and something went snap! in his groin. Incredible pain shot down both legs and he bent double, clutching himself. Flashbulbs went off behind his eyes. He stumbled around in small circles, holding himself awkwardly. Many groans. Much anguish. He leaned against the Rolls, and the pain began to subside; but he had broken something down there. After a few minutes he was able to stand semi-erect. His shirt was drenched with sweat. His deodorant was wearing off. Cars were swerving around the Rolls, honking incessantly, drivers swearing at him. He had to get the Rolls out of the middle of the street.

Still clutching his crotch with one hand, jacket hanging from him in tatters, beginning to smell very bad, William Weisel put his shoulder to the car, grabbed the steering wheel and strained once again; the wheel went around slowly. He readjusted himself, excruciating pain pulsing through his pelvis, put his shoulder against the window post and tried to push the behemoth. He thought of compacts and tiny sports cars. The Rolls moved a fraction of an inch, then slid back.

Sweat trickled into his eyes, making them sting. He huffed and lunged and applied as much pressure as the pain would permit. The car would not move.

He gave up. He needed help. *Help!*

Standing in the street behind the car, clutching his groin, jacket flapping around him, smelling like something ready for disposal, he signaled wildly for assistance with his free hand. But no one would stop. Thunder rolled around the Valley, and Weisel saw what looked like a pitchfork of lightning off across the flats where Van Nuys, Panorama City and North Hollywood lay gasping for water.

Cars thundered down on him and swerved at the very last moment, like matadors performing a complicated *verónica*. Several cars seemed to speed up, in fact, as they approached him, and he had the crazy impression the drivers were hunched over the wheels, lips skinned back from clenched teeth, like rabid wild things intent on killing him. Several nearly sideswiped him. He barely managed to hobble out of the way. One Datsun came so close that its side-view mirror ripped a nasty, raw gash down the entire right side of the Rolls. He cursed and gesticulated and pleaded. No one would stop. In fact, one fat woman leaned out of her window as her husband zoomed past, and she yelled something nasty. He caught only the word "Tolliver!"

Finally, he just left it there, with the hood up like the mouth of a hungry bird.

He walked the mile to his office, thinking he would call the Automobile Club to come and tow it to a station where it could be filled. He didn't have the time or the patience to walk to a gas station, get a can of fuel, and return to fill the tank. During the mile-long walk he even had time to wonder if he would be *able* to buy a can of gasoline.

Tolliver! God *damn* that old man!

There was no one in the office.

It took him a while to discover that fact, because he couldn't get an elevator in his building. He stood in front of one after another of the doors, waiting for a cage to come down, but they all seemed determined to stop at the second floor. Only when other passengers waited did an elevator arrive, and then he was always in front of the wrong one. He would dash to the open door, just as the others entered, but before he could get his hand into the opening to stop the retarder bar from slamming against the frame, the door would seem to slide faster, as if it possessed a malevolent intelligence. It went on that way for ten minutes, till it became obvious to him that something was terribly, hideously, inexplicably wrong.

So he took the stairs.

(On the stairs he somehow slipped and skinned his right knee as one of the steps caught his heel and tore it off his right shoe.)

Limping like a cripple, the tatters of his jacket flapping around him, clutching his groin, blood seeping through his pants to stain, he reached the eleventh floor and tried to open the door. It was, of course, for the first time in the thirty-five-year history of the building, locked.

He waited fifteen minutes and the door suddenly opened as a secretary, carrying some papers up one flight to the Xerox center, came boiling through. He barely managed to catch the door on its pneumatic closer. He stumbled frantically onto the eleventh floor and, like a man emerging gratefully from a vast desert to find an oasis, he fled down the corridor to the offices of the Weisel Construction Corporation.

There was no one in the office.

It was not locked. Was, in fact, wholly unattended and wide open to thieves, if such had chosen that office for plundering. The receptionist was not there, the estimators were not there, not even Belle, his wife, who served as secretary when he didn't want to hire a Kelly Girl, was there.

However, she had left him a note:

I'm leaving you. By the time you read this I will have already been to the bank and emptied the joint account. Don't try to find me. Goodbye.

Weisel sat down. He had the beginnings of what he was certain was a migraine, though he had never had a migraine in his life. He didn't know whether, in the vernacular of the United States Army, to shit or go blind.

He was not a stupid man. He had been given more than sufficient evidence that something malevolent and purely anti-Weisel was floating across the land. It was out to get him . . . had, in fact, *already* gotten him . . . had, in fact, made a well-ordered and extremely comfortable life turn into a nasty, untidy, noisome pile of doggie-doo.

And it was named *Tolliver*.

Fred Tolliver . . . ! How the hell . . . ? Who does he know that could . . . ? How did he . . . ?

None of the questions reached a conclusion. He could not even formulate them. Clearly, this was insanity. No one he knew, not Gene at the gas station, not the people in the cars, not Belle, not his staff, not the *car door* or the building's *elevators* even knew who Tolliver was! Well, Belle knew, but what the hell did she have to do with *him*?

Okay, so it *wasn't* going so good with Belle. So they *hadn't* really reconciled that innocent little thing he'd had with the lab technician at Mt. Sinai. So what? That was no reason for her to ditch a good thing. *Damn that Tolliver!*

He slammed his hand onto the desk, missed slightly, caught the edge and drove a thick splinter of wood into the fat of his palm, at the same time scattering the small stack of telegrams across his lap and the floor.

Wincing with pain, he sucked at the splinter till it came out. He used one of the telegram envelopes to blot the blood from his hand.

Telegrams?

He opened the first one. The Bank of America, Beverly Hills branch 213, was pleased to advise him they were calling due his loans. All five of them. He opened the second one. His broker, Shearson Hayden Stone Inc., was overjoyed to let him know that all sixteen of the stocks in which he had speculated heavily, on margin, of course, had virtually plummeted off the big board and he had to come up with seventy-seven thousand dollars by noon today or his portfolio was wiped out. It was a quarter to eleven by the wall clock. (Or had it, inexplicably, stopped?) He opened the third one. He had failed his est class and Werner Erhard himself had sent the telegram, adding in what Weisel took to be an unnecessarily gloating tone, that Weisel had "no human potential worth expanding." He opened the fourth one. His Wassermann had come back from Mt. Sinai. It was positive. He opened the fifth one. The Internal Revenue Service was ecstatic at being able to let him know they were planning to audit his returns for the past five years, and were seeking a loophole in the tax laws that permitted them to go back farther, possibly to the start of the Bronze Age.

There were others, five or six more. He didn't bother opening them. He didn't want to learn who had died, or that the state of Israel had discovered Weisel was, in actuality, Bruno "The Butcher" Krutzmeier, a former prison guard at Mauthausen, personally responsible for the deaths of three thousand Gypsies, Trade Unionists, Jews, Bolsheviks and Weimar democrats, or that the U.S. Coast and Geodetic Survey Department was gleefully taking this opportunity to advise him that the precise spot over which he sat was expected to collapse into the magma at the center of the Earth and by the way we've canceled your life insurance.

He let them lie.

The clock on the wall had, to be sure, stopped dead.

In fact, the electricity had been turned off.

The phone did not ring. He picked it up. Of course. It—like its friend the clock—was stone dead.

Tolliver! Tolliver! How was he *doing* all this?

Such things simply *do not* happen in an ordered universe of draglines and scoop-shovels and reinforced concrete.

He sat and thought dark, murderous thoughts about that old sonofabitch, Fred Tolliver.

A 747 boomed sonically overhead and the big heavy-plate window of his eleventh floor office cracked, splintered, and fell in around his feet.

Unknowing confluence of resonating emotions, Fred Tolliver sat in his house, head in hands, miserable beyond belief, aware only of pain and anger. His cello lay on its back on the floor beside him. He had tried playing a little today, but all he could think of was that terrible man Weisel, and the terrible bathroom that was filling with water, and the terrible stomach pains his feelings of hatred were giving him.

Electrons resonate. So do emotions.

Speak of "damned places" and one speaks of locations where powerful emotional forces have been penned up. One cannot doubt, if one has ever been inside a prison where the massed feelings of hatred, deprivation, claustrophobia and brutalization have seeped into the very stones. One can feel it. Emotions resonate: at a political rally, a football game, an encounter group, a rock concert, a lynching.

There are four billion people in the world. A world that has grown so complex and uncaring with systems and brutalization of individuals because of the inertia produced by those systems' perpetuation of self, that merely to live is to be assaulted daily by circumstances. Electrons dance. The emotions sing. Four billion, resonating like insects. The charge is built up; the surface tension is reached; the limit of elasticity is passed; the charge seeks release; the focus is sought: the weakest link, the fault line, the most tremblingly frangible element, AnyTolliver, EveryTolliver.

Like the discharge of the lightning bolt, the greater the charge on the Tolliver, the greater its tendency to escape. The force of the four billion driving the electrons in their mad dance away from the region of highest excess toward the region of greatest deficiency. Pain as electromotive force. Frustration as electric potential. The electrons jump the insulating gap of love and friendship and kindness and humane behavior and the power is unleashed.

Like the discharge of the lightning bolt, the power seeks and finds its focus, leaps the gap, and the bolt of energy is unleashed.

Does the lightning rod know it is draining off the dangerous electrical charge? Is there sentience in a Leyden jar? Does not the voltaic pile continue to sleep while current is drawn off? Does the focus know it has unleashed the anger and frustration of the four billion?

Fred Tolliver sat in misery, the cello forgotten, the pain of having been cheated, of being impotent against the injustice, eating at his stomach. His silent scream: at that moment the most dominant in the entire universe. Chance. It could have been anyone; or perhaps, as Chesterton said, "Coincidences are a spiritual sort of puns."

His phone rang. He did not move to pick up the receiver. It rang again. He did not move. His stomach burned and roiled. There was a scorched-earth desperation in him. Nine *thousand* dollars overcharge. Thirty-seven hundred dollars by the original contract. Twelve thousand seven hundred dollars. He had had to take a second mortgage on the house. Five more months than the estimated two Weisel had said it would take to complete the job. Seven months of filth and plaster dust and inept workmen tramping through his little house with mud and dirt and dropping cigarette butts on his floor.

I'm sixty-two years old, he thought, frantically. *My God, I'm an old man. A moment ago I was just middle-aged, and now I'm an old man . . . I never felt old before. It's good Betsy never lived to see me like this; she would cry. But this thing with the bathroom is a* terrible *thing, an awful thing, it's made me an old man, poor, in financial straits; and I don't know how to save myself. He's ruined my life . . . he's killed me . . . I'll never be able to get even, to put away a little . . . if the thing with the knees gets any worse, there could be big doctor bills, specialists maybe . . . the Blue Cross would never cover it . . . what am I going to do, please God help me . . . what am I going to do?*

He was an old man, retired and very tired, who had thought he could make it through. He had figured it out so he could just barely slide through. But the pains in the backs of his knees had begun three years before, and though they had not flared up in sixteen months, he remembered how he would simply fall down, suddenly, ludicrously, fall down: the legs prickling with pins and needles as though he had sat cross-legged for a long time. He was afraid to think about the pains too much. They might come back if he thought about them too much.

But he didn't really believe that thinking about things could make them happen. Thinking didn't make things change in the real world. Fred Tolliver did not know about the dance of the emotions, the resonance of the electrons. He did not know about a sixty-two-year-old lightning rod that leaked off the terror and frustration of four billion people, all crying out silently just as Fred Tolliver cried out. For help that never came.

The phone continued to ring. He did not think about the pains he had felt in the backs of his knees, as recently as sixteen months ago. He did not think about it, because he did not want it to return. It was only a low-level throbbing now, and he wanted it to stay that way. He didn't want to feel pins and needles. He *wanted* his money back. He *wanted* the sound of gurgling under the floor of the guest bathroom to stop. *He wanted William Weisel to make good.*

He answered the phone. It rang once too often for him to ignore it.

"Hello?"

"Mr. Tolliver? Is that you?"

"Yes, this is Fred Tolliver. Who's calling?"

"Evelyn Hand. I haven't heard from you about my violin, and I'm going to need it late next week . . ."

He had forgotten. In all the anguish with Weisel, he had forgotten Evelyn Hand, and her damaged violin. And she had paid him already.

"Oh, my gosh, Miss Hand, I'm awfully sorry! I've just had the most awful business going on these last months, a man built me a guest bathroom, and he overcharged me nine thousand dollars, and it's all broken and . . ."

He stopped. This was unbecoming. He coughed with embarrassment, giving himself a moment to gather his composure. "I'm just as terribly sorry and ashamed as I can be, Miss Hand. I haven't had a chance to get to the repairs. But I know you need it a week from today . . ."

"A week from *yesterday*, Mr. Tolliver. Thursday, not Friday."

"Oh. Yes, of course. Thursday." She was a nice woman, really. Very slim, delicate fingers and a gentle, warm voice. He had thought perhaps they might go to the Smorgasbord for a meal, and they might get to know each other. He wanted companionship. It was so necessary; now, particularly, it was so necessary. But the memory of Betsy was always there, singing softly within him; and he had said nothing to Evelyn Hand.

"Are you there, Mr. Tolliver?"

"Uh, yes. Yes, of course. Please forgive me. I'm so wrought up these days. I'll get to it right away. Please don't you worry about it."

"Well, I *am* rather concerned." She hesitated, as though reluctant to speak. She drew a deep breath and plunged on: "I did pay you in advance for the repairs, because you said you needed the money for bills, and . . ."

He didn't take offense. He understood perfectly. She had said something that otherwise she would have considered *déplacé*, but she was distraught and wanted to make the point as firmly as she could without being overly offensive.

"I'll get to it today, Miss Hand; I promise."

It would take time. It was a good instrument, a fine, old Gagliano. He knew he could finish the repairs in time if he kept at it without distraction.

Her tone softened. "Thank you, Mr. Tolliver. I'm sorry to have bothered you, but . . . you understand."

"Of course. Don't give it a thought. I'll call as soon as it's ready. I'll give it special attention, I promise."

"You're very kind."

They said their goodbyes and he stopped himself from suggesting dinner when the violin was ready. There was always time for that later, when appropriate. When the business with the bathroom was settled.

And that brought him back to the state of helpless fury and pain. That terrible man, Weisel!

Unknowing confluence of four billion resonating emotions, Fred Tolliver sat with head in hands; as the electrons danced.

Eight days later, in a filthy alley behind a boarded-up supermarket that had begun as a sumptuous gilt-and-brocade movie house in 1924, William Weisel sat in filth, trying to eat the butt of a stale loaf of pumpernickel he had stolen from a garbage can. He weighed ninety-seven pounds, had not shaved in seven days, his clothes were stained and torn rags, his shoes had been stolen while he slept, four days earlier, in the doorway outside the Midnight Mission, his eyes were rheumy and he had developed a terrible, wracking cough. The angry crimson weal on his left forearm where the bolt of lightning had just grazed him seemed to be infected. He gagged on the bread, realizing he had missed one of the maggots, and threw the granitelike butt across the alley.

He was incapable of crying. He had cried himself out. He knew, at last, that there was no way to save himself. On the third day, he had tried to get to Tolliver, to beg him to stop; to tell him he would repair the bathroom; to tell him he would build him a new house, a mansion, a palace, *anything*! Just stop this terror! *Please!*

But *he* had been stopped. He could not *get* to Tolliver. The first time he had set his mind to seeing the old man, he had been arrested by a California Highway Patrol officer who had him on his hot sheet for having left the Rolls in the middle of Ventura Boulevard. Weisel had managed to escape on foot, somehow, miraculously.

The second time he had been attacked by a pit bull while skulking through back yards. He had lost his left pant leg below the knee.

The third time he had actually gotten as far as the street on which Tolliver's house sat, but a seven-car pileup had almost crushed him beneath tons of thundering metal, and he had fled, fearing an aircraft carrier might drop from the sky to bury him.

He knew now that he could not even make amends, that it was inertial, and that he was doomed.

He lay back, waiting for the finish. But it was not to be that easy. The song of the four billion is an undending symphony of incredible complexity. As he lay there, a derelict stumbled into the alley, saw him, and pulled the straight razor from his jacket pocket. He was almost upon him when William Weisel opened his eyes. He saw the rusty blade coming for his throat, had a moment of absolute mind-numbing horror wash over him, spasmed into shock, and did not hear the sound of the cop's service revolver as the derelict—who had serviced over a dozen other such bums as Weisel in this same manner—was blown in half.

He woke in the drunk tank, looked around, saw the company to which he had been condemned, knew that if he lived it would be through years of horror, and began tearing off strips of rags from what remained of his clothing.

When the attendant came to turn the men out into the exercise area, he found William Weisel hanging from the bars of the door, eyes bulging, tongue protruding like a charred leaf from his mouth. What he could not reconcile was that no one in the cell had even shouted, nor raised a hand to stop Weisel. That, and the look of voiceless anguish on the dead man's face, as though he had glimpsed, just at the instant of death, a view of an *eternity* of voiceless anguish.

The focus could direct the beam, but it could not heal itself. At the very moment that Weisel died, Fred Tolliver—still unaware of what he had done—sat in his home, realizing finally that the contractor had done him in. He could never repay the note, would perhaps have to get work again in some studio, and probably would be unable to do it with sufficient regularity to save the house. His twilight years would be spent in some dingy apartment. The modest final hope of his life had been denied him: he would not be able just simply to get by in peace. It was a terrible lonely thing to contemplate.

The phone rang.

He picked it up wearily. "Yes?"

There was a moment of silence, then the voice of Miss Evelyn Hand came across the line, icily. "Mr. Tolliver, this is Evelyn Hand. I waited all day yesterday. I was unable to participate in the recital. Please have my violin waiting for me, repaired or not."

He was too stunned, too depressed, even to be polite. "Okay."

"I want you to know you have caused me great pain, Mr. Tolliver. You are a very unreliable and evil man. I want you to know I'm going to take steps to rectify this matter. You have taken money from me under false pretenses, you have ruined a great opportunity I had, and you have caused me unnecessary anguish. You will have to pay for your irresponsibility; there must be justice. I will make certain you pay for what you've done!"

"Yes. Yes, of course," he said, dimly, faintly.

He hung up the receiver and sat there.

The emotions sang, the electrons danced, the focus shifted, and the symphony of frustration went on.

Fred Tolliver's cello lay unattended at his feet. He would never get through, just barely slide through. He felt the excruciating pain of pins and needles in his legs.

No snowflake in an avalanche ever feels responsible.

—S. J. Lec

DARRELL SCHWEITZER

"Divers Hands"

Darrell Schweitzer (1952-) has been recognized as a leading writer, editor and critic in the fields of fantasy, horror and science fiction. His novels **The White Isle** *and* **The Mask of the Sorceror** *are powerful blends of heroic fantasy and horror, and* **The Shattered Goddess** *a dark fable of the far future. His short fiction has been collected in* **We Are All Legends, Tom O'Bedlam's Night Out, and Other Strange Excursions**, *and the World Fantasy Award-nominated* **Transients and Other Disquieting Tales**. *He has written critical books on the work of H. P. Lovecraft, Robert E. Howard, Stephen King and Lord Dunsany, compiled several interview collections in the* **Science Fiction Voices** *series, and edited the* **Discovering Classic Horror** *and* **Discovering Modern Horror** *essay miscellanies. Since 1988, he has served as the editor of the revived* **Weird Tales**.

Divers Hands

by Darrell Schweitzer

"In what battle was it, Sir Knight, and to what foe did you lose your hand? Did you slay him who maimed you thus?"

The speaker was seated before me, a short, hooded man with a copious gray beard. I could not see his face in the fading twilight. He was the last one to come that day into my tent, at the crossroads fair in the mountain country beyond the empire of the Greeks, which is called Byzantium. The circumstance was a strange one: I, Julian, of various names and titles, long since lost to chivalry and my God, was reduced to beggary, shunned by the folk of every land. Who would trust this grim, hook-handed knight in tarnished mail, whose shield and surcoat bore not the emblem of the cross? What is he doing here? Is he really a man, they would ask, or some creature out of the darkness? Why goes he not with his comrades, to the east to fight the pagans? At the fairground, in that tent in a strange land near a strange city, and speaking a tongue I knew but rudely, I seemed to fit in, at least for the moment. I could not admit to myself that mere existence had become an end in itself, and each hour of peace a worthy goal for a long quest.

To make a living I told tales of my travels and of the adventures of others, and sometimes when these failed I invented, but no one could tell when I lied and when I didn't. Ever popular was my sojourn in the land of darkness, where dwell folk marvelously transfigured, so that their heads grow beneath their shoulders, and their ears, appended to their arms, stretch wide like the wings of bats, enabling them to fly. Also there were the salt maidens of Antioch, whose tears filled up their entire forms, so that they were left pillars of salt, like Lot's wife, when they mourned a blasphemer struck dead by the Apostle Peter. As each tale concluded, the listener would drop a coin in the bowl I had set out—and the telling was rewarding in another way too.

Being a storyteller is like confessing to a priest—nay—more like the fool in the fable who buried his head among the reeds and whispered *King Midas has asses' ears*. Everyone knows, but it is a fanciful thing. Who believes what is said by the wind in the reeds? Thus one can be unburdened of truth. So I told the questioner the true answer:

"Long and long ago it seems, but not very long ago in fact, there was a knight who met the Devil face to face in a ruined hall deep in the forest, and there he gave himself to him, to ransom a maiden who had been wronged. This was, by his faith, and his faith was a terror to him thereafter, the only chivalrous thing he had done in his entire life, for all his ideals, all his training, all his deeds. And for this he was damned, so that the Devil did not take his soul just then, so sure a thing it was, but instead commanded him, *'Go wander the world which shall this day be made anew, and forever be a stranger, until at last you come to me.'* And in his travels he met an evil thing, which in the guise of a lady comforted him, but in truth drank away his blood and his years. When the thing was slain, as needs it must be, the knight woke from a blissful dream in those false arms, and was confused, and in misguided wrath killed his deliverer, and for this was again damned. Then, on one of the occasions when he wished his life would end, but knew it could not, lest the Devil have him at once, he sought the Vale of Mistorak in the farthest East, and there conversed with a spirit, but bought those words with his own flesh, and that is how he lost his hand."

"And was the bargain well made?" asked the listener. "Was the answer satisfactory?"

"If it were, would I be here in this tent telling such wild tales?"

The hooded one wheezed what was supposed to be a laugh.

"I have no coin for you," he said, "but in exchange, a tale of my own. There was a king, whose name was Tikos, who ruled over a very ancient land. To the castle of his fathers came all the great lords of the world at one time or other. Alexander came there as a boy, and saw the wonder of it, and when he grew older turned his armies away from it, toward the east. But at long last, through treachery wrought by the priests of a new god, against whom the old gods were powerless, the people seized the king and mutilated him according to their custom, cutting off his right hand so that he might never again raise a sword, cutting off his left so he could hold no scepter. Thus was the king reduced to misery and scorn, until he found a way to gain his revenge. He swore himself to a new master. He became *Nekatu*."

"*Nekatu?*"

"As such he had vast powers, including prophecy. It has been prophesied that the knight of your story will come to the castle of the king of mine, and learn what that word means."

With that, he rose and left the tent. The flap waved like a flag with his passing.

"Wait!" I sprang up and went after him, bursting out into the evening air. It was intensely cold already, as it gets so quickly in the mountains. Beyond the peaks, the sun had set in a splash of gold. Overhead, the stars were already out, and I was sure the chill wind I felt came from between them, from beyond the mortal earth, where winged demons freely traffic. Such a demon my listener must have been to get away so fast. There was no sign of him anywhere.

Nekatu, he had said. That was the first time I ever heard the term.

That night as I slept I was haunted by evil dreams, at first, a recurring vision of a meadow strewn with the newly slain, all of them rising up as I approached, their wounds unhealed, to fight again in hopeless misery. Their cries at last drove me from the dream, and I awoke, bewildered for an instant, finding my tent an unfamiliar place. Then I listened to the night noises, tethered horses stamping in the cold, the crackle of campfires, a dog barking, someone singing. Beyond all that, an owl hooted.

I slept again, and this time I was riding through a dark wood, where every tree seemed to lean low with the weight of monstrous menace crouched in the branches, and inhuman faces peered fleetingly between the trunks. I had seldom known such terror in the waking world. My horse wanted to rear up and bolt, and only with utmost effort could I retain control. I gave in to the animal's instincts some, letting it speed up to a trot, then a canter, and finally a full gallop, as its panic and mine were one, and we thundered through the forest in a rain of great clods of mud thrown up by the hooves, and still there were the feeling of suffocating dread, and the half-glimpsed forms between the trees. Then I turned around in the saddle and looked behind me, and saw that I was indeed pursued, by another knight clad all in black mail and a black surcoat, mounted on a black steed, with his visor raised and a bare skull for a face. Then I screamed, and awoke again into the tent, and there was absolute silence in the camp, with every ear turned my way. Was the strange knight wrestling with a demon in his bed? I knew I would have to leave in the morning, before the tale grew in the retelling and reached the ears of a priest, and too many questions were asked.

Just before dawn I dozed off again. I was still riding through the forest, the apparition just behind me, and I was exhausted, as if my dream self had been fleeing on the foam-flecked dream horse all the while I had been awake. The terror was still there, and every instant seemed my last, until finally the forest broke into an open plain where two rivers joined. Where they joined stood a walled town, and beyond it, with a river girding it on either side, was a lone mountain. Three of its sides were sheer cliffs, but on a fourth a road wound down, crossed a bridge, and entered the far side of the town. Atop the mountain perched a castle of black stone. As soon as I spied this place it seemed a great weight was lifted from me, and another glance over my shoulder revealed that my nemesis had vanished. I let my horse slow to a walk, and as I approached the town and castle, the sun rose behind me, out of the forest, banishing all evil.

The last thing I saw—and I don't know if I imagined or truly dreamed it—was the hooded stranger rising from where he sat over a steaming cauldron, stretching his cramped legs, while within all the things in my dreams, the knight, the horse, the forest, the castle, and even myself, sank slowly through the broth to the bottom and there dissolved away.

I had no more visions that night.

There were people milling about when I awoke the third time. When I emerged from my tent they steadfastly refused to look directly at me or speak a word, even if questioned. And I knew not to persist in questioning. Some were breaking camp, piling unsold goods into carts, making ready to go even before the fair was over. I didn't have to ask the reason. An ill omen. There would be no luck in this place, and perhaps a curse for those who lingered. Next year the fair would doubtless be held somewhere else.

I didn't linger either, but instead packed what supplies and money I had into saddle pouches and rode away, leaving my tent where it stood. I couldn't take it with me in any case. For all I cared, the old bread-seller from whom I'd bought it could have it back. He might want to wrestle a devil in there sometime.

I knew that in such dreams, from wherever sent, something of import had been revealed, if a little vaguely, as is the manner of dreams. But such things cannot be without meaning. Indeed, as had been prophesied, I rode west, and that very afternoon came to the forest I had seen. It was not as sinister as its dream self, but always in the periphery of my sight there was a suggestion of a shape that set me ill at ease. I glanced back now and again to see if I was followed. I was alone, but my steed was as nervous as I, and difficult to control.

Beyond the wood was a plain, as I had foreseen, and two rivers met, and a mountain reared above all. One could only reach the castle atop it by passing through the town, as if the castle were the innermost keep of a larger fortress surrounding it.

Soon I came upon peasants bringing their crops to market. The folk on this side of the forest seldom dared venture to the other, so they were not the same who had been at the fair, or so I hoped. There were all sorts going the same way: two priests—and I recoiled unconsciously at the sight of them—a boy with a mandolin slung over his shoulder, obviously a minstrel, and every variety of low-born person, afoot, astride mules and plow horses, or in carts.

As the traffic increased there were even a few of the wealthy in their ponderous, solid-wheeled carriages, surrounded by troops of men at arms. It occurred to me to seek employment as one such, but first I knew I must discharge whatever supernatural obligation had been laid on me, the dreams would continue, the skeletal rider overtake me as I slept, and at the very least I would awaken mad.

There was a soldier at the town's gate leaning lazily on a pike, asking each man what his business was. A farmer would drive up with a load of cabbages, announce that he'd come to sell cabbages, and be passed through with a bored wave. The nobles in their carriages would be known by the signs of their houses, inevitably on a banner carried by one of their horsemen, and not challenged at all.

In my case, it was not that simple.

"What do you want here?" Seeing that I wore a mail coat under my cloak and a steel cap on my head, and carried a sword, and eyeing the plain black shield that hung by my saddle, and all the while knowing by the most cursory glance that I was a foreigner, the guard stood up attentively, and raised his pike to block my way.

An equally cursory glance on my part revealed no other guards nearby, and none of the men at arms attending the carriages were close enough to come immediately to his assistance, or even ascertain at once what was going on.

So I reached up with my hand—my only hand, the hook being

hidden beneath the cloak—and pushed the pike away. At the same time I feigned a rage and glared at him.

"You filthy churl! How dare you question your betters?" My Greek was rough, but I was understood. The pike dropped limply away, and the fellow's mouth hung agape. He didn't know what to do, and alone he dared do nothing. So I took rein again in hand and spurred my horse quickly into the city before he could recover his wits. Almost as quickly I wondered if I had done the right thing. Would the guard brave his master's wrath and report his incompetence? Well, the die was cast, as Caesar had once remarked, and I had done what I had done. If my strange saga were known, I surely would not be welcomed here, but first I wanted to know what sort of place this was before seeking out its lord and making my way to the castle.

In the main square something was going on which wasn't standard trading or entertainment.

A large crowd had gathered and there was much excitement. I stood up in my stirrups to see more clearly. It was an execution. A man was being drawn and quartered between four separately harnessed oxen. Even over the yells of the mob I could hear his shrieks. As he hung there above the ground, and hooded executioners stood by with switches ready to prod the animals on, another, presumably the Master Executioner, had slit his belly open, yanked out an end of intestine, and begun coiling it around a stick. With every firm, jerking turn came another scream. Then one of the prisoner's arms slipped from the ropes and I saw why—he had no hand, so the wrist slid right out of the knot. Gesticulating furiously, the master rose from the disembowelling, kicked one of his assistants aside, and retired the rope, below the elbow this time.

As if this sight reminded them of something, the crowd began to shout with one voice a single word: *"Nekatu! Nekatu!"*

I sat down, startled. That was the second time I had heard the name, or term, or whatever it was, and I liked the circumstance even less well than I had the first. I took care that my own lack of a hand was concealed. I doubted this was the criminal's offense, but instinct counseled caution.

Disgusted, I rode around the edge of the square and along a narrow street filled with booths. Behind me the shouts of the crowd came to a crescendo, then stopped.

Now, most cities I have seen are vast caverns of wood and stone, and this one was no exception. Night begins early in a city. Even the great capital of Constantinople is lighted only around the palace and guard houses, and in a few principal squares. The common people grope like the blind through muddy, treacherous streets. In this place the upper storeys of the houses leaned over the back streets, the all but touching roofs shutting out all but the light of noontide. As I rode it was well into the evening, the fading sunset reflected only from those high gables and rooftops which caught the glow.

I came to a gap in the buildings, where I could get a full view of the castle on the hill beyond the town. Now it was silhouetted starkly against the western sky. Even as time passed, and the light faded even more, the placed remained dark. Not a torch was lit in a tower; not a lantern glowed from any window. It seemed simply impossible that it could be deserted with a thriving town at its feet.

"Hist!" someone whispered. "Don't be staring at that! Ye'll bring a curse down on yer head."

I looked down, astonished that anyone would speak to me in such a manner. It was an old woman, her hair a tangled white explosion, with a bundle of sticks on her shoulder.

"And what ill can come from looking at the house of your lord? Woman, do you speak treason against him?"

Her face all but split apart with an irregularly toothed grin.

"Our *lord*? Ha! Our mortal lord lives here in the town. Only the wicked call *him* lord!" To make herself more clear, she pointed at the castle with her free hand.

"Does Satan himself roost up there then?" I laughed back at her.

"'Tis no subject for a jest, good sir. That one they quartered today—that's what happens to people who take too much interest in evil places." She crossed herself hastily.

"For merely looking at it?"

She grinned again. Now I was sure she took me for a fool, for all my higher birth.

"He *went* there. He was *Nekatu*!"

As soon as she uttered that word, the exchange was no longer a joke. I leaned over in the saddle and faced her intently. Despite the gloom I could see her eyes well enough to tell she was suddenly frightened of me.

"I have heard of this *Nekatu* many times. Twice since I came here. Old woman, there is gold in this for you if you will kindly tell me what—may the saints preserve us—everyone is talking about. What is *Nekatu*?"

She put her hand to her mouth and said nothing. Ah, I thought. Her tongue is suddenly tied in knots. Thinking to loosen it, I reached into my purse for one of my few coins. But the leather thong was too tightly drawn. I couldn't get it open with one hand.

So without giving it any thought, I slipped the tip of my hook between the thong and the bag to work it loose.

And the woman screamed. At the sight of the hook she dropped her bundle and ran down the street shrieking "Nekatu! Help! Help! Another one! Nekatu!"

Instantly what seemed an empty alley filled with people. Some grabbed at my horse's reins. I drew my sword and slashed, and there was a howl of pain, but by then dozens of others had swarmed all around. Hands were pulling me from the saddle. My horse reared up in terror, which only helped them, even if a few skulls were split beneath the hooves. I tumbled over backwards out of the saddle and into the muddy street, striking furiously with sword and hook.

This had a temporary effect. No one was holding me when I hit the ground. I struggled to my feet. Whirling steel kept my foes temporarily at bay. None of them were armed with anything more fearsome than some of the old woman's firewood.

This changed almost at once. Nearby mail clinked, and I glanced quickly in the direction the crone had run. The pikes and steel helmets of the city guard were working their way through the jostling crowd.

With renewed fury I cut my way through the wall of my assailants. My horse had run off. I would have to escape on foot. An iron shoe in the groin, a chop at an upraised arm, a raking slash across the face with my metal hook, and I was no longer surrounded. A shout went up from the guards, and all the people regained their courage and surged after me. The chase went along that street into a narrower one, splashing through the mud, pushing passersby roughly aside until they understood what was happening, and joined in. The cry of *"Nekatu!"* seemed to be a kind of universal alarm, and every citizen stopped what he or she was doing and united against the common enemy.

My mail and my iron-covered shoes weighed me down, and I surely would have been overtaken before long had the chaotic fray not spilled into a lane so narrow that there was barely enough room to squeeze a cart along it—and there was a cart heading straight toward us.

Some of my pursuers hesitated, but I lunged forward with desperate speed. The cart driver drew rein, unsure of what was going on. Before he knew it I was alongside him. I flattened myself against a wall, then gave his horse a long, shallow swipe on the rump with my sword. Of course the enraged animal charged forward, completely out of control, right into the mass of my foes. As it clattered past, the protruding axles of the cart missed me by scarcely a span.

Breathing heavily, but still maintaining the strength which had brought me through countless battles, I came at last to the far end of the town, where a gate led to the bridge over the river, then to the winding road up the one less than utterly sheer side of the mountain. This gate was barred from the inside. Now the bridge itself was fortified, and a small number of soldiers thereon could surely prevent an enemy from climbing up onto it from barges. This side was otherwise completely inaccessible. The thick, slippery wall of the town dropped straight to the water's edge, leaving no more than a foot or two of muddy bank. In any case, I'd seen no indication that this was a time of war.

Not hesitating to ponder this idiocy of siege design in a town that seemed completely crazy anyway, I placed both shoulders beneath the massive wooden bar, and with all my strength forced it up until it rose free of its supports and fell to the ground with a thud. The gate swung outward and I staggered backwards through it, onto the bridge.

By now those who hadn't been trampled by the runaway cart had found me again. With long strides I ran across the bridge and part way up the mountain. Then I turned to look. They weren't following. The crowd now filled the gateway, but none would venture forth. A tangle of faces stared up at me, sullen and quiet. It only seemed fitting that people who so irrationally feared men who were missing hands, and who so shunned the castle around which their town was built that they condemned to death anyone who went there, should behave in so ridiculous a way. I was sure they were all lunatics. With a contemptuous snort, I turned and made my way up the mountain at a leisurely pace.

It was only after I had gone a ways and the castle loomed huge above me, blotting out the stars, that it occurred to me that the people might have been sensible after all. Could there be some danger lurking among those towers such that one going the way I was would be insured a more frightful doom than anything the executioner could contrive?

If so, I was in a terrible situation, like a man who cannot swim trapped on a burning ship. I could not return to the town. There was no way to go but up, into the castle I had first glimpsed in a dream. In that dream it had been a place of relief and refuge, but now I was not so sure.

There was a little door beside the main gate of the castle, with a heavy metal iron for a knocker. I clanged the thing until the sound must surely have echoed throughout the whole land.
There was a stirring within.
"*Nekatu*," I said.
A bolt slid aside and the door opened.
That is how I found refuge among the *Nekatu*.

II

"The phrase '*nekatu*' literally means 'messenger,' not in Greek, but in the older language of these people. As you see, I have made good my promise. As soon as you arrived here, you learned the definition."

The same hooded stranger who had come to my tent the night before now led me up a winding flight of stairs, and into a large room. I couldn't tell how large. He carried only a small oil lamp, and nothing was lighted. The castle was clearly in a state of considerable disrepair. I could dimly make out fallen beams, stones, and tattered draperies scattered about.

He put the lamp down on a bare wooden table, pulled out a high-backed chair, and indicated that I should sit. The only sounds were the scraping of the chair, the clank of my shoes, and the soft pad of his slippers. He stood and I sat absolutely still for a moment, and the only sound was a slight fizzling from the lamp. Then there was something else: a faint pattering, like the scurrying of rats. At first I thought it to be that, but there wasn't enough scratching. Too soft, without claws. More like many people drumming their fingers nervously on wood.

I watched my host's every move with utmost suspicion. All this had been his contrivance. He wanted something. I was being brought here as surely as a fish on a hook. To make the point that I was not utterly helpless, I did not sheathe my sword, which I had carried in hand all the way up the mountain, but placed it in clear view in front of me. It clattered, and for an instant the tapping sound in the background stopped. Then it resumed, somewhat closer.

The hood fell back, and a thin, bearded, ageless face was revealed. Atop silvery hair rested the thin band of a golden crown.

"King Tikos, I presume."

"The unhappy knight of the tale, I presume." Another chair was dragged, and he sat down across from me. "But let us set aside all pretense. Look at this."

He leaned forward into the light, pushed up both sleeves, and held his wrists up to the lamp, so I could plainly see.

"Look very closely," he said.

I let out an inadvertent grunt of astonishment. There was a thin line across both wrists, and he turned both hands over to show that these lines went all the way around. No one could have scars like that. They were *seams*.

"Scorcery! Not even the greatest doctors of a physic. . . ."

"Most not-so-noble knight, if your tale is as true as I think it is, you are not wholly godly yourself."

"That is . . . true. But how?"

"This is one of the many powers of the *Nekatu*."

"Messengers?"

"A kind of brotherhood, set apart from the rest of mankind. This is why I have brought you here, why I sought you out when I saw you in the fair and noticed that your left hand was missing."

"Are you some kind of ghoul that you are fascinated by mutilation? Go to the wars in the east, and you'll get your fill."

"No! No! You fail to understand! I offer you a great gift. Look again!"

He reached under the table and drew from someplace a wooden box. The hinged lid came open. Inside there was a left hand carven out of a single piece of crystal, glittering with a thousand facets. It was a stunning piece of work, something with which to ransom empires.

I was not at all sure that it was a trick of the poor lighting that the thing seemed to move. Had the fingers been entirely outstretched? Now they seemed somewhat curled.

"By a most secret art," he said, "I have learned to make these. Contrary to what the philosophers will tell you, that which glitters has substance. Each ray of light captured within the crystal is a living thing, giving the hand itself life. This hand I have exposed to the stars for a hundred nights, giving it the life of the *Nekatu*. When joined to a wrist it becomes as living flesh in all ways."

"Joined? How so?"

"It naturally adheres, as you shall see. Take off that hook and bronze cap, and be healed and whole again."

The intensity of his gaze, my exhaustion, and the perils I had passed through must have bewitched me, for I thought of little else but having a living hand again, even if there would be a seam around it. I forgot the treacherous, extreme outrageousness of my situation, the childishly obvious fact that the King was not doing this out of charitable commiseration over my wound.

Hardly realizing what I was doing, I pulled the hook and cap off my left wrist, exposing the healed stump. Tikos took the arm in his hand—I did not resist—and joined it to the crystal hand over the flame of the lamp.

I felt no pain. First there was a numbness, then a tingling, a sort of melting, as the flame licked over the wrist and hand, and the substance flowed like hot wax. Even as I watched the crystal lost its luster, the facets smoothing over, the color fading. It was turning into flesh. I seemed far away from everything, drifting in abstraction. I wondered in bemusement if this were tried on a Negro. Would the hue be right?

When the King let go, the hand seemed as if it had grown there. Thrilling at the sensation, I flexed the fingers, then made a fist and banged with all my might on the table. The sword and the lamp bounced.

"A miracle! I am restored!"

"Yes, miraculous. By the way, are you hungry? I doubt you've eaten."

I made no answer. It seemed such a silly question, like the hues of Negroes. Who could care about food now?

King Tikos snapped his fingers and a tray was set before me. My heart skipped a beat when I saw that it was placed there by *hands*, but nothing more. They floated in the air as if creatures were reaching through from some invisible world into our own.

"*Christ and Satan!*"

"Swear by whomever you like," laughed the King. "Why not Jupiter, Thor, Mithra, and Ahura-Mazda also? It'll do you as much good. Those hands, I can safely tell you now, are simply *Nekatu*, like yourself, only in a far more advanced stage of development. The body withers away—it is unimportant—and is absorbed entirely into the hand. Why has this not happened to me? I remain whole because the Master, whom we all serve—yes, even you now—wills it. I recruit new slaves for him, even if sometimes, like that fool in the town today, a few are lost. He tried to run away."

With a howl of rage and despair, and every curse I could think of garbled together, I grabbed my sword and lunged across the table at the laughing monster, bent on total dismemberment. But before

I could even get to my feet a frigid shock ran up my left arm and through my body. I staggered numbly for a second, the sword dropping from senseless fingers, then collapsed forward onto the table, smothering the lamp. That was the last thing I remembered.

For a second night then I was tossed like a cork on a sea of nightmares. At first there was complete darkness, and a feeling of being long dead and very *soft*, trapped far underground, and clawing my way to the surface, until all the putrid flesh of my body had been sloughed off, and only my diamond-hard *hands* emerged from the earth. Then the scene changed and I saw myself lying where I had fallen on the table, my left arm, with that accursed hand, dangling over the edge. Again came a numbness at the wrist, and a sensation of melting.

The thing dropped off, landing on the floor upright on its fingers, like a cat dropped from a rooftop. It stood there like a living thing—which indeed it was—and there was an instant of confusion and disorientation: I was wrenched from where I lay, drifting, falling, floating upward into warmth; and then I was looking up into the gloom at an enormous table with an unconscious giant sprawled over it, and the stump of a left wrist hanging over me.

My soul, my self, was now a prisoner in the hand. I was not in control. Another mind was at work. Following a way the fingers knew, I was carried away from the table and my body, into utter blackness as the hand passed through a tiny crevice in the wall. I could "see" nothing else until I/we/it emerged on the outside of the castle. All the while the sensations of fingertips on damp stone were intense, very real. Then there was the vast panorama of the town and surrounding countryside viewed from a height, and a brilliant full moon in the sky.

The hand wanted to avoid the light. It stayed in the shadows as much as possible as it climbed down the outside of the castle wall, each finger seeking and finding holds sufficient to sustain the weight of the thing. Like a monstrous spider it crept over the stone until it was just above the door through which I had first entered the castle. There followed a sickening, terrifying drop through space as the grip was released, then a jolt as the hand landed upright, as it had done beneath the table.

It crawled down that road up which I had come, scurrying as fast as a rat. For all the distance and its small size, it was at the barred gate of the town very quickly. The closed gate posed no obstacle. The rough outcroppings of the city wall were as sure as the rungs of a ladder. Up and over we went with practiced skill, and once more there was a drop, and the fingers sank the second joint in mud. Still the hand was not stopped. The fingers spread out, then curled, squeezing mud, then spread out in a kind of swimming motion until the fingertips reached more solid ground. This gave way to a paved street, and the filthy fingers paddled silently along the cobblestones, remaining always in the deepest shadows.

"Sight" was a confusing thing. At times I seemed to view the five fingers working, as if I were a tiny observer seated on the back, just behind the knuckles, and at other times the hand would stop, raise the index finger like an eyestalk, and I would get a sweeping view through that.

My waking self, Julian, the man who had been duped, had no idea where we/the hand intended to go, but there was a definite mission in the motion of the fingers. The hand came to certain intersections, and the index finger would scout about, then I would be going down a particular street, to a specific destination.

At last there was a wretched hovel propped between two brick buildings. A board was missing from the door, so the hand could enter without difficulty.

Within, the pattering which was definitely not a rat crossed the floor, steering a wide curve around the glowing coals of the firepit in the middle of the floor. Moonlight streamed through the smoke hole in the roof, and I could clearly discern a person asleep on a heap of straw on the far side of the room. It was the old woman who had carried the sticks.

Stealthily the hand made its way through the straw then began to climb the tattered blanket she had wrapped herself in. The hand began to climb the blanket onto her shoulder. The index finger stood straight up, again the "eye" of the creature, while the second and third fingers pinched cloth between them, as did the little finger and thumb. With these two grips the hand inched its way on top of her, then crept across her rising and falling body. I could feel her heartbeat beneath my fingertips as I moved down onto her breast, over the collarbone—

It was obvious what was intended. I desperately wanted to stop, to curl the fingers into a fist and drop into the straw, to shout a warning with all my breath. But I had no breath. My voice and lungs were back at the castle. I had no will, no control as the fingers slipped around the helpless crone's thin throat. Blood throbbed in her neck, but the skin felt like parchment.

Suddenly, with furious strength, the hand closed on her windpipe. She awoke, sat up wide-eyed in terror, let out a single gurgling cry, and then could utter nothing more. For a minute she writhed in the straw, flailing wildly after her unseen assailant and meeting only empty air, and then she lay still. The horror of the thing was not merely the death, or even my inability to prevent it, but that *I had done the deed.* As the hand strangled her I felt the muscles of a phantom arm, my arm, the arm of my body back at the castle, straining with the work. I felt the weight of my whole body pressed on the woman, pushing her down until her neck snapped like one of the sticks she had been carrying.

Someone stirred in another part of the room.

"Grandmother? Is that you?" Bare footsteps moved near the firepit, and a handful of rushes was lighted, then carried in my direction. I could see the face of a young girl as she bent over her grandmother, and the contortions of revulsion and mad terror at the sight of the thing still perched on the corpse. The light went out again as the rushes were dropped to the floor. The granddaughter screamed and was answered by shouts from without.

Instantly the hand knew what to do. With unbelievable agility it scrambled up the wall and was out another hole in the rotted wood. Then followed a drop into the muddy back street, and a scramble across to another house, and up a wall. From atop the neighboring roof it watched and gloated—yes, there was a definite feeling of that emotion in the second mind, joined to my own, which I could not escape.

"It has happened again! Grandmother!" the girl tried to explain to others through hysterical tears. *"Nekatu!"*

It was then that I came to understand some of the peculiar things about this town.

III

It was no surprise, but a dreadful, sickening certainty when I awoke the next morning on the table and there was mud on my left hand.

Revenge the King had said. In this way he wrought revenge on those who had overthrown him. No wonder there were no men-at-arms on his battlements. He had an army of *Nekatu* which was far more deadly.

I lurched to my feet and instantly fell. My legs would not support me. I was sick, exhausted, as if I had just completed a vast labor, and I realized that, as the King had said, the hand was beginning to absorb my vitality into itself. I dropped to my knees, grasping the edge of the table with my right hand. I left the other arm hanging limp. The thing seemed asleep. Now, by daylight, my body was my own.

Apparently there were limits. I had to stay alive long enough for the thing to steal my life away. It would take a while. I would have to be kept for a long time. The tray set down by the hands the night before was still there. On it were cold meat, bread, and cheese. A cup of wine stood beside it. This had *not* been there before.

My breakfast was laid out for me.

I spent the day exploring the castle. I could not go into the town, where I would be killed on sight. If I fled over the countryside, making my way down one of the cliffs with only one hand I could trust, I had no doubt the hand could bring me back, or at the very least deal with me the same way it had with the old woman. I could, at last resort, cast myself from the walls, or simply refuse to eat until I starved, but these were indeed last resorts. It is not like a warrior, *any* warrior, be he Christian knight or pagan savage, to surrender before the battle is joined. The enemy must be met, no matter how hopeless the odds.

So all day I wandered through the ruined halls of the castle. I found a library filled with books written in strange scripts. There were also a few in Latin, and these I glanced through. Most were treatises on magic, of vast age. One was dedicated: *To my Lord Nero, who taught me how to begin.* The same Nero who reigned shortly after Christ, and slew the apostles Peter and Paul. How long had it been since King Tikos lost his natural hands? Surely the folk of this town were not his subjects, but their remote descendants.

When twilight was drawing near, I knew my efforts were over for the day. Another night of helpless horror was to follow. But before anything happened I dragged an iron brazier I had found into the room where the wooden table was, then gathered up some dry rushes, bits of wood, and scraps of the fallen tapestries. I meant to keep the place lighted so I could see Tikos when he came to put the spell on me, and slay him if I could. I still had my sword.

Supper had been set in my absence. I ate while the familiar pattering passed back and forth behind the walls. Long shadows crossed the floor.

There was a footstep behind me.

283

"Ah, now that you've dined, it's time for another errand," said King Tikos.

Before I could even turn around, the cold blast overwhelmed me.

Many more died that night, but not in the town below. The mission was far stranger. I was in the company of a whole brigade of *Nekatu*, perhaps as many as fifty. Together we climbed *up* the outside of the castle, to the top of a tower. There a flock of black hawks were waiting, as still as carven gargoyles. Each hand climbed on the back of a bird, the thumb and forefinger hooked around the neck, the rest grasping the body. The feel was very familiar. I've handled falcons often.

There was a more terrifying drop than before as the bird I was riding fell into the abyss, heavy with its burden, struggling for flight. It flapped desperately, then caught the air and rose clumsily to join the others, all of them lurching in an equally heavy manner. Below, the fields and hills rolled. Moonlight gleamed on the two rivers. We followed one of them to its source in the mountains beyond a forest, then over the mountains until we came to the manor of some lord. The birds waited patiently on walls and window ledges while the passengers dismounted and went about their business. The hands worked in pairs this time, not necessarily left and right, but always in pairs. I was with a huge black member—answering my question about Negroes. Together we came to a chamber in which a man and a woman slept. Now the black hand did something which I had witnessed the first night, but had never been able to imitate. It floated in the air, as if attached to an invisible body, as those bringing the tray had done. It slid a sword from the scabbard which hung from the bedpost. All this while my own hand was climbing up the side of the bed, inching up a blanket. "A more advanced stage," the King had said. A *Nekatu* which still had a human body, a newcomer like myself, had not yet all the powers given to that fiendish brotherhood. I could not yet rise and float. I had to crawl.

The murder was done. I/the hand in which my self was trapped crept to the face of the man, then clamped tightly over his mouth while the black hand slit his throat from ear to ear with the sword. The lady slept through the whole deed, so swiftly and silently was it performed. Again I felt the weight of my whole body leaning over the bed, gagging my victim while my accomplice slew him.

The sword was placed gently on the floor and the two of us returned to the windowsill, there mounting our bewitched steeds. As if at a signal, the whole flock took off at once, bearing the army of *Nekatu* back to the castle of King Tikos. I was not told, but I knew that what I had participated in was not unique that night. In twenty-five rooms wives would wake up, soaked with blood, and scream as they found themselves sharing beds with still warm corpses. Could King Tikos hear the screams? Was he somehow nourished by the terror and death?

Once more I found myself in that room by the table, and a breakfast had been prepared for me. Where did he get the food? No stores could keep fresh all that time. Did he send *Nekatu* to rob butchers and bakers? Well, that was the most innocuous thing they would ever do.

I hated myself as I ate. It was all I could do not to vomit as I remembered what had happened. It was time, I told myself, to leap to an easy death, before more innocents perished. *I* was not innocent. I had many times longed for death. But then the familiar terror came. . . . After death—damnation, the eternal torments I could escape only for that brief time I lived. Like all men, I am ultimately selfish. I would sacrifice the whole world to escape Hell even for a short while. I could kill myself only on a sudden, saving impulse swifter than thought. If I reasoned what was right, just, and the moral thing to do, I would forget all about rightness, justice, and morality, and be paralyzed.

That day I continued to search the castle, hoping to find some secret thing by which I could justify myself.

And I was rewarded. There was a small door beneath what had once been a long bench. I made a torch out of wood, weeds from a courtyard garden, and scraps of cloth, lit it with flint and steel from the pouch on my belt, and descended into a vault. There I found twelve stone coffins, each of them with, curiously, an opening of about a span cut into the top.

No, not curious at all. A span is measured by the spread of a man's fingers.

Within were *Nekatu* of "a more advanced stage of development." When I slid the lid off the first coffin, I grew faint at the sight, but quickly gathered my courage. There lay an ancient, withered corpse, little more than skin stretched tight over bones, save that on one of the arms the shrunken skin blossomed out into a perfect living hand.

The fury of loathing gave me strength. I hacked at the thing with my sword, severing the hand, cutting again and again until the fingers were scattered and the whole body was a ruin. The skull splintered; the ribcage collapsed into slivers and chips. Only when nothing remained recognizable did I stop, sweat-covered for all the dampness of the vault, breathing heavily from my labor. After a pause I went on to the next one and destroyed it as thoroughly, but more methodically.

I was encouraged that my left hand was *my* left hand as I did this work. It did as my muscles commanded, and aided me in my task.

That night, however, the King again appeared from nowhere—I still had no idea how he did it—and more evil work was done. The army of *Nekatu* was abroad once more, and I noticed, and despaired as I saw, that some of them were crisscrossed with imperfectly healed scars. One or two even "limped" as they crawled on broken fingers. But they did what their master bade them. This time we came to a monastery, and, after stealing candles from the chapel altar, each of the *Nekatu* crept into a cell and burned out the eyes of the monk therein.

IV

When next I awoke, my vital essence was so drained I could not rise. I was getting rapidly weaker. My flesh was wasting away. Already I was as gaunt as a starving beggar, increasingly like the shrivelled corpse of the *Nekatu* in the coffins. Doubtless before long I would be unable to move at all, and many hands would carry me to those same or similar coffins, and place me in one of them. Only with utmost effort could I crawl to the chair, eat, and live for another day. Now I knew I could never fling myself from a parapet. I'd never reach the wall. So I sat there throughout the day, as sunlight shifted from window to window along the south side of the room.

I was very cold. Somehow I found the strength to rise after a while and light the brazier. I could think of nothing but warmth. For warmth, in my wretched condition, I would sell my soul. But my soul was already spoken for, so I had to provide for myself.

Thus I sat as evening fell, leaning against the back of the chair, my sword before me on the table, both hands in my lap, right on top of left in vain hope of restraining it. Beside me, the brazier sputtled and crackled. The smell of smoke was comforting, my single tie to earthly things? Whenever the flames burned low I fed them bits of straw, cloth, and splinters of rotten wood. A heap of fuel was within arm's reach.

King Tikos arrived. He did not come into the room; he was merely *there*. I thought the white spot in the air was a trick on my tired eyes, but it grew and took shape, and he was in the room with me. His slippers padded softly on the floor as he walked. All but soundless, a horde of *Nekatu* kept pace with him on extended fingers. There were more of them than I had ever imagined. They poured from the cracks and holes until the floor was covered. There were easily a thousand of them. How foolish to think my tiny group made up the whole army!

"It is time," said the King, "that our brother be brought fully into our fellowship. No waiting in the vaults for him. The Master is coming this night to claim and transform him."

He was speaking to the hands, not to me. I was merely an object to be dealt with. He paced back and forth as he spoke, the *Nekatu* scurrying this way and that after him like thousands of crabs come out of the sea just long enough to devour a drowned sailor the waves had washed up.

"We must wait, brothers. Have patience. The Master will come when the Master feels it is time. In the Master's world, beyond our own, time is not as we know it. I have been there as none of you have, and have seen, so believe me. Shapes and sounds and colors are all wondrously transformed, unrecognizably different. Senses are confused. One *hears* the color white, tastes the sweet twang of terror. A scream is like a soft caress *within* the body. Space, and time, and distance? These do not exist where the Master dwells, any more than depths exist in the world of a drawing on a page of parchment. Can one of those figures stand up, and walk out of the book? The Master can. You and I shall be able to also, in the end, when this world likewise belongs to the Master. That is why I worship him. That is why he is greater even than the God who created this universe. The Master walks between many universes. *Whence comest thou? From walking to and fro in the sum of cosmoses, and up and down in it, between the planes and angles.* That is why the Master is the Master.

"And yet," said the King, pacing back and forth in the semi-darkness amid the thousand disembodied hands, "and yet I do not fear the Master where I now stand, for he needs me, to become material in our world. To take on solid substance. *And the word was made flesh, and screamed among us.* He is not as powerful here as he is in the void between the voids."

I listened to all this with the dull incomprehension of a pig in the slaughterhouse overhearing the talk of two butchers. Surely Tikos was mad to talk of anything beyond the sphere of the Earth, the moon and sun moving around it, and the fixed stars in the spheres of the firmament beyond, but then I was surely mad to be dreaming this nightmare in which I now existed, and the whole world was mad to allow such thoughts to come to be, and God was mad, as I knew well, for having created it that way. *And the Earth was without shape and form, and darkness was on the face of the deep.* Ah! If only the Father had been truly wise, and not meddled!

"The Master comes!" There was a rippling of the air, like foam on the sea an instant before a great whale leaps from the depths. For the first time Tikos spoke to me: "Watch! Watch, Sir Knight, and listen, and observe the last thing you shall ever observe with mortal eyes and ears. Tonight on this night of nights, the last of the harvest moon, the Master comes into this chamber, and you will be within our grip. *Ours.* I am part of the Master. This is the ultimate secret. Now, as I have promised, you truly know the meaning of the work *Nekatu*. A messenger, a servant of the Master, a finger of his hand."

Literally. As I watched the whiteness in the air returned and surrounded the King. He stood still. A thousand hands paused on five thousand fingertips. Four columns of whiteness began to materialize around him, and as they did he lost his own shape. He was flowing together, arms melting into his body, his two legs become one. Like wax. A candle. *Lighted.* Fire. Dimly the association anchored in my mind.

A finger of the Master. Exactly. That was what he had become. The four other fingers appeared beside him, and he—the index finger—was lifted off the floor as the Master reared up. The Master was a huge hand, that of a giant as tall as the castle if any body had been present. Something reaching through the air out of an invisible world coexistent with our own.

The hand climbed up on the table. It was the size of a horse. The wood creaked under its weight.

All time seemed suspended, and in my abstraction, I noticed a curious thing. The finger which had been King Tikos had a red welt around it. Was the Master a kind of *Nekatu* of a larger world, not complete without the animate finger which was the king, or which he had become? Was this the ultimate bargain to which the maimed and outcast king had agreed so long ago, through which he gained his continual revenge?

Joined together, a voice in the back of my mind chanted. Candle. Wax. Welting. Fire. Wax. *Fire.*

Now my left hand, that which was *Nekatu*, had come alive. The rest of my body was too weak to obey any commands, so the hand was on the table, crawling toward the far end where the Master stood on fingertips a foot across, dragging me with it. Now my awareness was entirely in my head. The hand didn't need me, and moved of itself.

So I was pulled forward, across the table, toward the grasp of the Master.

I leaned forward. My chin touched the hilt of my sword, which was still on the table in front of me. With impossible strength the *Nekatu* hand was dragging me up out of the chair, onto the table. It passed the overturned oil lamp from the first night.

Fire. Wax. Melting.

In the remote regions of my mind, where thoughts were still my own, the idea came. I laughed at the brilliance of it. I was completely detached, my awareness floating. What was happening was not *really* happening. It was an intellectual exercise. I had always been good at things like chess. There was all the time in the world to carefully consider. Soon, someday, I would try—

I lost myself wholly for an instant, and *was* in the *Nekatu* hand, unheeded, but feeling the attraction of the Master, the call to union, a kind of lust—

—and was again myself, and in less than a split second the thoughts, the little voices, melted and turned and twisted upon themselves: Fire. Wax. Fire. Candle. Fire. Fire. *Fire.* . . .

The unexpected: a convoluted stratagem—again I slipped into blackness, was in hand for a longer interval, and the call was far, far stronger—and flashed back, perhaps for the last time, into the body and mind of the man Julian—the convoluted stratagem: while all attention was on my left hand, the *Nekatu*, the right hand was doing something.

In the realm of philosophical abstraction, detached from time and space, as an interesting exercise, the fingers of my *right* hand, my human hand, curled around the hilt of my sword as it lay there on the table.

With a sudden *thwunk!* the right hand brought the sword up and around and down, crashing into the tabletop, aimed at the *Nekatu* hand, but clumsily. It missed by less than the width of the blade.

The hand stopped, startled. The master stood there impassively. The thousand *Nekatu* on the floor remained motionless.

The grip on my left arm was relaxed for an instant. I was free. My body fell backwards into the chair, and with desperate effort I thrust the left hand into the flaming brazier.

The *Nekatu* hand recoiled. The Master stumbled backwards, and toppled off the end of the table, landing with a heavy thud on the floor, crushing those beneath him. Now a lifeless hand hacked apart during the day feels nothing, but a living one at night is different—and the Master directs all his hands, feeling as they feel.

Feeling as I feel. The hand did not go for my throat. The Master now writhed with the agonies of those he had crushed in his fall, and I, linked to them as a *Nekatu*, felt the same. It was in the fury of this pain that I was able to put my left hand back on the tabletop, then with my right, with the sword I still held, strike the mightiest blow ever struck in all the battles of mankind. I could have felled whole cities with it. The blade crashed down, through the wrist, just above the place where it joined the *Nekatu* hand. Honest agony followed. I was severed from the Master—it was mortal blood that flowed now from the stump. Only my own body.

I screamed, and in screaming woke fully into myself. Thick in the midst of the fight, instinct took over. The Master stood up once more, trembling on his pale, flabby fingers and began to crawl back up onto the table. I hurled the brazier at him, and again he retreated from the flames. I lifted the table with my bleeding stump, and the hand that still held the sword, and flipped it over on top of him. I sheathed the sword, and hurled handfuls of kindling onto the heap. There was some oil left in the lamp which now poured out and kept the fire going until it could catch on the wood.

All this while the *Nekatu* stood motionless on the floor, waiting for commands. I trampled them with my iron shoes.

All this while blood was gushing from my left arm. It was only as I fell forward, to the very edge of the flames now licking over the upside-down table that I realized my death was moments away. To this day I am amazed that I was able to do anything as rational as reaching forward with the bleeding arm, forcing the wound into the fire, and closing the wound. This new pain somehow gave me strength enough to rise from my feet and stagger down the winding stair, through the door, and out of the castle.

I was mad. I screamed. I howled. I laughed. I was as far from myself as I had been on the midnight missions of the *Nekatu*. There was that remote part of me which knew what was going on, but the rest raged in a frenzy of pain, fear, and sub-bestial fury.

Do you believe in miracles? *Speak not!* Any words are lies! *You know!*

Was it not a miracle that when I came to the bottom of the mountain road, with the castle burning fiercely behind me, the people of the town opened their gates and let me pass? "He is dead," I said, not knowing if the Master even *could* die. I think they feared me more than King Tikos. I think they took me for some new demon more terrible than the old. They opened the gate before I could blast it with a thunderbolt. They brought my horse to me. To appease my wrath? To get rid of a dread savior delicately before his unknown will be known? They saw my wounded wrist and knew I was no longer *Nekatu*, and they saw the glare from the castle above. Was this not a miracle?

Was it not a miracle that I found myself, when for the first time in a very long while I could think coherently, riding across a meadow far to the west of the city, beyond the mountains, a place I had once spied from the air, it seemed, in a dream?

And what else could it have been but a miracle, which brought me at last to a monastery of blind monks, who discovered by feel the wound on my arm, and said, "Look brothers, he is afflicted even as us," while carrying me to a bed and stumbling to fetch medicines?

Later, when again I was reduced to beggary, I refrained from telling stories, lest I somehow forget myself and accidentally relate how I lost my left hand twice.

ORSON SCOTT CARD

"Eumenides in the Fourth-Floor Lavatory"

Orson Scott Card (1951-) won the John W. Campbell Award for best new science fiction writer in 1978 and made science fiction history when his novel **Ender's Game** *(based on his first published story) and its sequel* **Speaker for the Dead** *each won the Hugo and Nebula Awards in 1985 and 1986, respectively. He has since extended the Ender series into a trilogy with* **Xenocide**. *A versatile writer who works in a variety of genres, he is the author of the fantasy novel* **Hart's Hope**, *the historical tale* **A Woman of Destiny**, *and the multi-volume Worthing Chronicle sequence, which splices fantasy elements into a science fiction scenario. His epic Tales of Alvin Maker saga, which includes* **Seventh Son, Red Prophet**, *and* **Prentice Alvin**, *is set in an alternative American past in which magic works. The tales gathered in his* **Maps in a Mirror: The Short Fiction of Orson Scott Card** *include "Eumenides in the Fourth-Floor Lavatory" which, along with his novels* **The Lost Boys** *and* **The Treasure Box**, *represent an infrequent foray into dark fantasy.*

Eumenides in the Fourth-Floor Lavatory

by Orson Scott Card

Living in a fourth-floor walk-up was part of his revenge, as if to say to Alice, Throw me out of the house, will you? Then I'll live in squalor in a Bronx tenement, where the toilet is shared by four apartments! My shirts will go unironed, my tie will be perpetually awry. *See what you've done to me?*

But when he told Alice about the apartment, she only laughed bitterly and said, "Not anymore, Howard. I won't play those games with you. You win every damn time."

She pretended not to care about him anymore, but Howard knew better. He knew people, knew what they wanted, and Alice wanted *him*. It was his strongest card in their relationship—that she wanted him more than he wanted her. He thought of this often: at work in the offices of Humboldt and Breinhardt, Designers; at lunch in a cheap lunchroom (part of the punishment); on the subway home to his tenement (Alice had kept the Lincoln Continental). He thought and thought about how much she wanted him. But he kept remembering what she had said the day she threw him out: "If you ever come near Rhiannon again I'll kill you."

He could not remember why she had said that. Could not remember and did not try to remember because that line of thinking made him uncomfortable, and one thing Howard insisted on being was comfortable with himself. Other people could spend hours and days of their lives chasing after some accommodation with themselves, but Howard was accommodated. Well adjusted. At ease. I'm okay,

I'm okay, I'm okay. Hell with you. "If you let them make you feel uncomfortable," Howard would often say, "you give them a handle on you and they can run your life." Howard could find other people's handles, but they could never find Howard's.

It was not yet winter but cold as hell at three A.M. when Howard got home from Stu's party. A "must attend" party, if you wished to get ahead at Humboldt and Breinhardt. Stu's ugly wife had tried to be tempting, but Howard had played innocent and made her feel so uncomfortable that she dropped the matter. Howard paid careful attention to office gossip and knew that several earlier departures from the company had got caught with, so to speak, their pants down. Not that Howard's pants were an impenetrable barrier. He got Dolores from the front office into the bedroom and accused her of making life miserable for him. "In little ways," he insisted. "I know you don't mean to, but you've got to stop."

"What ways?" Dolores asked, incredulous yet (because she honestly tried to make other people happy) uncomfortable.

"Surely you knew how attracted I am to you."

"No. That hasn't—that hasn't even crossed my mind."

Howard looked tongue-tied, embarrassed. He actually was neither. "Then—well, then, I was—I was wrong. I'm sorry, I thought you were doing it deliberately."

"Doing what?"

"Snub—snubbing me—never mind, it sounds adolescent, just little things, hell, Dolores, I had a stupid schoolboy crush—"

"Howard, I didn't even know I was hurting you."

"God, how insensitive," Howard said, sounding even more hurt.

"Oh, Howard, do I mean that much to you?"

Howard made a little whimpering noise that meant everything she wanted it to mean. She looked uncomfortable. She'd do anything to get back to feeling right with herself again. She was so uncomfortable that they spent a rather nice half-hour making each other feel comfortable again. No one else in the office had been able to get to Dolores. But Howard could get to anybody.

He walked up the stairs to his apartment feeling very, very satisfied. Don't need you, Alice, he said to himself. Don't need nobody, and nobody's who I've got. He was still mumbling the little ditty to himself as he went into the communal bathroom and turned on the light.

He heard a gurgling sound from the toilet stall, a hissing sound. Had someone been in there with the light off? Howard went into the stall and saw nobody. Then looked closer and saw a baby, probably about two months old, lying in the toilet bowl. Its nose and eyes were barely above water; it looked terrified; its legs and hips and stomach were down the drain. Someone had obviously hoped to kill it by drowning—it was inconceivable to Howard that anyone could be so moronic as to think it would fit down the drain.

For a moment he thought of leaving it there, with the big city temptation to mind one's own business even when to do so would be an atrocity. Saving this baby would mean inconvenience: calling the police, taking care of the child in his apartment, perhaps even headlines, certainly a night of filling out reports. Howard was tired. Howard wanted to go to bed.

But he remembered Alice saying, "You aren't even human, Howard. You're a goddamn selfish monster." I am not a monster, he answered silently, and reached down into the toilet bowl to pull the child out.

The baby was firmly jammed in—whoever had tried to kill it had meant to catch it tight. Howard felt a brief surge of genuine indignation that anyone could think to solve his problems by killing an innocent child. But thinking of crimes committed on children was something Howard was determined not to do, and besides, at that moment he suddenly acquired other things to think about.

As the child clutched at Howard's arms, he noticed the baby's fingers were fused together into flipper-like flaps of bone and skin at the end of the arm. Yet the flippers gripped his arms with an unusual strength as, with two hands deep in the toilet bowl, Howard tried to pull the baby free.

At last, with a gush, the child came up and the water finished its flushing action. The legs, too, were fused into a single limb that was hideously twisted at the end. The child was male; the genitals, larger than normal, were skewed off to one side. And Howard noticed that where the feet should be were two more flippers, and near the tips were red spots that looked like putrefying sores. The child cried, a savage mewling that reminded Howard of a dog he had seen in its death throes. (Howard refused to be reminded that it had been he who'd killed the dog by throwing it out in the street in front of a passing car just to watch the driver swerve; the driver hadn't swerved.)

Even the hideously deformed have a right to live, Howard thought, but now, holding the child in his arms, he felt a revulsion that translated into sympathy for whoever, probably the parents, had tried to kill the creature. The child shifted its grip on him, and where the flippers had been Howard felt a sharp, stinging pain that quickly turned to agony as it was exposed to the air. Several huge, gaping sores on his arms were already running with blood and pus.

It took a moment for Howard to connect the sores with the child, and by then the leg flippers were already pressed against his stomach, and the arm flippers already gripped his chest. The sores on the child's flippers were not sores; they were powerful suction devices that gripped Howard's skin so tightly that they ripped it away when the contact was broken. He tried to pry the child off, but no sooner was one flipper free than it found a new place to hold even as Howard struggled to break the grip of another.

What had begun as an act of charity had now become an intense struggle. This was not a child, Howard realized. Children could not hang on so tightly, and the creature had teeth that snapped at his hands and arms whenever they came near enough. A human face, certainly, but not a human being. Howard threw himself against the wall, hoping to stun the creature so it would drop away. It only clung tighter, and the sores where it hung on him hurt more. But at last Howard pried and scraped it off by levering it against the edge of the toilet stall. It dropped to the ground, and Howard backed quickly away, on fire with the pain of a dozen or more stinging wounds.

It had to be a nightmare. In the middle of the night, in a bathroom lighted by a single bulb, with a travesty of humanity writhing on the floor, Howard could not believe that it had any reality.

Could it be a mutation that had somehow lived? Yet the thing had far more purpose, far more control of its body than any human infant. The baby slithered across the floor as Howard, in pain from the wounds on his body, watched in a panic of indecision. The baby reached the wall and cast a flipper onto it. The suction held and the baby began to inch its way straight up the wall. As it climbed, it defecated, a thin drool of green tracing down the wall behind it. Howard looked at the slime following the infant up the wall, looked at the pus-covered sores on his arms.

What if the animal, whatever it was, did not die soon of its terrible deformity? What if it lived? What if it were found, taken to a hospital, cared for? What if it became an adult?

It reached the ceiling and made the turn, clinging tightly to the plaster, not falling off as it hung upside down and inched across toward the light bulb.

The thing was trying to get directly over Howard, and the defecation was still dripping. Loathing overcame fear, and Howard reached up, took hold of the baby from the back, and, using his full weight, was finally able to pry it off the ceiling. It writhed and twisted in his hands, trying to get the suction cups on him, but Howard resisted with all his strength and was able to get the baby, this time headfirst, into the toilet bowl. He held it there until the bubbles stopped and it was blue. Then he went back to his apartment for a knife. Whatever the creature was, it had to disappear from the face of the earth. It had to die, and there had to be no sign left that could hint that Howard had killed it.

He found the knife quickly, but paused for a few moments to put something on his wounds. They stung bitterly, but in a while they felt better. Howard took off his shirt; thought a moment, and took off all his clothes, then put on his bathrobe and took a towel with him as he returned to the bathroom. He didn't want to get any blood on his clothes.

But when he got to the bathroom, the child was not in the toilet. Howard was alarmed. Had someone found it, drowning? Had they, perhaps, seen him leaving the bathroom—or worse, returning with his knife? He looked around the bathroom. There was nothing. He stepped back into the hall. No one. He stood a moment in the doorway, wondering what could have happened.

Then a weight dropped onto his head and shoulders from above, and he felt the suction flippers tugging at his face, at his head. He almost screamed. But he didn't want to arouse anyone. Somehow the child had not drowned after all, had crawled out of the toilet, and had waited over the door for Howard to return.

Once again the struggle resumed, and once again Howard pried the flippers away with the help of the toilet stall, though this time he was hampered by the fact that the child was behind and above him. It was exhausting work. He had to set down the knife so he could use both hands, and another dozen wounds stung bitterly by the time he had the child on the floor. As long as the child lay on its stomach, Howard could seize it from behind. He took it by the neck with one hand and picked up the knife with the other. He carried both to the toilet.

He had to flush twice to handle the flow of blood and pus. Howard wondered if the child was infected with some disease—the white fluid was thick and at least as great in volume as the blood. Then he flushed seven more times to take the pieces of the creature down the drain. Even after death, the suction pads clung tightly to the porcelain; Howard pried them off with the tip of the knife.

Eventually, the child was completely gone. Howard was panting with the exertion, nauseated at the stench and horror of what he had done. He remembered the smell of his dog's guts after the car hit it, and he threw up everything he had eaten at the party. Got the party out of his system, felt cleaner; took a shower, felt cleaner still. When he was through, he made sure the bathroom showed no sign of his ordeal.

Then he went to bed.

It wasn't easy to sleep. He was too keyed up. He couldn't get out of his mind the thought that he had committed murder (not murder, not murder, simply the elimination of something too foul to be alive). He tried thinking of a dozen, a hundred other things. Projects at work . . . but the designs kept showing flippers. His children . . . but their faces turned to the intense face of the struggling monster he had killed. Alice . . . ah, but Alice was harder to think of than the creature.

At last he slept, and dreamed, and in his dream remembered his father, who had died when he was ten. Howard did not remember any of his standard reminiscences. No long walks with his father, no basketball in the driveway, no fishing trips. Those things had happened, but tonight, because of the struggle with the monster, Howard remembered darker things that he had long been able to keep hidden from himself.

"We can't afford to get you a ten-speed bike, Howie. Not until the strike is over."

"I know, Dad. You can't help it." Swallow bravely. "And I don't mind. When all the guys go riding around after school, I'll just stay home and get ahead on my homework."

"Lots of boys don't have ten-speed bikes, Howie."

Howie shrugged, and turned away to hide the tears in his eyes. "Sure, lots of them. Hey, Dad, don't you worry about me. Howie can take care of himself."

Such courage. Such strength. He had gotten a ten-speed within a week. In his dream, Howard finally made a connection he had never been able to admit to himself before. His father had a rather elaborate ham radio setup in the garage. But about that time he had become tired of it, he said, and he sold it off and did a lot more work in the yard and looked bored as hell until the strike was over and he went back to work and got killed in an accident in the rolling mill.

Howard's dream ended madly, with him riding piggy-back on his father's shoulders as the monster had ridden on *him*, tonight—and in his hand was knife, and he was stabbing his father again and again in the throat.

He awoke in early morning light, before his alarm rang, sobbing weakly and whimpering, "I killed him, I killed him, I killed him."

And then he drifted upward out of sleep and saw the time. Six-thirty. "A dream," he said. And the dream had awakened him early, too early, with a headache and sore eyes from crying. The pillow was soaked. "A hell of a lousy way to start the day," he mumbled. And, as was his habit, he got up and went to the window and opened the curtain.

On the glass, suction cups clinging tightly, was the child.

It was pressed close, as if by sucking very tightly it would be able to slither through the glass without breaking it. Far below were the honks of early morning traffic, the roar of passing trucks, but the child seemed oblivious of its height far above the street, with no ledge to break its fall. Indeed, there seemed little chance it would fall. The eyes looked closely, piercingly, at Howard.

Howard had been prepared to pretend that the night before had been another terribly realistic nightmare.

He stepped back from the glass, watched the child in fascination. It lifted a flipper, planted it higher, pulled itself up to a new position where it could stare at Howard eye to eye. And then, slowly and methodically, it began beating on the glass with its head.

The landlord was not generous with upkeep on the building. The glass was thin, and Howard knew that the child would not give up until it had broken through the glass so it could get to Howard.

He began to shake. His throat tightened. He was terribly afraid. Last night had been no dream. The fact that the child was here today was proof of that. Yet he had cut the child into small pieces. It could not possibly be alive. The glass shook and rattled with every blow the child's head struck.

The glass slivered in a starburst from where the child had hit it. The creature was coming in. And Howard picked up the room's one chair and threw it at the child, threw it at the window. Glass shattered, and the sun dazzled on the fragments as they exploded outward like a glistening halo around the child and the chair.

Howard ran to the window, looked out, and watched as the child landed brutally on the top of a large truck. The body seemed to smear as it hit, and fragments of the chair and shreds of glass danced around the child and bounced down into the street and the sidewalk.

The truck didn't stop moving; it carried the broken body and the shards of glass and the pool of blood on up the street, and Howard ran to the bed, knelt beside it, buried his face in the blanket, and tried to regain control of himself. He had been seen. The people in the street had looked up and seen him in the window. Last night he had gone to great lengths to avoid discovery, but today discovery was impossible to avoid. He was ruined. And yet he could not, could never have, let the child come into the room.

Footsteps on the stairs. Stamping up the corridor. Pounding on the door. "Open up! Hey in there!"

If I'm quiet long enough, they'll go away, he said to himself, knowing it was a lie. He must get up, must answer the door. But he could not bring himself to admit that he ever had to leave the safety of his bed.

"Hey, you son-of-a-bitch—" The imprecations went on but Howard could not move until, suddenly, it occurred to him that the child could be under the bed, and as he thought of it he could feel the tip of the flipper touching his thigh, stroking and getting ready to fasten itself—

Howard leaped to his feet and rushed for the door. He flung it wide, for even if it was the police come to arrest him, they could protect him from the monster that was haunting him.

It was not a policeman at the door. It was the man on the first floor who collected rent. "You son-of-a-bitch irresponsible pig-kisser!" the man shouted, his toupee only approximately in place. "That chair could have hit somebody! That window's expensive! Out! Get out of here, right now, I want you out of this place, I don't care how the hell drunk you are."

"There was—there was this thing on the window, this creature. . . ."

The man looked at him coldly, but his eyes danced with anger. No, not anger. Fear. Howard realized the man was afraid of him.

"This is a decent place," the man said softly. "You can take your creatures and your booze and your pink stinking elephants and that's a hundred bucks for the window, a hundred bucks right now, and you can get out of here in an hour, an hour, you hear? Or I'm calling the police, you hear?"

"I hear." He heard. The man left when Howard counted out five twenties. The man seemed careful to avoid touching Howard's hands, as if Howard had become, somehow, repulsive. Well, he had. To himself, if to no one else. He closed the door as soon as the man was gone. He packed the few belongings he had brought to the apartment in two suitcases and went downstairs and called a cab and rode to work. The cabby looked at him sourly, and wouldn't talk. It was fine with Howard, if only the driver hadn't kept looking at him through the mirror—nervously, as if he was afraid of what

Howard might do or try. I won't try anything, Howard said to himself, I'm a decent man. Howard tipped the cabby well and then gave him twenty to take his bags to his house in Queens, where Alice could damn well keep them for a while. Howard was through with the tenement—that one or any other.

Obviously it had been a nightmare, last night and this morning. The monster was only visible to him, Howard decided. Only the chair and the glass had fallen from the fourth floor, or the manager would have noticed.

Except that the baby had landed on the truck, and might have been real, and might be discovered in New Jersey or Pennsylvania later today.

Couldn't be real. He had killed it last night and it was whole again this morning. A nightmare. I didn't really kill anybody, he insisted. (Except the dog. Except Father, said a new, ugly voice in the back of his mind.)

Work. Draw lines on paper, answer phone calls, dictate letters, keep your mind off your nightmares, off your family, off the mess your life is turning into. "Hell of a good party last night." Yeah, it was, wasn't it? "How are you today, Howard?" Feel fine, Dolores, fine—thanks to you. "Got the roughs on the IBM thing?" Nearly, nearly. Give me another twenty minutes. "Howard, you don't look well." Had a rough night. The party, you know.

He kept drawing on the blotter on his desk instead of going to the drawing table and producing real work. He doodled out faces. Alice's face, looking stern and terrible. The face of Stu's ugly wife. Dolores's face, looking sweet and yielding and stupid. And Rhiannon's face.

But with his daughter Rhiannon, he couldn't stop with the face.

His hand started to tremble when he saw what he had drawn. He ripped the sheet off the blotter, crumpled it, and reached under the desk to drop it in the wastebasket. The basket lurched, and flippers snaked out to seize his hand in an iron grip.

Howard screamed, tried to pull his hand away. The child came with it, the leg flippers grabbing Howard's right leg. The suction pad stung, bringing back the memory of all the pain last night. He scraped the child off against a filing cabinet, then ran for the door, which was already opening as several of his coworkers tumbled into his office demanding, "What is it? What's wrong? Why did you scream like that?"

Howard led them gingerly over to where the child should be. Nothing. Just an overturned wastebasket, Howard's chair capsized on the floor. But Howard's window was open, and he could not remember opening it. "Howard, what is it? Are you tired, Howard? What's wrong?"

I don't feel well. I don't feel well at all.

Dolores put her arm around him, led him out of the room. "Howard, I'm worried about you."

I'm worried, too.

"Can I take you home? I have my car in the garage downstairs. Can I take you home?"

Where's home? Don't have a home, Dolores.

"My home, then. I have an apartment, you need to lie down and rest. Let me take you home."

Dolores's apartment was decorated in early Holly Hobby, and when she put records on the stereo it was old Carpenters and recent Captain and Tennille. Dolores led him to the bed, gently undressed him, and then, because he reached out to her, undressed herself and made love to him before she went back to work. She was naïvely eager. She whispered in his ear that he was only the second man she had ever loved, the first in five years. Her inept lovemaking was so sincere it made him want to cry.

When she was gone he did cry, because she thought she meant something to him and she did not.

Why am I crying? he asked himself. Why should I care? It's not my fault she let me get a handle on her. . . .

Sitting on the dresser in a curiously adult posture was the child, carelessly playing with itself as it watched Howard intently. "No," Howard said, pulling himself up to the head of the bed. "You don't exist," he said. "No one's ever seen you but me." The child gave no sign of understanding. It just rolled over and began to slither down the front of the dresser.

Howard reached for his clothes, took them out of the bedroom. He put them on in the living room as he watched the door. Sure enough, the child crept along the carpet to the living room; but Howard was dressed by then, and he left.

He walked the streets for three hours. He was coldly rational at first. Logical. The creature does not exist. There is no reason to believe in it.

But bit by bit his rationality was worn away by constant flickers of the creature at the edges of his vision. On a bench, peering over the back at him; in a shop window; staring from the cab of a milk truck. Howard walked faster and faster, not caring where he went, trying to keep some intelligent process going on in his mind, and failing utterly as he saw the child, saw it clearly, dangling from a traffic signal.

What made it even worse was that occasionally a passerby, violating the unwritten law that New Yorkers are forbidden to look at each other, would gaze at him, shudder, and look away. A short European-looking woman crossed herself. A group of teenagers looking for trouble weren't looking for him—they grew silent, let him pass in silence, and in silence watched him out of sight.

They may not be able to see the child, Howard realized, but they see something.

And as he grew less and less coherent in the ramblings of his mind, memories began flashing on and off, his life passing before his eyes like a drowning man is supposed to see, only, he realized, if a drowning man saw this he would gulp at the water, breathe it deeply just to end the visions. They were memories he had been unable to find for years, memories he would never have wanted to find.

His poor, confused mother, who was so eager to be a good parent that she read everything, tried everything. Her precocious son Howard read it all, too, and understood it better. Nothing she tried ever worked. And he accused her several times of being too demanding, or not demanding enough; of not giving him enough love, or of drowning him in phony affection; of trying to take over with his friends, of not liking his friends enough. Until he had badgered and tortured the woman so that she was timid every time she spoke to him, careful and long-winded and phrasing everything in such a way that it wouldn't offend, and while now and then he made her feel wonderful by giving her a hug and saying "Have I got a wonderful mom," there were far more times when he put a patient look on his face and said, "That again, Mom? I thought we went over that years ago." A failure as a parent, that's what you are, he reminded her again and again, though not in so many words, and she nodded and believed and died inside with every contact they had. He got everything he wanted from her.

And Vaughn Robles, who was just a little bit smarter than Howard and Howard wanted very badly to be valedictorian and so Vaughn and Howard became best friends and Vaughn would do anything for Howard and whenever Vaughn got a better grade than Howard he could not help but notice that Howard was hurt, wondered if he was really worth anything at all. "Am I really worth anything at all, Vaughn? No matter how well I do, there's always someone ahead of me, and I guess it's just that before my father died he told me and told me, 'Howie, be better than your dad. Be the top.' And I promised him I'd be the top but hell, Vaughn, I'm just not cut out for it. . . ." And once he even cried. Vaughn was proud of himself as he sat there and listened to Howard give the valedictory address at high school graduation. What were a few grades, compared to a true friendship? Howard got a scholarship and went away to college and he and Vaughn almost never saw each other again.

And the teacher he provoked into hitting him and losing his job; and the football player who snubbed him and Howard quietly spread the rumor that the fellow was gay and he was ostracized from the team and finally quit; and the beautiful girls he stole from their boyfriends just to prove that he could do it and the friendships he destroyed just because he didn't like being excluded and the marriages he wrecked and the coworkers he undercut and he walked along the street with tears streaming down his face wondering where all these memories had come from and why, after such a long time in hiding, they had come out now. Yet he knew the answer. The answer was slipping behind doorways, climbing lightpoles as he passed, waving obscene flippers at him from the sidewalk almost under his feet.

And slowly, inexorably, the memories wound their way from the distant past through a hundred tawdry exploitations because he could find people's weak spots without even trying until finally, memory came to the one place where he knew it could not, could not ever go.

He remembered Rhiannon.

Born fourteen years ago. Smiled early, walked early, almost never cried. A loving child from the start, and therefore easy prey for Howard. Oh, Alice was a bitch in her own right—Howard wasn't the only bad parent in the family. But it was Howard who manipulated Rhiannon most. "Daddy's feelings are hurt, sweetheart," and Rhiannon's eyes would grow wide, and she'd be sorry, and whatever Daddy wanted, Rhiannon would do. But this was normal, this was part of the pattern, this would have fit easily into all his life before except for last month.

And even now, after a day of grief at his own life, Howard could not face it. Could not but did. He unwillingly remembered walking by Rhiannon's almost-closed door, seeing just a flash of cloth moving quickly. He opened the door on impulse, just on impulse, as Rhiannon took off her brassiere and looked at herself in the mirror. Howard had never thought of his daughter with desire, not until that moment, but once the desire formed Howard had no strategy, no pattern in his mind to stop him from trying to get what he wanted. He was *uncomfortable*, and so he stepped into the room and closed the door behind him and Rhiannon knew no way to say no to her father. When Alice opened the door Rhiannon was crying softly, and Alice looked and after a moment Alice screamed and screamed and Howard got up from the bed and tried to smooth it all over but Rhiannon was still crying and Alice was still screaming, kicking at his crotch, beating him, raking at his face, spitting at him, telling him he was a monster, a monster, until at last he was able to flee the room and the house and, until now, the memory.

He screamed now as he had not screamed then, and threw himself against a plate glass window, weeping loudly as the blood gushed from a dozen glass cuts on his right arm, which had gone through the window. One large piece of glass stayed embedded in his forearm. He deliberately scraped his arm against the wall to drive the glass deeper. But the pain in his arm was no match for the pain in his mind, and he felt nothing.

They rushed him to the hospital, thinking to save his life, but the doctor was surprised to discover that for all the blood there were only superficial wounds, not dangerous at all. "I don't know why you didn't reach a vein or an artery," the doctor said. "I think the glass went everywhere it could possibly go without causing any important damage."

After the medical doctor, of course, there was the psychiatrist, but there were many suicidals at the hospital and Howard was not the dangerous kind. "I was insane for a moment, Doctor, that's all. I don't want to die, I didn't want to die then, I'm all right now. You can send me home." And the psychiatrist let him go home. They bandaged his arm. They did not know that his real relief was that nowhere in the hospital did he see the small, naked, child-shaped creature. He had purged himself. He was free.

Howard was taken home in an ambulance, and they wheeled him into the house and lifted him from the stretcher to the bed. Through it all Alice hardly said a word except to direct them to the bedroom. Howard lay still on the bed as she stood over him, the two of them alone for the first time since he had left the house a month ago.

"It was kind of you," Howard said softly, "to let me come back."

"They said there wasn't room enough to keep you, but you needed to be watched and taken care of for a few weeks. So lucky me, I get to watch you." Her voice was a low monotone, but the acid dripped from every word. It stung.

"You were right, Alice," Howard said.

"Right about what? That marrying you was the worst mistake of my life? No, Howard. *Meeting* you was my worst mistake."

Howard began to cry. Real tears that welled up from places in him that had once been deep but that now rested painfully close to the surface. "I've been a monster, Alice. I haven't had any control over myself. What I did to Rhiannon—Alice, I wanted to die, I wanted to die!"

Alice's face was twisted and bitter. "And I wanted you to, Howard. I have never been so disappointed as when the doctor called and said you'd be all right. You'll never be all right, Howard, you'll always be—"

"Let him be, Mother."

Rhiannon stood in the doorway.

"Don't come in, Rhiannon," Alice said.

Rhiannon came in. "Daddy, it's all right."

"What she means," Alice said, "is that we've checked her and she isn't pregnant. No little monster is going to be born."

Rhiannon didn't look at her mother, just gazed with wide eyes at her father. "You didn't need to—hurt yourself, Daddy. I forgive you. People lose control sometimes. And it was as much my fault as yours, it really was, you don't need to feel bad, Father."

It was too much for Howard. He cried out, shouted his confession, how he had manipulated her all her life, how he was an utterly selfish and rotten parent, and when it was over Rhiannon came to her father and laid her head on his chest and said softly, "Father, it's all right. We are who we are. We've done what we've done. But it's all right now. I forgive you."

When Rhiannon left, Alice said, "You don't deserve her."

I know.

"I was going to sleep on the couch, but that would be stupid. Wouldn't it, Howard?"

I deserve to be left alone, like a leper.

"You misunderstand, Howard. I need to stay here to make sure you don't do anything else. To yourself or to anyone."

Yes. Yes, please. I can't be trusted.

"Don't wallow in it, Howard. Don't enjoy it. Don't make yourself even more disgusting than you were before."

All right.

They were drifting off to sleep when Alice said, "Oh, when the doctor called he wondered if I knew what had caused those sores all over your arms and chest."

Eumenides in the Fourth-Floor Lavatory

But Howard was asleep, and didn't hear her. Asleep with no dreams at all, the sleep of peace, the sleep of having been forgiven, of being clean. It hadn't taken that much, after all. Now that it was over, it was easy. He felt as if a great weight had been taken from him.

He felt as if something heavy was lying on his legs. He awoke, sweating even though the room was not hot. He heard breathing. And it was not Alice's low-pitched, slow breath, it was quick and high and hard, as if the breather had been exerting himself.

Itself.

Themselves.

One of them lay across his legs, the flippers plucking at the blanket. The other two lay on either side, their eyes wide and intent, creeping slowly toward where his face emerged from the sheets.

Howard was puzzled. "I thought you'd be gone," he said to the children. "You're supposed to be gone now."

Alice stirred at the sound of his voice, mumbled in her sleep.

He saw more of them stirring in the gloomy corners of the room, another writhing slowly along the top of the dresser, another inching up the wall toward the ceiling.

"I don't need you anymore," he said, his voice oddly high-pitched.

Alice started breathing irregularly, mumbling, "What? What?"

And Howard said nothing more, just lay there in the sheets, watching the creatures carefully but not daring to make a sound for fear Alice would wake up. He was terribly afraid she would wake up and not see the creatures, which would prove, once and for all, that he had lost his mind.

He was even more afraid, however, that when she awoke she *would* see them. That was the only unbearable thought, yet he thought it continuously as they relentlessly approached with nothing at all in their eyes, not even hate, not even anger, not even contempt. We are with you, they seemed to be saying, we will be with you from now on. We will be with you, Howard, forever.

And Alice rolled over and opened her eyes.

TANITH LEE

"Red as Blood"

The work of Tanith Lee (1947-) is remarkable for its free interplay of ideas from fantasy, horror and science fiction. She is a prolific novelist and short story writer with many multi-volume sagas to her credit, including her **Tales from the Flat Earth** *and "The Secret Books of Paradys" trilogies. She is renowned for her inventive uses of the vampire theme, in the science fiction diptych* **Sabella, or the Blood Stone** *and* **Kill the Dead**, *and in her current three-volume "Blood Opera" series, which consists of* **Dark Dance, Personal Darkness,** *and* **Darkness, I.** *Her short fiction collections include* **The Gorgon and Other Beastly Tales, Dreams of Dark Light,** *and* **Women as Demon**. *"Red as Blood" was nominated for the Nebula, World Fantasy and British Fantasy Awards.*

Red as Blood

by Tanith Lee

The beautiful Witch Queen flung open the ivory case of the magic mirror. Of dark gold the mirror was, dark gold as the hair of the Witch Queen that poured down her back. Dark gold the mirror was, and ancient as the seven stunted black trees growing beyond the pale blue glass of the window.

"*Speculum, speculum,*" said the Witch Queen to the magic mirror. "*Dei gratia.*"

"*Volente Deo. Audio.*"

"Mirror," said the Witch Queen. "Whom do you see?"

"I see you, mistress," replied the mirror. "And all in the land. But one."

"Mirror, mirror, who is it you do not see?"

"I do not see Bianca."

The Witch Queen crossed herself. She shut the case of the mirror and, walking slowly to the window, looked out at the old trees through the panes of pale blue glass.

Fourteen years ago, another woman had stood at this window, but she was not like the Witch Queen. The woman had black hair that fell to her ankles; she had a crimson gown, the girdle worn high beneath her breasts, for she was far gone with child. And this woman had thrust open the glass casement on the winter garden, where the old trees crouched in the snow. Then, taking a sharp bone needle, she had thrust it into her finger and shaken three bright drops on the ground. "Let my daughter have," said the woman, "hair black as mine, black as the wood of these warped and arcane trees. Let her have skin like mine, white as this snow. And let her have my mouth, red as my blood." And the woman had smiled and licked at her finger. She had a crown on her head; it shone in the dusk like a star. She never came to the window before dusk; she did not like the day. She was the first Queen, and she did not possess a mirror.

The second Queen, the Witch Queen, knew all this. She knew how, in giving birth, the first Queen had died. Her coffin had been carried into the cathedral and masses had been said. There was an ugly rumor—that a splash of holy water had fallen on the corpse and the dead flesh had smoked. But the first Queen had been reckoned unlucky for the kingdom. There had been a strange plague in the land since she came there, a wasting disease for which there was no cure.

Seven years went by. The King married the second Queen, as unlike the first as frankincense to myrrh.

"And this is my daughter," said the King to his second Queen.

There stood a little girl child, nearly seven years of age. Her black hair hung to her ankles, her skin was white as snow. Her mouth was red as blood, and she smiled with it.

"Bianca," said the King, "you must love your new mother."

Bianca smiled radiantly. Her teeth were bright as sharp bone needles.

"Come," said the Witch Queen, "come, Bianca. I will show you my magic mirror."

"Please, Mama," said Bianca softly, "I do not like mirrors."

"She is modest," said the King. "And delicate. She never goes out by day. The sun distresses her."

That night, the Witch Queen opened the case of her mirror.

"Mirror, whom do you see?"

"I see you, mistress. And all in the land. But one."

"Mirror, mirror, who is it you do not see?"

"I do not see Bianca."

The second Queen gave Bianca a tiny crucifix of golden filigree. Bianca would not accept it. She ran to her father and whispered: "I am afraid. I do not like to think of Our Lord dying in agony on His cross. She means to frighten me. Tell her to take it away."

The second Queen grew wild white roses in her garden and invited Bianca to walk there after sundown. But Bianca shrank away. She whispered to her father: "The thorns will tear me. She means me to be hurt."

When Bianca was twelve years old, the Witch Queen said to the

King, "Bianca should be confirmed so that she may take Communion with us."

"This may not be," said the King. "I will tell you, she has not even been christened, for the dying word of my first wife was against it. She begged me, for her religion was different from ours. The wishes of the dying must be respected."

"Should you not like to be blessed by the church," said the Witch Queen to Bianca. "To kneel at the golden rail before the marble altar. To sing to God, to taste the ritual bread and sip the ritual wine."

"She means me to betray my true mother," said Bianca to the King. "When will she cease tormenting me?"

The day she was thirteen, Bianca rose from her bed, and there was a red stain there, like a red, red flower.

"Now you are a woman," said her nurse.

"Yes," said Bianca. And she went to her true mother's jewel box, and out of it she took her mother's crown and set it on her head.

When she walked under the old black trees in the dusk, the crown shone like a star.

The wasting sickness, which had left the land in peace for thirteen years, suddenly began again, and there was no cure.

The Witch Queen sat in a tall chair before a window of pale green and dark white glass, and in her hands she held a Bible bound in rosy silk.

"Majesty," said the huntsman, bowing very low.

He was a man, forty years old, strong and handsome, and wise in the hidden lore of the forests, the occult lore of the earth. He would kill too, for it was his trade, without faltering. The slender fragile deer he could kill, and the moonwinged birds, and the velvet hares with their sad, foreknowing eyes. He pitied them, but pitying, he killed them. Pity could not stop him. It was his trade.

"Look in the garden," said the Witch Queen.

The hunter looked through a dark white pane. The sun had sunk, and a maiden walked under a tree.

"The Princess Bianca," said the huntsman.

"What else?" asked the Witch Queen.

The huntsman crossed himself.

"By Our Lord, Madam, I will not say."

"But you know."

"Who does not?"

"The King does not."

"Or he does."

"Are you a brave man?" asked the Witch Queen.

"In the summer, I have hunted and slain boar. I have slaughtered wolves in winter."

"But are you brave enough?"

"If you command it, Lady," said the huntsman, "I will try my best."

The Witch Queen opened the Bible at a certain place, and out of it she drew a flat silver crucifix, which had been resting against the words: *Thou shalt not be afraid for the terror by night. . . . Nor for the pestilence that walketh in darkness.*

The huntsman kissed the crucifix and put it about his neck, beneath his shirt.

"Approach," said the Witch Queen, "and I will instruct you in what to say."

Presently, the huntsman entered the garden, as the stars were burning up in the sky. He strode to where Bianca stood under a stunted dwarf tree, and he kneeled down.

"Princess," he said. "Pardon me, but I must give you ill tidings."

"Give them then," said the girl, toying with the long stem of a wan, night-growing flower which she had plucked.

"Your stepmother, that accursed, jealous witch, means to have you slain. There is no help for it but you must fly the palace this very night. If you permit, I will guide you to the forest. There are those who will care for you until it may be safe for you to return."

Bianca watched him, but gently, trustingly.

"I will go with you, then," she said.

They went by a secret way out of the garden, through a passage under the ground, through a tangled orchard, by a broken road between great overgrown hedges.

Night was a pulse of deep, flickering blue when they came to the forest. The branches of the forest overlapped and intertwined like leading in a window, and the sky gleamed dimly through like panes of blue-colored glass.

"I am weary," sighed Bianca. "May I rest a moment?"

"By all means," said the huntsman. "In the clearing there, foxes come to play by night. Look in that direction, and you will see them."

"How clever you are," said Bianca. "And how handsome."

She sat on the turf, and gazed at the clearing.

The huntsman drew his knife silently and concealed it in the folds of his cloak. He stopped above the maiden.

"What are you whispering?" demanded the huntsman, laying his hand on her wood-black hair.

"Only a rhyme my mother taught me."

The huntsman seized her by the hair and swung her about so her white throat was before him, stretched ready for the knife. But he did not strike, for there in his hand he held the dark golden locks of the Witch Queen, and her face laughed up at him and she flung her arms about him, laughing.

"Good man, sweet man, it was only a test of you. Am I not a witch? And do you not love me?"

The huntsman trembled, for he did love her, and she was pressed so close her heart seemed to beat within his own body.

"Put away the knife. Throw away the silly crucifix. We have no need of these things. The King is not one half the man you are."

And the huntsman obeyed her, throwing the knife and the crucifix far off among the roots of the trees. He gripped her to him, and she buried her face in his neck, and the pain of her kiss was the last thing he felt in this world.

The sky was black now. The forest was blacker. No foxes played in the clearing. The moon rose and made white lace through the boughs, and through the backs of the huntsman's empty eyes. Bianca wiped her mouth on a dead flower.

"Seven asleep, seven awake," said Bianca. "Wood to wood. Blood to blood. Thee to me."

There came a sound like seven huge rendings, distant by the length of several trees, a broken road, an orchard, an underground passage. Then a sound like seven huge single footfalls. Nearer. And nearer.

Hop, hop, hop, hop. Hop, hop, hop.

In the orchard, seven black shudderings.

On the broken road, between the high hedges, seven black creepings.

Brush crackled, branches snapped.

Through the forest, into the clearing, pushed seven warped, misshapen, hunched-over, stunted things. Woody-black mossy fur, woody-black bald masks. Eyes like glittering cracks, mouths like moist caverns. Lichen beards. Fingers of twiggy gristle. Grinning. Kneeling. Faces pressed to the earth.

"Welcome," said Bianca.

The Witch Queen stood before a window of glass like diluted wine. She looked at the magic mirror.

"Mirror. Whom do you see?"

"I see you, mistress. I see a man in the forest. He went hunting, but not for deer. His eyes are open, but he is dead. I see all in the land. But one."

The Witch Queen pressed her palms to her ears.

Outside the window the garden lay, empty of its seven black and stunted dwarf trees.

"Bianca," said the Queen.

The windows had been draped and gave no light. The light spilled from a shallow vessel, light in a sheaf, like the pastel wheat. It glowed upon four swords that pointed east and west, that pointed north and south.

Four winds had burst through the chamber, and three archwinds. Cool fires had risen, and parched oceans, and the gray-silver powders of Time.

The hands of the Witch Queen floated like folded leaves on the air, and through dry lips the Witch Queen chanted.

"Pater omnipotens, mittere digneris sanctum Angelum tuum de Infernis."

The light faded, and grew brighter.

There, between the hilts of the four swords, stood the Angel Lucefiel, somberly gilded, his face in shadow, his golden wings spread and blazing at his back.

"Since you have called me, I know your desire. It is a comfortless wish. You ask for pain."

"You speak of pain, Lord Lucefiel, who suffer the most merciless pain of all. Worse than the nails in the feet and wrists. Worse than the thorns and the bitter cup and the blade in the side. To be called upon for evil's sake, which I do not, comprehending your true nature, son of God, brother of The Son."

"You recognize me, then. I will grant what you ask."

And Lucefiel (by some named Satan, Rex Mundi, but nevertheless the left hand, the sinister hand of God's design) wrenched lightning from the ether and cast it at the Witch Queen.

It caught her in the breast. She fell.

The sheaf of light towered and lit the golden eyes of the Angel, which were terrible, yet luminous with compassion, as the swords shattered and he vanished.

The Witch Queen pulled herself from the floor of the chamber, no longer beautiful, a withered, slobbering hag.

* * *

Into the core of the forest, even at noon, the sun never shone. Flowers propagated in the grass, but they were colorless. Above, the black-green roof hung down nets of thick, green twilight through which albino butterflies and moths feverishly drizzled. The trunks of the trees were smooth as the stalks of underwater weeds. Bats flew in the daytime, and birds who believed themselves to be bats.

There was a sepulcher, dripped with moss. The bones had been rolled out, had rolled around the feet of seven twisted dwarf trees. They looked like trees. Sometimes they moved. Sometimes something like an eye glittered, or a tooth, in the wet shadows.

In the shade of the sepulcher door sat Bianca, combing her hair.

A lurch of motion disturbed the thick twilight.

The seven trees turned their heads.

A hag emerged from the forest. She was crook-backed and her head was poked forward, predatory, withered, and almost hairless, like a vulture's.

"Here we are at last," grated the hag, in a vulture's voice.

She came closer, and cranked herself down on her knees, and bowed her face into the turf and the colorless flowers.

Bianca sat and gazed at her. The hag lifted herself. Her teeth were yellow palings.

"I bring you the homage of witches, and three gifts," said the hag.

"Why should you do that?"

"Such a quick child, and only fourteen years. Why? Because we fear you. I bring you gifts to curry favor."

Bianca laughed. "Show me."

The hag made a pass in the green air. She held a silken cord worked curiously with plaited human hair.

"Here is a girdle which will protect you from the devices of priests, from crucifix and chalice and the accursed holy water. In it are knotted the tresses of a virgin, and of a woman no better than she should be, and of a woman dead. And here—" a second pass and a comb was in her hand, lacquered blue over green—"a comb from the deep sea, a mermaid's trinket, to charm and subdue. Part your locks with this, and the scent of ocean will fill men's nostrils and the rhythm of the tides their ears, the tides that bind men like chains. Last," added the hag, "that old symbol of wickedness, the scarlet fruit of Eve, the apple red as blood. Bite, and the understanding of sin, which the serpent boasted of, will be made known to you." And the hag made her last pass in the air and extended the apple, with the girdle and the comb, toward Bianca.

Bianca glanced at the seven stunted trees.

"I like her gifts, but I do not quite trust her."

The bald masks peered from their shaggy beardings. Eyelets glinted. Twiggy claws clacked.

"All the same," said Bianca. "I will let her tie the girdle on me, and comb my hair herself."

The hag obeyed, simpering. Like a toad she waddled to Bianca. She tied on the girdle. She parted the ebony hair. Sparks sizzled, white from the girdle, peacock's eye from the comb.

"And now, hag, take a little bite of the apple."

"It will be my pride," said the hag, "to tell my sisters I shared this fruit with you." And the hag bit into the apple, and mumbled the bite noisily, and swallowed, smacking her lips.

Then Bianca took the apple and bit into it.

Bianca screamed—and choked.

She jumped to her feet. Her hair whirled about her like a storm cloud. Her face turned blue, then slate, then white again. She lay on the pallid flowers, neither stirring nor breathing.

The seven dwarf trees rattled their limbs and their bear-shaggy heads, to no avail. Without Bianca's art they could not hop. They strained their claws and ripped at the hag's sparse hair and her mantle. She fled between them. She fled into the sunlit acres of the forest, along the broken road, through the orchard, into a hidden passage.

The hag reentered the palace by the hidden way, and the Queen's chamber by a hidden stair. She was bent almost double. She held her ribs. With one skinny hand she opened the ivory case of the magic mirror.

"*Speculum, speculum. Dei gratia.* Whom do you see?"

"I see you, mistress. And all in the land. And I see a coffin."

"Whose corpse lies in the coffin?"

"That I cannot see. It must be Bianca."

The hag, who had been the beautiful Witch Queen, sank into her tall chair before the window of pale, cucumber green and dark white glass. Her drugs and potions waited, ready to reverse the dreadful conjuring of age the Angel Lucefiel had placed on her, but she did not touch them yet.

The apple had contained a fragment of the flesh of Christ, the sacred wafer, the Eucharist.

The Witch Queen drew her Bible to her and opened it randomly. And read, with fear, the word: *Resurcat.*

It appeared like glass, the coffin, milky glass. It had formed this way. A thin white smoke had risen from the skin of Bianca. She smoked as a fire smokes when a drop of quenching water falls on it. The piece of Eucharist had stuck in her throat. The Eucharist, quenching water to her fire, caused her to smoke.

Then the cold dews of night gathered, and the colder atmospheres of midnight. The smoke of Bianca's quenching froze about her. Frost formed in exquisite silver scroll-work all over the block of misty ice that contained Bianca.

Bianca's frigid heart could not warm the ice. Nor the sunless, green twilight of the day.

You could just see her, stretched in the coffin, through the glass. How lovely she looked, Bianca. Black as ebony, white as snow, red as blood.

The trees hung over the coffin. Years passed. The trees sprawled about the coffin, cradling it in their arms. Their eyes wept fungus and green resin. Green amber drops hardened like jewels in the coffin of glass.

"Who is that lying under the trees?" the Prince asked, as he rode into the clearing.

He seemed to bring a golden moon with him, shining about his golden head, on the golden armor and the cloak of white satin blazoned with gold and blood and ink and sapphire. The white horse trod on the colorless flowers, but the flowers sprang up again when the hoofs had passed. A shield hung from the saddle-bow, a strange shield. From one side it had a lion's face, but from the other, a lamb's face.

The trees groaned, and their heads split on huge mouths.

"Is this Bianca's coffin?" asked the Prince.

"Leave her with us," said the seven trees. They hauled at their roots. The ground shivered. The coffin of ice-glass gave a great jolt, and a crack bisected it.

Bianca coughed.

The jolt had precipitated the piece of Eucharist from her throat.

Into a thousand shards the coffin shattered, and Bianca sat up. She stared at the Prince, and she smiled.

"Welcome, beloved," said Bianca.

She got to her feet, and shook out her hair, and began to walk toward the Prince on the pale horse.

But she seemed to walk into a shadow, into a purple room, then into a crimson room whose emanations lanced her like knives. Next she walked into a yellow room where she heard the sound of crying, which tore her ears. All her body seemed stripped away; she was a beating heart. The beats of her heart became two wings. She flew.

She was a raven, then an owl. She flew into a sparkling pane. It scorched her white. Snow white. She was a dove.

She settled on the shoulder of the Prince and hid her head under her wing. She had no longer anything black about her, and nothing red.

"Begin again now, Bianca," said the Prince. He raised her from his shoulder. On his wrist there was a mark. It was like a star. Once a nail had been driven in there.

Bianca flew away, up through the roof of the forest. She flew in at a delicate wine window. She was in the palace. She was seven years old.

The Witch Queen, her new mother, hung a filigree crucifix around her neck.

"Mirror," said the Witch Queen. "Whom do you see?"

"I see you, mistress," replied the mirror. "And all in the land. I see Bianca."

RAMSEY CAMPBELL

"Mackintosh Willy"

Ramsey Campbell (1946-) was only eighteen years old when his first collection, **The Inhabitant of the Lake and Less Welcome Tenants,** *was published. His second collection,* **Demons by Daylight***, a landmark in modern horror fiction, is a series of thickly textured stories in which decaying urban landscapes, supernatural and nonsupernatural menaces, and the tortured psyches of his character fuse to form a suffocating atmosphere of dread. Campbell has been recognized as one of the premiere writers of short contemporary horror fiction, and the range of his skills at this length are on display in* **The Height of the Scream, Dark Feasts, Waking Nightmares, Strange Things and Stranger Places,** *and the World Fantasy Award-winning omnibuses* **Dark Companions** *and* **Alone with the Horrors***. Campbell has tried a wide variety of themes and approaches to horror in his novel-length work, including supernatural horror in* **Incarnate** *and* **The Parasite***, psychological suspense in* **The Face That Must Die***, the serial killer story in* **The Count of Eleven***, the tale of supernatural possession in* **The Influence***, the crime thriller in* **The One Safe Place***, and visionary horror* **Midnight Sun***. "Mackintosh Willy" won the World Fantasy Award for best short story of 1979.*

Mackintosh Willy

by Ramsey Campbell

To start with, he wasn't called Mackintosh Willy. I never knew who gave him that name. Was it one of those nicknames that seem to proceed from a group subconscious, names recognized by every member of the group yet apparently originated by none? One has to call one's fears something, if only to gain the illusion of control. Still, sometimes I wonder how much of his monstrousness we created. Wondering helps me not to ponder my responsibility for what happened at the end.

When I was ten I thought his name was written inside the shelter in the park. I saw it only from a distance; I wasn't one of those who made a game of braving the shelter. At ten I wasn't afraid to be timid—that came later, with adolescence.

Yet if you had walked past Newsham Park you might have wondered what there was to fear: why were children advancing, bold but wary, on the red-brick shelter by the twilit pool? Surely there could be no danger in the shallow shed, which might have held a couple of dozen bicycles. By now the fishermen and the model boats would have left the pool alone and still; lamps on the park road would have begun to dangle luminous tails in the water. The only sounds would be the whispering of children, the murmur of trees around the pool, perhaps a savage incomprehensible muttering whose source you would be unable to locate. Only a game, you might reassure yourself.

And of course it was: a game to conquer fear. If you had waited long enough you might have heard shapeless movement in the shelter, and a snarling. You might have glimpsed him as he came scuttling lopsidedly out of the shelter, like an injured spider from its lair. In the gathering darkness, how much of your glimpse would you believe? The unnerving swiftness of the obese limping shape? The head which seemed to belong to another, far smaller, body, and which was almost invisible within a gray Balaclava cap, except for the small eyes which glared through the loose hole?

All of that made us hate him. We were too young for tolerance—and besides, he was intolerant of us. Ever since we could remember he had been there, guarding his territory and his bottle of red biddy. If anyone ventured too close he would start muttering. Sometimes you could hear some of the words: "Damn bastard prying interfering snooper . . . thieving bastard layabout . . . think you're clever, eh? . . . I'll give you something clever . . ."

We never saw him until it was growing dark: that was what made him into a monster. Perhaps during the day he joined his cronies elsewhere—on the steps of ruined churches in the center of Liverpool, or lying on the grass in St. John's Gardens, or crowding the benches opposite Edge Hill Public Library, whose stopped clock no doubt helped their draining of time. But if anything of this occurred to us, we dismissed it as irrelevant. He was a creature of the dark.

Shouldn't this have meant that the first time I saw him in daylight was the end? In fact, it was only the beginning.

It was a blazing day at the height of summer, my tenth. It was too hot to think of games to while away my school holidays. All I could do was walk errands for my parents, grumbling a little.

They owned a small newsagent's on West Derby Road. That day they were expecting promised copies of the *Tuebrook Bugle*. Even when he disagreed with them, my father always supported the independent newspapers—the *Bugle*, the *Liverpool Free Press:* at least they hadn't been swallowed or destroyed by a monopoly. The lateness of the *Bugle* worried him; had the paper given in? He sent me to find out.

I ran across West Derby Road just as the traffic lights at the top of the hill released a flood of cars. Only girls used the pedestrian subway so far as I was concerned; besides, it was flooded again. I strolled past the concrete police station into the park, to take the long way round. It was too hot to go anywhere quickly or even directly.

The park was crowded with games of football, parked prams, sunbathers draped over the greens. Patients sat outside the hospital on Orphan Drive beside the park. Around the lake, fishermen sat by transistor radios and whipped the air with hooks. Beyond the lake, model boats snarled across the shallow circular pool. I stopped to watch their patterns on the water, and caught sight of an object in the shelter.

At first I thought it was an old gray sack that someone had dumped on the bench. Perhaps it held rubbish—sticks which gave parts of it an angular look. Then I saw that the sack was an indeterminate stained garment, which might have been a mackintosh or raincoat of some kind. What I had vaguely assumed to be an ancient shopping bag, resting next to the sack, displayed a ragged patch of flesh and the dull gleam of an eye.

Exposed to daylight, he looked even more dismaying: so huge and still, less stupefied than dormant. The presence of the boatmen with their remote-control boxes reassured me. I ambled past the allotments to Pringle Street, where a terraced house was the editorial office of the *Bugle*.

Our copies were on the way, said Chrissie Maher the editor, and insisted on making me a cup of tea. She seemed a little upset when, having gulped the tea, I hurried out into the sudden rain. Perhaps it was rude of me not to wait until the rain had stopped—but on this parched day I wanted to make the most of it, to bathe my face and my bare arms in the onslaught, gasping almost hysterically.

By the time I had passed the allotments, where cabbages rattled like toy machine-guns; the downpour was too heavy even for me. The park provided little cover; the trees let fall their own belated storms, miniature but drenching. The nearest shelter was by the pool, which had been abandoned to its web of ripples. I ran down the slippery tarmac hill, splashing through puddles, trying to blink away rain, hoping there would be room in the shelter.

There was plenty of room, both because the rain reached easily into the depths of the brick shed and because the shelter was not entirely empty. He lay as I had seen him, face upturned within the sodden Balaclava. Had the boatmen avoided looking closely at him? Raindrops struck his unblinking eyes and trickled over the patch of flesh.

I hadn't seen death before. I stood shivering and fascinated in the rain. I needn't be scared of him now. He'd stuffed himself into the gray coat until it split in several places; through the rents I glimpsed what might have been dark cloth or discolored hairy flesh. Above him, on the shelter, where graffiti which at last I saw were not his name at all, but the names of three boys: MACK TOSH WILLY. They were partly erased, which no doubt was why one's mind tended to fill the gap.

I had to keep glancing at him. He grew more and more difficult to ignore; his presence was intensifying. His shapelessness, the rents in his coat, made me think of an old bag of washing, decayed and moldy. His hand lurked in his sleeve; beside it, amid a scattering of Coca-Cola caps, lay fragments of the bottle whose contents had perhaps killed him. Rain roared on the dull green roof of the shelter; his staring eyes glistened and dripped. Suddenly I was frightened. I ran blindly home.

"There's someone dead in the park," I gasped. "The man who chases everyone."

"Look at you!" my mother cried. "Do you want pneumonia? Just you get out of those wet things this instant!"

Eventually I had a chance to repeat my news. By this time the rain had stopped. "Well, don't be telling us," my father said. "Tell the police. They're just across the road."

Did he think I had exaggerated a drunk into a corpse? He looked surprised when I hurried to the police station. But I couldn't miss the chance to venture in there—I believed that elder brothers of some of my schoolmates had been taken into the station and hadn't come out for years.

Beside a window which might have belonged to a ticket office was a bell which you rang to make the window's partition slide back and display a policeman. He frowned down at me. What was my name? What had I been doing in the park? Who had I been with? When a second head appeared beside him he said reluctantly, "He thinks someone's passed out in the park."

A blue-and-white Mini called for me at the police station, like a taxi; on the roof a red sign said POLICE. People glanced in at me as though I were on the way to prison. Perhaps I was: suppose Mackintosh Willy had woken up and gone? How long a sentence did you get for lying? False diamonds sparkled on the grass and in the trees. I wished I'd persuaded my father to tell the police.

As the car halted, I saw the gray bulk in the shelter. The driver strode, stiff with dignity, to peer at it. "My God," I heard him say in disgust.

Did he know Mackintosh Willy? Perhaps, but that wasn't the point. "Look at this," he said to his colleague. "Ever see a corpse with pennies on the eyes? Just look at this, then. See what someone thought was a joke."

He looked shocked, sickened. He was blocking my view as he demanded, "Did you do this?"

His white-faced anger, and my incomprehension, made me

speechless. But his colleague said, "It wouldn't be him. He wouldn't come and tell us afterwards, would he?"

As I tried to peer past them he said, "Go on home, now. Go on." His gentleness seemed threatening. Suddenly frightened, I ran home through the park.

For a while I avoided the shelter. I had no reason to go near, except on the way home from school. Sometimes I'd used to see schoolmates tormenting Mackintosh Willy; sometimes, at a distance, I had joined them. Now the shelter yawned emptily, baring its dim bench. The dark pool stirred, disturbing the green beards of the stone margin. My main reason for avoiding the park was that there was nobody with whom to go.

Living on a main road was the trouble. I belonged to none of the side streets, where they played football among parked cars or chased through the back alleys. I was never invited to street parties. I felt like an outsider, particularly when I had to pass the groups of teen-agers who sat on the railings above the pedestrian subway, lazily swinging their legs, waiting to pounce. I stayed at home, in the flat above the newsagent's, when I could, and read everything in the shop. But I grew frustrated: I did enough reading at school. All this was why I welcomed Mark. He could save me from my isolation.

Not that we became friends immediately. He was my parents' latest paper boy. For several days we examined each other warily. He was taller than me, which was intimidating, but seemed unsure how to arrange his lankiness. Eventually he said, "What're you reading?"

He sounded as though reading was a waste of time. "A book," I retorted.

At last, when I'd let him see that it was Mickey Spillane, he said, "Can I read it after you?"

"It isn't mine. It's the shop's."

"All right, so I'll buy it." He did so at once, paying my father. He was certainly wealthier than me. When my resentment of his gesture had cooled somewhat, I realized that he was letting me finish what was now his book. I dawdled over it to make him complain, but he never did. Perhaps he might be worth knowing.

My instinct was accurate: he proved to be generous—not only with money, though his father made plenty of that in home improvements, but also in introducing me to his friends. Quite soon I had my place in the tribe at the top of the pedestrian subway, though secretly I was glad that we never exchanged more than ritual insults with the other gangs. Perhaps the police station, looming in the background, restrained hostilities.

Mark was generous too with is ideas. Although Ben, a burly lad, was nominal leader of the gang, it was Mark who suggested most of our activities. Had he taken to delivering papers to save himself from boredom—or, as I wondered afterward, to distract himself from his thoughts? It was Mark who brought his skates so that we could brave the slope of the pedestrian subway, who let us ride his bicycle around the side streets, who found ways into derelict houses, who brought his transistor radio so that we could hear the first Beatles records as the traffic passed unheeding on West Derby Road. But was all this a means of distracting us from the park?

No doubt it was inevitable that Ben resented his supremacy. Perhaps he deduced, in his slow and stolid way, that Mark disliked the park. Certainly he hit upon the ideal method to challenge him.

It was a hot summer evening. By then I was thirteen. Dust and fumes drifted in the wakes of cars; wagons clattered repetitively across the railway bridge. We lolled about the pavement, kicking Coca-Cola caps. Suddenly Ben said, "I know something we can do."

We trooped after him, dodging an aggressive gang of taxis, toward the police station. He might have meant us to play some trick there; when he swaggered past, I'm sure everyone was relieved—everyone except Mark, for Ben was leading us onto Orphan Drive.

Heat shivered above the tarmac. Beside us in the park, twilight gathered beneath the trees, which stirred stealthily. The island in the lake creaked with ducks; swollen litter drifted sluggishly, or tried to climb the bank. I could sense Mark's nervousness. He had turned his radio louder; a misshapen Elvis Presley blundered out of the static, then sank back into incoherence as a neighboring wave band seeped into his voice. Why was Mark on edge? I could see only the dimming sky, trees on the far side of the lake diluted by haze, the gleam of bottle caps like eyes atop a floating mound of litter, the glittering of broken bottles in the lawns.

We passed the locked ice-cream kiosk. Ben was heading for the circular pool, whose margin was surrounded by a fluorescent orange tape tied between iron poles, a makeshift fence. I felt Mark's hesitation, as though he were a scared dog dragged by a lead. The lead was pride: he couldn't show fear, especially when none of us knew Ben's plan.

A new concrete path had been laid around the pool. "We'll write our names in that," Ben said.

The dark pool swayed, as though trying to douse reflected lights.

Black clouds spread over the sky and loomed in the pool; the threat of a storm lurked behind us. The brick shelter was very dim, and looked cavernous. I strode to the orange fence, not wanting to be last, and poked the concrete with my toe. "We can't," I said; for some reason, I felt relieved. "It's set."

Someone had been there before us, before the concrete had hardened. Footprints led from the dark shelter toward us. As they advanced, they faded, no doubt because the concrete had been setting. They looked as though the man had suffered from a limp.

When I pointed them out, Mark flinched, for we heard the radio swing wide of comprehensibility. "What's up with you?" Ben demanded.

"Nothing."

"It's getting dark," I said, not as an answer but to coax everyone back toward the main road. But my remark inspired Ben; contempt grew in his eyes. "I know what it is," he said, gesturing at Mark. "This is where he used to be scared."

"Who was scared? I wasn't bloody scared."

"Not much you weren't. You didn't look it," Ben scoffed, and told us, "Old Willy used to chase him all round the pool. He used to hate him, did old Willy. Mark used to run away from him. I never. *I* wasn't scared."

"You watch who you're calling scared. If you'd seen what I did to that old bastard—"

Perhaps the movements around us silenced him. Our surroundings were crowded with dark shifting: the sky unfurled darkness, muddy shapes rushed at us in the pool, a shadow huddled restlessly in one corner of the shelter. But Ben wasn't impressed by the drooping boast. "Go on," he sneered. "You're scared now. Bet you wouldn't dare go in his shelter."

"Who wouldn't? You watch it, you!"

"Go on, then. Let's see you do it."

We must all have been aware of Mark's fear. His whole body was stiff as a puppet's. I was ready to intervene—to say, lying, that I thought the police were near—when he gave a shrug of despair and stepped forward. Climbing gingerly over the tape as though it were electrified, he advanced onto the concrete.

He strode toward the shelter. He had turned the radio full on; I could hear nothing else, only watch the shifting of dim shapes deep in the reflected sky, watch Mark stepping in the footprints for bravado. They swallowed his feet. He was nearly at the shelter when I saw him glance at the radio.

The song had slipped awry again; another wave band seeped in, a blurred muttering. I thought it must be Mark's infectious nervousness which made me hear it forming into words. "Come on, son. Let's have a look at you." But why shouldn't the words have been real, fragments of a radio play?

Mark was still walking, his gaze held by the radio. He seemed almost hypnotized; otherwise he would surely have flinched back from the huddled shadow which surged forward from the corner by the bench, even though it must have been the shadow of a cloud.

As his foot touched the shelter I called nervously, "Come on, Mark. Let's go and skate." I felt as though I'd saved him. But when he came hurrying back, he refused to look at me or at anyone else.

For the next few days he hardly spoke to me. Perhaps he thought of avoiding my parents' shop. Certainly he stayed away from the gang—which turned out to be all to the good, for Ben, robbed of Mark's ideas, could think only of shoplifting. They were soon caught, for they weren't very skillful. After that my father had doubts about Mark, but Mark had always been scrupulously honest in deliveries; after some reflection, my father kept him on. Eventually Mark began to talk to me again, though not about the park.

That was frustrating: I wanted to tell him how the shelter looked now. I still passed it on my way home, though from a different school. Someone had been scrawling on the shelter. That was hardly unusual—graffiti filled the pedestrian subway, and even claimed the ends of streets—but the words were odd, to say the least: like the scribbles on the walls of a psychotic's cell, or the gibberish of an invocation. DO THE BASTARD. BOTTLE UP HIS EYES. HOOK THEM OUT. PUSH HIS HEAD IN. Tangled amid them, like chewed bones, gleamed the eroded slashes of MACK TOSH WILLY.

I wasn't as frustrated by the conversational taboo as I might have been, for I'd met my first girlfriend. Kim was her name; she lived in a flat on my block, and because of her parents' trade, seemed always to smell of fish and chips. She obviously looked up to me—for one thing, I'd begun to read for pleasure again, which few of her friends could be bothered attempting. She told me her secrets, which was a new experience for me, strange and rather exciting—as was being seen on West Derby Road with a girl on my arm, any girl. I was happy to ignore the jeers of Ben and cronies.

She loved the park. Often we strolled through, scattering charitable crumbs to ducks. Most of all she loved to watch the model yachts, when the snarling model motorboats left them alone to glide over the pool. I enjoyed watching too, while holding her warm, if rather clammy, hand. The breeze carried away her culinary scent. But I couldn't help noticing that the shelter now displayed screaming faces with red bursts for eyes. I have never seen drawings of violence on walls elsewhere.

My relationship with Kim was short-lived. Like most such teenage experiences, our parting was not romantic and poignant, if partings ever are, but harsh and hysterical. It happened one evening as we made our way to the fair which visited Newsham Park each summer.

Across the lake we could hear shrieks that mingled panic and delight as cars on metal poles swung girls into the air, and the blurred roaring of an ancient pop song, like the voice of an enormous radio. On the Ferris Wheel, colored lights sailed up, painting airborne faces. The twilight shone like a Christmas tree; the lights swam in the pool. That was why Kim said, "Let's sit and look first."

The only bench was in the shelter. Tangles of letters dripped trails of dried paint, like blood; mutilated faces shrieked soundlessly. Still, I thought I could bear the shelter. Sitting with Kim gave me the chance to touch her breasts, such as they were, through the collapsing deceptively large cups of her bra. Tonight she smelled of newspapers, as though she had been wrapped in them for me to take out; she must have been serving at the counter. Nevertheless I kissed her, and ignored the fact that one corner of the shelter was dark as a spider's crevice.

But she had noticed; I felt her shrink away from the corner. Had she noticed more than I? Or was it her infectious wariness which made the dark beside us look more solid, about to shuffle toward us along the bench? I was uneasy, but the din and the lights of the fairground were reassuring. I determined to make the most of Kim's need for protection, but she pushed my hand away. "Don't," she said irritably, and made to stand up.

At that moment I heard a blurred voice. "Popeye," it muttered as if to itself; it sounded gleeful. "Popeye." Was it part of the fair? It might have been a stallholder's voice, distorted by the uproar, for it said, "I've got something for you."

The struggles of Kim's hand in mine excited me. "Let me go," she was wailing. Because I managed not to be afraid, I was more pleased than dismayed by her fear—and I was eager to let my imagination flourish, for it was better than reading a ghost story. I peered into the dark corner to see what horrors I could imagine.

Then Kim wrenched herself free and ran around the pool. Disappointed and angry, I pursued her. "Go away," she cried. "You're horrible. I never want to speak to you again." For a while I chased her along the dim paths, but once I began to plead I grew furious with myself. She wasn't worth the embarrassment. I let her go, and returned to the fair, to wander desultorily for a while. When I'd stayed long enough to prevent my parents from wondering why I was home early, I walked home.

I meant to sit in the shelter for a while, to see if anything happened, but someone was already there. I couldn't make out much about him, and didn't like to go closer. He must have been wearing spectacles, for his eyes seemed perfectly circular and gleamed like metal, not like eyes at all.

I quickly forgot that glimpse, for I discovered Kim hadn't been exaggerating: she refused to speak to me. I stalked off to buy fish and chips elsewhere. I decided that I hadn't liked her anyway. My one lingering disappointment, I found glumly, was that I had nobody with whom to go to the fairground. Eventually, when the fair and the school holidays were approaching their end, I said to Mark, "Shall we go to the fair tonight?"

He hesitated, but didn't seem especially wary. "All right," he said with the indifference we were beginning to affect about everything.

At sunset the horizon looked like a furnace, and that was how the park felt. Couples rambled sluggishly along the paths; panting dogs splashed in the lake. Between the trees the lights of the fairground shimmered and twinkled, cheap multicolored stars. As we passed the pool, I noticed that the air was quivering above the footprints in the concrete, and looked darkened, perhaps by dust. Impulsively I said, "What did you do to old Willy?"

"Shut up." I'd never heard Mark so savage or withdrawn. "I wish I hadn't done it."

I might have retorted to his rudeness, but instead I let myself be captured by the fairground, by the glade of light amid the balding rutted green. Couples and gangs roamed, harangued a shade half-heartedly by stallholders. Young children hid their faces in pink candy floss. A siren thin as a Christmas party hooter set the Dodgems running. Mark and I rode a tilting bucket above the fuzzy clamor of music, the splashes of glaring light, the cramped crowd. Secretly I felt a little sick, but the ride seemed to help Mark regain his confidence. Shortly, as we were playing a pinball machine with senile flippers, he said, "Look, there's Lorna and what's-her-name."

It took me a while to be sure where he was pointing: at a tall, bosomy girl, who probably looked several years older than she was, and a girl of about my height and age, her small bright face sketched with makeup. By this time I was following him eagerly.

The tall girl was Lorna; her friend's name was Carol. We strolled for a while, picking our way over power cables, and Carol and I began to like each other; her scent was sweet, if rather overpowering. As the fair began to close, Mark easily won trinkets at a shooting gallery and presented them to the girls, which helped us persuade them to meet us on Saturday night. By now Mark never looked toward the shelter—I think not from wariness but because it had ceased to worry him, at least for the moment. I glanced across, and could just distinguish someone pacing unevenly round the pool, as if impatient for a delayed meeting.

If Mark had noticed, would it have made any difference? Not in the long run, I try to believe. But however I rationalize, I know that some of the blame was mine.

We were to meet Lorna and Carol on our side of the park in order to take them to the Carlton cinema, nearby. We arrived late, having taken our time over sprucing ourselves; we didn't want to seem too eager to meet them. Beside the police station, at the entrance to the park, a triangular island of pavement, large enough to contain a spinney of trees, divided the road. The girls were meant to be waiting at the nearest point of the triangle. But the island was deserted except for the caged darkness beneath the trees.

We waited. Shop windows on West Derby Road glared fluorescent green. Behind us trees whispered, creaking. We kept glancing into the park, but the only figure I could distinguish on the dark paths was alone. Eventually, for something to do, we strolled desultorily around the island.

It was I who saw the message first, large letters scrawled on the corner nearest the park. Was it Lorna's or Carol's handwriting? It rather shocked me, for it looked semi-literate. But she must have had to use a stone as a pencil, which couldn't have helped; indeed, some letters had had to be dug out of the moss which coated stretches of the pavement. MARK SEE YOU AT SHELTER, the message said.

I felt him withdraw a little. "Which shelter?" he muttered.

"I expect they mean the one near the kiosk," I said, to reassure him.

We hurried along Orphan Drive. Above the lamps, patches of foliage shone harshly. Before we reached the pool we crossed the bridge, from which in daylight manna rained down to the ducks, and entered the park. The fair had gone into hibernation; the paths, and the mazes of tree trunks, were silent and very dark. Occasional dim movements made me think that we were passing the girls, but the figure that was wandering a nearby path looked far too bulky.

The shelter was at the edge of the main green, near the football pitch. Beyond the green, tower blocks loomed in glaring auras. Each of the four sides of the shelter was an alcove housing a bench. As we peered into each, jeers or curses challenged us.

"I know where they'll be," Mark said. "In the one by the bowling green. That's near where they live."

But we were closer to the shelter by the pool. Nevertheless I followed him onto the park road. As we turned toward the bowling green I glanced toward the pool, but the streetlamps dazzled me. I followed him along a narrow path between hedges to the green, and almost tripped over his ankles as he stopped short. The shelter was empty, alone with its view of the decaying Georgian houses on the far side of the bowling green.

To my surprise and annoyance, he still didn't head for the pool. Instead, we made for the disused bandstand hidden in a ring of bushes. Its only tune now was the clink of broken bricks. I was sure that the girls wouldn't have called it a shelter, and of course it was deserted. Obese dim bushes hemmed us in. "Come on," I said, "or we'll miss them. They must be by the pool."

"They won't be there," he said—stupidly, I thought.

Did I realize how nervous he suddenly was? Perhaps, but it only annoyed me. After all, how else could I meet Carol again? I didn't know her address. "Oh, all right," I scoffed, "if you want us to miss them."

I saw him stiffen. Perhaps my contempt hurt him more than Ben's had; for one thing, he was older. Before I knew what he intended he was striding toward the pool, so rapidly that I would have had to run to keep up with him—which, given the hostility that had flared between us, I refused to do. I strolled after him rather disdainfully. That was how I came to glimpse movement in one of the islands of dimness between the lamps of the park road. I glanced toward it and saw, several hundred yards away, the girls.

After a pause they responded to my waving—somewhat timidly, I thought. "There they are," I called to Mark. He must have been at the pool by now, but I had difficulty in glimpsing him beyond the glare of the lamps. I was beckoning the girls to hurry when I heard his radio blur into speech.

At first I was reminded of a sailor's parrot. "Aye aye," it was croaking. The distorted voice sounded cracked, uneven, almost too old to speak. "You know what I mean, son?" it grated triumphantly. "Aye aye." I was growing uneasy, for my mind had begun to interpret the words as "Eye eye"—when suddenly, dreadfully, I realized Mark hadn't brought his radio.

There might be someone in the shelter with a radio. But I was terrified, I wasn't sure why. I ran toward the pool, calling, "Come on, Mark, they're here!" The lamps dazzled me; everything swayed with my running—which was why I couldn't be sure what I saw.

I know I saw Mark at the shelter. He stood just within, confronting darkness. Before I could discern whether anyone else was there, Mark staggered out blindly, hands covering his face, and collapsed into the pool.

Did he drag something with him? Certainly by the time I reached the margin of the light he appeared to be tangled in something, and to be struggling feebly. He was drifting, or being dragged, toward the center of the pool by a half-submerged heap of litter. At the end of the heap nearest Mark's face was a pale ragged patch in which gleamed two round objects—bottle caps? I could see all this because I was standing helpless, screaming at the girls, "Quick, for Christ's sake! He's drowning!" He was drowning, and I couldn't swim.

"Don't be stupid," I heard Lorna say. That enraged me so much that I turned from the pool. "What do you mean?" I cried. "What do you mean, you stupid bitch?"

"Oh, be like that," she said haughtily, and refused to say more. But Carol took pity on my hysteria, and explained, "It's only three feet deep. He'll never drown in there."

I wasn't sure that she knew what she was talking about, but that was no excuse for me not to try to rescue him. When I turned to the pool I gasped miserably, for he had vanished—sunk. I could only wade into the muddy water, which engulfed my legs and closed around my waist like ice, ponderously hindering me.

The floor of the pool was fattened with slimy litter. I slithered, terrified of losing my balance. Intuition urged me to head for the center of the pool. And it was there I found him, as my sluggish kick collided with his ribs.

When I tried to raise him, I discovered that he was pinned down. I had to grope blindly over him in the chill water, feeling how still he was. Something like a swollen cloth bag, very large, lay over his face. I couldn't bear to touch it again, for its contents felt soft and fat. Instead I seized Mark's ankles and managed at last to drag him free. Then I struggled toward the edge of the pool, heaving him by his shoulders, lifting his head above water. His weight was dismaying. Eventually the girls waded out to help me.

But we were too late. When we dumped him on the concrete, his face stayed agape with horror; water lay stagnant in his mouth. I could see nothing wrong with his eyes. Carol grew hysterical, and it was Lorna who ran to the hospital, perhaps in order to get away from the sight of him. I only made Carol worse by demanding why they hadn't waited for us at the shelter; I wanted to feel they were to blame. But she denied they had written the message, and grew more hysterical when I asked why they hadn't waited at the island. The question, or the memory, seemed to frighten her.

I never saw her again. The few newspapers that bothered to report Mark's death gave the verdict "by misadventure." The police took a dislike to me after I insisted that there might be somebody else in the pool, for the draining revealed nobody. At least, I thought, whatever was there had gone away. Perhaps I could take some credit for that, at least.

But perhaps I was too eager for reassurance. The last time I ventured near the shelter was years ago, one winter night on the way home from school. I had caught sight of a gleam in the depths of the shelter. As I went close, nervously watching both the shelter and the pool, I saw two disks glaring at me from the darkness beside the bench. They were Coca-Cola caps, not eyes at all, and it must have been a wind that set the pool slopping and sent the caps scuttling toward me. What frightened me most as I fled through the dark was that I wouldn't be able to see where I was running if, as I desperately wanted to, I put up my hands to protect my eyes.

MICHAEL BISHOP

"Seasons of Belief"

Although generally considered a science fiction writer, Michael Bishop (1945-) has made a career out of crossing back and forth between the horror, fantasy and science fiction genres. His novels **A Funeral for the Eyes of Fire, The Secret Ascension,** *and the Nebula Award-winning* **No Enemy But Time** *deploy the traditional science fiction themes of interplanetary adventure, alternate universes and time travel in stories that pose questions regarding human identity and social responsibility.* **Who Made Stevie Crye?** *is a darkly comic self-reflexive critique of horror fiction, and* **Unicorn Mountain** *a moving fantasy parable about coming to terms with terminal illness. In his World Fantasy Award-nominated novel* **Brittle Innings**, *he reworked the Frankenstein theme for an odyssey of self-discovery set in the world of minor league baseball. Some of his best short fiction has been collected in* **Blooded on Arachne, One Winter in Eden,** *and* **At the City Limits of Fate.** *"Seasons of Belief" is, like his masterful tale "Icicle Music," a brief story that draws horror unexpectedly from its holiday setting.*

Seasons of Belief

by Michael Bishop

In the dead of winter, in a high-ceilinged room in a drafty, many-gabled house, a family had gathered to pass the twilight hour after supper. Father was reading a book, Mother was busy with thimble and needle at her quilting frame, and the children were stretched out in front of the room's copper-colored space heater with their crayons and several big yellow-gray sheets of newsprint.

It was not long before their bedtime. The silence in the room had grown as thick and muffling as the coverlets of snow on the house's gables and windowsills. In everyone's mind was the half-formed thought that the first word spoken into this stillness would seem as loud and unexpected as a Fourth of July firecracker.

In everyone's mind, that is, except Stefa's. Stefa was five. She had suddenly grown tired of drawing trees across her paper and of worrying about explaining to everyone else what her fine, treelike trees were *really* supposed to be. Father would mistake them for people, Mother for tornadoes or big green bananas, and Jimbo, willfully, for scribbles. Stefa was also tired of sharing the crayons, even though the box contained at least a hundred of them. Only a few were good honest colors like red, yellow, blue, green, and orange. All the rest were impostors like burnt sienna, aquamarine, raw umber, goldenrod, or colors equally shady; and what, exactly, were they *good* for?

Stefa threw her good honest green crayon on the floor and watched it roll under the space heater. "Tell us a story," she demanded.

Her brother, Jimbo, who was seven, jumped as if a Fourth of July firecracker had just exploded. But after looking disapprovingly at

Stefa, he turned to his parents and repeated his sister's request: "Yes, tell us a story. We're tired of drawing."

"Your turn," said Mother, looking directly at her husband. "Last night I told them about roller-skating to the circus."

The children hurried across the room and crumpled the pages of Father's book climbing into his lap. When they were finally settled on either side of him in the big green chair, Stefa said:

"A scary story, please."

"All right," Father told them, finally adjusted to their presence. "This is a story about the grither—because Stefa wants a scary story."

"What's a grither?" Jimbo asked.

"A grither is a creature," began the children's father, "who lives in the wreck of an ancient packet ship in the ice floes of the Arctic Circle. There is only one grither in the entire world, and each time he hears his name spoken aloud by any member of the human population, he sets off to find that impertinent person and make sure that he never says his name again. He has very, very good ears, the grither does, and he cannot tolerate being the object of anyone's gossip."

"Don't tell *this* story," Stefa cautioned her father. "I don't want you to tell it."

Mother looked up from her quilting frame. "It may be too late to stop him, Stefa. Your father has already mentioned the grither's name, and the creature is probably on his way to our house right this very moment."

"He's only just started," the father said. "It'll take him a while to get here, of course, and if I'm careful to keep this story short, the grither may not be able to reach our house before I've finished. He depends on hearing his name several times to get to where he needs to go."

"Don't tell it," Stefa pleaded, hoping that her father would go on to the last possible moment before their safety was irrevocably compromised and the grither sprang into the room to devour them.

"Do you know why the grither is called a grither?" Father asked, looking first at Stefa and then at Jimbo.

"Why?" the children asked together.

"Because the grither has fists as big as basketballs and arms as long as boa constrictors. When he finally locates the human busybodies who have been tossing his lovely name around, he opens up his fists, reaches out his arms, and—*grithers'em in!* Just like that,

Stefa and Jimbo, just as if he were hugging his cousins at a family reunion—*he grithers'em in!*"

Jimbo and Stefa shuddered and pressed themselves more tightly against their father.

"Is the grither a bigfoot?" the boy asked.

"No," Father responded. "The grither isn't a bigfoot, or an abominable snowman, or any of those other doubtful monsters that people sometimes think they've seen. The grither has never been seen by *anyone*—except, of course, by the people whom he grithers in and gobbles up. And those unfortunate folks are no longer around to tell us what he looks like."

"What does he look like?" asked Jimbo.

"Well, besides his basketball fists and boa-constrictor arms, the grither has a body as tall and supple as a poplar tree. You can see right through him, though, as if he were made of melting, colorless gelatin. He looks a little bit like a plastic road map because inside his legs and arms and chest and face you can see the tiny red and blue veins that twist through his body and help to hold him together. The blue's for fear, the red's for rage, and these feelings, flowing through his veins, help to keep him warm, too. As you may imagine, it's very chilly in the hold of a packet ship stuck in the pack ice—much chillier, my children, than it ever gets here."

"Then why doesn't he leave?" Stefa objected.

"He does," Father said. "Every time he hears anyone speaking his name aloud. When I first started telling this story, the grither snaked his way out of that shipwrecked vessel's hold, slithered over the gunwales, and began loping across the blue-white Arctic deserts toward the sound of our voices. He doesn't like gossip, as I've already told you, but he's always glad for the chance to go somewhere to stifle it. He's coming now. Listen."

"No!" shrieked Stefa, covering her ears and shutting her eyes. But even so she could hear the sighing of the wind in the naked oaks—a sound as sinister as a siren at midnight.

"Where is he now?" Jimbo asked. The boy peered at the room's solitary, icy window, sneaked a look at the door, and glanced suspiciously at the innocent ceiling.

"That's hard to say," Father replied. "But as he comes to get whoever's gossiping about him, he always sings this song." And, narrowing his eyes and doing something strange to his voice, Father showed them how the song was sung:

337

"I am the grither, gruesome and hungry.
Here I come, folks,
All the while grimacing.
You cannot escape me—it's simply impossible.
Don't even try.
I am the grither, crude and most grum.
Pleading is useless.
So are your prayers—also your rabbit's feet.
The grither is greedy
For only one thing:
To silence your gossip, folks.
That's why this song says
Your moments are numbered.
I'm quite sorry for you.
I'm quite sorry for you.
So please do accept
My most heartfelt apologies."

Scandalized, Stefa protested, "That doesn't even *rhyme!* There aren't no sound-alikes!"

"'Any,'" Mother interjected.

"There aren't *any* sound-alikes," Stefa corrected herself.

"That's true," Father admitted. "And the grither doesn't sing very well, either."

"But where is he now?" Jimbo asked.

Father tilted his head and listened to the sound of the grither's song as it was apparently borne to him on the sighing winter wind. "Maine," he said. "The grither's in Maine—but he's heading relentlessly south and taking all the shortcuts he knows."

"Stop!" cried Stefa. "Don't tell any more!"

"It's cheating," said Father, "if you don't finish the story. You just have to be sure to finish it before the grither arrives—that's the main thing. Now that the grither's on his way, it would be terribly unfair to leave him stranded in Bangor. He doesn't like short trips, you know."

"It isn't fair to the people in Maine, either," Mother pointed out. "He's always traipsing back and forth through their state, and we can't allow that revengeful critter to impose on their hospitality any more than he already manages to."

"No, we can't," Father agreed.

"Well, then," said Stefa impatiently, "please hurry up and finish telling the story."

"Yes," said Jimbo. "Maybe you can leave him stranded in New Jersey or Virginia. Virginia's a pretty state."

"That's an idea," said Father, contemplating this notion. "All right, then. I'll go on with my story. You may be wondering where the grither came from in the first place. Well, the fact is—"

Just then the telephone—which hung from a wall in the kitchen, right next to the pantry door—began to ring. Stefa thought that the burring noise it emitted was exactly the sort of sound you could expect a statue in the park to make, if only statues could come alive in the cold to shiver and suffer.

"Would you mind getting that?" Mother asked Father. "I've almost finished quilting this square."

"Oh no!" cried Jimbo and Stefa in unison.

Father shrugged amiably, eased himself out of the big green chair, and disappeared into the kitchen to make the phone stop ringing. He caught it on the sixth or seventh burr.

Stefa and Jimbo, with a warm dent between them in the cushion, looked at each other and made worried faces. They lived in the South, but not *that* far south, and the grither was descending upon them like a ravenous avalanche. Stefa could not understand her parents' lack of concern—they were usually very sensible people.

"Where is he now?" she moaned. "Where is he now?"

"Boston, maybe," Mother said, without looking up from the quilting frame. "Or Philadelphia, if he's flying."

"Flying?" said Jimbo. "How?"

"Well," said Mother, briefly pursing her lips as she forced the needle through two layers of cloth and the cotton batting between them, "the grither's ears—which are invisibly small to start with—get bigger and bigger each time his name is spoken. By the time it's been spoken ten or twelve times, they're big enough to carry him wherever he's going; a pair of miraculous, transparent wings." Mother took off her thimble, kissed her thumb, and tugged thoughtfully at her ear lobe. "I'd imagine our grither's over Philadelphia, or maybe Baltimore, by now. He ought to have an extremely nice pair of ear-wings—we've been gossiping about him for quite some time."

"Daddy!" Stefa screamed at the kitchen. *"Daddy!"*

Father came strolling back into the living room with his hands in his pockets. "Here I am," he said. He sat down between the children.

"Hurry," Stefa advised him. "Finish telling the story."

"Who was that?" Mother asked, nodding her head toward the kitchen and the telephone.

"I don't know," Father responded mysteriously. (Stefa was not sure if he had winked at Mother or not.) "Someone who knows who we are and who wondered if we were home. I said we were, of course."

"Was it the grither?" Jimbo asked, his face betraying both excitement and alarm.

"I don't know that, either. You see, Jimbo, the caller didn't say who he was and I've never heard the grither speak before. How do you suppose I ought to be able to recognize his voice?"

"You sang his silly song," Stefa reminded him.

"Right," Father said. "But that was from memory."

Neither Stefa nor Jimbo understood the precise meaning of this explanation, but it kept them from asking any more questions about the grither's voice. It didn't, however, keep them from worrying about the telephone call.

Pounding her kneecaps, Stefa urged Father to finish the story.

"Washington, D.C.," Mother noncommittally informed her family. "I believe he's over Washington."

"Please," said Stefa.

"Well," said Father, trying to take up where the telephone call had interrupted him, "the grither came into existence when a royal packet ship steaming between Boston, Massachusetts, and Portsmouth, England, was blown ridiculously off course by a storm and driven up Baffin Bay toward the Pole. Not a soul aboard that ship survived—but before they all drowned or froze to death, they lifted their voices into the storm to remind the heavens that they were under the King's protection. The grither was born from the fear, rage, and disappointment of those who died. And it has ever since been merciless to those who speak its name because the storm was merciless to those who had to die to give the grither life."

"Is that all?" asked Stefa.

"Richmond, Virginia," said Mother. "He's soaring over Richmond—on his way to Winston-Salem."

"No," said Father, looking at his little girl. "Not quite all. The story goes that the grither won't cease to exist until—"

There was a knock on the door. Mother looked at Father. Stefa and Jimbo looked at each other. The wind, as it curled around the gables of the house, set the walls and floorboards a-creaking. The light bulb hanging from its cord in the center of the room began to bob and dance.

And a voice beyond the door was singing:

> "The grither is greedy
> For only one thing:
> To silence your gossip, folks.
> That's why this song says
> Your moments are numbered.
> I'm quite sorry for you.
> So please do accept
> My most heartfelt apologies."

When the singing was finished, the knocking on the door grew louder and louder.

"Who's going to answer it?" asked Father.

Stefa and Jimbo shrank back against the big green chair's bolster cushion and gave their father disbelieving looks. When Mother saw their fear, she in turn gave Father a look of reproach and warning.

"I'm sorry," Father began contritely. "It's really just—"

But the door banged open with a crash, a huge furry figure leapt through the opening with a roar of Arctic air, and the double row of tiny blue flames in the space heater rippled and guttered as the same voice that had been singing the grither's song cried out in malevolent glee:

"GOTCHA!"

The entire family gasped as a single person. Father, indeed, jumped out of his chair.

Then they all saw that the figure who had sprung through the door was Stefa and Jimbo's grandfather, dressed for the season in a raccoon coat and a Russian hat. Coming into the high-ceilinged room behind him, Grandmother had the practicality and presence of mind to close the wide-thrown door.

"Grandfather sometimes gets carried away," she apologized.

"I telephoned to say we were coming," said Grandfather unrepentantly, winking at Mother. "Didn't this husband of yours tell the children?"

Father's mouth was still open. He had neither the practicality nor the presence of mine to close it.

"I've finished with this," said Mother, rising from her quilting frame. "Let's go into the kitchen for coffee and doughnuts." She led Grandmother and Grandfather, scolding each other and laughing, out of the dim and drafty living room to the comfort of the kitchen table.

"Where's the grither?" Stefa demanded of her father, wiping tears of fright from her eyes. "Where's the *real* grither?"

"Yes," said Jimbo. "What about the rest of the story?"

Father closed his mouth and put his hands in his pockets. Then he opened his mouth and said very slowly:

"I hope neither of you really believes in the grither. You don't, do you?"

"No-o-ohh," the children managed.

"Good," boomed Father jovially. "Because if you don't believe in what isn't, it can't do you any harm. Can it?"

Stefa and Jimbo looked at each other. In unison, each prompted by the other, they doubtfully shook their heads.

"It's almost bedtime. Come into the kitchen for milk and doughnuts, and then we'll go up to bed." Father paused before leaving and looking at the floor. "But first pick up your crayons, please."

Alone in the high-ceilinged living room, Stefa and Jimbo got down in front of the space heater to pick up their scattered crayons—the aquamarines and goldenrods as well as the reds and blues.

"Winston-Salem isn't too far from here," Jimbo said as they gathered up the crayons. "I've seen it on a map at school."

And Stefa whispered miserably, "I wonder where the grither is right now." For Stefa believed in the grither, and what she believed in could certainly do her harm, couldn't it?

"Look," said Jimbo, and he pointed at the rime-coated window across the room. In the final moments of dusk, with the electric glare of the light bulb glinting off the glass, the window was veined with slender threads of red and blue, and the glass itself seemed to be melting—just like leftover Jell-O when no one has put it back in the refrigerator.

But because they weren't a bit surprised, Stefa and Jimbo didn't even scream. . . .

MJF BOOKS
Is Proud to Bring You

A Century of Science Fiction
A Century of Mystery
A Century of Fantasy
A Century of Horror

The four series collects the greatest stories written during the twentieth century in each genre. Each volume's cover is illustrated by a well-known artist, printed on acid-free paper, and sturdily bound to last for years. The Series Editor is Martin H. Greenberg, America's most renowned anthologist. Mr. Greenberg has been the Guest of Honor at the World Science Fiction Convention and The World Fantasy Convention, and the recipient of the Ellery Queen Award for lifetime achievement for editing in the mystery field. He also was a member of the Board of Advisors of the Sci-Fi Channel, a basic cable network that launched in September 1992. To oversee the four series, he has recruited top editors Robert Silverberg (Science Fiction and Fantasy), David Drake (Horror), and Marcia Muller and Bill Pronzini (Mystery).
The Century series has been conceived to offer the reader only the very best, in collectible books of lasting value.

Available Now:

A Century of Science Fiction: 1950-1959

Featuring stories by Robert Silverberg, Fritz Leiber, Ray Bradbury, James Blish, Walter M. Miller, Jr., Philip Jose Farmer, Arthur C. Clarke, Philip K. Dick, Isaac Asimov, Theodore Sturgeon, Marion Zimmer Bradley, and others

A Century of Mystery: 1980-1989

Featuring stories by Tony Hillerman,
Frederick Forsyth, Ruth Rendell, Janwillem van de Wetering,
George V. Higgins, Lawrence Block, Bill Pronzini,
Clark Howard, Marcia Muller, Peter Lovesey, and others

A Century of Fantasy: 1980-1989

Featuring stories by Roger Zelazny, Andre Norton,
Orson Scott Card, Harlan Ellison, Joe Haldeman,
George R.R. Martin, Ellen Kushner, Alan Dean Foster,
Larry Niven, Ursula K. Le Guin, and others

A Century of Horror: 1970-1979

Featuring stories by Richard Matheson, David Drake,
Robert Bloch, Brian Lumley, Joyce Carol Oates,
Ray Bradbury, Michael Bishop, Harlan Ellison,
Orson Scott Card, Tanith Lee, Ramsey Campbell, and others

Available At Your Local Bookstore